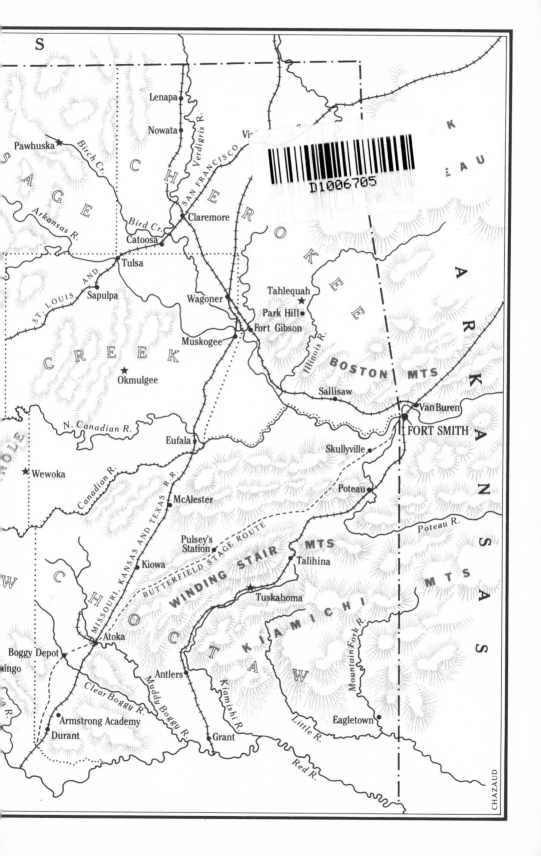

The Whipping Boy

The Whipping Boy

Speer Morgan

HOUGHTON MIFFLIN COMPANY

BOSTON · NEW YORK · 1994

For information about permission to reproduce selections from this book,
write to Permissions, Houghton Mifflin Company, 215 Park Avenue South,
New York, New York 10003.

Library of Congress Cataloging-in-Publication Data

Morgan, Speer, date.

The whipping boy / Speer Morgan.

p.   cm.

ISBN 0-395-67725-4

I. Title.

PS3563.O87149W49   1994   93-40836

813'.54 — dc20   CIP

Printed in the United States of America

MP 10 9 8 7 6 5 4 3 2 1

Endpaper map by Jacques Chazaud

Book design by Melodie Wertelet

ACKNOWLEDGMENTS

Thanks to John Sterling and Esther Newberg, who keep the faith, and to the National Endowment for the Arts, whose fellowship came along just in time.

This one is for
Caitlin Derbyshire Morgan

The Whipping Boy

·Prologue·

MID-MORNING on a late fall day in 1894, the sun was almost visible in thin clouds, and the sky over western Arkansas looked as if it was about to clear after days of on-and-off rain. But the air suddenly turned cool, with the quickening feel of more weather on the way. Within an hour the sun's halo disappeared, as two massive prongs of cold approached along the Arkansas River Valley from the east and the Indian Territory to the west, pushing wet southern air away from the earth in majestic anvil-shaped clouds.

In Fort Smith, a young murderer named Johnny Pointer was to be hanged at noon on the lawn of the old U.S. courthouse, a few hundred yards from the Arkansas River. It was the first execution ordered by Judge Isaac C. Parker in over a year, the longest interruption in his otherwise lethal twenty-year record on the bench. Newspapers from as far away as Boston had sent stringers for the event, which wasn't unusual for a Parker hanging. In a nation enveloped in a depression, a good hanging offered promise of spectacle, lurid detail, moralizing, sentimentality, and all the other elements of the best order of journalism.

A lot of sightseers from the Cherokee and Choctaw Nations had come over to see the white man hanged. It was ginning season, and some of the farmers were taking the occasion to bring in their cotton. There was a recently opened bridge across the Arkansas River that they could use, instead of the ancient log-and-plank barge operated by a disagreeable old man, who'd been subjecting his riders to the same jokes for over four decades — foul, ancient jokes which some people actually swam the river to avoid. Now people could just trot right across the bridge, high above the unpleasant old coot and his flyblown ferry.

At 10:30, hangman George Maledon appeared on the scaffold, a man of such slight build that he looked like a white beard on a stick. He adjusted the rope's length and checked the trap mechanism, which momentarily hushed the crowd when it chunked open. Farm wagons drifted slowly up the street, with rawboned children sprawled across bales that were destined for the factors along Garrison Avenue. Advertisers milled among them, cheerfully yelling that they were paying more than any other factor in town. In truth, there was nothing cheerful about the price of cotton in 1894, which, after decades of decline, was scraping along at less than fifty dollars a bale.

The streets must have afforded curious sights to the Indian and boomer kids — zinc-sheathed telegraph and telephone poles along one side, buildings as high as six stories, a horsecar track, and the big crowd, variously described in news accounts as "more than five hundred souls" and "well above fifteen hundred." Monte sharks and patent-medicine salesmen were doing business along the street north of the old courthouse lawn — watchfully, since at previous hangings some had been arrested and fined. There were dippers milling in the crowd to steal watches and money. Men emerged from alleyways wiping their mouths with coat sleeves.

On the south side of Rogers Avenue rough three-tiered bleachers had been erected, and thirty-four orphan boys from the Choctaw Armstrong Academy dressed in plain butternut uniforms stood on the wooden planks, brought here by their missionary principal to witness, while still young and uncorrupted, the fruit of crime. Since their orphanage was in the farthermost sticks of the southwestern Choctaw Nation, where the only women were wraithlike crones who came once a week to wash the clothes, many of the boys were in fact concerned less with the fruits of crime than the amazing women promenading through the crowd behind their formidable madams in bright, deeply slashed pastel dresses.

At 11:47, Johnny Pointer, convicted of murdering two livestock-thief cohorts in separate incidents — shooting them through their heads while they lay asleep — was taken from the courthouse jail and with great difficulty led to the gallows. He complained, pushed, pulled, and fell on the ground, protesting that he was being mistreated, that he wanted his lawyer, that his dear mother had not visited him and he would not leave the world without seeing her one last time.

Pointer had been a cause célèbre in the local papers, partly because there hadn't been a hanging in a while. Also, Parker's usual clientele were whites and breeds illegally roaming the Indian Nations, hiding from the law, selling whiskey, stealing livestock, who one day got a little too drunk in a one-horse town like Nicksville, Claremore, Cloud Chief, Pitcher, White Bread, who went on a rampage, murdering somebody or several somebodies, and woke up in jail. Compared to these smelly types, Johnny Pointer was a member of the royalty, raised in a middle-class family, a white boy who had "gone astray and deserved mercy," as one newspaper put it. Other papers described him as a spoiled, treacherous, murdering brat — a "traitor to his race" — who deserved worse than hanging. There were four newspapers in Fort Smith and dozens of others on both sides of the border, all keen to gain readers and trying to outdo each other at ferocity of opinion and sensationalism, much of it conjured out of whiskey-empurpled imaginations.

Johnny Pointer's protestations silenced the crowd. Dragged onto the high gallows by six stern deputy marshals, his knees and boots clunking against each of the thirteen steps, the prisoner rejected the advice of one of the deputies to take it like a man by sitting down and bursting into copious tears. The marshals briefly conferred, then picked him up bodily so Mr. Maledon could slip his carefully tarred rope over Pointer's head and secure the knot under his left ear. Maledon normally tied his client's legs and placed a black bag over the head, but this time he did neither. Pointer was putting up such resistance that he wanted to finish the job as quickly as possible.

Desperately, Pointer got his hands loose and clasped his arms around one of the marshals at just the moment the diminutive hangman sprang the trap, "retarding the felon's fall," as one reporter described it, "and causing the struggling marshal almost to plunge through with him."

The newspapers gave wildly different accounts of what happened on the gallows and among the crowd after this point, but the primary fact was not disputed: the man who was to be skillfully ejected into hell at the hour of noon refused to die for forty-three minutes — a record by a good mark, even in the ample history of the Fort Smith gallows.

A half-hour after Johnny Pointer's mortal struggle began, Judge Parker was fetched at a board meeting of the Belle Grove School and asked what should be done about the unfortunate spectacle. His answer, as recorded by one reporter, was, "Let the son of a b—— go all night. You may hire an orchestra for all I care."

In earlier days, when Parker's court was located in the old officers' quarters of Fort Smith, and his dungeon below it, he held sole appealless jurisdiction for all murder, robbery, assault, and whiskey cases involving whites and non–full bloods in seventy-four thousand square miles of western Arkansas and the Indian Nations. On a number of occasions, Parker had saved the district money by sending two to five men at once to the gallows. New courts lately had been established in the Indian Nations and the white-settled Oklahoma Territory, and Parker's district was now whittled down, his authority shrunk. His cases were now subject to appeal, many were overturned, and Parker himself had gotten into bitter, public disagreements with federal officials over policy and management in the Indian Nations. Influential men in the United States government, including members of the Supreme Court, the solicitor general, the Congress, and the president, all regarded the now white-haired, dropsy-plagued judge as undesirable. In one of his more politic statements on the issue, the solicitor general said that Parker was "overzealous in convictions and executions, particularly of whites and half-breeds who he claims disturb the peace and dignity of the Indian Tribes." Parker's somewhat less politic response was that "The solicitor general of the United States doesn't seem to be aware of the fact that it is against the law for whites and nontribal members to roam around the Indian Nations confiscating Indian lands, stealing livestock, and killing people. I advise him to read the treaties."

In 1894, in a fancy new gingerbread-gothic federal building located several blocks away from his old courtroom, Parker still kept up his accustomed schedule, holding court from daylight until dark six days a week. He would retire a little over a year after the Johnny Pointer hanging, with 174 convictions and 160 actual executions or jail deaths, the largest number of any judge in U.S. history, but his more remarkable accomplishment may have been how long he could talk, off the cuff, about disorderliness, drunkenness, murder, theft, rape, and the destruction of the Indian Nations by lawlessness. When delivering the death sentence to Johnny Pointer, he had subjected the poor hangee to the usual long lecture, at the end holding out hope for him that our Lord, whose Court could offer the only appeal, might afford one last chance for eternal mercy to whoever repented his sins and took his punishment humbly.

Johnny Pointer, refusing to die, showed no inclination to follow this advice.

The tone of the newspaper descriptions of his forty-three-minute execution varied from the blackest moral outrage to the most whimsical carnival irony, making it hard to tell what the mood really was. It was noted that a large number of people in the crowd became ill, some with nausea, others with chills and fever and "sudden, catastrophic indigestion." Most of them did remain throughout the event, despite the increasing cold, the darkening sky, and the rain, which started after noon. A few younger witnesses mocked the hanging man in macabre cavortings around the gallows. This would later result in a peculiar high-kneed, walking dance called the Johnny Pointer, popular among children and teenagers in the border country as late as the 1950s.

The rain wasn't heavy at first, but several of the news stories telegraphed out of Fort Smith that evening noted the ominous weather.

So began the flood of 1894.

♦

An event in its own way extraordinary happened to Tom Freshour, one of the boys on the Armstrong Academy bleachers. Someone took a photograph of the thirty-four Choctaw orphans who'd been brought here to see what happened to criminals, but the photograph was a dud, the boys' faces all like clouds of light and shadow. It is impossible to guess which of them is Tom Freshour; being sixteen or seventeen (his birth date was not known), he must be one of the four or five tallest boys. The front door and window of the building behind the orphans, however, are perfectly in focus, as if the photograph had been intended to be of DEKKER HARDWARE. A Closed sign hangs on the big double door, evidence of Dekker's status as a wholesaler, since no retailer in that terrible depression year would have shunned the traffic brought by a hanging.

Sometime during Johnny Pointer's long demise, the front door of the building in this photograph opened, and through it walked the usher of young Tom Freshour's fate in the person of one Mr. Bob MacGinnis, hardware salesman. MacGinnis had been sent out to find errand boys. Seeing the entire bleachers of candidates, MacGinnis went up to them and announced, "Any of you want work? I need three boys." Most of them would probably have delivered a message to hell to get away from the spectacle on the gallows and the cold rain they were being forced to stand in, but MacGinnis's appearance was so sudden, his request so unexpected, that none responded.

For these boys, raised in the stolid, regimented gloom of an orphanage in the remote woods of the Indian Territory, it had been a day of perpetual wonders, new sights and sensations one after another starting at six o'clock that morning. First the trip on the train, which had caused some of the boys to get sick, others to hold on to their seats in fear. Few of them had ever traveled except on their two feet or riding a plow mule, and hurtling along at fifty miles an hour had been breathtaking. Then there was the spectacle of the crowd at the hanging, a throng of people including women costumed in the most unbelievable fashion, with the whole front of their dresses open in such a way that invited one to wonder what was in there — about which few of the boys had clear ideas. Stories circulating at the academy regarding the female sex came from boys who were under eight years old (the academy would take no older) who'd had sisters before becoming orphans, and their descriptions were passed on with such inaccuracy that girls sprouted all kinds of strange anatomical features. Tom Freshour had sometimes sneaked off to the scalding shed and passed time with one of the washing ladies on the day she worked, at least giving him some contact with the opposite sex. But this hardly softened the blow of seeing these powdered, perfumed, white-skinned creatures with their dresses gapped down the front. In addition to these shocks there had been the hanging (to these boys actually not the strangest of the day's events), the surging hysteria of the crowd, and now this nervous-looking man who'd suddenly appeared asking for volunteers for what? A job?

Failing to get any response, MacGinnis found their principal, a pokerfaced missionary named James Schoot, and told him that he needed three boys for regular employment.

The prospect of having three fewer to feed on his tight budget surely must have delighted the principal, although he was always anxious about losing "moral control" over the boys. Reverend Schoot was rigorous about moral control, which he administered liberally, regularly, at the drop of a hat, to their flesh. A teacher who briefly worked at the orphanage noted in his diary that Reverend Schoot "commonly held regular weekly disciplinary floggings as well as daily beatings. I have seen some boys beaten as often as six times per day." Handling so many beatings every day along with all of his other responsibilities must have been tiring work for the Reverend, and one would think he'd be happy to have fewer to perform; but if he worried about releasing the three boys, that would be understandable, since one of them might go into the world, get a pistol, come back to the Armstrong Academy, and pay him back for several thousand whippings.

Mission headquarters, however, would doubtless be pleased when he reported that three older charges had been gainfully employed in the world, so he swallowed whatever concerns he had and prepared to make a bargain. He demanded that the boys' first month's wages be sent to him, for which consideration he gave up all responsibility and control. MacGinnis agreed to this condition, he and the Reverend shook hands, and the boys were on their own.

In this way Tom Freshour, Hack Deneuve, and Joel Mayes were released from the cloistered orphanage, the only place they had ever known, into the world.

Part One

Part One

· 1 ·

A S A SALESMAN who had worked at Dekker Hardware for more than twenty years, W. W. "Jake" Jaycox was present for the regular monthly sales meeting being held that day at the store. Neither he nor any of the other salesmen was aware of exactly what was going on across the street. Even later, Jake remained uninterested in the story of Johnny Pointer's hanging, despite the fact that he'd been across the street when it happened. Jake was pragmatic, hardheaded, and indifferent to how a man died who had shot a couple of his pals in the head while they were asleep. Having sold hardware in the Indian and Oklahoma territories for twenty-some years, Jake took a dim view of outlaws and lawmen, criminals and courts — and he devoted as little thought to any of them as possible.

The "big office," where the salesmen were waiting, was on the east side of the building, and their view didn't include the gallows. All they could see out the window was the Dekker wagon yard, which was packed with hacks and farm wagons of every description. When the rain started after noon, Jake wondered why the lot didn't begin to clear out, but he wondered more about why Mr. Dekker was late for the sales meeting — which never had happened before in his memory. He could see Mr. Dekker's plain Studebaker wagon and his son Ernest's fancy team parked in the crowd of other rigs, making him suspect that the two of them were in the old man's office, across the display room on the other side of the building. But punctual sales meetings were a sacred event, and he couldn't imagine why the old man would be so late if he was already here, unless he was having an extremely serious talk with his son.

For years, Jake had hoped that Ernest Dekker would find employment elsewhere. If his father got sick or feeble and Ernest took over, the place would surely go to hell. Ernest was not a hardware man. He was a gambler and socialite who dressed sharp and loafed around town with the straw-hat-and-palm-fan crowd, bird hunting, fishing, playing cards, watching horse races, chasing skirts, dabbling in investment schemes, talking real estate. But none of his interests had anything to do with hardware. Dekker Wholesale sold more than twenty-seven thousand separate items, including heavy hardware, sporting goods, enamelware and tinware, pumps, house and commercial furnishings, mechanics' tools, and farm implements, and Ernest didn't know a compression cock from a croquet set. He had never worked at the front desk or in the stockroom, nor had he gone out on the road. Exactly what he did on his occasional visits to the store Jake didn't know. Lately he had been hanging around Charles McMurphy, the treasurer, so apparently he helped with the figures, although Jake couldn't see Ernest stooping to such a lowly occupation as adding and subtracting. As vice president he pulled down a far higher salary than any of the salesmen, but he'd never to Jake's knowledge sold a stick of merchandise.

Waiting for the meeting to start, Jake daydreamed that the old man was finally in there giving Ernest what he'd long deserved, an invitation to get a job somewhere else. Shrewd and plain-dealing with most people, Mr. Dekker had always been soft on Ernest, probably because he was his only living son. Another son had died at the age of ten, and his one daughter had married and moved away years before. They had little in common: the father was a rough-and-ready commercial pioneer, while his son was of the leisured class. The old excuse for Ernest was that he had wild oats to sow, but now that he was near forty, that had worn thin.

The white sky had turned black, the office was dark, and Jake noticed that two or three wagons had torn out of the yard in an awful big hurry. He assumed it was just the weather. The waiting teams were restive, rattling the traces and whinnying as if they didn't particularly want to be pulling home in a storm. Peculiar noises were coming from the direction of the gallows, but none of the salesmen walked out front to see what was going on. The old man had been known to fire a salesman for going to the privy during one of these meetings, so they all stuck tight in the darkening room, chewing, waiting, wondering.

Bob MacGinnis was complaining about how poor things had got in his district. MacGinnis had been hired recently to replace J. D. Plagman, who'd committed suicide at the Wyandott Hotel in Texarkana, apparently because he was unable to sell hardware in southwest Arkansas — a sad fact, since the Angel of Commerce herself couldn't have sold much hardware after more than a year of the Panic. MacGinnis was not doing any better than Plagman had before he shot himself. "It's deader'n a nut down there," he said. "Nobody buyin much as nails."

Jack Peters wheezed in his high voice, "That's the way it is everywhere. The boom in Oklahoma Territory is a damn bust."

Dandy Pruitt and Marvin Beele both threw in their two cents about how low the Indian Nations had got. "What little you sell, you can't count on being delivered. Trains ain't running half the time," Marvin said, quickly bobbing his head down and bull's-eying the spittoon.

When Mr. Dekker finally did walk into the big office, at nearly a quarter after twelve, Jake was further mystified. The old man always started meetings urgently, by saying, "Let's see if you sons of bitches have sold any hardware this month." Today he came in and sat down and looked at them — toward them — with no particular expression except what appeared to Jake to be a kind of light glowing around his eyes. He said nothing. Mr. Dekker was a lean man of average height, tending to bald, with a fierce sharp beak of a nose and close-set eyes. He was waiting for somebody else to arrive.

After a time, Ernest came in. With one eyebrow floating high and a flushed look, the vice president took out a pre-rolled cigarette and put it into a black ivory holder. Jack Peters, the salesman for Oklahoma Territory, leaned out to light it. Unlike his father, Ernest was substantial in size, and he put on magisterial, impatient airs around "inferiors." He looked over the men and asked

Bob MacGinnis to come outside. After talking with MacGinnis for a few minutes, Ernest returned alone. The salesmen looked around at one another suspiciously. This was a very odd start for a sales meeting.

At last Mr. Dekker said, "You'd better tell em."

Ernest glanced at his father and took the ivory holder from his mouth. "All right," he said briskly. "Sorry to be the bearer of bad tidings, men, but it appears the Panic has finally got to us. The Mercantile Exchange Bank has called in our credit. They have demand notes and we have no choice but to meet them."

Jack Peters made a little *oof* sound, like he'd been hit in the gut. Marvin Beele rolled his eyes around to Jake. Pete Crapo of central Arkansas merely continued to look puzzled, his normal expression. Jake noticed that the old man, with head cocked back and eyes slightly narrowed, watched Ernest closely.

Ernest scowled at his cigarette. "Mr. Bradley, chief teller, notified us this morning. It was completely unexpected."

Jake knew something of Bradley. He'd seen him around town, running in the same crowd as Ernest.

Ernest continued, "I don't have to tell you how precarious this situation is. We'll have to take immediate action, or they'll seize our merchandise and shut us down. You realize we have no choice in the matter. We're declaring war against debt. We'll have to collect all accounts. Those of you who don't succeed I'm going to have to let go. I'm giving some of you couriers and I want you to keep em damn busy."

Couriers? As Ernest talked on, Jake's disbelief mounted. Heat ascended the back of his neck. He couldn't believe the old man would even listen to the idea of making an all-out collection sweep now. Nobody in the territory had any money. It was shipping season after a bad harvest on top of a panic. Arkansas, Oklahoma, and all of the Indian Nations were in turmoil. The stores were tighter than he'd ever seen them. Business was in hibernation. The store owners were operating on bank debt and faith that the Panic would end.

And why had Ernest taken over the meeting?

MacGinnis came back in the office pushing three rangy-looking half-breeds. They were shivery and green around the gills.

MacGinnis looked like he'd seen a ghost. "The man they're hanging over there ain't dead yet!" he said breathlessly. "He's been alive since twelve noon. Goddamnit, he's up there walkin, like . . . like he can't get up a flight of stairs!"

"Maybe he's going the wrong way," Ernest said. "He ought to turn around and try the other direction. Where'd you find these boys?"

"They're from the Choctaw orphanage near Durant. Principal's out there waiting to talk to you."

"Are you young men Christians?" Ernest asked.

"Yes sir," two of them barked, skinny boys blinking their eyes and squinting through the gloom, as if they had no idea where they were. The third, who was taller and stouter, a well-featured young man, said nothing at all. He looked around the room with what appeared to be defiant silence.

The boys stood dripping before the scowling, chewing, tense salesmen.

"Choctaws, huh?" said Ernest Dekker. "Good. You can generally trust them for courier work better'n white boys."

Peters wheezed a little laugh, and an awkward silence followed.

"We use couriers in town," Ernest said. "Now I want some of you men — the ones with the most money to collect — to have your own personal couriers. We can't count on the express or the post offices in the Nations. I want you men out there working the customers, and I want these couriers to make continuous delivery of everything over a hundred dollars. We have to show the bank, every day, that we're on the right track."

Marvin bobbed his head down and spat.

Then Jake cleared his throat and spoke. Unconsciously, he turned to the old man. "Our customers are behind, but there aren't many holding out on us. About the only kind of paper anybody's got right now are customer IOUs and mortgages. We start hittin em hard now and we'll have a lot of closings."

Ernest flourished his cigarette. "You men have been complaining so long that you sound like a flock of old soldiers at the courthouse. You ain't collecting debts because you've gotten lazy. You're so spoiled by the boom that you don't know how to take a little slowdown. Mr. Dekker, sitting before you now, sold hardware

· 15 ·

off the back of a buggy when the only other white peddlers on the road were the kind with kegs in their wagons. He was out there with a buggy full of pots and pans, and not just sellin, he was collecting his debts."

The old man looked uneasy at being the object of Ernest's oration, but still he said nothing. Jake wished he'd at least speak. Had the bank knocked the wind out of him?

"You, Jaycox. Eighteen months ago you were probably moving stock by the carload down in the Choctaw Nation —"

"I haven't traveled the south route for seven years —"

"You're used to fat times, that's the plain fact! This is your first taste of hardscrabblin, gentlemen, and I don't know whether you're real salesmen or not. We'll just have to see."

Jake wanted to reply that he was a "real salesman" when Ernest Dekker was still wearing knee britches, and furthermore, Ernest had never been any kind of salesman, so how'd he get to be such an expert? But Mr. Dekker Senior was looking at him with an expression that suggested he stay quiet.

◆

On the night train headed over the Kiamichi Mountains, Jake was in a dark mood. His newly hired "courier" sat beside him. After the meeting, Ernest Dekker had taken the new couriers off and talked to them about their new job. Jake had been assigned the biggest of the three, the one called Tom Freshour. He didn't say much and he stared a lot — particularly at females, of whom there happened to be one striking example in their car. To Jake's questions he gave stiffly polite but brief answers. He had a way of dimming his eyes and staring off to discourage conversation. He seemed to Jake tight-strung, sitting upright, almost as if he was at attention, even when dozing.

Jake needed this shavetail following him around like he needed a Chinese footman.

It was raining hard, thunder rattling the windows, as the train crawled up the ridgelike mountain. Today's queer sales meeting had lasted well into the afternoon, and Jake had actually left before it was quite over in order to hightail up to his boarding house, get a travel grip, then rush back to the train station with the young man in tow. At the station people had all been talking furiously about what a nail-curler the hanging had been, but Jake was so preoccupied by what had happened at the store that he hadn't been curious.

Tom Freshour nodded off by the time they reached Talihina, and he slept with a restless, worried look, his head repeatedly jerking upright. He looked to be a half-breed, maybe quarter. The shirt and pants he was wearing were a cheap, thin grade of cotton, his soft-soled shoes had holes in them, and he shivered a little as he sat there nodding. Jake eventually moved to a seat across the aisle so he could spread out.

Couriers! If Ernest had ever been across the river on anything but bird-hunting trips, he might know that no matter how bad the express companies had got, you could always find a way. You could even mail cash, if you had to, by tearing it in two and sending it from two different places. Instead of paying a few dollars, the store would be buying train tickets, which would end up costing a good hunk of whatever money they could collect. Oh, but this was an all-out emergency, Ernest had insisted, and they needed to start making deposits right away.

Equally galling was the fact that Ernest had assigned Jake to collect what they called the south route, the Choctaw Nation, which hadn't been his territory for seven years. He was supposed to immediately collect "at least twenty percent of the account balance" being carried in the district. Ernest was shuffling the salesmen between territories because he thought it would be easier for them to be tough on customers they didn't know so well. Furthermore, the bank suggested that they employ some scheme whereby the men could collect those stores that had no cash by trading the merchandise mortgages that Dekker held on them for the property mortgages that the stores held against their customers; but the bank was "still working on the details."

That was the point at which Jake begged out to catch the train. He'd go south. He'd try to collect. But heaven help Dekker Wholesale Hardware and Supply. This sudden shift of authority to Ernest was truly strange. Why he should take over, Jake couldn't figure, unless this credit call had just knocked the stuffing out of the old man. Nor did he understand why Ernest appeared to relish it so much and had such a big plan all ready to lay out: couriers, shifted districts, twenty percent collections, mortgage switches — had he made all that up on the spot?

Jake gazed at the sleeping boy and simmered. He would have no pension to look forward to if the store went down. How the store could stay solvent under Ernest Dekker he didn't know. As they approached the high point in the Kiamichi, rain had turned to hail, chunking into the side of the car like rocks.

To make his mood worse, Jake had the extremely vexing thought — he didn't believe it, but it occurred to him — that he could be wrong. It was true that the accounts had been getting further behind every month and a business couldn't subsist forever on its reserves, panic or no panic. It was also true that however strange the plan was, at least it stood up to the problem. Whether he was acting like a fool or not, Ernest was at least acting. All these thoughts were irksome.

The storm was beating against the south side of the train with a vengeance. It was a real deluge. A window up the aisle was cracked open, and hail bounced off the transom into the car. As the train clattered slowly down the mountain, he wondered about the full-blood villages out there in the storm, hid off in the hills, little gatherings of leaky, fleabag huts without fireplaces or outhouses. The full bloods fed themselves by hunting, scratching gardens out of poor hill soil, and collecting government money. Back when he'd covered this territory, Jake had tried to sell hardware in a couple of full-blood towns, but the pickings were slim with no stores to speak of, just a few blacksmiths.

Yet the Choctaw and Cherokee were the "rich" tribes, and fortunes in cotton had been built forty years ago down this way and on the Red River. When Jake had traveled this district, there were still a handful of Choctaw growers trying to keep up the old plantation style, with house servants and fancy carriages. But that kind of thing had generally gone the way of the cotton market. In 1894 "cotton farmer" was another way to say poor folk.

On lower ground, the hail gave way to rain, and they crept into Tuskahoma, past the capitol, a two-story brick building with a mansard roof, lighted in the downpour by brilliant trees of lightning.

Jake noticed Tom Freshour was awake, and looking disconcerted. "Capitol of the Choctaw Nation," Jake said across the aisle. "Ever see that before?"

"No sir," the boy said, blinking his eyes dully.

"The legislature meets there," Jake said.

"Yes sir."

Talkative devil.

Tuskahoma town consisted of a stunted row of false-front buildings on one side of the track, and across from it, down near the bank of the Kiamichi River, some older buildings including a blacksmith shop, a warehouse, and a hotel. Farms were strewn in no particular order on the surrounding hills, most of them with a few acres of valley cropland. The only person Jake was supposed to collect from here was John Blessing, but there was no way he could see him tonight.

Stepping off the car, Jake headed straight into the station house. The agent was gone. A gasoline stove sat hissing on the counter, and around the room were stacked crates, bales of new barbed wire, a saddle, and a case of saw blades from Dekker Hardware that was being leaked on through the roof. Jake shoved it out of the drip. When he turned around, the woman in their car Tom had been watching was standing there.

"Hello," she said, smiling.

Jake was too surprised to smile back. "Hello."

Tom Freshour took one look at her and turned away.

"Do you know where I could find a good hotel?"

"I know where a hotel is. Wouldn't necessarily call it good, ma'am." He hesitated a minute longer, not looking forward to getting soaking wet. The OK Hotel was where he'd always stayed when he traveled this route, and he hoped it was still in operation.

They headed across the muddy street, down the hillside through blowing, cold sheets of rain. The OK was still there, and Mrs. Oke, the gnarled root of a woman who owned the hotel, was up busying around taking care of leaks, stuffing cracks, taking up rag rugs, and glancing nervously out the windows.

"Awful wet out there," Jake said, setting down his grip.

"Black as a pocket," Mrs. Oke said.

"How have you been doing?"

"Oh, I'm all broke down and puny," she said, looking up at him with a glitter in her rheumy eyes. She was littler than ever — probably weighed all of eighty pounds. "Ain't me I'm worried about tonight, it's that river."

Jake signed his name to the register. "You remember me?"

"Course I do. You're Mr. Hardware. This your family?"

"No ma'am, I'm a bachelor. This is Tom. He's a new hand. And this lady's looking for a hotel."

She winked at Jake. "That boy's too handsome for the hardware business, hey?" She collected their fifty cents, lighted a hurricane lantern, then leaned toward Jake and said in hushed tones, "Got some deputies here tonight with a prisoner. Penny pinchers! Worried me to death tryin to get my price down." She took up the lantern and led them upstairs to a one-bed room, made a pallet on the floor for Tom, and got a couple of pans for leaks that were coming through the roof. A layer of old thin shakes was the only thing between them and the weather. Mrs. Oke left them to take care of the woman.

Jake decided that the weather was too terrible for him to go to the outhouse, so he peed out the window and the boy followed suit. "Don't get your pecker wet," Jake said.

Tom looked wary. "I won't, sir."

Jake took off his sopping clothes and put on his spare long johns. It occurred to him that the boy had no dry clothes, in fact no luggage at all. Having lived by himself, mostly in boarding houses, for thirty years, Jake wasn't accustomed to worrying about somebody else's domestic needs, but he dug out an undershirt and a pair of pants from his valise and offered them. Tom looked at the clothes, then at Jake, with the same unvarnished blankness, at first making no effort to take them.

"You want something dry?"

He took them, but instead of putting them on, laid them beside his pallet.

Jake shut down the wick and settled into the shuck mattress. The boy quickly knelt by the flickering window and said the Lord's Prayer aloud, so hurriedly that it sounded like nine or ten long words: ". . . forthineisthekingdom thepowerandtheglory foreveramen."

It was a thunder-rattled night, with fat raindrops unrelievedly beating on the roof, and Jake remained in a fitful state, smelling the bedbug-repelling kerosene soaked into the bedsteads, listening to the drip pans, worrying about how in the Sam Hill he was going to collect money from any of these stores. Jake remembered the Panic of '73, and this one was worse. In '73, he'd still been young enough not to worry, as long as his belly didn't get too empty. Still, he remembered how lucky he'd felt not to have a family to feed.

Through the night he fretted and tossed. Sometime before the first paleness of day, a thunderbolt shook the walls, and he rolled over and saw the boy at the window, outlined in a sky walking with fire. He had taken off his wet shirt, and in the lightning Jake saw a thick network of scars on his back. A good-sized kid. Tall. Maybe sixteen, hard to tell. Jake wondered about him in a dreamy kind of way — where he'd come from, how he'd been orphaned. He looked again through half-shut eyes and noticed that the boy turned toward him, stepped quietly over the pallet, now came swiftly toward the bed and was suddenly there above him. A dim fear went through Jake's mind, but he was just at the cusp of sleep. A boy with that many scars on his back could be a rotten apple. But he lay momentarily frozen between indecision and plain sleepiness, and before he had made up his mind to sit up, the boy stole away. Soon Jake tumbled headlong into a brief sleep full of vivid dreams.

Only to be waked up by banging and yelling, after what seemed like less than an hour. He put his feet on the floor — the boy wasn't in the room — and he walked over to the window. The sun wasn't up yet, but he saw in lantern reflection out a window what the boy had been watching.

The Kiamichi had become a river sure enough, out of its banks and roaring, and the hotel was sitting in the edge of it. A chicken house floated by, crowned by one forlorn leghorn. The door to the room swung open and Mrs. Oke poked her head in.

"Movin out!" she croaked. "Need help!"

· 2 ·

FOR TOM FRESHOUR the last twenty-four hours had been like a dream — the long walk from the orphanage at Bokchito to Durant, the train ride from there to Fort Smith, and the hanging, then going into a big old building and standing before a roomful of nervous, chewing men, and being given a job, and told that he would never return to the academy, just like that. And again a train into the territory, and staying the night in an atticlike room with a salesman named Mr. W. W. "Jake" Jaycox while it rained without end. The whole world outside the Armstrong Academy was like a dream, only more sudden, more amazing, more full of strangeness. And this morning Tom's shivering and the gnawing hunger in his belly felt very real, but slogging up the cold, rain-swept hill carrying furniture seemed both real and dreaming — the real of the cold against his skin in the fantastic dreamy unendingness of the rain.

Lanterns burned smoky and high around the common room of the OK Hotel. Water was over the floorboards and the old woman waded around, gathering up smaller things. A man carrying a huge wooden display grip with *El Dorado Chemical & Drugs* in sweeping red letters was helping move some of it. There were three others: a white prisoner with loosened leg manacles and two white men with badges. The deputies slouched in the common room, rolling cigarettes and passing a bottle back and forth. The old woman kept fussing at the ones who were helping, as they hauled food safe, tables, dressers, and even some beds out the door and up the hill.

"*Apela!*" She went down the little hall to the first-floor room and pounded on the door. "Wake up! Come out! Hurry."

Mr. Jaycox appeared, walking as stiffly as a table down the stairs, looking grizzled and grumpy, blinking at the water that covered the floor. "Good God almighty," he muttered. Soon he was helping Tom muscle a chest of drawers and parts of beds up the slippery hill, dropping things, getting their feet stuck in the mud. The drug salesman and the prisoner — the deputies called him "cedar thief" — continued helping, too, while the two deputy marshals did not.

They bucked the furniture to a building behind John Blessing's General Merchandise. Back at the hotel, the water was more than ankle-deep. Mrs. Oke now was being followed around by the shorter of the deputies, who wanted to get back last night's room fee in payment for the labor of their prisoner. He was a fast-talking, snaky man with two big hogleg guns strapped backwards to his waist.

She had her cash box under her arm but wasn't about to hand back any money. "*Ch sinti!* Go away, you penny pincher!" she said angrily.

Mr. Jaycox picked up a lantern and walked between them. "This place is flooding out."

The door to the downstairs room opened and out came the woman they had met last night. She wore a high collar and a starched grey skirt, the hem of which floated in the water. It wasn't as if her appearance was unexpected, but to Tom the sight of her was troubling. High-arched eyebrows, green eyes, and dark hair done up in a bun with stray curls down her temples — she was the most beautiful woman he had ever seen, though he hadn't seen many. He wanted to look away from her but found it impossible to do so. It occurred to him that she was from the city, the big city — an odd thought since, as far as he knew, he had never known anyone from a big city, much less a woman. The one woman he had really known was seventy-some years old and did not speak the same language he did, so they had done little talking. Yet however ill equipped he was to come up with such an opinion, still he thought it: big city.

She looked at both Mr. Jaycox and him with almost a smile. "I hope you're well this morning, Mr. Jaycox," she said, and while he looked momentarily bemused by this, she glanced around the somber disorder of the room, showing no sign of fear, hiked up her skirt and actually led them out of the hotel.

They all trailed up the hill and stood on the roofed porch of Blessing's store. Cheerless, begrudging, greenish light began filtering through clouds that showed no sign of letting up. Near the train depot, a man in a big-wheeled hack was mired up to the axle, his mare struggling wildly under the continuously booming thunder, and Tom went over and helped him push it out. People all around the village were crawling out of damp nests. A few were trudging back and forth, carrying things up from low-lying houses and buildings.

The young woman and Mrs. Oke, still clutching her cash box, remained on the porch watching the hopeless situation of the hotel, while others went inside and huddled around the stove. The prisoner and two deputies were soon grousing about this and that, the shorter deputy about the widow not refunding his money, the timber thief about having to do all the work.

The taller deputy, who had a woeful, guilty look, seemed mainly concerned about breakfast. "Git no sleep, work all mornin helpin her, you'd think she'd git us somethin . . ."

"*Who* worked all morning?" the timber thief said. "Neither one of you dogberries knows *how* to work."

Townspeople trailed into the store a few at a time looking for help or consolation, clusters of refugees bringing more household items to the high ground, including bundles of clothes, chairs, broken-down beds, and some animals left outside — chickens, a little herd of goats, some cows. A couple of men wanted to "borrow" chicken wire from the store owner to make a temporary pen on the high ground behind the store, and he gave it to them. People talked quietly about who'd been washed out, who'd lost livestock, and where they could move things. The men made and lighted cigarettes, and the room smelled of sumac, tobacco, wet clothes, and upset nerves.

The young woman from the hotel stood beside Mrs. Oke on the porch; a moment earlier she had come inside and looked around. Tom noticed that no one spoke to her. The deputies and the timber thief quit quarreling and watched her in a sullen, walleyed way.

The short deputy poked Tom in the shoulder and said, with a dirty-toothed grin, "Like to git a little of that?"

"I beg your pardon?" Tom said.

"Oh ho! Listen to that, Wayne. We have an educated one here. He's so smart he don't know what I'm talking about."

"Tom," Mr. Jaycox said sharply, "could you come over here, please." He was sitting on a box back from the fire. He motioned Tom to sit next to him, then said quietly, "You probably ought to keep away from them."

"Yes sir."

After a moment he said, "Tom, did you talk to that young woman?"

"No I didn't, sir."

The salesman looked puzzled. "I don't think I know her. I guess Mrs. Oke must have mentioned my name to her."

"Yes sir."

"You can call me Jake if you'd like."

"Thank you, sir."

Mr. Jaycox looked around the store and sighed.

Grim-faced, with mud to their knees, two more families from low-lying houses showed up, bringing things with them, and the store was now littered with wet furniture, wet bundles of clothes, wet and dismal people of all ages. Drips plinked down and buckets were accidentally knocked over on the floor.

Mr. Jaycox spoke so no one but Tom could hear him. "Looks like John Blessing's down to bartering pumpkins and sweet corn. This place is as sparse as a hillbilly's teeth. When I sold goods here, he was getting to be one of the best general merchants in the Nation." Jake shook his head. "Today ain't the time for collecting. Not with what's going on here."

Tom watched the owner. He had dark bags under his eyes. When he sold something he didn't ask for cash; he just wrote the figures in his big account book, larger in size than the "book of sins" kept by Reverend Schoot but with the same thick black cover. In all the confusion of traffic, people were asking the storekeeper for loans of this and that, help, or advice. He tried to accommodate them, but he looked debilitated and strained. Nervously, fussily, he checked the buckets he'd set around the room to catch drips.

A thin, wavering cry came from the porch, and everyone in the room fell quiet — statues in a dimly lit room marbled with smoke. Several of them moved at once, crowding out to the front porch, and Tom followed, just in time to see the hotel they had slept in last night jolt and shudder and be swept away by the flood. The old woman cried out again — a thin, high, eerily familiar sound. The big building pivoted sideways and headed ponderously downstream on its foundation of logs, floating for some distance like a ship before doing a slow, staggering dip, tipping over and starting to break apart. Another building nearby was being shaken and torn by the force of the current. The warehouse next to the hotel had already collapsed into the river, and the downslope half of Tuskahoma appeared to be pretty much gone. Mrs. Oke's cry cut through the rain.

Tom was standing painfully close to the young woman, who gave off a heat that he could feel through the wet air. She turned and looked at him — slowly, actually raking her eyes up across him — and he backpedaled a step, tripped over a boot scraper, and fell hard on his tailbone. Humiliated, he got up quickly.

Mr. Jaycox came over. "I think we're going to have to call this trip a bust and try to catch a train back. The bridges are either going to be under water or blocked by ballast trains pretty soon. We'd be floating around out here till the cows come home. I'm just going to say hello to John Blessing. Come over and meet him."

Tom saw the young woman move a step, as if about to speak to Mr. Jaycox, but he didn't notice her.

The owner was behind his counter, wet and grim. He was a stout man, at least half-blood, with a scar cut deeply into his chin. When they walked over, Blessing stayed behind his counter, looking unfriendly. "What are you doin here, sellin rowboats?" Blessing said without preface, swallowing his words off short, as if they tasted bad in his mouth.

Mr. Jaycox held out a hand to shake, and Blessing barely touched it. "No sir. This is still Dandy's territory."

"You travelin Guthrie?"

"Guthrie and north of there," Mr. Jaycox said.

"Makin a lot of money in the white settlements?"

"Not lately."

"That's where all the money is. Sure ain't down here."

Mr. Jaycox smiled and shook his head. "Most of the money in Oklahoma Territory stays on the keno tables, John. Half the people in Guthrie moved out a couple of weeks ago for the Outlet rush."

"The free land," Blessing said sarcastically. "They'll have ours soon."

"Meet Tom Freshour, John. He just came on with us."

Blessing looked morosely toward the door. "So Dekker is hiring Indian boys to sell hardware? Must be in a bad way."

Mr. Jaycox looked taken aback. "Well now, John, that's a heck of a thing to say."

The storekeeper looked suspicious. "You ain't here to collect money from me, are you?"

"I'm just stopping off to say hello. I'll talk to you later."

"But that's what you're here for, isn't it," Blessing demanded.

"I'm not going to pester you, John. You've been a good customer for a long time, and I can see what's goin on here today —"

This apparently was the wrong thing to say, because Blessing gritted his teeth and slammed his fist onto his account book so hard the glass cases rattled. "So you *are* here to dun me!"

Mr. Jaycox appeared startled at his sudden fury.

"What you wanta do, confiscate my stock, eh? Let me tell you something. You can have it!" He shoved a heavy sack across the counter, hitting the salesman in the leg, scattering tenpenny nails all over the floor. A rope tree with coils of different-sized manila sat on his counter, and he picked up the end close to him and with a powerful spasmodic contraction of his shoulders flipped it toward them. It hit the floor next to Mr. Jaycox's boot.

"Damnation, John —"

"Wanta shut me down, eh? Take my store. Ya can have it! Debtsandall!" He again pounded the accounts book. "Take — eh, eh!" He seemed breathless, his head bobbing and eyes blinking in a slow, strange way. "Ya can have it!" He pointed at the account book.

Stepping backwards, the store owner bumped into his medicine shelf, reached into a box, and pulled out a pistol. It looked like the old wartime cap-and-ball revolver that Tom had seen the Reverend use. "Take it!" he shouted, the scar on his chin livid. He waggled the pistol at them.

Remarkably fast, the crowded store was emptying of people. Blessing remained behind his counter, eyes narrow, with the pistol aimed at Mr. Jaycox.

"Tom, we better be leaving." He put a hand on Tom's shoulder and Tom did what he did, backpedaling slowly until they had made it onto the porch.

"Take the damn thing!" John Blessing roared.

♦

The first thing Tom noticed outside was that the young woman in the grey skirt and Mrs. Oke had apparently gone down the hill to get something, because now they were starting back up the hill. The two deputies remained, peeking through the front window, talking about the store owner, who was threatening now to kill himself and anybody who came in the door.

"It's against regulations to pull a gun in a post office," said the short one with two pistols.

"Naw, now —" said the tall one.

"This here's a goddamn post office, ain't it? He can't kill hisself in there. If he's breaking postal regulations, we haul him to Guthrie. It's a good hunderd fifty miles, times six cents, plus the federal bounty. That's real money, mister."

The arrested man, sitting down against the wall, snorted, "He's a Indin. He can commit suicide anyplace he wants to."

"You're wrong there, cedar thief," the short deputy said. "He can't do it in a post office. It don't make no difference what kind of Indin he is."

"How in the hell are you going to *git* to Guthrie?" the cedar thief said vehemently. "Rivers are floodin, and you're too *cheap* to buy a ticket even if the trains was runnin, you and your damn six cent a mile! Besides which, I ain't goin two hunderd mile across the damn country chained to some son of a bitch that's tryin to kill hisself!"

"I don't know," the tall deputy said worriedly. "I think we oughter leave . . ."

Peering intently through the rain, Tom saw Mrs. Oke with the young woman beside her carrying a suitcase, struggling toward the porch, sinking up to her shins in the street. Mrs. Oke held a little box of knickknacks. The woman stepped onto the porch first, and Mr. Jaycox was moving to warn her away when four or five shots came off so fast that Tom hardly had time to flinch. Out of the corner of his eye he glimpsed something coming through the door, a large black thing, flying like a saw blade cut loose from its axle, and the woman was knocked back off the porch into the mud, quick as a steer hit in the head with a sledgehammer.

It was Mr. Blessing's account book, hurled out the door with such force that she probably hadn't even seen it.

Mr. Jaycox went to her and knelt down. He yelled at Tom to help him.

· 3 ·

GET OUT OF HERE," came the hoarse voice from inside the building. "All of you!"

Back against the wall near the front door, a foolish grin on his face, the short deputy yelled, "I'm arresting you for shootin in a post office!"

"I do whatever I want to in my own store, *hatak hata.*"

Blash!

A bullet cut through the rain, and Jake instinctively ducked, dropping the woman back into the mud.

"Boy, she don't look good," the short deputy said, with the same goofy grin on his face.

The color had quickly left her face, her expression crumpled. The big black ledger lay flopped open by her head with several bullet holes in it. Blessing had shot his own ledger, then hurled it out the door. Jake couldn't see any wounds besides an ugly, deep bruise on her temple. The boy was kneeling next to her in deep mud, his hands held out, not quite touching her.

"Come on," Jake said. "We better get her out of the street before she drowns."

"Is she shot?" the short deputy asked, grinning stupidly.

"Listen," Jake said, "if you keep ragging that man in there, he'll just get madder. He's off on a jag. Leave him alone. Let him cool off."

"Indin goes off his rocker, there's hell to pay," the short deputy said, waving one of his .45s toward Jake. "This here is the law's work." The tall deputy crouched on the other side of the doorway.

Jake scooped up the woman and took her to the storage building behind the store. Mrs. Oke and Tom followed. It was an old dwelling house, stacked haphazardly with merchandise — kitchen cabinets, bundles of clothes, Bibles, mirrors, standing coat hooks, spittoons. The woman's face remained ashen. The heavy binding of the ledger must have hit her right where she lived. Jake again looked for signs of other wounds, but saw none. Mrs. Oke found a horse blanket, wrapped her in it, and sent the boy to get the doctor. Outside, the deputy continued nagging John Blessing.

"Cain't pull a gun in a federal post office, mister."

"Leave me alone! I have dynamite!"

Jake had remained calm until now, but he found himself standing outside, mad, with his heart pounding hard. It was no wonder people hated the law, when they hired these malletheads and paid them nothing but travel bounties and rewards. He was pacing in and out the door when Tom returned. The one doctor in town had taken a call miles away during the night and wasn't back. Mrs. Oke looked up at Jake and shook her head. "Don't know what to do," she said quietly. The woman's eyes were drawn up, and Jake knelt and felt her pulse. She had only a small cut on her temple, but beneath it was the deep, spreading bruise.

"Come on out!" the deputy yelled at Mr. Blessing.

Jake cursed under his breath, and was just standing to go outside when a tremendous thud hit the wall. Glass and part of the wooden frame of the window blew out, shards spraying across the floor. The first thought Jake had was that lightning had struck the wall, although the smell coming through the window quickly told him differently.

"Clear the glass off!" he shouted, pointing to the woman. The boy and Mrs. Oke helped brush away the glass and undid the blanket. Mrs. Oke loosened her clothes. Jake went outside the shed. The sulfurous stink of powder dynamite lay thick in the rainy air; part of the store's back wall and roof and all of the windows had been blown out.

Jake was the first one inside the smoking store, and he found what was left of John in a corner. He dragged him out onto the front porch, then went back inside and took a piece of calico off a shelf to put over the storekeeper's face. His tattered, blackened legs stuck out below. The explosion had shredded his trousers into smoking rags hanging off his still-intact galluses. With his hat pulled low over his eyes, Jake knelt by the steaming corpse, dizzy from his own pulse.

The timber thief, who had been sitting against the wall near the front door, continued to sit there, looking stunned but unhurt. The deputies had escaped visible injury, although the one with two guns looked even more unhinged than before. He walked up to the corpse and, to Jake's amazement, pushed it with his toe. "What I told you. The son of a bitch ruint the post office. We'll haul him to Guthrie for the pelt."

His tall, morose partner glanced at him with wifely recrimination. "Naw, we oughter get out of here."

Jake stood up and fixed the short one with a baleful look. "That man has seven sons and about twenty cousins. They'll be showing up here real soon. Lay a finger on his body and you won't know who snuffed the candle."

This seemed to make some impression on the knucklehead. His partner kept urging that they get out of town, and eventually the two faded away, prisoner in tow, into the storm.

Jake heard the sound of a whistle coming from the south. The night train from Texas had made it through. He went back in the storage room. The woman's color was much better now, but the lump on her temple really was ugly.

Mrs. Oke stood up to Jake, close, with her head down. "My fault."

"It ain't your fault," Jake said.

"Carry her to Fort Smith to see the doctor. Please do that, Mr. Hardware. I'm too old, hey?"

The train went by, slowing to a stop at the little platform. Jake didn't have much time to make up his mind. "Come on, kid. I guess we better take her with us. You get her by the feet."

The woman was limp as a rag, and it wasn't easy toting her to the train. Tom acted het-up, bumbling and confused, and it nearly broke Jake's back getting her through the mud, onto the platform, and into the car. Finally aboard, they laid her across a seat, took the wet horse blanket from around her, and wrapped her in a slightly less wet coat from Jake's valise, not much use when her dress was sopping. He wiped the mud from her face with his handkerchief. The left eye, below her swollen temple, was bloodshot.

As the train got under way, Jake looked down and saw Mrs. Oke standing in the door of the station house, and he pushed up the window and yelled, "Do you know what her name is?"

Mrs. Oke made no sign or response. Shawl wrapped tightly around her head, she gazed in Jake's direction with the implacable blankness of a full blood, as if losing her hotel had returned her to the primitive fate that all these years she'd worked to avoid.

They took off briskly up the hill — only the engine, a mail car, and two passenger cars. This train was the first luck he'd had that day. They made it handily over the fog-enshrouded Kiamichi Mountains, and Jake imagined they'd be in Fort Smith inside of two hours. But down the other side, in the lowlands, the roadbed was covered by water in several places, and they had to slow down.

Across the aisle, Tom looked uneasy. He kept staring at the woman, who had slipped until her head was tilted backwards, her long neck revealed, curly black hair in disarray, mouth slightly open. Her color was a little better.

"Fix her so her head ain't dangling down like that," Jake said.

The boy didn't seem to hear him.

"Go straighten her up before she hurts her durn neck."

Tom moved to do so, but he seemed afraid to touch her, and Jake fumed when he had to get up and do it himself. This courier that big shot Dekker had foisted off on him was about as much use as a mule collar hanging around his neck, what with keeping him awake at night, not doing what he was asked, and never saying enough to let you know what was going on in his head. To heck with him. To heck with em all. Jake moved to a seat in the rear of the car, shut his eyes, and tried to take a nap.

·4·

EVERY TIME Tom looked at her, he couldn't take his eyes away. She was awake some of the time now, rising occasionally, squinting as if she had a severe headache.

The train entered the bottomlands at a crawl. Rain was still coming down in sheets. Tom saw whole endless fields covered in water, with islands of land here and there. Stranded cattle stood up to their bellies, unable to make it to higher ground because of fences or potholes. Farther out, the water looked dead calm, but in places along the train's roadbed it flowed in a river-like current. When he heard the wheels pushing through water, Tom stuck his head out the window and saw that they were headed into what looked for all the world like a giant, trackless lake planted mysteriously with trees. Lonely clusters of squatters' shacks stood in the flood, surrounded by floating debris of all kinds, and the train had slowed to such a pace that he could see it all — barrels, dead chickens, snakes. On the roof of one shack sat a wet cat with his tail curled up around him, looking down at the water.

Below Talihina, where they were barely moving through the water, a huddle of people on the roadbed flagged down the train. The engineer stopped and they pushed onto the cars — a soggy crowd, mixed breeds and whites, mournful-looking men with the black-scarred faces of coal miners, farmers, women in bonnets with sleeping and crying babies, and fretting, bird-chested, hookworm-skinny children. Farther along, the train ran into another and still another flock, adding more than thirty people in all to their car. The women were lugging tins of beans and tomatoes and bits of this and that — lard buckets full of radishes and potatoes and any other kind of food they could find to take. The men carried saddles, boxes and sacks of clothes, axes, rolled-up screen wire, kerosene lanterns, shotguns.

Mr. Jaycox, buffeted by people jamming themselves and their belongings into the seats and aisle around him, had apparently given up trying to take a nap. The sodden throng gave up a fearsome ammonia-smelling fog of bodies, kid pee, vegetables, and who knows what else. After the third bunch had scrambled on board, Tom noticed that the woman was sitting halfway up, looking around in bewilderment at the crowd. She was awake but dazed. A short, rough-looking man shoved her upright and sat next to her, and she gazed at him in woozy astonishment.

"Get your hands off of me," she said, pushing him back.

"What the hell?" he sputtered.

"You smell bad," she said.

"Why —"

Mr. Jaycox got up and elbowed toward her. "She has a head wound. She's injured."

"She'll git a wound all right, talkin to me like that," the man snarled. "No got-damn woman —"

"You smell like a skunk," she stated; Tom could hear her plainly despite the hubbub. Face pallid, hair tangled and wet, one eye bloodshot, she looked wild as a wounded mustang. Mr. Jaycox eventually managed to bring her up with Tom and him, although by the time he got there, someone had already stolen his seat, and there was more confusion getting the man out, and getting her, Tom, and himself settled into two seats — the boy squashed against the window, her in the middle, and Mr. Jaycox on the aisle. She seemed to have very little idea where she was or what was happening. Brief fits of talking came up and passed, but her expression was forlorn. She muttered things neither of them could understand. Being awake seemed to tire her out; soon her head lolled onto Tom's shoulder, and she fell into a delirious, worried sleep.

Her blouse undone at the top by Mrs. Oke, white unmentionables visible, muddy clothes in disarray, she went from cold and stiff to feverish and limber, then back to cold. With her pushing against him in the seat, Tom felt his tool of generation (as Reverend Schoot called it) rising up hard as a stick in his wet pants. At the Armstrong Academy, his tool never got him into anything but trouble. When it went off in dreams, it was deceptively pleasant at the moment, but when cots were examined and evidence was found, it was worth between ten and fifteen lashes, depending on the Reverend's mood. Tom tried to avoid this by masturbation. He abused himself despite the fact that it was bad for him, made his brain heavy and dull, caused exhaustion of the nerves, weakened memory, bad posture, narrow-chestedness, flabby muscles, consumption, paralysis, heart disease, and in some cases suicide. It was bad for him, but he did it only to avoid the nightly emissions. Most of the older boys at the orphanage had a dim grasp of the primitive facts about human reproduction, but it was taboo as a subject of jokes or conversation. The Reverend had his spies among the boys, and you had to be very careful about what you said.

He squirmed in the seat in an effort to get farther from the woman, but there was no place to go. She was touching him in several places, her head leaning onto his shoulder, hair in his neck, and her arm down loosely at her side, hand against his leg.

Suddenly she pulled her head up and announced, "I have to go."

Tom looked out the window, as if he hadn't heard her.

"I was afraid this would happen," Mr. Jaycox said. "Help me, Tom."

They got her up and pressed her through to the back of the car. The water closet had run over, but several desperate people were nevertheless waiting to use it. She moaned as they pushed through the crowd. The train kept stopping entirely so the engineer could assess the depth of water ahead, and Mr. Jaycox said, "Tom, we're going to have to take a chance here. Make way, please." They propelled her out the door and down the steps. It was nearly dark, and there wasn't a dry spot of land anywhere within reach, and lightning was still cracking as if the storm had just started. The track was a good hand's depth below the surface. They were standing in a lake. To Tom's dismay, Mr. Jaycox advised her to relieve herself right there.

After some confusion, she had in fact drawn down her scanties and was dangling from their grasp, one on each side, south pole nearly touching the water, but she did not do her business. "Don't have much time, ma'am. This train's gonna start back up," Mr. Jaycox said. She looked out to the side, puzzled at what must have seemed in her delirium like an endless expanse of brown water. Four or five little boys hung out the window, watching with interest.

"You said you needed to go. Now's your chance!"

"I'm . . . dead?" she mumbled.

"No ma'am, you aren't dead. I doubt that you'll need to do this when you're dead."

"I'm a dead duck," she sighed.

Every way they looked was some kind of critter — prairie chickens, rabbits, snakes — trying to find a perch above the water. A very live snake was swimming vigorously toward them. It was a blacksnake, and it came right for her leg, nuzzled against it, and tried to climb for higher ground.

She looked at it dully. "Thas a snake?"

"Yes ma'am, but it's just a blacksnake. He's looking for something to climb up. Now if you'll go ahead and finish, I'll get you out of here."

"Lemme loose, you two!"

"Go ahead, now. Drain the lizard. Let er go —"

She finally did so, while the boys who were leaning out the window continued to look on seriously. The train was slowly moving on now, and they stood her up, unraveled the snake from her leg and pitched it away, struggled her back aboard, and pushed her through the crowd. Children were wailing. A man somewhere in the car was in a coughing frenzy.

It was completely dark when they idled through the mining town of Poteau, which was flooded out by the very river they were supposed to cross ahead. The train stopped on a dry patch just outside town, and passengers piled out, some so tired they just sat or lay down on the roadbed. The light of sheltered campfires reflected from a nearby hill, and word passed around that most of Poteau's few hundred citizens had retreated to high ground. Some of the miners decided to stay and join them, fearful of the big Poteau River crossing ahead. The train waited for the better part of an hour and Tom, passing through the crowd, heard all kinds of speculations about what lay ahead, from the most ominous to the rosiest: the track was good to the north, it was completely washed out, the roadbed was steadily higher, it was steadily lower, the bridge into Fort Smith had disappeared, it was ten feet above the water — everyone seemed to have a different, extreme idea, and the engineer took his time making up his mind. All wires were down, and there was no way to check by telegraph.

A little band of locals who had spotted the train showed up and wanted to get on, but the sooners who'd already been in the car defended their spots as fiercely as if they owned the railroad line. Pushing and yelling fights broke out in the darkness, and Tom was afraid the woman was going to wake up again with some other terrible problem — or that she would die before they made it to Fort Smith.

"My stomach's so empty it hurts," Mr. Jaycox said.

A woman with a pokeful of onions between her legs sat in the seat in front of them. Mr. Jaycox leaned over and asked her if she'd take a nickel for a couple of onions. He gave one to Tom and they sat there peeling and munching on them.

The injured woman's condition kept worrying Tom. After they'd all reloaded, the conductor walked along beside each car with a lantern and called, "Can't tell how the bridge is ahead, but however it is, it'll just get worse. I'm taking this engine in. Anybody don't want to chance it ought to get off here." He took out his watch and looked at it. "You have two minutes!"

There was more pushing as a handful of passengers decided to get themselves and their belongings off the train. A single gas lamp was lit somewhere in the car, providing dim light, and when the train started to move, the woman grew wakeful and started mumbling and cursing again. She tried to sit up straight. She flung her arms and legs around with as little concern as a baby, one leg going over Mr. Jaycox's until she was half in his lap, and she pushed directly against Tom's thighs.

If it was possible to die of blushing, Tom was a goner. He was immobilized, every muscle in his body stiff. When she sank headfirst, completely dead weight, into his lap, he looked down, truly scared, at the top of her muddy, damp head. Mr. Jaycox reached over and felt the pulse in her neck. He straightened her head so she could breathe. "Just leave her be." He glanced sourly at Tom. "I wish that engineer would just take us wherever we're going, either to Fort Smith or the bottom of the Poteau River. I'm about to the point I don't care which."

At a settlement called Cameron, on the shoulder of a hill, three more passengers who were afraid of the last bridge jumped off the slow-moving car.

Tom heard more anxious talk about logjams and fallen bridges.

Near midnight, the murmuring in the car died away as they finally approached the Poteau River bridge into Fort Smith. A woman with a nervous, reedy voice started saying "The Lord is my shepherd," and others joined in. In the blackness of night they could see nothing, and the river was so loud and close that the train already seemed to be under water. Partway out came an immense shudder. "The Lord is my shepherd" died away. Even the babies stopped crying. Tom quit trying to look out. Couplings clattered against each other as the bridge wobbled and swayed in the river with the current and the weight of the train. The steady *ch-ch-ch* of steam from the engine turned peculiar, then stopped altogether.

"Regulators are under water!" somebody said.

They lost power, and when he felt the car's vibration change and heard a loud splashing of water, Tom realized they were in it high above the wheels, plowing through the river on deeply submerged track. Water poured in from cracks in the floor planking.

He had been in feverish worried excitement since the woman fell on him. He was less anxious about the river than he was about her. She lay slumped on him, her bosom crushed against his leg, her head rubbing and jerking in his lap with the wild motions of the train. Sweat ran down his face like tears, and he squirmed in the seat, wanting both to get away and not to get away. The feeling of euphoria in his lower extremities was so potent that he seemed almost to float above the seat. He looked down at her head, trying to decide whether to move it, then his breath caught and in the momentary silence of the car, his was the only cry — startled, unintentional, brief.

Steam could be heard bubbling out the regulators, and the crowd gave up a ragged cheer. They'd made it across the bridge. The engineer stopped immediately when they reached Coke Hill, a high spot on the river end of Fort Smith, and the cars were still draining water as passengers piled off. Tom extricated himself and tried to stand up, but his body was numb, his knees rubbery, and he could hardly get out of the seat.

· 5 ·

JAKE HAD NEVER been so happy to step off a train in his life. Located a couple of hundred yards west of Parker's gallows, Coke Hill was a little settlement off to itself, occupied by two bleak saloons, a ramshackle two-story hotel of dubious reputation called the Belle Point, and a huddle of poor dwelling houses. He hurried over to the hotel and secured a porter with a rig.

The porter took the highest route, his mare trotting sure-footedly through the streams of water in the brick streets. In the coolness the woman was briefly wakeful, mumbling and cussing, but still unable to talk sense. The boy acted sleepy and confused. Jake felt markedly better despite his exhaustion and hunger, moving briskly through the clean, cold air. As he'd expected, the low end of town was thoroughly flooded at the confluence of the Poteau and Arkansas rivers. The ground floor of the Dekker building was bound to be under.

St. John's Hospital was out Second Street, a modest house with tall windows and a picket fence around it. A red flag with black letters hung by the entrance: SMALL POX. A young man with a hat pushed back on his head and a patch of hair hanging down his forehead sat on the front step underneath the flag, calmly puffing on a pipe. The rain had momentarily stopped.

"Doctor in?"

"I'm Doc Eldon. Who is that?"

"Jake Jaycox."

"What brings you?"

"I have a patient for you."

"Wouldn't have smallpox, would he?"

"It's a she. No, she doesn't."

"I can't do a thing for her, Mr. Jaycox. We've been under quarantine going on four days. I wouldn't even want to examine her."

"Where can I take her?"

"What's the trouble?"

"Hit in the head. Can't seem to wake up."

"Does she know her own name?"

"I'm not sure."

"Well, ask her."

Jake turned and asked what her name was. She gave no answer, and after a moment the boy, on whose shoulder she leaned, said grimly, "Sleeping again."

"Probably has a concussion," the doctor said quietly. He sat there a while nursing his pipe, looking out into the night, the SMALL POX sign waving slightly in the breeze above his head. "Can she stand up?"

"Not on her own."

The doctor shook his head. "I don't know what to tell you. I can't see her. I've got eleven people packed in Vaseline in here."

"I've heard there's a lying-in hospital on Seventh Street."

Eldon hesitated. "Yep. That's Doc Finch. He'll be about all you'll find tonight. I've had people by here every few minutes. Doctors will be out all over town."

"So you reckon that's the place to go?"

Eldon again hesitated, and gave a little shrug. "Well, he'll be there, anyway."

With that precarious recommendation, on they went to Seventh Street, where Jake asked the porter to wait while they took the woman inside, with hopes of leaving her.

Finch's "hospital" was as busy as Muskogee on a Saturday night. A trail of blood led to a partly shut door, behind which someone was yelling, "Ashes, linen! Hurry up!" Jake learned from others in the waiting room that the doctor was trying to stop the bleeding of a boy who had chopped a hunk out of his ankle.

Around the room were several kids, some wailing, with mothers trying to calm and shush them. A couple of fathers sat on the back bench, stiff and sleepy, faces emptied of all expression. Jake wondered, as he often had, what it was like to be perpetually tormented by sick and dying children, having to bring them to these carbolic- and liniment-reeking rooms, and so often having to bury them. He'd never had a wife, partly for that reason. To have a family was to sign up for the army of illness and death.

Tom Freshour sat straight-backed but sleepy on a bench with the woman listing against him, her eyes closed. Even with her leaning on him and his own eyes almost shut, the boy still sat up straight.

The chief nurse was an angry-faced woman who regarded the three of them with icy displeasure, and her scowl worsened when Jake admitted they didn't know the injured woman's name. A fat, full-bearded man careened into the waiting room and glanced around with a wild glint to his eye. His nose was livid, and he smelled and looked like a back-alley drunkard. He was the doctor, it turned out. He took a couple more children by the arms and dragged them into the back room. The chief nurse remained behind her desk, surveying people in the room with disapproval. Two other nurses scuttled here and there, doing the work of the place.

Jake regretted even coming here. The woman would get better medical care under a railroad trestle than in this sawbones' joint. By now he was so tired that he could have walked out the door and gone to sleep in a mud puddle in the yard. For a while he stood there looking at the boy, who gazed in sleepy bewilderment at him. Jake let out a big sigh. "Come on. We can't leave her in this place."

♦

Mrs. Peltier was as decent and kind a landlady as ever lived — as long as her rules weren't broken. Jake had lived at her Bachelors' House for thirteen years and was not shy about knocking on her door in the middle of the night. She woke up and attended to the woman without complaint, taking her into the spare bed in her own parlor.

Jake and the boy sat in exhausted silence at the little table in Mrs. Peltier's kitchen. They shared a loaf of bread, a couple of apples, and bottles of strawberry-flavored soda water from the icebox. After watching Jake, Tom eventually reached for the bright red soda. He drank it, looked at it in sleepy amazement, and wolfed down some bread.

"What will happen to her, Mr. Jaycox?" he asked, blinking his eyes slowly.

Jake shook his head. "I never heard of anybody killed by an accounts book before, but you never can say for sure."

The boy looked away from Jake, into his strawberry soda.

"By the way, you can call me Jake."

"Yes sir." The boy's eyelids soon descended, and he fell asleep sitting upright, in mid-chew. Jake had to help him up. He pushed him upstairs.

A note had been shoved under Jake's door. Helped to the couch, Tom curled up and went to sleep. His clothes were still wet, but the room was warm enough, and Jake let it be. He walked over to the note on the floor, hesitated, then decided that it was probably from the store, and he didn't want to see it. Not tonight. He noticed Tom's face, a little rounder and more like a child's when he was asleep. But he wasn't a boy. He was a young man who just didn't quite know it yet. Jake went in and shut his own door to merciful, private quietness. Finally.

♦

At 6:30 the next morning, Jake and Tom were slogging down Rogers Avenue fortified by a good boarding-house breakfast. Mrs. Peltier had judged their patient improved, sleeping soundly and with better color. It was still cloudy but not raining, the streets quiet, horsecars not running. The note Jake had waited until morning to read was somewhat mysterious. It said simply, "Jake, I need to see you as soon as you get back. Ralph Dekker." A block away from the Dekker building they hit the floodwater, and it was thigh-deep by the time they got to the front door. Directly across the street, the old courthouse jail sat on its privileged hillock a couple of feet above the flood. The last block of Rogers Avenue sloped sharply downhill to the train station, which had completely disappeared, roof, chimney, and all, beneath the flood.

The sandbagging around the store building was so far under that Jake didn't even see it until he bumped into it. The front door was open to the water. Around the large front sales room floated sundry items of stock and trash, a couple of spittoons, and one rat swimming for its life, among the carcasses of many others. The sales desk barely stuck out of the water. A worker paddled a johnboat piled with stock from the sports equipment shelves toward the rear of the big room.

The narrow stairs were busy with haggard, wet men who looked like they'd been at work for hours. Jake and the boy went for the elevator, which was about to go up with three huge boxes of shotgun loads in the middle of the platform. The elevator operator was Edgar Wyatt, a short black man with massive shoulders who pulled and braked the ropes that drove the fifteen-foot-square wall-less platform up and down the unguarded shaft between floors. Jake and the boy clambered onto it from the water. The basement, normally visible through the big space on all sides of the elevator, was a giant vessel of water.

"Get everything out from below?" Jake asked.

"Nosuh," Edgar said. "Been workin since in the night, but the river risin so fast, can't keep up with it. It start to comin in, got to thundering down this hole. One of the mens almost got washed down."

"Is Mr. Dekker here?"

"They all been comin and goin." He began pulling the ropes. "Some of em on the shippin floor."

"I'll just get off there. Could you put this boy to work, Edgar? He can help with carrying."

"Yessuh. Them other two new ones already workin."

He pulled the thick up-rope and the mechanism groaned and creaked as they ascended the half-floor to the shipping floor. Murky daylight drifted through the nearly closed big shipping doors that opened onto the railroad spur on the east side. Sitting at the big flat construction table were three salesmen — Jack Peters, Marvin Beele, and Dandy Pruitt — all looking as whipped and gloomy as cur dogs. Ernest Dekker had them in some kind of meeting. Ralph Dekker was nowhere in sight.

Jake walked off the back side of the elevator, out of their sight, and stood in the shadows by the long row of coat hooks. The two Arkansas salesmen weren't there. A short, fat man with a derby hat sat beside the salesmen at the shipping desk. Jake had seen him around before, and believed that he was a lawyer. He was looking straight ahead with eyes dead as fish bait, the stub of a cigar sticking out the middle of his mouth. A heap of papers lay on the desk in front of him. Ernest, freshly shaved and powdered, wearing a dapper sportsman's waistcoat, waved around his black ivory cigarette holder, holding forth about collections. Jake heard snatches: ". . . on them with all fours. Hit em direct, no apologizing. Make it plain and clear, if they don't have cash, we'll take the mortgages . . ."

Jake wondered where the old man was. He heard the elevator descend again, and as it went by he took a glance to see if Mr. Dekker might be on it. No such luck. The salesmen looked pretty uncomfortable. Marvin Beele was churning hard on his quid.

Ernest turned the meeting over to the lawyer, whose tongue flicked out and ran over his lips. His voice was tight, constricted, high, and not clearly audible to Jake. ". . . real estate property . . . white men can own improvements. These here forms . . . get him to sign . . ." Jake strained to hear as the lawyer held up a printed document and pointed at the bottom of it. After a while, his tongue snaked out and he plugged the cigar back into the middle of his mouth, apparently finished.

Marvin spat over his shoulder in the direction of the open port before asking a question, to which the lawyer answered, "Whatever improvements they got themselves and whatever customers' property mortgages they're holdin."

Ernest had picked up one of the forms. ". . . doing them a favor . . ."

When Jake heard the elevator coming back up, he hopped onto it. He held up his hand with a warning look so Edgar wouldn't say anything. After they'd glided above the third floor, he asked, "Where'd you last see Mr. Dekker, Edgar? I'm supposed to find him."

"I took him to the fifth earlier this mornin. Hadn't seen him since."

"That's where I want to go, then."

When they got to the top floor, Jake saw Mr. Dekker sitting in a chair by a window on the southwest wall of the building. He picked his way hesitantly between barrels of nails, approaching the old man.

Mr. Dekker looked up and gave a little smile. "Look out there, Jake," he said, waving toward the window.

It was a strange sight — the confluence of the rivers turned into a vast brown moving plain, with this building at the edge of it and the Indian Nation far, far on the other side. Across Coke Hill, the upper works of the bridge Jake had crossed last night were halfway under the flood, jammed with debris. The new Arkansas River bridge wasn't visible from this window, but Jake reckoned you could probably dangle your feet in the river from it.

Mr. Dekker looked distant, wrapped in his own thoughts. Before the takeover by his son, he would have been running all over the store giving everybody hell, and here he was sitting on his backside staring out on the view like an old soldier on the front porch. For a long time he remained silent.

Finally Jake said, "I got back late last night. Saw your note this morning."

The old man's face clouded a little. "How'd you get back?"

"Last train. Damn engineer took us over that." He nodded toward the Poteau bridge.

Mr. Dekker smiled again weakly and took a slow breath. "You know, Jake, one of the worst things can happen to a man is to realize he was doing something all wrong just at the minute it's taken out of his hands. Must be why some people get so scared when they're dying."

Jake sat down on the edge of a bin stuffed full of washboards.

The old man continued to look bemused, as if he was thinking about events that had happened a long time ago. "You may not know this, but Ernest is pretty good pals with some of the young fellows at the bank. They cooked this up together. The bank's having problems right now, that's no secret. But instead of calling in a little debt from all their main accounts, they're calling the whole kit and caboodle off us. Ernest talked to the Young Turks at Mercantile and convinced them our situation was getting worse with me running the store, and he made them a proposition. If they'd put him in charge, he'd guarantee to find a way to meet a good part of our debt."

Jake was surprised not by the facts but by how plainly Mr. Dekker was describing it. "Can they do that?"

"Well, they did do it, whether they can or not. They'll declare us in default at the end of next month if I don't step down. That's the way they put it to me."

Jake looked out the window over the flooded river plain, trying to resist his urge to comment. "That's goddamn blackmail."

"I've been around and around it, Jake, and there's not much I
can do. It's a call loan. I visited Shelby White yesterday. He's the
head of the Mercantile board, but of course he's on their rope.
We've known each other long enough for him to tell me the
whole story, anyway." Mr. Dekker allowed a brief bitterness to
color his expression.

"What makes them think Ernest can get water from a dry
hole?" Jake said heatedly. "They're just going to take Dekker
down. What good'll that do?"

"Depends on how desperate they are for cash. We have the
building and stock, and we've got some real estate here and there.
If Ernest fails and we go bust, they'll pull a quick twenty or twenty-
five thousand from a fire sale off our carcass, which would be that
much more cash than they have today. And there'd be another
benefit, too. Every debtor in town would have the stuffing scared
out of them. Whatever tune the Mercantile called, they'd line up
like choirboys to sing it. Although . . ." He shook his head.

"What?"

"It doesn't quite all add up." Mr. Dekker looked uncertain.
"Anyhow, if we owed a lot of different creditors, they couldn't do
this. But we don't. Ernest's been working with McMurphy, and I
let them concentrate all our suppliers' debts at the bank. They've
got us in their pocket, and it's my fault for not watchin the store
closer."

"So he's been planning this?"

"Course he has."

Jake searched his face for the gall that he himself felt. "Well,
what do you think about it?"

Mr. Dekker allowed a melancholy smile. "I guess I could be
proud of him. He's takin the risk, all right. You boys don't collect,
his future won't look good. Course, neither will yours or mine."

"Well, if my first effort to collect was any sign, we might as well
hang it up." Jake told him about what had happened with John
Blessing.

Mr. Dekker asked a few questions, then sat in another long silence. "Well, now he's got a scheme to collect mortgages at stores
where you men can't get cash. The bank's going along with it. He

hired some two-dollar lawyer. They're setting up all kind of new arrangements." Bitterness had edged back into Mr. Dekker's expression, although his tone remained mild. "Well, Jake. I guess there's a time when the old guard passes. It happens different ways, but it always happens."

"That how you look at it?"

Mr. Dekker pushed up his hat and stared out the window at the devastation of the flood below. "Boy oh boy. How much of that train station's going to be left?"

Jake was extremely vexed by Mr. Dekker not putting up a fight. But it wasn't his business; he was just the hired help around here. "Did you want to see me about something?"

The old man glanced at him. "I wanted to talk to you before you saw Ernest. I know you don't like him, and you'll most likely think about quitting over this business. I wouldn't blame you. But I want to ask you not to, as a favor to me. Ernest doesn't talk much to me. When he's doing something, I'm lucky to find out about it. If you stay on, I'll have somebody in the sales force I can trust to keep me up on what's going on."

"I don't mean this disrespectfully, Mr. Dekker, but Ernest shouldn't be put in charge of the store under any circumstances. I don't care what kind of scheme he's got going. You're just over sixty. There's plenty of time for a real hardware person to learn the ropes."

He shook his head. "We can't have the bank foreclosing on us December thirty-one. They've cast that die, and they ain't foolin around. Ernest is playing his hand — that's a fact. And he does have his ducks lined up. Only way I could stop it today would be to shut the store, and I've decided not to do that. I'm layin back, Jake."

"Layin back to fight, or give up?"

Mr. Dekker sighed and gave him a little smile. "Hell of a deal, ain't it? My own son."

Jake studied him. He hadn't answered the question, but there was something just a bit cagey to his expression. From that small promise — a look in the old man's eye — Jake made his decision. "All right. I won't quit without talking to you first. Unless he fires me."

"Oh, he won't do that," the old man said blandly.

· 6 ·

A S THE FLOOD waxed and waned, everybody in the big
building toted merchandise and office records upstairs, then
hardly got a breath before it was time to move it all back
downstairs. Tom worked much of the time with the other two
boys from the academy, Hack Deneuve and Joel Mayes. Hack and
Tom had been friends ever since Tom could remember. A few
of the academy boys occasionally skipped out on field work and
met in the woods to play a war game they called Cherokee and
Choctaw, and Tom and Hack would be captains of the opposing
sides — Tom always Cherokee. They took on names like Darius
and Xerxes, from one of the history books in the Reverend's
small library, and they made swords and spears and had pretend
battles in the trackless bottomland around Bokchito.

After years of classes, field work, beatings, and near-complete
isolation, now they were free, with jobs, launched into the world
of men so suddenly that they hardly knew yet how to talk about
it. Hack and Joel were staying temporarily with Edgar, the elevator
man.

A steam engine was set up to pump out the basement, and for
days its steady throbbing through the building seemed to mimic
the tension in the place. Ernest Dekker went around ordering
workers to move items from every floor to different locations,
reshuffling the store's stock, at first away from the flood, then, it
seemed to Tom, jamming it all together near the shipping floor.
Old Mr. Dekker continued to sit by a window on the top floor,

as if he were uninterested in these big changes. "Old man actin queer," said Edgar Wyatt. "I never seen him so quiet and off to hisself."

The huge store was dark inside, with jets of gaslight widely spaced along the walls. Sweating, grunting men trundled merchandise that had gotten wet outside to the wagon yard to dry in the sun, then back to the bins and shelves. The academy boys were fascinated by all of it — rows and rows of shiny new grease-smelling plows, scythes, coils of rope and screen wire, cases of stove polish, roof caps and radiators made of planished iron, kitchen machines of every sort, including coffee and spice mills with big flywheels on the side, kraut and meat cutters, sausage stuffers, butter molds with swans and stars on them, large nickel- and porcelain-plated water coolers, wooden iceboxes of every size and description, hand-powered machines for washing clothes, fishing tackle, rifles, pistols, tools, wagon and carriage work, hinges, hoses, steam fittings, corrugated roofing, and items whose names Tom didn't know, with only numbers or manufacturers' names on them. In dusty corners of the building he ran his hands over these mysterious things — levers connected to strange devices, heavy machines with cranks, hinged cooking devices with a top and bottom and little squares in them. Tom had not known such a luxury of exotic things existed in the whole world, much less in one building. Hearing the elevator rising or someone coming up the stairs, he hurried away to avoid getting caught by the cigarette-waving boss, who strode around the floors cursing the men, threatening to fire them for slacking. Tom noticed Hack looking at Ernest Dekker with a lost, confused look.

The store was like the orphanage in some ways. It had about as many employees as the orphanage had boys, and the boss was greatly feared, like the Reverend, only he fired you instead of putting you down on the stock and whipping you. Getting fired was worse than getting beaten, Tom figured, because you were cast out into the world. He understood the seriousness of that.

At Mrs. Peltier's boarding house, his thoughts were occupied by the woman who was recovering upstairs. Saying prayers at night, he couldn't keep his thoughts on the subject for daydreaming about her. His Divine Father, whom he never had exactly pictured, kept slipping away in favor of the woman upstairs. As he knelt by the couch, in fact, his Divine Father didn't have much pull at all compared with the woman upstairs. During the little time he actually slept, weird dreams poured through his head. Tom had always had vivid dreams and nightmares, but now they were laced with images of her. She would be lying down, her hair out on the ground, eating an apple, her mouth a thread of scarlet. Or she would be a tower, her eyes as large as green pools, and he would climb up her neck.

He strongly wanted to go to the parlor and see her, and he managed to do so a couple of times by taking water and food to her room. The lump on her temple seemed to be going down, leaving a greenish bruise. She smiled at him the second time he went, and all that night he turned every which way on the couch, feeling strangely hot, thinking about her.

Reverend Schoot had preached about the serpent poisons of the female sex. Women were the offspring of Eve, bitter as wormwood, sharp as a two-edged sword, to be feared and put out of one's thoughts. The lust that they inspired could destroy the body and eat up the soul. At the very least, the lust for woman threw off the compass of righteousness. To his knowledge, Tom had never had a strong compass of righteousness, but whatever kind he did have was sure gyrating.

Tom could tell that the woman was on Jake's mind, too. Afternoons, they worked past dark and came back for late suppers in the kitchen, and Jake always asked Mrs. Peltier about her, first thing. Had she said her name yet? Was she better? The landlady's tone regarding her patient seemed to grow less sympathetic each day. Tuesday, she answered Jake's inquiry with a look and no more, leaving an embarrassing silence, and by Wednesday she clearly had lost all sympathy for the patient. "Oh, she talks all right."

"What about?" Jake asked.

Mrs. Peltier glared at him a minute before answering. "She ought to stay in bed, but she wants to get up and wander around all the time. Doesn't pay a whit of attention to me. Treats me like a hired woman! Last night I was putting witch hazel on her and she said she was tired of me bothering her."

On Thursday, the landlady had become openly unhappy about running a hospital on top of a boarding house, and very tired of the increasing interest her "bachelors" had in the woman. They were all men in late middle or old age — three of them retired — and Tom was amazed at how much time they had just to sit around talking and being curious. Mrs. Peltier insisted that Jake try to send a telegram to Tuskahoma requesting information about her, so that relatives could be found to take charge of her. He tried, but lines into the territory were still dead. Early that evening Mrs. P sent for a doctor, and according to the way it was told by the men at dinner, he had given his patient a poultice and two doses of what he called "brain stimulant," to be taken the next morning if she wasn't better.

Mr. Potts was fidgety. The oldest of the bachelors, Potts always sat at the head of the table wearing a boiled shirt, wing collar, cravat, and silver tie pin. Tom's impression of Potts was that he was always cheerful, sometimes to an almost alarming degree. But tonight he kept shaking his head and looking worried. Mr. Taylor, a retired pharmacist, leaned down the table and told Jake, "I seen him make up that pill, and it looked like blue mass to me. I guess he figures her brain is in her digestion."

"That's a doctor for you," Jake said. "Just selling his powders."

The flood was receding by Friday, and the whole river end of town smelled like decaying animals. Tom's job that day was to help haul out more than a foot of muck that covered the first floor and to find dead rats and fish in the building. Although some carcasses could be smelled but not found, he cleared out more than a wheelbarrow full. That evening, Jake and Tom again got home in time to eat supper with the others at the boarding house. Tom knew the bachelors' names by then, although he'd said little but good morning or good evening to any of them. They were, besides Jake, Messrs. Haskell, Albert, Ferris, Taylor, and Potts — and it seemed that their mood tonight was awfully quiet and nervous at the table.

"What's everybody so talkative about?" Jake asked. No one answered, and as Jake muttered something about what a friendly bunch of scalawags they were, Tom saw the door fly open and there she stood, wearing nothing but Mrs. P's old dressing robe, askew on her body, the belt loose and doing little to hold it together. Tom fetched up off his chair as fast as if something had bit him in the rear end, crashing against the table, causing dishes to rattle and glasses wobble. There he remained, amazed, frozen in a half-cocked position, trying, out of automatic reticence, not to look below her green eyes, or her mouth — absolutely no lower than the top of her white neck. Yet he found it impossible not to notice regions below that.

"I've been poisoned," she announced.

The men around the table stopped in mid-chew, all reaching of arms and mastication halted, as they gazed at the extraordinary sight. Mr. Potts began coughing, choking on his sweet potato. Standing by the table with a bowl of green beans, Mrs. Peltier said, "You are not dressed properly for the dining room!"

"I'm dying," she complained miserably.

Mrs. Peltier set down her green beans with a clatter and rushed toward her as if to push her out of the room.

"Oh, keep away from me!"

"You can't be in here in front of the gentlemen in this condition."

"All day long I've been in the lavatory. That doctor poisoned me."

"That wasn't poison. That was your brain stimulant!"

"If that was my brain, it's all gone now."

Mr. Potts coughed louder.

"Young lady, you are not dressed —"

"Oh, shut up." She turned on her heel and exited the room, leaving them in stunned silence.

Mrs. Peltier picked up an empty bowl and gathered herself together. After a moment she said portentously, "Mr. Jaycox, may I speak with you?"

Looking grim, Jake followed her into the kitchen. Over Mr. Potts's continued coughing, Tom heard her whispering furiously and Jake mumbling something back, and then her coming back more loudly, "Well, you have to get her out of the boarding house!"

"I told you," Mr. Taylor said. "That doctor give her a double dose of blue mass. That's enough to set a horse straight."

"You okay, Potts?" Mr. Haskell asked.

"It's been twenty year since I seen anythin like that, Yankee," Mr. Potts said in a tight voice, rubbing his throat and finally getting his sweet potato all the way down. He took a drink of water. "Liked to strangled me."

Tom was still frozen in a half-standing position, and Mr. Haskell, next to him at the table, put a hand on his forearm. "Sit down, Tom. It's passed."

◆

Tom didn't sleep again that night.

He worried that Mrs. Peltier was going to throw the woman out of her boarding house, and perhaps throw him out, too, if things didn't get "back to normal" — a phrase he heard her say several times. He didn't want to leave this place, because he'd begun to feel at home here. There was so much to like about his new life.

He liked the amazing wealth of things at the store, liked the energy of working among men. He liked not having to parse sentences and practice penmanship and memorize history dates and Latin verbs and recite the Twenty-third Psalm and the proverbs, and not having to listen for the umpteenth time to the toiling recitations of other boys. He liked not having to witness the stubby hand of the Reverend during these recitations, tirelessly marking down little strokes in his "book of sins," in order later to punish each of them with the birch or the belt or the horsewhip according to an exact accounting of their failures. The Reverend always raised his eyebrow and gave a quiet, satisfied grunt when he made marks in the book. Tom had what one of the many teachers who passed through the academy (they always quit or were fired after a brief time) had called a God-given talent for memorizing passages, so the black marks in his account usually had been for other things — impudence, irreverence, blasphemy, backsliding, uncleanness, haughtiness, each of which merited a certain number of lashes or other punishments, like going without food for two days or being locked in the windowless basement, where Tom sometimes thought he could hear the moaning ghosts of soldiers who'd died in the building when it was a hospital during the Civil War. Tom's God-given talent had not helped him evade the Reverend's constant eye.

Except for the teachers who came and went too quickly to have much influence, the boys who lived at the orphanage at Bokchito were about the only ones who knew about its internal workings, and they were the least equipped to understand it. Few of them had much memory of living anywhere else, and those who did remembered little but the gnawing of empty stomachs. Tom didn't remember even that, so his only points of comparison were from passages in books in the library and from his few encounters with the outside — with the washerwoman, or going to Durant on market day.

The academy library was a dusty closet near the Reverend's office with a few shelves of books, and Tom had read all of them more than once — books personally chosen by the Reverend to uplift the Christian reader, though not too far or too high above the solid foundations of Presbyterian thought. It was in fact a dreary collection, but Tom had no way of knowing that, since he'd never read a book outside it. At least he did have books to read. Mostly they were about the Bible and Christian thought and Christian living and Christian habits and Christian martyrs and even Christian hygiene. One book, kept not in the library but in the quarantine room, was called *The Exemplary Lives and Joyful Deaths of Several Young Children,* and he had read it once while sick. The first chapter came to the "inevitable conclusion," through the "new science of statistical reasoning," that hell was populated primarily by children. Other chapters described — in imaginative and colorful language — what awaited children who had committed sins, like playing with pets on Sunday or thinking ungodly thoughts. Descriptions of joyful deaths were few and vague, while the descriptions of their sufferings in hell were painted in excellent detail.

Literature in the library included *The Grave* by Robert Blair and *Elegy in a Country Churchyard* by Gray. *The Analects of the Great Romans* caused a stirring in him, especially the brisk narrative of the Gallic Wars by Julius Caesar. There was a biography of John Calvin which spoke of Paris and Geneva and other faraway places. His favorite book was Herodotus's *History of the Persian Wars.* Here and there in nooks and crannies of this otherwise desolate little group of books were moments of triumph, love, or happiness that Tom read about with interest and puzzlement. The Reverend severely discouraged such emotions except when they involved the conversion experience — which Tom and the majority of the other boys never had.

For now, Tom was still too close to the academy even to hate it. Perhaps at some time in the future he'd understand that the place he grew up in was a cold fortress against the outside world, commanded by a man who cared more about the health of his Christian soldiers' souls than their lives, and more about his own need than either. Maybe Tom would be knowledgeable enough in the ways of the world to figure out how it was that Reverend James Schoot got away with running the academy however he pleased, effectively as distant from the Presbyterian Mission's headquarters as the banks of the Yangtze River, and how it was that the otherwise competent Choctaw government never did anything about the Armstrong Academy — never sent an inspector, never complained, never responded to the outrages that were vividly described in letters written by the teachers who quit the place. Perhaps the tribe did nothing about the academy because it did not seem unlike many other mission-run schools. Perhaps they did nothing about it because they were overwhelmed by other concerns — intensifying lawlessness, a flood of white riffraff who were illegally occupying their land in increasing numbers, a major crop that had come to be nearly worthless, and most recently the ominous Dawes Commission, gathering like a black cloud in Muskogee, said to be hiring hundreds of clerks in preparation for the final liquidation of their government and their domain. Amid such concerns, maybe the Choctaw government was satisfied that the efficient-acting Reverend was handling the orphan boys.

What Tom did know at this point was that he was away from the academy, things were different, life was moving on in a more promising way. His feelings were like a cottonwood seed that had burst open and was being blown in every direction by the wind. There were moments when his heart would begin pounding for no apparent reason, as if something big was about to happen — good or bad, he couldn't tell.

Oddly, he and the other two boys didn't talk much at work. They had been friends at the academy, particularly Tom and Hack, but instead of sticking together and talking about their new jobs, they hardly spoke at all. At first he didn't realize how much they were avoiding one another. One day near the end of work Tom was on the fourth floor loading frying pans onto a cart, and he looked up to see Hack across the gloomy, rough-pillared room, staring into a sunset. Hack turned from the window, saw Tom, and without a word quickly disappeared from view, but even in that brief moment, across the big room, Tom felt a mysterious charge of aversion between them. He walked slowly up the long aisle to the window where Hack had been looking southwestward, beyond the courthouse and river, across the low rolling hills of the Choctaw Nation toward Bokchito.

At the end of each day's work, Tom lay awake in the boarding house, tired, excited, listening to the wind outside and to the sounds of the house, wondering if the woman upstairs was awake or asleep, getting up and pacing the room and gazing out at the yellow light coming from a saloon down the street.

And he did like the boarding house. He liked walking home from work with Jake, past the hydrangea bushes onto the scroll-sawed porch. He liked the fading flowered wallpaper in Jake's sitting room, now temporarily his room, and the towel, pitcher, and soap dish on a stand where he could wash up before dinner, and the smells of food coming up through the floor. And the free private hot bath, allowed twice a week in the big lion-claw bathtub on the first floor — far superior to the "washdowns" at the orphanage, where all the boys at once were ordered outside to have cold well water poured over their heads. The boarding house had its own orderliness: the meals with Mrs. Peltier, lounging in the parlor at night, where Messrs. Haskell, Albert, Taylor, Ferris, and sometimes Jaycox played dominoes for matchsticks. The more elderly Mr. Potts, who was too easily addled, often just watched. Comfortable in their game, they'd glance at Tom with amiable neutrality and invite him to play. They accepted him easily and wanted nothing from him. Sometimes they dismissed him, saying things like "Go away, you young buck. I know what's on a young buck's mind." It was usually Mr. Jacob Haskell who said something like this, and Tom gloried in it. Haskell was a little older than Jake, short of stature, and, despite his joking with Tom, generally a shy man. Although they had no real conversations, Tom had a feeling of friendship with him.

There was some ongoing strife among the boarders. Mr. Potts's brainless cheerfulness got to them all at times. Haskell was the only one among them who had been a Yankee soldier, and Potts was always blithely tormenting him about it. Mrs. Peltier had her moods, too, and she was unbending about her rules. When you crossed her, that was it. Tom was frankly afraid of the landlady, but that wasn't much to complain about given the atmosphere of acceptance and tolerance in her house.

And he liked the nearby presence of the nameless woman upstairs. He liked that very much. But she was the big worry, too. Mrs. Peltier told Jake that she couldn't have a woman flouncing around her house without the proper clothes on, it didn't matter how injured she was. A lady kept herself covered neck to ankles, and she most certainly did not present herself to a crowd of men in a loose night robe.

Jake said that he couldn't throw the woman into the street while she was still recovering.

That was not her concern, Mrs. Peltier declared.

Several days of unpleasant standoff followed, and the landlady made it plain that she was waiting for him to do as she said. She became colder each day, and her dinners became smaller, hitting all the bachelors where they lived. Her normally munificent table shrank fast, with fewer vegetables, smaller portions of meat, and no desserts. Jake muttered at one of these poor dinners that they'd soon be fighting for food like common boarders. It had happened before, he later told Tom: when one of the men indulged in the bottle or started bringing women to a room, the food quickly went downhill. "Damn good way to get everybody on her bandwagon," he muttered.

♦

One evening the landlady also stopped making a plate for the woman. They could see about that themselves with food from the table, she informed them. Jake asked Tom to get a plate together and take it to her.

When Tom went up, she was still confused and tired, possibly more from the aftereffects of the "brain stimulant" than from her injury, and she didn't look as if she was ready to eat. A day later, she was better. She sat up in bed and began to nibble at her things while he stood watching her. She eventually said, "What are you looking at?"

"The plate — I'll wait for it."

"That old ice wagon hates me." She made a face at a chicken wing.

He didn't reply.

"She thinks I'm a whore." She looked up and said in a different tone, "My memory's back."

"It is?"

"Coming back, anyway." She put down the chicken wing and looked at him appraisingly. "It's the queerest thing. Have you ever lost your memory?"

"Yes ma'am. Before I was four years old."

She looked incredulous. "No one remembers what happened when they were babies."

"Well, I remember everything else," he said hesitantly.

"Who are you?"

"Tom Freshour," he said, looking at the floor.

"Well, I know that," she said impatiently. "I mean who are you? Mr. Jaycox isn't your father?"

"No ma'am. Until two weeks ago, I lived in the Armstrong Academy."

"What's that?"

"It's a home for boys."

"An orphanage?"

"Yes ma'am. A school and orphanage."

"What happened to your parents?"

"I don't know. That's the part I can't remember."

"An orphan . . ." she repeated softly, looking down the bedspread. "At least it's not your fault."

"I beg your pardon, ma'am?"

She still looked down. "So you work with Jake at the hardware store?"

"Yes ma'am." He couldn't believe how easily she was talking to him. He couldn't believe the color of her eyes.

"Have you met many of the people down there?"

"Where?"

"Where you work! The hardware store."

He blushed. "Oh, yes. Most of them."

"What kind of man is Mr. Dekker?"

Tom was surprised at the question. "There are two of them, father and son. I don't know them really. I'm just a runner and stockroom worker."

"What's the father like?"

"I don't really know, ma'am."

She looked at him curiously. "How old are you, Tom?"

Tom had neither a birthday nor a precise age. Such things were considered frivolity at the academy, although he'd read and heard enough about birthdays to be embarrassed that he couldn't answer her. "I guess I have to go back downstairs now," he said, and retreated from the room.

Lying on the couch that night, Tom tossed and turned again, thinking about her, trying to anticipate other questions she might ask him. But now that she was recovering, would she soon be leaving?

◆

The next evening Jake stayed very late at the store, and Tom got together the plate and carried it up the stairs, started to knock, and, seeing her through the partly open door, hesitated outside. She was not in bed but sitting at a table, a lamp before her, writing on a piece of paper, Mrs. Peltier's dressing gown loose on her shoulders. Tom couldn't get over the sight of her.

When he knocked, she looked up and quickly turned over the piece of paper. He came in and set the plate down on the table. She looked at him and smiled. Her eye was no longer bloodshot, and the only thing that seemed to remain of her injury was the disappearing bruise on her temple.

"Sorry about yesterday," she said.

"Sorry?"

"I wasn't very thoughtful when I asked about your age. I'm still curious, though. Are you about eighteen?"

"About sixteen," he said.

"Mmm," she said, looking at him with a little smile. "You're a big boy for sixteen."

He smiled back numbly. "Yes ma'am."

"Samantha King," she said, the lamp glowing yellow in her face.

"I beg your pardon?"

"My name is Samantha King. Call me Sam, if you'd like. You didn't ask me yesterday."

"Samantha King," he repeated hesitantly.

She stood up and walked confidently to the window. "Is Jake here?"

"He had to stay late at the store."

"Is he going into the territory again soon?"

"I think so, ma'am."

"Would you ask him to come talk with me when he comes back?"

It was two hours later before Jake arrived. A cool wind from the northeast was sweeping Texas Avenue when Tom met him on the porch and told him about her apparent full recovery. Jake looked dazed, and at first Tom assumed that it was because of his news. When Tom told him her name, Jake just stared and said vaguely, "We're hitting the road again. I guess we'll have to do something with her, or Mrs. P'll starve her out." Without another word he went into the house and up the stairs to talk with Miss King, and came back down to tell Tom that she'd be riding the train with them, perhaps as far as Guthrie.

Tom was happy to hear that.

"Says she's okay. Says she left her suitcase in Tuskahoma and wants to collect it."

Jake had been worrying about one thing or another for the entire brief time that Tom had known him, and tonight he seemed even more deeply preoccupied. From little things he'd said, Tom understood now that it had mostly to do with the store.

The next day, while Jake went to Dekker's for final instructions for the trip, he sent Tom to buy the tickets, theirs to Durant, on the St. Louis and San Francisco, and hers to Guthrie on the same train.

·7·

JAKE HAD BEEN unresponsive to the news about Miss King's improvement because he'd just had a brief but extraordinary talk with Ralph Dekker, after which he'd wandered the streets alone for an hour in a state of mild shock. That evening, word had come to him from Edgar Wyatt, the elevator man. "Old man wanta see you after six. By his window." By his window was where Mr. Dekker had been for two weeks, his silent presence somehow like a judgment above the beehive of activity presided over by his son. Nervous jokes had been passing around that maybe the old man had finally sprung a leak.

Jake had climbed the narrow stairs to find Mr. Dekker sitting in the gloom, looking out his window at the oncoming night. His voice gravelly and thin, he continued to gaze over the darkening land. "I've thought about it a good while now, and decided that what he's doing is wrong. I'm going to stop it if I can. He's got the bank boys with him, so it won't be easy. I'll have to travel to St. Louis and do a little money finagling. I have to tell you, Jake, I've found out some other particulars, and Ernest plays a more dangerous game than I thought. If he stays, it'll be over my dead body. Right now, I'm asking you just to stay with the program. Don't do anything different than he asks. Just act like you're following his orders."

He'd turned and looked at Jake then, his eye and expression not quite visible in the somber light. "I already talked to Dandy about this, just to make sure he's with us. I was going to talk to

Marvin, but made up my mind against it. I'm picking friends careful now. The rest of them can go to hell for all I care. Jake, I want you to start thinking about running the store. You're my man. Start thinking about the way you'll do it. Even if we get out of this mess, God knows we'll have problems."

Running the store was beyond any ambition Jake had ever had. He had daydreamed now and again about what he'd do if he was boss — who he'd like to see fired, and the like — but never to the point of losing any sleep over it. It was truly outside the range of his expectations. Why wouldn't Mr. Dekker himself take the store back in hand? Or if he was fixed on giving it over, why not to a younger man like Dandy? Why turn it over to an old horse like him?

But Mr. Dekker made it clear when he was finished talking that he would appreciate not answering a lot of questions, so Jake asked none at all. He just took a deep breath and said, "All right, I'll think about it," and walked back down the murky aisle to the narrow stairs, feeling a chill on his spine as he went down. Mr. Dekker had come to a decision, and the implications to Jake were almost too big to take in. At the moment it overshadowed the news about Miss King.

The next day, Tuesday, at the store Jake was as nervous as a fiddler. Mostly it was due to this new thing on his mind, but the atmosphere of the place gave him the willies. People were acting suspicious, glancing at each other funny ways, and Peters, the only other salesman who hadn't yet caught a train, was jabbering and bragging so much that Jake finally told him to save some of his breath for breathing. Ernest knew how to bring out the worst in a man.

They were to leave for the territory on Wednesday morning. Miss King asked if she could go with Tom on a quick visit to a clothing store before their train, and Jake reckoned she could. He'd meet them at the station.

Stopping at Dekker to get his final instructions, Jake was surprised when the treasurer, McMurphy, told him to concentrate on the far western part of Choctaw country, in the Fringe. The trade was relatively poor over there. While Jake was talking to McMurphy, Ernest opened his office door, saw him, and quickly closed it again. Jake was glad to be shut of this place for a while, no matter if he was going on a collection trip. He saw no sign of Ralph's buggy in the yard and wondered if he had already left for St. Louis.

Jake walked down the hill to the depot, which had been half washed away. The entire frame part of the structure had been flattened by the swirling flood, leaving the brick walls. A gigantic gar, over nine feet long, was hanging from the big limb of a nearby tree, from a block and tackle. The monster fish had somehow been trapped inside the brick baggage room. The old ticket seller and baggage man were in high spirits. Having their workplace demolished made them happier than Jake had seen them in years.

To his exasperation, Miss King and Tom Freshour hadn't shown up by the time of the first call, but at last a rig clattered down the hill with about a minute to spare. She alighted, wearing a brown wool skirt with jacket, tailored white shirtwaist, and tan hat with feather. Alongside her was a well-dressed, tallish young man, dark of complexion, wearing a full ready-to-wear suit about the color of her skirt, including collar and string tie and a new pair of polish-leather shoes — all of which he sported with a sheepish look and a peculiar sideways twist to his body, shy about the new duds. He gave Jake a furtive glance, as if pleading with him not to make any comments.

Jake couldn't resist. "Who the heck is this?"

"May I introduce you to Mr. Thomas Freshour," Miss King announced.

Jake wondered how she'd paid for all of it, but didn't ask.

As their train joggled across a landscape still pockmarked by temporary ponds of water, he noticed that Tom quickly became drowsy, his lack of sleep over the last several days apparently catching up with him in the gentle rattling and swaying. Miss King drew the attention of the handful of men on the train, even as she sat completely still, staring out the window. There was something about this young woman, now that she was getting well — a gathering purposefulness, Jake thought. Mrs. Peltier had become convinced that she was a floozie — an "Irish woman," as the landlady put it. She was the sort of woman who presented a challenge just by her presence. In his earlier days, he had met a few like her, and won the battle by retreating from the field.

Jake was curious about Samantha King, but his mind was as

cluttered as the Dekker shipping floor right now, and he didn't want to put anything else into it. She'd be leaving soon, going about her business. Which was good, he figured, for the young man helping him. Jake had noticed the way Tom had been noticing her. But she was too much for a kid like him. A young man shouldn't be introduced to females like this. He ought to start with a homelier neighborhood example to get his bearings set . . .

As they curved southward, the old man's talk with him kept going through his mind. Mr. Dekker wanted Jake to go along with Ernest until he'd made his trip to St. Louis and gotten together the money necessary to pay off the debt. Jake was under the impression that the old man's original financing had been from banks in St. Louis, so it made sense that he was going there.

The store had problems, all right, but Jake figured that if it could weather the depression, they'd pull through. The flood hadn't ruined that much stock. Stains on the walls, the loss of some records — these were minor hindrances, and the store did get a free rat-exterminating job out of it. Ernest's "reorganization" of the stock would probably end up costing more than the flood. He'd been jamming everything either on or close to the shipping floor, as if he was expecting to sell it all next week, for what reason Jake couldn't guess, since it would make it hard to find items when merchandise started moving a little faster in March.

Jake had been going along with the program, just like the old man asked him to do, following instructions, studying accounts, and getting them straight to the penny. They'd had to attend daily meetings presided over by Ernest, his stubby little bulldog of a lawyer, and, on two occasions, Bradley, of the bank, who preached to the salesmen about how to get the accounts collected. Jake would sooner have gone outside and picked corn out of corral dust than go to these meetings. Although Ernest had no experience in the territory, he had a lot of strong opinions: The days of carrying no-account customers were over. They were declaring war on debt. This was a crusade. No prisoners would be taken. The new business era of the twentieth century was around the corner, when money would be made by the bold use of capital. To solve Dekker's problem, he and responsible officials at the bank were going to offer the salesmen incentives to collect. And what's more, they had devised a plan whereby most customers who didn't have cash could satisfy their debts through paper transactions.

It worked this way: Dekker customers who couldn't immediately pay at least half their debt in cash — as few could — were to be given the option of signing "mortgage transfer agreements." These documents exchanged the standard merchandise mortgages previously held by Dekker against them for property mortgages — either the store owners' own business properties or the mortgages that stores were holding against their customers' debts. Almost all the substantial merchants held mortgages on the land of their regular customers, acting as banks where few banks existed.

This got a little complicated, Ernest's lawyer had allowed, since it was still illegal for outsiders to own tribal land, so the mortgages in the Nations officially applied only to "improvements" — buildings, not land — "until such time as ownership of the attendant property is provided by law," when the tribes finally gave up the ownership of lands. In the sales territories in Arkansas, Kansas, and the white-settled Oklahoma Territory around Guthrie and Enid, the transfers did attach actual real estate now, or claimed to.

The whole thing amounted to Dekker's foreclosing on its customers' debts but accepting as payment the mortgage-based debts that they held on their own customers — "at our rate," the lawyer said. Jake didn't know enough about property law to judge whether these mortgage transfer agreements were legal, but he did know enough about human nature to dread trying to make customers hand over other people's land.

Ernest and the bank had foreseen that problem and had devised a "generous incentive plan," which by itself could make some of the salesmen "financially independent," according to the lawyer. Salesmen were to be paid ten cents per acre in outright cash for every acre up to five thousand that they put under mortgage, and fifteen cents thereafter. Furthermore they would receive a two-cent bonus on land within more desirable areas. Jake noticed that some of the salesmen, who until then had acted glum and confused, began to wake up and pay attention to the details.

The rate of transfer of property to debt would normally be twenty-five cents per acre. A store with two hundred fifty dollars of unpayable debt needed to hand over paper on about a thousand acres for it. For this simple shuffling of paper the salesman was to get two hundred dollars cold cash, three hundred if the property was within certain fixed areas, receivable on a weekly basis and fully backed by the bank. Jake again noticed the expressions of the salesmen: Dandy frowning, Pete Crapo looking bewildered but excited, fat Jack Peters nearly giving off steam, he was figuring arithmetic so fast behind his eyes.

The retailer had the advantage of then owning his Dekker-supplied stock free and clear. "After that," the lawyer said, "he can stay in bidness or he can fail, it don't make no different to us. Hell, he can up and leave with the merchandise as far as we care, because we're holding something that won't go away."

Jake's brief Monday night talk with Mr. Dekker presided over his daydreaming. He remembered every word of the old man's speech to him, and all over again he felt the prickle of both elation and dread that he'd felt as he descended the dark stairs.

◆

By the time they stopped at Tuskahoma station, Tom had succumbed to what looked like deep sleep, and Jake got out to help Miss King look for her suitcase. They had a five-minute stop, and he searched around the little platform while Miss King went over to the storage shed behind poor Mr. Blessing's store. On the platform Jake bought a nickel bag of popcorn from a boy who was there meeting trains — the only sign of enterprise. The town felt sodden and bleak. Four or five men lounged along the false fronts next to the boarded-up hulk of Blessing's store. The downslope part of Tuskahoma now consisted of tin rubble and the scattered log remains of the OK Hotel, and the whole place was as empty and sleepy as a ghost town.

Jake stuck his head inside the station house and saw a muddy suitcase sitting by itself on the floor.

Miss King was on the other side of the train; Jake hesitated, decided to look for himself, and opened the suitcase a crack. He saw a glint of metal and opened it slightly more, discovering a five-shot Smith & Wesson pistol and box of .38-caliber smokeless bullets, which made him doubt that the suitcase was hers. But it also carried women's clothes, and he saw a piece of paper, which he unfolded. The scribbled notes on it confounded him sufficiently that he sat there staring at it until the hissing of steam alerted him to get back aboard. He folded up the paper and put it into his pocket, then closed the suitcase and took it to the train.

Already back in the car, Miss King was delighted. "Where'd you find it?"

"In the station," Jake said gruffly. "Sittin right there. Didn't take a genius." Jake reckoned he'd take his time and look over that piece of paper more closely later. He didn't have the energy to worry about anything else right now.

♦

A little past noon they arrived at Grant, not far from the Texas border. They were supposed to have a three-hour wait before switching to the once-a-day straight west to Durant, where Jake planned to rent a rig and travel around, hitting some customers but taking his time about it. From Durant, Miss King was supposed to continue on to Guthrie, or wherever she was going.

The Grant station operator, a full blood with a smooth face and long hair, was hunched over a clattering telegraph machine on his desk, just finishing a message. He glanced up at them, and didn't respond at all to Jake's hello. People sure had gotten friendly in Choctaw country. The depot was dirty and unpleasant, with flyspecked windows, a door that slammed hard each time it was used. Three older men sat near the stove, working hard at disregarding a sign on the wall that said USE THE SPITTOON. Miss King's appearance caused them to work even harder. The train was scheduled to come through soon, but the operator acted unsure about when it would in fact arrive.

Miss King chose to wait in the street rather than stand around in the spitting den. Jake and the boy walked over to call on George Marston, of Marston & Sons General Implements, which was just across the way. Marston ran a tool store, blacksmith shop, and wagon yard. Three wagons were parked this way and that outside, and a small pack of razor-backed dogs were trotting around nearby, grazing on some trash in the street.

When Jake had first traveled in this territory, Marston had been a blacksmith, and he'd built up the implement dealership over years of hard work. Dandy had mentioned that the "& Sons" on his sign no longer applied, one son having died of a sickness and another gone off somewhere. The Red River was only a few miles away from here, and during the long cotton slump of the last years, a lot of people had crossed it and never come back. Marston was a white man married to an Indian, well established but not particularly prosperous.

They found him at work on an axle, and he didn't act too friendly when he saw Jake. He barely nodded when Jake introduced Tom. Customers had a way of smelling "collection," so Marston's cool reception didn't surprise Jake. What did surprise him was that when he eventually worked his way around to the subject of the mortgage transfer, Marston agreed with little hesitation to sign it and give Jake the papers on three customers' properties. "None of them are good for it, anyway," he said almost angrily. "I been holdin that paper for over two year. Just show me where you want me to sign."

"Now, you understand it gives Dekker Company a hold on that land until the bill's cleared up. And I have to take the land papers —"

"I'll sign the damn thing." He hustled to a back room and came out with a pencil and three land-use warrants. Jake sat down and wrote out the land descriptions, and Marston hurriedly scratched his name in big block letters across the bottom of the transfer. When they'd finished, Jake asked if he could rent a wagon for a few days if the train was held up, and Marston said he didn't have any for rent.

Jake was puzzled at how easily Marston had signed over the land, but as he and Tom walked out of the place, he realized something about Ernest's scheme. A lot of store owners were so strapped for cash and worn out from being unable to collect from their customers that they would take the deal.

Back at the depot, the door slammed behind them, and the stationmaster looked at Jake suspiciously. Jake wondered if word had passed down the line that he'd had something to do with John Blessing's death. Telegraphers were like a knitting club, shooting news, gossip, and lies around the Nation fast as lightning.

Jake knew about grudges from growing up in the hill country of northern Arkansas, but they had a very serious way of going about them in the Indian Territory. *Achowa,* they called it — blood feud — and instead of broken arms, swollen heads, cuts, and hurt feelings, which made up the balance of feuding in Jake's home country around Bentonville, out here people got shot, houses burned down, children scalped, and neighbors massacred. Over the years, at Indian stores, he'd heard tales of seemingly unending feuds resulting from the murder of some family member or friend, or from some dispute over good bottomland. Bitter memories never died, and young men fired by liquor would vindicate foul deeds, imagined or real, done to their relatives as far back as fifty years.

Jake saw in the quick glance of one of the old men in the station that something was going on here. One of them got up and looked out the window, as if expecting to see somebody outside.

The train to Durant definitely wasn't running, due to problems on the track south of here. Jake asked when it would be running, and the tight-lipped stationmaster said, "May be several days."

Jake went back outside to tell Miss King and Tom the news. Carrying their luggage out, he remembered the note that was folded in his pocket.

· 8 ·

THE THREE OF THEM stood oddly close together in the
November afternoon light, a wind picking up, white clouds
rolling from the south over their heads, Tom now fully wakened from his train sleep to the sight of Miss King's glorious
breeze-ruddied face. Jake wasn't saying much, but then Jake
nearly always seemed preoccupied. Looking at Miss King was to
Tom like eating some good food, and as the wind blew a few loose
wisps of hair round her face, a strand of it almost touched him,
and he smelled the scented soap she had used — lavender, lime,
he did not know its name.

He would never forget this moment of the three of them
standing there. He was finally over the edge, completely head
over heels for her, although his ideas about the relations of
women and men were so sketchy that he did not think of it as that,
did not think of it as anything, really, but merely kept drifting toward her, as if she were a magnet and he an iron filing, and he was
washed over with an unexplainable, curious, elaborate warmth
from his head to his feet.

She told Jake that she wanted to travel on with them instead of
being stuck here. Jake looked neutral. "I have a little money," she
said. "I'll help rent a buggy."

"George Marston has stopped renting," Jake said. "Aren't a lot
of other places to choose from."

Grant consisted of a mud-packed street and eight or ten buildings, half of which looked unoccupied.

"Then we should buy one," she said.

"Cost more than I've got," Jake said irritably.

"I'm glad to help. I do have a little money."

Jake's heavy gaze stayed on her a while longer, and Tom got the distinct impression that he wanted to say something to her, but he sighed and looked away. "Guess we don't have any choice unless we want to stay in this friendly place."

They walked eastward, knocking on the doors of farmhouses, inquiring whether someone would rent or sell them a rig. Tom's heels were blistered by the time they found a prospect a mile out of the village — a wily-looking older man sitting in a latticeback chair against the front of his shack, wearing an enormous turban, several handkerchiefs knotted loosely around his neck, a thick layering of brightly colored shirts, and a knee-length robe.

Despite the fact that Tom was by race an Indian, or part Indian, he didn't know much about the tribes of the Nation, his education having been limited to such things as English grammar, the Bible, and white Dissenter history, but he'd seen these turbaned men before — Seminoles, they were called — on grocery day when they got to ride from Bokchito into Durant. This man was as tall as Jake, and drinking from a crockery jug something that smelled like coal oil. He and Jake were soon talking, and he offered them a plain flatbed farm wagon with missing wheel spokes, patched-together harness (laid out in the dirt), and two grey-faced, ratty-coated old mules who were indignant at being taken out of the pasture this time of the afternoon and made to stand together for harnessing. They bucked and twitched and rolled their eyes as the man struggled to get them both into collars. Tom had spent enough hours behind mules in the academy's corn field to not like the look of these two.

Finally having done it, the man stood back and wiped his brow, sweating despite the cool wind. Children had been coming out of the house, first two, then three, then another, and another — the older ones dressed in robes not unlike those of their stately, mildly inebriated father, except their robes were not as thick with underlayers as his. Apparently the very youngest got no clothes at all, because among the gaggle of children were two little girls, utterly naked, and Tom couldn't keep his eyes from brushing down their bellies to the strange, decisive cleft below.

Jake and the man squatted down to bargain on the ground, which especially interested the older boys, as Jake twice put money down and both times was rejected. Eventually he got up and went over to check the mules' teeth. The farmer sat back on his haunches, looking peacefully into the distance, with the pile of money before him. "God almighty," Jake said, scowling into one of the mules' mouths. The other one refused to allow his mouth to be opened. Caught by the nose, he snapped viciously, and Jake gave up and walked around the rig, examining the underside. Then he ambled over to Tom and Miss King. "That one's got piano keys for teeth. I'd walk to Guthrie before I'd give him more than I've put down."

Without a word, Miss King turned her back, unbuttoned the top of her dress, withdrew something — several bills — and went straight over and laid them down with Jake's offer.

The old man looked fleetingly at it, scooped it all up, and quickly sprang into action, grabbing suitcases and loading them up. In the blink of an eye they were ready, and the man ambled into his house to put his money up.

"Boy, you sure primed his pump," Jake said. "How much did you give him?"

She smiled and gave no answer.

"I don't mind making a fool of myself in a horse trade, but I like to know how much of a fool."

"Twenty dollars," she said innocently, climbing onto the seat.
"Now I know."

"Call me the fool if you want. It's my money."

Tom got into the back, and Jake got up next to Miss King and took the reins. "Hey-up, hey! Get on! Hey!"

The mules didn't move, didn't so much as raise their ears. Jake pushed back his hat and sat there for a moment. "Let's go!" He popped the reins on their backs.

They stayed put.

The Seminole came out of his cabin carrying a large coffee-pot, and said, "Hafta talk Indian."

"Well, you might have told us that," Jake said disgustedly, getting back down from the seat. "Tom, see if you can make these durn mules move. If you can't, we'll take our money back."

Tom didn't talk Indian much better than Jake did. It wasn't allowed at the academy, although some of the boys spoke a little pidgin Choctaw on the sly, the "trade language," and he'd learned a few phrases from the washing lady. But he was more than happy to sit by Miss King, hip to hip, on the small driver's seat.

"*Kanima!*"

No luck. The Seminole stepped off his porch, poured coffee into a cracked dog's bowl, and brought it over to the mules who, first one and then the other, unhesitatingly sucked it up.

"*Aiya!*" the farmer yelled, whacking one of them on the nose with his open palm, and both mules raised their old fuzzy ears halfway up and inched out. Tom rattled the traces and scolded them along. For a while, Jake walked alongside them like an ox driver, and all of the children, including the naked ones, followed, making a ragtag parade, the father bringing up the rear, holding the bowl. "Cold coffee, good for mules," he said.

Jake climbed into the back of the wagon, muttering, "I've seen it all."

Down the road the children eventually fell away. The mules became more reticent and twitchy, and Tom had to keep snapping the reins and yelling. The animals were not only half deaf, or pretending it, but they worked against each other, one slowing while the other pulled, raking out sideways in the traces, nipping at each other and carrying on. The road was a slippery, potholed, muddy ribbon through the grassland, and the only time the mules hurried was at the roughest spots. They trotted smartly through holes and mud puddles and over rocks, throwing Tom and Miss King back and forth against each other like marbles in a can.

The countryside was flat and low here, surprisingly different from the hilly country around Bokchito, which probably wasn't more than thirty miles away. When Tom thought of how close they were, and that they were actually getting closer, it made him uneasy. Jake situated himself in the back of the wagon as they slipped and slid through the village, scattering dogs out of the way, and finally headed out the road toward Durant. Going through the sleepy little town, Tom caught a glimpse of only one man, leaning against the wall of Marston & Sons.

Jake was propped against the suitcases. "So you're going to Guthrie?" he shouted above the rattle.

"Yes," she said indifferently.

"I've got a lot of calls between here and there. You'll want to be taking the first train you can get."

"I'd like to travel with you the whole distance," she said. "I won't get in your way."

After a moment Jake said, "You interested in this kind of thing?"

"What's that?"

"Hardware business."

"I'm interested in business, in general. Whoops." Thrown against Tom, she pushed on his leg to right herself.

It was hard for them to talk above the noise of the wagon, even when going slowly, and Jake said nothing else. Trudging into the red sunset down an increasingly thin road, the mules made several stands at going no farther, and when Tom got off and tried to lead them, they reared their heads, snapped at him, and pulled backwards, thumping against the wagon and threatening to tear up the old harness lines, so he followed the example of the farmer and popped one of them on the nose. He was soon back on the seat, squeezed against Miss King. It was sweet torture, her thighs against his.

By dusk they had traveled all of six or seven miles. Miss King's feathered hat flew off twice, and when she gave up wearing it, strands of her hair blew in the chilly wind, tickling the side of Tom's face. In the fading light they stopped so she could get out a wrap, and Tom noticed how Jake glanced at her as she opened the suitcase.

By nightfall, the mules had gone through whatever mysterious process of mule thinking necessary to reconcile themselves to their immediate fate, and they were actually moving along at a good walking pace. They had made it through the Muddy Boggy Creek and climbed into low hills of blackjack oak and meadowland. A deer crossed in front of them, its white rosette tail floating off into the dark woods. Blackbirds fussed from nearby. The road was a dim track in places, and Tom was not always sure he was sticking to it. He might take a wrong turn at some branch and get them lost in the woods or even end up at Bokchito, a possibility he didn't relish. Being this close to the academy made him anxious in the extreme.

"Shouldn't we stop?" Miss King asked. "How can you see the road?"

Jake spoke up from the back. "Long as these mules are still walking, I figure we should take advantage of it. They'll be dying their natural deaths anytime."

The clouds had slowly cleared and stars appeared in a thick canopy of light. Jake was dozing in the back, and it was almost as if Tom and Miss King were riding through the darkness alone.

"I'm hungry," she said.

"I am, too," Tom quickly agreed. The night made him feel even closer to her, but he couldn't think of how to keep the conversation going. They rode on in silence.

After another hour of bumping and rattling down the dark trail, the mules were back to their earlier tricks, and when they came upon a large abandoned house, Jake roused and said they should stop for the night. The house, built of home-fired brick, had large porches on both sides. The front door was hanging open, but the musty smells of animals and wood rot didn't invite them to go inside. They coaxed the mules into a meadow, and Tom set about tethering them while Jake and Miss King made a fire. One of the animals nipped Tom on the shoulder while he was trying to get off the harness, and he was tempted to leave them in it. By the time he had finished, the fire was going in a little culvert protected from the wind.

"Quite a house," Miss King said.

"Old plantation place," Jake said.

She looked off toward the dark shape against the night sky. "When I see an old house like that, I always wonder where the family is, whether they're as dead and forgotten as the house they used to live in."

"I reckon more than one family lived there. Choctaws settled down here over fifty years ago."

"What do you think happened to the people?"

"Price of cotton probably drove em off," Jake said. "Them and everybody else. There were plantations all up and down here in the old days. Full-blood Choctaws riding around in fancy carriages with drivers and footmen."

"Indians had slaves?" Miss King asked.

Jake fired up a small cigar. Tom sat back quietly listening. "Ones around here did. They were big cotton farmers. After the war, a lot of freedmen stayed in the area — freedmen and poor Indians — staking out little farms where plantations used to be. Most of em didn't make it. By the time I started covering this territory, they were starting to drift off. They grow cotton cheaper in India or someplace." He sighed and looked out as if trying to see beyond the firelight. One of the mules brayed at the night. "Those are the oldest, ugliest animals I've ever seen this side of the rendering plant."

"So you traveled this territory?" Miss King asked.

"I didn't travel too much down in this corner, even when it was in my territory."

"Why?"

"Good times were gone in the cotton country. Wasn't anybody down here with any money. Nobody building. Not many blacksmiths, even. Most of the business fell into the eastern part of the Choctaw country. Now, just west and north of here you get to the Fringe. There are some customers out there, but you can't count on em staying put and staying alive."

"What's the Fringe?"

"Choctaw, Chickasaw, Seminole. Crisscross of different boundaries, each one with different courts and police — lighthorse, they call em. And the white whiskey towns. You get a lot of lowlifes hidin out there where the law can't reach them. Pretty good place to get killed. Hell's Fringe, they call it."

She looked away into the night and said quietly, "Why are you here if there's no business?"

Jake puffed vigorously on the little cigar. "You know, I shouldn't do all the talking. I still don't hardly know a thing about you."

Jake's tone toward Miss King was even and neutral, but Tom heard something of a challenge.

She held her hands out to the fire. "What would you like to know?"

"Well . . . where are you from? Where's your family?"

"St. Louis. I don't have any remaining family."

"Sorry to hear that."

"It doesn't matter," she said. A puzzled frown went across her face, not a conspicuous expression except for the fact that Tom hadn't seen her make it before now. They all gazed somberly into the fire a moment, before she looked back up and said, "Please call me Sam."

"So. Do you plan to settle in Guthrie?" Jake asked. Tom was getting the impression that Jake was being cool toward her.

"I want to take a look at Guthrie. I'm thinking about starting a hotel."

Jake showed surprise. "Buying or building?"

"I don't know yet. I'm still just thinking about it."

"Better get flood insurance," Jake said.

She laughed. A surge went through Tom, so powerful that he had to look off at the stars.

"Reckon it'd be kind of chancy, way things are," Jake added.

"Oh?"

Jake took the cigar out of his mouth. "Guthrie may be the capital, but it's been dead lately. Got three or four big hotels already that aren't doing so good. Now, Perry and Enid are a different story. They're crying for hotels. Enid has ten thousand people in it, and the buildings are just coming up. Trouble is, there isn't much cash out there."

"You seem to know this country well."

Jake smiled a little. "I've been traveling west of the river for about twenty-five years, but I can't say I know it all that well. Nobody does. Changing too fast. Booms and busts travel like firestorms. When it busts, it really busts. Five years ago I would have thought Guthrie was getting bigger'n Fort Smith. Bigger'n anything. Now it's dead as a sinker doughnut, a lot of people moving north to the good cropland in the Outlet. Down here in the old Choctaw country" — Jake nodded toward the abandoned house — "well, you can see what's happened to that. Civilized Tribes say they want to keep what's left of their land — call it Sequoyah. Keep their own separate state between Oklahoma Territory and Arkansas. I don't know. There's always some kind of mess. Runnin boomers out, then lining them up and runnin them in. Never can tell whether you're on the edge of the future or the ruin of the past. Hell of a place to try to set up a new hotel."

"Maybe I ought to go in business with you."

Jake didn't respond, although Tom sensed that he wanted to. Again, an uncomfortable silence.

"Were you ever married?"

Jake laughed incredulously. "Married? Not as far as I remember."

Tom watched her eyes in the firelight. After a while she said, "I'm not really fixed on hotels. My mother owned one."

"Oh? I've been to St. Louis a time or two. Maybe I saw it. What hotel was it?"

She hesitated, then said, "The King."

He thought a minute and shook his head. "Why'd you leave St. Louis for this durn place?"

"I had reasons," she said quietly, as if to discourage any further talk about it.

Jake threw the cigar into the fire and stood up. "I guess we'd better try to get some sleep."

They put more sticks onto the fire and tried to find comfortable places on the ground. She took out her suitcase and offered Jake and Tom pieces of her clothing, dresses, to sleep under, which made Jake laugh more strenuously than Tom had ever seen before. Jake turned down the offer, and Tom felt bound to do the same, although it would have been inexpressibly wonderful to sleep with her clothes covering him. "Suit yourselves," she said. Tom took off his uncomfortable new shoes, collar, and tie, and curled up not more than ten feet from where she was, raising his head a few times and looking at her surreptitiously.

Sometime late in the damp of night, unable to sleep, Tom went up to the two-lane road to take a pee, and while there he had the odd feeling that someone was nearby. He looked off toward the woods and could almost feel the closeness of the academy, as if it were just through the trees. The night smelled the same here as it did at Bokchito — the same oak and ash forest, the same softly calling owls. Tom suddenly fell into complete, heart-pounding wakefulness, and he had the overpowering urge to run, he did not know why, just to run anywhere. He tried to force himself to walk back to their camp spot but veered off through the wet grass, walking faster until he really was running, southward across a field. He ran beyond the ruined house before he tripped and fell on his face and lay there, gulping air.

At Bokchito, many times he had awakened in the night with this impulse to run, almost as compelling as the desire to breathe. This was the first time he'd actually done it, and now there was no longer anything to run from. Realizing that he hadn't said a night prayer, he rolled over and said it on his back, looking at the stars. Walking back to the camp, Tom heard an animal snort and went over to the mules. They were dead asleep, silent except for the heavy whisper of their breathing. Tom raised his head and looked around. The noise had sounded farther away.

When he finally slept, not long before sunrise, he dreamed that Samantha King was riding beside him through smoking red light, as if the sunset had caught fire across the land. A raking, hot wind was blowing in their faces, his heels were on fire, the mules kept disappearing and reappearing in the billowing light, and they were somehow hitched to and pulling the entire Armstrong Academy building, filled with silent boys, the Reverend glaring from the upper balcony like the captain of a ship looking out at sea. In the dream he was very aware of how heavy the building was, and how improbable it was that the mules could keep pulling it.

◆

Jake got them up early, when there was just a hint of light in the east. Tom tried to put on his collar and tie, was unable to, and put them into his pocket. The new shoes were painful on his heels, but he assumed this was the price you paid for good hard-leather shoes. The mules refused to wake up and stand together for the harness, and he had to whack and push and pull them, and even after he got them together, they had a way of turning their heads or moving just enough to prevent the harness. Old mule tricks like twisting their ears had no effect on them. Tom finally had to hobble one tight and virtually pick the other up and set him in a different place. When he got the harness on, he noticed to his embarrassment that Miss King was standing there watching him, smiling.

By midday they'd gotten bogged down several times and had to push, had to lay paths of sticks and rocks ahead of the wagon and push it from behind in shin-deep mud, had to move and skirt fallen trees, had to coax and yell at the mules, and a couple of times to backtrack. They had no food, and their only water was from sulfurous, hard-water streams. When they at last rode into Durant, they were as haggard and dirty as gypsies in a rainstorm. Tom was too tired to feel anxious about Durant — about the fact that this was the town, the only town, he had known in his previous life.

Jake got rooms for them in the Red Rock Hotel, where the hotelkeeper was a white man who smiled a lot, showing off four gold teeth. Jake talked him into serving them an early supper. It was cornmeal mush, cold potatoes, and cucumber pickles, which they ate in voracious communal silence. Afterward Jake and Tom sat on the front porch, while Miss King disappeared for a rest. Tom took off his shoes, and Jake smoked an evening cigar, quickly growing heavy-eyed. "I'm turning in early. There's something I need to tell you."

Tom looked at him through the haze of his own exhaustion.

"If anybody asks you any questions about Dekker Hardware, don't answer them, don't even try to. That includes Miss King. Any kind of questions at all. Now, we ought to be starting out early in the morning. I think we'll keep those useless mules at least until we get to Guthrie."

Tom was confused but at the moment too inert to ask any questions. Jake got up stiffly and walked into the hotel. Tom's stomach was full, he was glad to have his shoes off, and his body was strangely pleasured by soreness. He remained in the cane chair, looking out at Durant's main street. Students who did well in their recitations were allowed to ride here with the Reverend to do Tuesday shopping — a mixed blessing, since one had to be close to Reverend Schoot all day. Bider's General Merchandise, directly across from where he now sat, was the place where they always bought supplies, and many times Tom had waited outside with the two or three other lucky boys of the week while the Reverend strutted inside to place his orders. The Reverend usually had the three boys stand outside in a line, "at ease," until he'd made the week's acquisitions, then he would come to the door and allow — order — them to walk up the street to "see the sights." This stroll up the long block of the dirt street was their reward for good schoolwork. There were seldom very many people in town on

Tuesdays besides the few regulars hanging around outside the pool hall, so the sights didn't change much from week to week.

Near sunset, Miss King appeared on the porch, looking sleepy from her nap, and she asked Tom to escort her to a nearby bathhouse. When he got up she took him by his arm. "I see you gave the shoes up."

"No," he hurried to say. "I just took them off for a while."

The pool hall had the usual congregation of squatters and leaners. Tom could smell them twenty feet away. He'd been taunted by them just about every time he and the other two boys marched up and down the street in their weekly moment of freedom.

"Eh, *han-shulush!* Where you get *na hollo ahoyo!*" one yelled, and a couple of them snickered aloud, but their tone was different now, envious rather than scornful.

The bathhouse itself — just the sight of it — was an even more direct contact with his past. He was walking toward the box-and-strip shack as he had often done before, and he got the queasy feeling that he was actually walking into his past. The Indian woman who ran the bathhouse had dark, sun-leathered skin. Tom had occasionally spoken to her before, but he expected she did not recognize him this evening. He'd often wondered about her — whether she had a husband or children, how she'd ended up here. The academy boys called her Apache, but they didn't really know anything about her.

Miss King paid her. The woman heated water on an open fire that was smoldering out back, and ushered them into a tiny room with two corrugated metal tubs separated by a ragged piece of canvas thrown over a line. She carried in buckets of heated water and said peremptorily, "Take off," and when Tom hesitated — he hadn't thought he'd be taking a bath, too — she grabbed the top button of his shirt and tugged at it. "Take off!" She had a broad, flat, ageless face, high cheekbones, and fierce black eyes.

She waved the back of her hand at him and pushed through the canvas, he quickly stripped down and got into the tub, and she brought in more buckets of the hot, milky, pungent water, pouring it into his tub, then into Miss King's on the other side of the canvas, then she disappeared for a while, leaving them alone in the steamy shack. The only sound was the slight lapping of water. Light coming through a small, yellow-papered window reddened in the winter sunset. The Indian woman came in and lit a kerosene lantern on Tom's side, and another on Miss King's. The smell was sweet to Tom. Miss King sighed, and he glanced through a triangular tear in the canvas and saw her in the lantern-lit steam from the breasts up.

He leaned his head back and looked at the roof. He had the peculiar image of himself exploding out of the tub, going clear through the roof of the shack.

"Tom?"

"Yes ma'am."

"How old do you think I am."

"I don't know."

"Make a guess."

He swallowed. "Well . . . twenty-five years old."

"I'm twenty-three."

He wasn't sure how to respond to this revelation.

"Will you stop calling me 'ma'am'?"

"Yes ma'am — I mean yes."

The Indian woman came into Miss King's side and started washing her with strong-smelling soap. Tom heard her groan with pleasure and again looked through the tattered canvas. Twenty-three? She lay back in the tub as she was being thoroughly soaped up on the shoulders, breasts, and down her stomach. His penis had risen and broken through the surface of the milky water and gone tight against his stomach, and when the washerwoman came through the canvas, he scooted down to hide it under the water.

She took him firmly by the shoulders and pushed him forward in the tub, then started rubbing his back with a big bar of lye soap, across his shoulders and up his neck, then downward, making vigorous small strokes over his muscles and the little ridges of scars on his back. Finishing at the top of his buttocks, she again took him by both shoulders and pushed him back against the sloped tub. He quickly pulled up his knees. She splashed water on his face, then moved from there on downward, to his chest and stomach. She washed all the way down, knocking against his hard penis and taking no more notice of it than anything else. She then turned to his feet, and beginning with his toes worked up his legs and across his thighs and around his buttocks and genitals, even briefly the length of his penis, washing it! Still holding it, she turned her implacable, knowing black eyes on him for a moment, and gave him just the shadow of a look, almost a smile.

That was all. She was gone.

A woman had taken hold of his hard penis. He lay there in the steam, not even wanting to peek through the canvas, he felt so strange. And she had recognized him.

"Jake doesn't like me," Miss King sighed.

Tom breathed the mist. He couldn't think what to say. There was something at once calming and exciting about her lazy tone. The entire central part of his body was tingling with anticipation.

"Tom?"

"What?"

"Do you know why Jake doesn't like me?"

"No!" Tom said. "He likes you fine."

"How's your bath?" she asked.

"Very good."

"Tom, did you know that you're a handsome young man?"

He stared at the slow, curling flame of the hurricane lamp.

"You're not very experienced with women, are you?" she said.

Experienced? With women? He knew that women and men mated in a way similar to the animals, they "knew" each other, and he had read and been told that it carried great peril when done for the wrong reasons, or too often, or not in the right way, and could cause the loss of ambition, the plague of alcohol, destruction of nerve cells, and other calamities — even, according to the first book of the Bible, the direct intervention of a wrathful God. But the precise details of how men and women went about "knowing" each other, or indeed why they did it at all when it involved such awful menace, he didn't fully understand.

"Tom?"

"What?"

"Did you hear me?"

"Yes."

"Have you ever seen a woman's body?"

Oh, Lord. Tom sank into the tub until his head was under water, his legs dangling out the other end. He stayed under there awhile until he had to come out for a breath of air. When he did so, she was standing in the lantern light, on his side of the curtain, her wet skin showing through a sheetlike towel, wrapped around her and knotted at the breast. The towel covered her only down to mid-thigh, long legs reaching out. "This is a woman's body," she said. She was turned a little to the side, and then she moved to face him directly, and he got a little closer to understanding why people took the chance despite the peril. She came and knelt beside him on the slippery clay-packed floor, and one part of his mind was racing while another was gently floating like the flame of the hurricane lamp in the clouds of the steamy little room. He desperately wondered whether he should try to find something to cover himself or whether he should just give up.

"Poor boy, what happened to your back?"

"The mule bit me. It's okay."

"I mean these scars."

She eventually reached out and lazily touched him on the chin, gently pushing his mouth closed. Her hand moved to his chest and then down the muscles of his front to his belly. His penis was standing out of the water, and when she reached down and touched it he moaned aloud, no longer capable of worrying what she thought. He gave up. He was completely in her hands. But she wrapped her fingers around it so briefly and with such a light touch and then allowed the hand just to float there in the water beside it, touching it lightly, bumping against it with her knuckles, no more. He wanted to reach out and tear off the sheet wrapped around her.

"You're getting more experienced by the hour," she said.

Tom contemplated this for the better part of a half-second and said, "Yes." He nodded, tensing his buttocks so that her floating fingers would touch him.

She knitted her brow and looked directly at him with her green eyes. "Tom, I want to keep traveling with you on to Guthrie."

Tom closed his eyes.

"Jake knows how business is done here. And he knows so many people. I need to learn from him. I need to learn as much as I can."

She said other things, but Tom didn't really hear her. He was too busy having a hard-on. In fact, rather than having a hard-on, he was a hard-on from his neck to his knees — hard-buttocked, tense, painfully stiff, a furious electric Presbyterian hard-on of the worst sort, sixteen inches from her casual gaze. She was so cool, as if this sort of thing was as common as a drink of water, the daily stuff of life, while he had become a rending, tumbling roar of emotions. Samantha King seemed unaware of it, and that unawareness was exotic to him, and totally baffling. She said something else that he didn't hear. He barely even heard the sound of her voice through the havoc racing through his body, and he openly moaned.

He was on a plateau. She was looking at him abstractedly. "Tom?" she said. "Did you hear me?"

"Yes," he lied, his hips levitated almost out of the water.

She looked at him again with the slow smile. "Poor boy." Taking his penis firmly in her hand, she moved it up and down, and before she had done so more than five times, it exploded in a pumping fountain of milky fluid halfway to the roof.

♦

Stupefied, Tom got out of the tub. His foot caught against the edge of it, splashing water all over the place, and he fell flat on his tailbone in the slippery, rock-hard clay. She had gone on before him, and eventually he stumbled out of the shack, past the old woman at her fire, and walked alone up the street.

Part Two

· 9 ·

THE NEXT MORNING, Jake sat awhile on the edge of the bed, remembering who and where he was. Kidneys sore and joints stiff, he gazed at the light coming through the window and realized that he'd slept more than twelve hours. A pillow was on the floor where Tom had apparently slept. Jake hadn't heard the boy come in, but last night he'd been so tired that he wouldn't have heard a locomotive go by his bed.

He found the piece of paper that he'd taken from Miss King's suitcase, and went to the end of the hallway where there was a primitive indoor water closet, really an outhouse on stilts leaning against the outside wall, built above the narrow ravine behind the hotel. It swayed a little as he stepped into it.

Jake sat down gingerly on the cool wood and perused the piece of paper in dim light coming through a hole in the wall. He didn't know whether to ask her what it was all about or just to forget it. It was nothing but a list of scrawled names. At the top were men who worked for Dekker Hardware, including Ernest, Jack Peters, Marvin Beele, and Jake, and below were the names of three others, among whom Jake saw no particular connection except that they were all pretty successful local businessmen. One was the man who owned the big bakery that often yeasted the town's air, another operated a factory that made fancy gift boxes.

Jake had thought that Samantha King was an accident in his life, but she'd come from St. Louis with his name on a list. He'd put off asking her about it yesterday, because there was too much else going on. He folded the note back up, figuring he'd better make room for it today. It probably wasn't that important, but he couldn't understand why she hadn't said anything about it.

Back in the room, a basin was already filled with water and there was a small dim mirror for shaving. Brushing up the soap, he glanced out the window and saw more people on the street than usual for a weekday. When he dried off his face, he glanced outside again and noticed Miss King step off the hotel porch and walk up the street.

In the dining room, Tom was sitting in a cane-backed chair reading a newspaper, *The Anti-Monopolist,* with furrowed brow. BOY TRAMPLED, WORRY DROVE HER TO DEATH, CAPITALIST CLASS USES PINKERTONS, announced headlines on the first page.

"Had breakfast?"

"Nosir!" Tom slapped the newspaper shut and jumped out of his chair onto his feet. His short black hair stuck up off his head in patches, and the clothes Miss King had bought him were as rumpled as if he'd slept in them.

"Didn't mean to startle you."

When they sat down at a table, Tom was still clutching the newspaper, first putting it in his lap, then onto the floor. Tom acted queer at meals. His posture would get ramrod straight, and before he would speak a single word he always put down his fork and knife. Today he seemed even more self-conscious, if that was possible.

"Get a good night's sleep?" Jake asked him.

"No sir," Tom said.

Jake almost laughed. He'd noticed before that Tom generally told the truth rather than giving the usual polite answer. It was one of the things he liked about him. "What's on your mind, then?"

Tom didn't seem to know how to answer him, although he looked as if he wanted to.

Breakfast was a poor affair of brown, watery coffee, *pashofa* — meal and stringy meat — with sweetened grape juice poured over it, and some kind of old hard bread. Tom glanced repeatedly toward the door, a worried, almost wild look to his eye.

"Did Miss King tell you what she was doing?"

Tom looked at him and said, in a wondering voice, "What she was doing?"

Jake stopped chewing. "Yeah. I noticed her leaving the hotel."

"You did?" Tom said, his skin darkening in what looked like a blush.

Jake sighed. "Just eat your breakfast. We have a day ahead."

The hotel proprietor came in and spilled some more rusty coffee into their cups and cheerfully announced, "They caught Charley Bryant. Brought him in early this mornin. He's over there dying right now."

"Who's that?"

"Never heard of Blackface Charley Bryant?" The proprietor grinned at Jake disbelievingly, showing off his gold teeth.

"Can't say I have."

"Robbed the Katy at least four times. Bunch of people are in town just to see him."

"Four robberies. What is that, a week's worth for the Katy?" Jake said drily. He hadn't liked the Katy when he'd sold the Choctaw Nation, and Dandy Pruitt liked it even less now that he had the territory. Dandy called it a religious railroad: every time you put a customer's order on it, you got down on your knees and prayed that it wouldn't be lost, crushed, or unloaded in Texas.

After breakfast, Tom remained as weird and peaked as before, and Jake wondered what was under his skin. He sent Tom out to get the team ready, and went off by himself to call on the first account.

Bider's, across from the Red Rock, was the biggest merchant in the area. Mr. Bider was a prickly, stingy, complaining little man who'd given Jake hell as a salesman. Now he claimed to be too busy to talk — and in fact there were quite a few ladies coming into the store — so Jake waited. Bider made him wait so long that when he finally did step over for a talk, Jake felt fine about collecting eighty-five dollars as well as some mortgage papers from him.

Tom had finished with the mules and was waiting for Jake outside, and the two of them spent an hour walking around discovering that two other storekeeps had gone out of business. The best Jake could tell, they'd both sold out their merchandise and walked away from their debts. This wouldn't have happened in the Choctaw Nation a few years ago. It wouldn't even have been imaginable.

The fourth storekeeper was Mr. Josephus Bargain, whose store hadn't changed much since Jake was last here, with uncut trees growing close to it, a flock of geese standing around its sagging front porch, dust and darkness inside, and a smell of creosote. Joe was a lanky old catfish of a man, probably half Indian but looking like a Mexican with his droopy, elaborate mustachios, remnants of his years as a cowboy. He wasn't a big general retailer, but he'd always done well with a few items. He owed about four hundred dollars.

"Ain't you dead yet?" Jake said, smiling. For some mysterious reason Joe had always loved to be kidded about mortality.

He looked up with no trace of an expression except in the glittering of his eyes. "Why, you son of a bitch, I'll go to your funeral! Who's the boy?" After the introductions, Tom retreated to look around the store while Joe continued his task — dipping ropes in a barrel of some kind of preservative and stiffener. Joe was the only store owner Jake knew who made quite a good trade selling lariats. Jake had talked with cowboys as far away as the Outlet who claimed to buy their lariats from Joe Bargain.

"Wanta know my secret?"

"Yeah. What is that stuff, kerosene? Creosote?"

"Ain't talking about my formula," Joe said, tying off the ends of another length. "I'm talking about the secret to a long life."

"Guess I'd like to know that, too."

Joe glanced at him and over toward the boy, and announced, "Always wear plenty of clothes."

"That's it?"

"That's the main part of it. Some people believe drinking water'll do it. Water out here'll kill you. Never drink it. Damn stuff'll eat out your insides."

"Last time I was by here, you told me to drink a glass of sarsaparilla every day. Still believe that?"

"Well, that does help the heart," Joe said thoughtfully. "There's a lot to it when you get down to the fine details."

The glitter dimmed from the old storekeeper's eyes when Jake sat down and told him briefly about the crisis at the store and read the mortgage transfer agreement. "I don't personally care if you sign over any property or not, Joe. I'm just delivering the message. Ernest Dekker told me to inform stores that he'd foreclose on the merchandise if they didn't pay up or sign."

"That what he said?"

"Afraid he did."

"Who the hell is Ernest Dekker? Ralph die?"

"Ralph didn't die. Ernest is his son, and he's taking over the store."

"Well, if he does die, send me a telegram. Ralph and me have a bet on who's going to call on the other one's widow."

"Afraid you won't win that one. Mrs. Dekker's been dead —"

"Yeah. I used to read the Dearly Departeds out of Fort Smith . . . She was from St. Louis, wasn't she?"

"Mrs. Dekker? I believe she was from South Carolina."

"Oh, well," Joe mused, playing with his mustache, "must have been somebody else." He went silent for a minute. "You know, Ralph was fool enough to set me up in business. He give me credit and a loan for a building when I didn't have so much as a stick to put it against." Joe stared into his fumey barrel, quiet a moment, then burst out, "It's the goddang politicians! I've been at the back end of three thousand head of cattle that smell better'n what they're doing in Muskogee."

"You talking about Senator Dawes's commission?"

"That's right. Dawes. Indian Nations are done with, Jake. They're sellin the land, stealing it, every last goddang acre. Already took half of it."

"I hear this idea of keeping a separate state for the Five Tribes might catch on."

Joe snorted. "They're whistling through their assholes about that. Senator Dawes wants the land and he'll get it."

"Government's giving good money for it. Maybe it's not a bad deal, with everybody being so broke. I know some Cherokees who'll be glad to be holding a couple hundred dollars from the sale of the Outlet. Particularly the younger ones."

"Yeah, I remember being young and stupid, too." Joe looked up from the barrel and squinted at Jake intently. "Certain parties ain't even waiting for the senator to do his work, you know. I had the Choctaw agent come by here the other day asking if I wanted to lease my little piece of bottomland."

Jake thought about that a minute. He'd heard of big leases from the tribes, but never from individuals. "For range?"

"This ain't rangeland, it's cropland. For a 'consortium,' he called it." Joe stood up and quickly coiled the length of rope and hung it on the wall. "I asked him who's in this consortium. Said he couldn't put names to the principals. Said that was confidential. I told him I don't do bidness with somebody won't tell me their names. Fifteen cent an acre, ten-year lease, including minerals, with the right to buy it — that's what he wanted. Told me that my land-use warrant wasn't no kind of deed anyway, and I'd be lucky to get that. I'd better take what I could get."

Tom had come over closer and was listening. Jake frowned, turning this over in his mind. "These are whites leasing land from people?"

"Yeah, and the damn Indian agent doing their work!"

"Against the law, ain't it?"

Joe glanced at him and just shook his head. "What law? Before Dawes? After Dawes? White? Indian? There ain't any law, Jake. That thing you're carrying, what does it say?" He pointed at the mortgage transfer.

Jake felt suddenly warm with embarrassment. He took a deep breath. "The bank's calling the shots, Joe. We don't have any choice but to bring in customer debt, or get mortgages that satisfy them. That's what they tell me. Now, I won't ask you to sign it if you'll give me a good part of what you owe. It's up to you."

"How much of my land do you want me to sign up?"

"You owe about four hundred. They're offering twenty-five cents an acre. That'd be sixteen hundred acres."

"Bull shit," Joe Bargain said. "What about these poor bastards that owe you two or three thousand bucks. How they gonna put their hands on eight thousand acres?"

"You can sign over land warrants you're holding from customers, as long as the land has improvements on it."

"I tell you what you do, Jake. What's this young Dekker's name?"

"Ernest."

"You give him a message from Joe Bargain. Tell him he shouldn't be asking storekeepers to sign over people's land unless he wants to get those storekeepers shot. You can also tell him they'll be ice water in hell before I sign over any mortgages I'm holding on customers."

Jake nodded slowly. "All right, Joe, what can you pay me?"

Joe ended up giving him eighty-five dollars and not signing. He also gave Jake some parting advice about traveling. "North of here, keep an eye out. Lot of these sodbusters didn't get no land, and they're scattering in all directions. They come limping in here every day, begging potatoes and such. One wagon leaves, another be coming down the road. Sorriest-looking bunch of white people I ever did see. Kind that pick up stakes every six months and never make a crop. Lot of em claim they've been robbed and such."

When Jake and Tom walked back toward the center of town, Jake kept having the feeling something odd was going on, something over and above the confusion of the town. He felt almost as if he was being watched. The traffic was mostly women and their kids, some of them carrying a package or bouquet of flowers, and congregating at the little log shack that served as the local jail. Several men wearing Oklahoma Territory badges sat on the ground outside, smoking and playing cards, and he went over and asked what all the excitement was.

"Charley Bryant's in there," said one of them, nodding at the shack.

"I'll be," Jake said noncommittally.

"Never hear of Blackface Charley Bryant?"

"Not until today."

"Well, he's worth a thousand dollars," said the deputy, with a one-fanged smile.

Out of curiosity, Jake and Tom poked inside the stifling shack, which was crowded mostly with women and kids. A short man with a weak chin, thinning hair, and a go-to-hell mustache lay on a blanket against the slat wall, with what looked like about a dozen wounds in him, all packed or dressed but some still bleeding. He was surrounded by flowers, cakes, and unopened gifts. Jake found himself standing next to a bone-skinny woman with stringy hair, age maybe sixteen, with a front tooth missing and a baby on her shoulder. She was a white woman, but the women here were mostly mixed bloods, with babies or kids hanging tight to their dresses. The jail shack was thick with rose water and sweat, people sniffling, whispering, and crying. "It's a shame," one murmured over and over, "such a shame." There was a mood of expectation in the crowded room. Jake never understood why the women worshiped these outlaws so much.

Mr. Bryant opened his eyes and glanced around nervously. Someone produced a bottle of rye and poured a little down his throat. He swallowed and croaked, "Let it be known I kilt nine men!"

The skinny mother beside Jake sighed, with a bright look in her eyes.

"How many?" another asked.

"I did, I kilt nine men," groaned Charley Bryant.

"Oh, my!" said another. "Nine of em."

One of the women near the dying outlaw produced a pair of scissors and quickly leaned over and snipped off a lock of his thinning hair. "Are you ashamed for a life of sin?" asked a sterner voice.

Bryant looked to be working hard to stay conscious. "I never kilt no women. I always loved a good woman."

"Tell us about the men you killed," demanded the stern voice.

He didn't seem to know where to start.

"Were they all bad men?" a more timid voice prompted.

"The worst." He coughed. "Gamblers, thieves, woman-rapers."

"Are you ashamed?" repeated the stern voice.

"Not one bit," said Blackface Charley Bryant.

Several of them sighed at once. The one who was kneeling beside Charley Bryant poured some more whiskey down his throat. "You done what you had to, Charley."

♦

Jake and Tom had just walked out the door when they caught sight of Miss King hurrying down the street toward the hotel. The deputies all stopped playing cards and stared at her.

"Good morning," she said with a smile.

"Mornin," Jake said in a subdued tone. Tom looked embarrassed again. She volunteered that she'd been to the telegraph office. "Wire somebody back home?"

She answered without hesitation. "Raymond Phillips. He's the closest I have to a family now in St. Louis. He was my guardian after my mother died." She added, "Ray gave me your name before I left St. Louis."

"Oh?"

"Yes, Ray gave me a list of men he thought might have business experience in the Oklahoma Territory."

They stopped beside the wagon, where Tom leaned against the wall and picked up his newspaper again.

"Don't believe I recall a Raymond Phillips." Jake was surprised that she was answering the very question he'd put off asking her.

"He heard your name from someone. Maybe your employer."

"So this man knows Ralph Dekker?" Jake asked.

"Ray's a lawyer, and he deals with all kinds of businessmen. He knows people in Fort Smith."

It might have been merely the coincidence of her answering the question that was on his mind, but something about this bothered Jake. And then again, it sounded like it could be the simple truth.

Tom remained with his head still stuck in the newspaper.

"Good morning, Tom," Miss King said. "Did you have a good night's sleep?"

Tom kept his head buried in his paper. The two mules, brushed down to their grey-coated glory, stood nearby, dozing in the traces.

"No ma'am," he said.

·10·

THE ANTI-MONOPOLIST was the first newspaper Tom had ever really read, although he had glanced over the headlines of papers left around the smoking parlor at Mrs. Peltier's. Suffering, lurid crimes, labor strikes, political turmoil, misery, hunger, orphans in the streets, families in desperate straits all around the United States — Reverend Schoot called such things "messages from an evil world," which was why he forbade newspapers at the academy. Tom had gone through the paper's ten pages several times, devouring it all, notices as well as news — advertisements for "summer camps" and for other papers with intriguing names like *RipSaw, Sledgehammer,* and *The Appeal to Reason.* But his curiosity about things in the newspaper occupied the thinnest, flickering surface of his mind. What he was really thinking about was Sam King and what happened with her in the bathhouse last night.

When it was time to go, she climbed up beside him, pushing against him on the little seat, giving him a brief, cool smile. A tingling of pleasure and fear and inexplicable sorrow went through him. He avoided looking directly at her, not knowing if he could stand another day of being this close to her.

Apparently the mules had decided that today was a nonworking day, and they started very slowly, lugging through Durant as if they were pulling a ten-ton wagon. Rolling past the bathhouse, Tom sat rigid on the seat, aware that Sam glanced at him, wishing she would stop looking at him, wishing she wouldn't stop, ever.

They ground along past the pool hall, where today a lone man wearing a black duster was leaning against the unpainted wall, hat low over his face.

♦

Tom decided to call the mules Grant and Lee. The biter was Grant; Lee was the less openly irritable of the two, but a deeper treachery lurked in his rheumy eye, as he waited for the chance to do major damage to someone. Finally beginning to wake up on the road, the two grizzled, annoyed creatures clashed and pulled against each other. After a while they started trying a new trick, to the surprise of all three of their passengers: in rutted, potholed stretches in the road their ears slowly perked up, and they walked faster and faster into a trot. Tom figured that they'd decided to risk broken legs in an effort to shatter a wheel or bounce their passengers out.

Tom controlled the mules the best he could, and Sam grabbed hold of him, of his leg or whatever was available, and held on for dear life. Jake wedged himself into the back in an effort to avoid falling out. As they rattled down the road, Jake's mood unaccountably turned better. He seemed glad to have left Durant.

Tom loved it, wobbling and bouncing through the ruts with Sam holding on to his thigh.

"Why are they running?" Sam asked, straightening herself back up on the seat.

"They heard me talking about the glue factory," Jake yelled.

"Well, they didn't do this yesterday."

"Probably talked it over last night."

"I don't believe they talk much," Tom said. "Their names are Grant and Lee."

Jake and Sam both laughed, to Tom's surprise. He didn't typically make jokes.

They turned north on the old Butterfield Route, the "Texas Road," the very same road that Mrs. Peltier's rooming house was on, a hundred fifty miles away in Fort Smith. By midday they reached Boggy Depot, a village of abandoned buildings and quietness as deep as the forest that surrounded it. Seven or eight fine old houses were scattered around the hills.

"Busy little town until the railroad came in twelve miles from here," Jake said. "Made a wallflower out of it. We've only got one customer left here."

It was a blacksmith and harness dealer. He was clean-shaping a handle when they arrived, and he kept working. He shook his head impatiently when Jake talked to him about collecting on his outstanding debt. "No English," he said, holding his hammer away from his body threateningly.

"If you won't pay on the debt and you don't sign, they may close out your merchandise mortgage."

Jake went on and explained the mortgage transfer agreement, and the blacksmith only narrowed his eyes slightly and went back to hammering on the handle. He didn't care to be polite. But when they were about to leave, he suddenly quit his forge and offered them all a drink from his well, as if deciding at the last minute to be friendly. He smiled unconvincingly, first at Jake, then Tom. "Thirsty? Want water?"

Sam, leaning against the wagon with her arms crossed, said she certainly did, and the blacksmith pumped water and offered the bucket first to Jake, then Sam, and finally Tom, who drank half a bucket despite the awful taste and smell of it and the sour looks both Sam and Jake were still making. The blacksmith smiled broadly now, as if pleased at how much they had enjoyed his water.

When Tom offered some to the mules, they sniffed it but wouldn't drink. Jake looked worried. "That stuff tastes like coal mine tailings."

"Are there coal mines here?" Sam asked, still making a face.

Jake got out a handkerchief and blotted at his mouth. "All you'd have to do is widen out the mouth of that well and you'd have the start of one."

Back on the wagon, Sam turned to Jake. "He didn't want to talk to you, did he?" she said.

"I don't blame him." Jake sounded generally disgusted.

"Why?" Sam asked.

"Askin somebody to sign away their own property is bad enough. Would you want to sign away your customers' property?"

Going out of Boggy Depot, the mules returned to their slow pace. "So why do you want him to sign this thing?"

"You're askin the wrong person." Jake still sounded annoyed.

"They say the bank wants better mortgages. We've always used merchandise mortgages. If they don't pay, after while we take the stock back. I've had to do it quite a few times, and I don't mind it, either. Now they don't pay, we're gonna take land."

"You don't think it's fair?" Sam asked. Tom glanced at her and noticed that she was staring ahead. The wagon creaked along, the mules again acting their ages. Jake didn't answer her for a moment, and Tom glanced back.

"We're changing the rules on them right when they're at their weakest. Nobody has any money to speak of. The price they're puttin to the land ain't fair. I don't call any of it fair. They have a word for people that sneak out and claim a quarter section of land before the gun goes off. They call em sooners. I guess you'd call this sooner than sooner. The land ain't even signed away from the tribe."

Tom was curious about why Jake was now talking freely with Sam about business, after having told him not to. Jake couldn't see her face, but Tom could, and he saw her eyes — a look in them as if a light had unexpectedly shone into them. She started to say something and then stopped; her mouth came open and after a pause she asked, "Who's they?"

"Beg pardon?"

"You said 'they' decided to do this. Who are you talking about?"

"Well, it ain't Mr. Dekker, I'll tell you that," Jake said. "He wouldn't turn on his customers like this."

"So he's an honest man?"

Jake seemed too peeved to talk further about it. She started to say something else, but decided not to.

Later that day, they were hungry and stopped at a farm shack.

"Hello the house!" Jake yelled. A woman eventually peeked around a rough wooden door, and he asked if they could buy some dinner from her.

The lady presented them each with a trencher of bread with lard drippings and something that tasted like scrambled prairie-chicken eggs with pumpkin mashed into it. The house was dark, lighted by a single coal oil lamp, and it had a packed earthen floor. Kerosene had been spilled on the floor to combat fleas, and Tom was not used to the strong smell of it. The kind lady hovered around them, concerned about whether they liked the food. She had given Jake larger portions. They ate off a long single plank in the tiny, dirty, sagging, windowless house. After a lifetime of terrible food, Tom didn't mind it, but Miss King looked less comfortable, and ate only a few bites. Children stood around watching them with luminous eyes.

One of them, a scrawny boy ten years old, sidled toward Tom with a shy smile. "My father ran away," he said in Choctaw, and to his surprise Tom understood him.

"When?"

"Long time ago," the boy said. "He went that way." He pointed up the road in the direction they were headed, still smiling. "He will never come back."

The lady wouldn't take payment for her hospitality, so Jake gave her a dollar to "buy a gift" for her kids, and they were back on the road. Sam acted a little woozy, as if the food wasn't agreeing with her. Jake, too, began to look under the weather. After a couple of miles they met a farm wagon coming fast the other way, with a man and woman on the seat and all form of possessions tied onto the back. The woman's face, as they rattled and bounced past, looked as if she'd seen a ghost. Just ahead, a group of people were camped in a walnut grove. They were whooping and yelling, the smell of liquor thick in the air. Three young men lurched from the campsite toward them, and Jake said, "Don't slow down, Tom."

The young men approached the wagon and walked along beside it. *"Na homi! Oka homi!"* they yelled. *"Oka homi!"*

Tom snapped the reins.

"Oka homi!" One of them came around in front of the team and stood in the way, smiling stupidly. He took out a knife and held it up in the air. Grant bit at him and actually got a nip of his arm, and he shrieked and moved out of the way, causing his two cohorts to break up in laughter. The young men were ragged, stinking, bleak beneath their hilarity. The one with the knife made an ineffectual swing at them as they passed by.

Sam glanced back at them. "Why were they saying 'Oklahoma'?"

" *'Oka homi,'* " Jake said. "Red water. Whiskey. They wanted us to refill their jugs."

"I don't feel good," Sam said.

Soon they were passing other travelers on the road, wagons with bony children trooping along behind them, and Jake said that they were probably settlers who'd not found land in the Outlet rush. "My stomach's a little upset, too," Jake admitted.

As if she'd been waiting for someone else to mention it, Sam got down from the wagon and immediately vomited. She couldn't sit upright, so Tom helped her into the back — Jake and Sam side by side, puckered and sick and ill complexioned.

"Wasn't the food," Jake said sourly. "That blacksmith gave us bad water. I knew better'n to take it."

Jake was as sick to his stomach as Sam was. They had to stop several times. Tom remained well despite having drunk a lot of the water, and he drove the mules on through the fading afternoon. The animals had gotten tired, and they no longer tried to run through the rough spots in the road. By late afternoon all of them were exhausted and wanted to stop, but they needed drinking water. On top of it all, Tom could not shake the strange feeling that they were being followed. Every time they momentarily stopped, he'd hear a sound behind them, some rustling or shuffling or stepping.

"Turn to Violet Springs," Jake said grimly. "It's a damn whiskey town, but we don't have any choice."

They had passed into an edge of the Seminole Nation and were now close to the border of Oklahoma Territory. They came to a good-sized river with an untended cable ferry across it. The mules refused to approach it. They had apparently decided they'd done enough work for one day. Tom tried every Indian word he could think of, he whacked them on the nose, he pulled them. Then Jake said, "Get em a drink of the river water," and Tom did so, by cupping his hands and bringing up a little, first to one, then the other. The mules liked the water very much, but rather than going on down to the ferry they just stood there, waiting for him to bring more handfuls. He had to stand in front of them with drinks, successively closer to the river, until it was right under their nose, and finally in a rush they clattered onto the ferry, where there was a watering trough nailed onto the planks. Tom started to drink a handful of the river water himself and Jake stopped him. "Don't you drink it. They run cows up the Canadian."

Tom turned a big winding gear that pulled the log-and-plank raft on its cable across the river, rippling dark under the purple sky. In the middle of the river Sam said in a calm but strange voice, "I have a terrible headache." Just as they hit the other side, Tom saw someone arriving at the opposite bank, but it was too dark to tell anything about him.

"That man has been following us all day," Tom said.

Jake glanced toward him and only grunted.

As they approached Violet Springs, Tom heard piano sounds somewhere in the distance, and headed in their direction. It was almost dark when he came to the cluster of buildings that seemed to form the center of town. There was no main street, just buildings and shacks facing different directions. Pianos seemed to be playing in almost every lighted place, and voices drifted from here and there. Tom found what looked like a town well, but it was surrounded by mud, and when he got down and approached it, he made out dark shapes all around. It was a pig wallow. One of the pigs got to its feet, came over, and started nuzzling and pushing at Tom's leg. Its grunting breath smelled alcoholic, and it appeared to be begging for something.

"This water's no good," Tom said. "There's a herd of pigs here."

"Get us a bed," Jake said out of the darkness. "You can't be very choosy. This is a rough place."

Tom felt his way to the nearest lighted building, a saloon. A man leaning against the wall outside — the first person he talked to — directed them to a nearby hotel, and when Tom inquired about a doctor, the man said that he was one himself. He would get his bag and come over as soon as possible. Luck seemed to be with them.

♦

A group of women were sitting around the hotel's parlor, smoking cigarillos, some drinking out of stemmed glasses, and Tom thought it must be a place where the people who worked in the saloons stayed. The woman who ran the hotel wore a single purple plume in her hair and a low-cut, tightly fitting, tiger-striped dress that came all the way up to her knees. The other women, younger, were in costumes with their breasts pushed up almost out of them;

one woman had a white pet rabbit in her lap. The room was a mist of perfume. A man who looked like a ranch hand was staggering around among them like a grasshopper jumping against the walls of a can, raising his front lip, showing his teeth, laughing in a high whinny. He sounded like he had a cold, as well as being drunk. "Now, why won't you give ol Pede some free onion? No money, so what. Trade you this sombitch fer one liddle hunk of happy valley." He pulled out a six-shooter and aimed it loosely at one of the women, laughing the goofy, high-lipped laugh. She sat very still and quiet, watching him, the white rabbit panting in her lap. The woman who ran the desk walked over and touched his elbow. "Time for you to leave, honey. Go on. Come back when you ain't so drunk." She had a gravelly, authoritative voice.

He thrust his jaw out at her like a young boy. "Whadif I doan wanna?"

"Well, hon, I have a shotgun behind this counter, and the last person that give me trouble I had to shoot and feed to the pigs. Now, you wouldn't want me to do that to you, would you?"

The man eventually ricocheted out the door, his pistol still dangling from his hand.

Tom told the desk lady that his companions were sick.

She gave him a look. "What kind of sick?" She questioned him closely, and only after Tom convinced her that they didn't have something catching did she take his money. "Fever season's mostly over, but I've got to be careful," she said. "I'm running a hospital around here, much sickness as I have to deal with."

Tom helped Jake and Sam up to the room. First he helped Jake up the stairs, but Sam was completely out, and he had to carry her like a baby. The tiger-skin lady watched curiously as he lifted Sam, who was pale, her hair all loose and hanging down. Aware of his own clumsiness, Tom went up the steps extremely carefully. With Jake taking up most of the bed, and already asleep, he had to put her on the very edge of it, go around and try to pull Jake over, then run back around and push her a little farther, until he'd managed to get her safely berthed.

The hotel continued to be busy with people going in and out, up and down the single flight of stairs to the six-room corridor. Men shuffled through the halls after the costumed women, and Tom finally began to realize what kind of hotel this was. He had heard such places named: a den of prostitution, a house of ill fame, a palace of sin. He was aware, broadly, what a prostitute was: someone who gave her body to be fouled by male lust. After almost two weeks of being in the grip of male lust, Tom now had a better idea of what it was, and he understood why men went to such places. Indeed, all he had to do was look at Sam on the bed — even in her bedraggled, dirty, half-dead state — and it made him think of the unbelievable occurrences of last night. He paced the small room, and looked out the window. Where was the doctor?

He was about to go out and search when the doctor arrived, a skinny, baggy-eyed man who kept sighing and scratching himself and adjusting his hat. He appeared to be uninterested in examining Jake or Sam. He didn't even ask any questions about them.

"My prices are good," said the doctor, looking at him with yellow eyes. "Two hangover treatments usually cost you four dollars. I'm givin it to you for three."

"They don't have hangovers, sir," Tom said. "They drank bad water."

"Same difference," the doctor said. "If you want a treatment, too, I'll add it for only a dollar and fifty cent."

"I'm not sick," Tom said.

"Never can tell when a tone-up will help. I treat a lot of these girls right here in this hotel. You ask them about my medicine." The doctor's kit was strangely simple. All he carried in it was a little bottle of white powder, a flask of water, a small, flat pan in which he cooked up the powder with water, and a large syringe and needle. Tom had had a smallpox vaccination, but this was a much bigger needle. He paced back and forth by the window while the doctor cooked the medicine over the lantern — scraggly beard and wild eyebrows weird in the yellow light, casting a large shadow on the wall behind. As he approached Sam's arm with the syringe, Tom suddenly put himself in the way, his heart crashing in his chest. "What kind of doctor are you?"

Holding the needle up, the man narrowed his eyes at him. "Why you asking me that now?"

"I want to know," Tom said.

"They call me Dr. Pain. There used to be eight of us in this town. Now there's only five, and I'm the best. I got people coming all the way from Guthrie fer my treatments."

"I don't want you to do that."

"You'll have to move out of the way. I got other people to see."

"No sir," Tom said. "I want you to leave here."

"I've done got the medicine cooked up. I can't waste it."

Tom was not calm. All he could think was to stop the man. "Go away!" he said, taking a step closer. "Don't touch them."

Scowling at him, the man went over to the room's single chair and sat down, rolled up a cuff, and stuck the needle into his own leg, slowly pushing in the syringe. As he was leaving, he snarled through his beard, "Somebody's in town looking fer you people. I might just have to let him know where you're at."

Tom stood around the room wondering what to do. Both Sam and Jake remained asleep, but neither of them looked good. Sam's skin was blanched and shiny. Jake was restless, and he kept tossing and toiling around in the bed, threatening to knock Sam onto the floor. They needed something. It was a noisy place — Tom kept hearing laughter, what sounded like moving furniture, and occasional yelling. He was overwhelmed by an urge to go to sleep. He had done this all wrong. He sank down on the floor and leaned against the wall for a moment's rest and fell asleep.

He dreamed that he was floating under warm green water, able to see through it for some distance. Ahead of him, he saw a cross-shaped thing and swam toward it. As he approached, it kept disappearing, sometimes reappearing on the left, sometimes the right, but ever closer, until suddenly it — she — was right before him with her arms out, her hair floating wildly out from her head, her body naked and vividly white in the green water, her eyes open and fixed on him . . .

◆

Popping noises. Gunshots, Tom realized as he came awake. His eyes blinked open and fixed on a lamp wick, almost burned down. He stood up, at first disoriented. How long had he slept? Sam and Jake were still on the bed. The hotel had fallen quiet. He hurried down the stairs. The tiger woman who'd rented them their room was still in the parlor, alone now, with her feet propped up on a chair. The plume had fallen from her hair onto the couch.

She yawned and stretched. "You must be a hot-blooded young man getting up in the middle of the night. Want a haircut?"

Haircut? "No ma'am. I need something for Jake and Sam. I tried to get them some water earlier, but there were pigs —"

"Don't mention those damn things. I don't even want to hear about em." She waved a hand in disgust. "They're drunkards, every one." She sighed. "You'd think the least a hog could do would be to stay sober. They eat mash put out behind the whiskey mill over here on the branch. Nighttimes, they hang around the well and go trotting around begging whiskey. People give it to em and think it's funny. I saw one old sow out there knock a man down to get at his open bottle. Saloons selling bottle water are happy to have these hogs around to ruin the well, of course, because they make as much money selling water as whiskey. Which I call immoral."

Tom appreciated her explanation but felt he needed to do something as soon as possible. "They were sick to their stomachs all afternoon. I never got them any water."

"That's two things you forgot. You left your team outside, too. I took care of it. You can fetch them at the stable when you need them."

"Thank you, ma'am. I'm just worried about Sam and J —"

From outside came three more shots, and someone not far away screamed in what sounded like mortal pain. From somewhere else came laughter, casual sounding, as if at a slight joke. "Idiots," the woman said. She stood up and quickly smoothed out her dress. "One of these days I'm goin back to St. Louis, before one of em shoots me. Come on, I'll take a look-see."

After she had looked more closely at Jake and Sam, the tiger woman suggested a cure. "Potato," she said, looking curiously at Sam. "Both of them need to eat a raw potato with a lot of salt on it, then afterwards good drinking water. Old Missouri cure for the pukes." She delivered this advice in a flat tone, as if reciting something she'd said many times before. Her eyes were fixed on Sam, almost as if she recognized her. There was no food in the hotel, and Tom had to go to one of the joints, looking for potatoes and fresh bottle water. "Careful out there," she warned, glancing up at him. "They've been at it again tonight."

The saloons that made up most of the town were spread around, and he found one nearby, a one-room building with no front porch and a floor low to the ground. One step up and he was in a smoky room with a kerosene chandelier suspended from the ceiling, eight or ten tables, mostly empty, wet-smelling saw-dust-covered floor, and a piano player dully pounding out the same ragtime sound that he'd heard coming from saloons in Fort Smith. On the wall behind the bar, obscure in the smoke, hung a large picture of a naked woman, reclining on a red couch with her legs intriguingly separated. A man was patrolling around with an ax handle in his hand, and he came over to Tom.

"Got a gun on you?"

"No sir." He cleared his throat. "Do you have any potatoes?"

The man looked not directly at Tom but just to the side of him, like Tom had seen Indians doing, although this was a very large and ugly white man. Slapping the ax handle in his paw, he said, "Give you five seconds to be out the door, asswipe. I had enough crazy flatheads in here."

Flush with embarrassment, Tom retreated. Flatheads? Unconsciously he felt the top of his head. He had done something wrong, but there was no time to worry about it. He stumbled through darkness to the next saloon, where another piano player was banging away. Here the naked woman on the wall, while as large as the one in the previous saloon, was standing by a lamp rather than lying on a couch, and striking a pose with her bottom cocked up, looking over her shoulder, hair past her waist. This saloon had more people than the other. Women moved around the room, some of them getting drinks from behind the bar, sitting in laps of card players, lighting cigars with big lucifer matches that they scratched slowly under the tables. Tom noticed that Indian bloods and whites played at separate tables. There was a big man patrolling this saloon, too, and Tom avoided him and went straight to the bartender. No food for sale, he said, but he did have water for fifty cents a bottle. He put a bottle on the bar and Tom drank the entire thing without pausing. Watching him with hooded, impersonal eyes, the bartender seemed to remember something and asked, "You ain't with them from Fort Smith, are you?"

"Yes."

"Better clear out of here."

"I beg your pardon?"

"Go on, git out! Go on! I don't want no more trouble tonight."

Tom backed out of the place, startled, and stood outside listening to the plink-plinking of pianos and the pig noises. He was beginning to wonder if he'd find any potatoes. The next saloon had a porch, which he discovered in the darkness by hitting it, shin-high, and sprawling across it. Not moving until the spasm in his leg receded, he took a minute to think. He was getting nowhere. Apparently he'd never find what he was looking for by just going in and innocently asking for it. He got up, took a deep breath, and entered the saloon. This time he acted less timid. He paid no attention to the naked woman on the wall or anything else about the place. He went right up to the bar and said to a bearded bartender, "I want six potatoes, a little salt, and three bottles of water. I'll pay you three dollars."

The bartender looked at him with a moment's consternation, but when Tom took out three dollars and put it on the bar, he got results. A woman was sent out and soon returned with potatoes. He put them with a salt shaker into his pockets and went outside in the first hint of morning light, clutching the bottles. Squinting through the darkness, he was hurrying toward the hotel when someone came toward him riding what at first looked like a strangely disfigured horse that became more disfigured the closer it came. It passed him at no more than ten feet, and he could not believe what he saw: a man in a bowler hat sitting on what looked like a gigantic fat bird with a tiny head on a hugely long neck. The bird trotted by smartly on two long, thick bird legs, a saddle strapped around its body. Tom was looking over his shoulder at this mirage when he tripped over something and hit the ground, number two for the night.

The pigs were on him out of nowhere. He had no warning, heard no sound — they were merely there, instantly, snuffling at his head and at his pockets with their flat, wet, stinking noses. He scrambled around to get the bottles, and all the way to the hotel they were as close on his heels as a pack of dogs. A couple of them followed him through the door, to the extreme aggravation of the tiger lady. She got a broom and cursed and whacked them toward the door. She finally chased them out and slammed the door, and pointed at him. "Them things have been drunk so long they don't know inside from outside. They come in here again, and I'm going to invite em all to a goddamn barbecue. You git your potatoes?"

"I saw a man outside riding —"

"A bird?" she finished for him. "That's old Bobby Joe Dyer. He's got him a saddle ostrich. Watch out, though, he's been known to kill a man for making fun of that bird. This town is full of the most peculiar people this side of the Barnum and Bailey."

The lady got a pocketknife from a drawer, and the two of them went upstairs. She gave Tom the knife and told him to peel the potatoes while she woke up Sam and Jake. When they had been gotten awake enough, the lady coaxed them to eat. "Make you feel better right away," she said in a rough but soothing voice. "I can guarantee the potato cure." Propped up on the bed, side by side, they took little nibbles at first and after a while had downed a half bottle of water apiece. Tom was surprised at how well it worked. They didn't get sick to their stomachs again. Tom munched on his own salted potato and felt better. The tiger lady was in and out of the room, checking on them, over the couple of hours it took. Tom noticed that she kept exchanging odd looks with Sam. Jake had gone off to the outhouse when the tiger lady finally asked, "Where you from, hon?"

Sam hesitated before saying, "St. Louis."

The lady sniffed and looked away, one brief gesture that again seemed to Tom like a recognition. She looked out the window into the blue sky, her gaze fixing far away.

· 11 ·

JAKE EVENTUALLY rallied, got dressed, and went to see
about the mules. After parking them beside the building, he
squatted against the wall in the sun, gathering his strength for
the day. He didn't feel all that poorly considering he'd been
poisoned yesterday. His bunkmate appeared to be doing pretty
well, too. Earlier this morning, he'd looked over at her and realized that she didn't look at all bad.

Dandy had a couple of customers here they had told Jake to
hit, but he didn't intend to spend another hour in this worthless
place. McMurphy had told him that this was one of the "preferred
areas" for collection, but he'd about had it with customers treat-
ing him like he had the typhoid fever, not saying hello or goodbye, committing suicide or trying to poison him. This mortgage-
collecting business was strictly for the birds.

Someone rode up to the hotel, and Jake happened to step
around the corner of the building just in time to see him go in the
front door. If the man had turned his head, he'd have seen Jake.

Yesterday at the river, Tom had pointed out that someone was
following them, and this close up Jake realized who he was.

Over the years, he had seen Deacon Jim Miller around the saloons in Fort Smith and heard more stories about him than he
cared to recall. Half of what was said about him was Saturday afternoon drunk talk, and Jake disdained both the man and the
conversation about him. But here he was, all duded up, strict and
tidy, just like you always heard he dressed when he was on a job.

And he had been following them.

Jake went to a side window, glanced in, and saw that the madam, still standing at her desk, looked like her plug had been pulled, and the floozie with the rabbit had put her face into her hands. Jake started thinking real hard. He had no gun. He had a couple of old guns back home but generally avoided them except for occasional hunting — which some called peculiar for a salesman in the territory. Deacon Jim Miller used a gun with as much reticence as most men used a toothpick.

He talked in a high, tight voice that Jake could hear through the open window. "Somebody I need to talk to? Name of Jaycox? Would you happen to know where he is?"

Miller stood there, utterly still. A surge of anger shot through Jake like electricity out of a dynamo, the feeling of outrage and disbelief that he'd experienced before only on those few occasions when his life had been threatened.

Jake saw a bush of hard-dried burrs next to the hotel and picked a couple of them. Pushing up the saddle and blanket on Deacon Miller's horse, he put the burrs under them. The horse didn't like that at all and, almost before Jake could untie him, started stirring and snorting and bucking. Pretty soon he was going in a circle, swapping ends, and as the burrs dug in deeper he began to sure enough buck, pump-handling all over the street, causing the drunk pigs that lay around the well to squeal wildly and scatter in all directions.

Jake watched through the window until Miller had gone out the door to catch his horse, and he went inside, fast, to collect Samantha and Tom. Everyone was frozen in a whore-parlor tableau. The floozie on the loveseat still had her face in her hands. The only thing moving was her rabbit's nose. The madam, pale as a dish, said, "You better get out of here, cowboy."

Jake went in and took the stairs three at a time, rushed down the hall to the room, and got Tom and Samantha. "Come on down and out the back door." He got Samantha's suitcase and pulled out the five-shot revolver that he knew was in it. Tom was still wordless. The three of them hurried back down and went out the back. "You drive better'n me," Jake told Tom. "Head for the river crossing."

The mules were amazingly cooperative. At a near trot, they

made it to the crossing inside of ten minutes, where their luck held: the ferry was on this side of the river. The man who operated the ferry, a debauched-looking breed who was leaning back on a jury-rigged chair smoking a big hand-rolled cigarillo, was on the job today. He raised an eyebrow but didn't stand up. "Three people, two heavy mule, one wagon. Cost you eighty-five cent."

The ferry was hardly ten yards into the river when Jake saw Miller coming, not in any particular hurry, ambling down to the river edge on the now unburred horse. "I have a message for you," he said in his odd, tight voice. "Best come back over here."

"Get in the water behind the raft," Jake said to Tom and Samantha. They didn't do so, of course, and he pushed Samantha overboard. He waved his arm then at Tom, and he went over, too, and they both came up sputtering, grabbing hold of the side. Jake checked the cylinder on Samantha's Smith & Wesson.

"I hope you're ready to use that," Jim Miller said with a dirty smile. His high voice carried menacingly, easily, across the slow-moving river. He took out his gun and pulled off one shot that skipped off the top of the water with a whine. "Ferryman!" he shouted. "Bring em back. Right now or you're in serious!"

The ferryman started turning the crank to take them back.

Jake took a couple of steps toward him with the gun trained on his gut. The ferryman stepped backwards and fell into the river. He immediately began swimming away.

The next shot from Miller went through the back of the wagon and wooden seat. Jake crouched down behind the wheel and pulled off two rounds, knowing it was hopeless with a three-inch barrel on a wobbly platform. Miller didn't look worried as he slid off his saddle. Trying not to show too much of himself, Jake went for the crank on the winding gear and turned it, pulling them across on the cable.

They were just past halfway when Miller unhurriedly got down in the sand with a little rise in front of him. Jake was a sitting duck, but the next shot was for Tom, so close that Jake at first thought he was hit. "Both of you get around behind the ferry," Jake shouted.

As Tom and Samantha pulled their way around the side of the raft, Miller shot again and the mules started rearing and pushing this way and that. They couldn't fall off the front because of the big, fixed watering trough, but if they pushed backwards hard enough, they would go into the water.

The next shot from Miller was the kind of experience that Jake had heard old soldiers describe but never quite believed true. He saw the bullet, or distinctly thought he did, and in the immense smallness of that instant knew that something had changed, some extremely basic fact, maybe that he was dead. This cerebration took place before he heard and felt the snap at his ear. It had clipped the ear, which didn't hurt exactly, although soon he could feel the warm blood dripping off his earlobe and chin.

Jake was beyond desperate. Nothing like this had ever happened to him before. He felt like he'd fallen off a cliff and was plummeting through thin air, trying to learn how to fly. Miller's horse had trotted down the edge of the river and now wheeled around and was ambling back, sniffing the water like a dog, looking for the shallowest way across. Jake pulled off two careful shots and the poor thing made a noise and fell with an unpleasant thump to the ground.

There was a moment's pause before Miller screamed, *"You bastard, you killed my trotter!"* He stood up, fired wildly, and ran over to see about his animal. Jake took the chance to stand up and crank hard and fast on the wheel.

The mules did just what he was afraid they'd do, but they were already in the shallows of the other side, and the wagon's back wheels dropped off the raft and hit ground. He stood up in their faces and got one of them by the nose and pushed him backwards off the ramp. They stalled and he pinched their noses hard and pulled them struggling through the water up to dry land. *"Aiya! Aiya!* Come on!" Tom and Samantha waded up after him, and a couple more shots from Miller ate the air wide of the mark.

Over the bank there was a trail following the river, and they struck out westward. Jake didn't question for a minute whether Miller would follow them. He'd go back to town, get a horse, and turn right around. Once across the river, he could gain on them quickly. The Santa Fe line was to their west, whether ten or twenty-five miles away Jake didn't know, but they had a chance of getting to it before dark if the mules and wagon held out, and if they could lose Miller.

They went for a while down the riverside road, then in a rocky place went over the shoulder of a hill and headed southwest. Wet and shivering, they stopped in a grove of leafless pecan trees to put on dry clothes, Tom and Jake with their backs turned to Samantha.

Tom, shivering, wild-eyed, was having trouble figuring out the shirt, and Jake helped him get it on. "Why was that man shooting at us?"

"I don't know. Better get the dry clothes on."

Tom clamped his teeth together, trying to stop shivering. The scars on his back were livid in the cold wind.

"Who is he?" Samantha asked, surprisingly unruffled.

"He's lowlife, he's a killer, that's about all I know about him." Jake turned to Tom and looked the boy in the eyes. "Can you keep your mind on driving these mules? We need to cover some ground. I don't want him catching us."

Tom looked back down the trail, his teeth gritted. "He looked like he was dressed for church."

Jake looked around the hills. "They call him the Deacon because he dresses up and acts polite when he's doing a job. They say he gets downright embarrassing-polite before he kills a man."

"Do you know him?" Samantha asked.

Jake shook his head. "I know of him."

Samantha's coat had been lost somewhere, probably when the wagon hit the river, and she'd put on a simple cotton dress. Everything about her condition, her unfettered body, hair wet and kinked up and loose on her head, showed how young and comely and free acting she was. Before they got back on the wagon, Jake saw her take hold of Tom and try to hug him, like a mother would hug a scared child, but Tom was stiff as a tree, as if he'd never been faced with a hug before. Jake piled into the back, Samantha got up beside Tom on the seat, and he got the mules moving. Jake was impressed by the way Tom handled the team despite what had happened.

Jake reloaded the pistol, put the remaining bullets into his coat pocket, and kept the lookout.

They hit the old government road to Fort Sill and took it straight west to Pauls Valley, on the Santa Fe line in the Chickasaw Nation. It took about three and a half hours of brisk traveling. Pauls Valley was in relatively open country, and near it they passed an Indian cemetery with a cluster of aboveground graves like tiny houses. Close to the railroad track a group of what looked like Shawnee were camped in three wretched coal-blackened box shacks that had probably been built for the trackmen of the Santa Fe twenty years ago. Nearby was a pile of buffalo and cattle bones, as tall as a house, doubtless awaiting shipment to a fertilizer factory. Jake often saw this along the rail lines in the western territory: destitute Indians collecting bones for some white man, who sold them by the carload in Kansas City. The town of Pauls Valley had a big sky and open feel to it. On the main street were several newish buildings including a large whitewashed IOOF building. A cattle pen near the rail depot held a few skinny animals. Jake kept an eye out for fear that somehow Deacon Miller had got there before them.

At the depot, a hand-lettered sign was posted by the door:

$$ GOOD MONEY FOR BONES $$
SEE THE AGENT INSIDE.

Sitting against the building on the sunny side were a gaggle of Indian men with the half-dead look of faithful drunkards. The first thing Jake noticed inside, on the counter, was a display board with several different-sized empty bottles with prices underneath, from ten cents to fifty. It was a widely used method by whiskey sellers throughout the territory: the liquor itself was discreetly out of sight. The ticket agent, a prosperous-looking man with a shrewd gleam in his eye, said that a train from Fort Arbuckle was three hours late but was expected anytime. Jake asked him whether there might be someone in town who'd buy a mule team and wagon. The agent went outside, took one look at the mules, and without hesitation walked right back in. "I'm afraid not. You couldn't find nobody to feed that old team through the winter." Then he added, "I'd be glad to go to the trouble of disposing them for you. Afraid that's about all I could do for you."

"I'll bet you would," Jake said. Rail agents got his goat, always cheating and scheming. He asked how much a ticket to ship the team with them to Guthrie would cost, and the agent looked at him as if he was crazy. "You mean to haul *those* animals on the train?"

"That's what you sell, ain't it? Train tickets? Or do you just sell whiskey?" Jake wasn't in a mood to be fooled with. The agent gave him a look and flipped open his pricing book. Jake laughed at the amount he quoted. "You fellows ought to spend more effort getting your trains on time, or getting your shipments where they're supposed to go, instead of sitting around figuring out one more way to put the screws to your customers."

The agent started to reply, but when he saw Jake reach into his wallet, he kept silent, eyes on the money.

During their brief wait, Jake went outside rather than stay in the same room with the agent. At the moment, he didn't feel like talking — about anything. Tom brought the mules a bucket of water, which they sucked down like it was the last liquid on earth. Tom petted them on their noses while they drank. Jake noticed how Samantha was looking at Tom.

The sun was setting in the mountain of white bones when the evening northbound pulled into town. Tom brought the mules up to the trackside ramp. They'd seen no sign of Miller since the river, but Jake wasn't convinced they'd shaken him.

♦

On the train to Guthrie the three of them finally talked about what had happened. They figured out that Deacon Miller had been following them at least from the Choctaw Nation, possibly even all the way from Fort Smith. Jake couldn't guess why a hired gun might be after him. Possibly because of John Blessing. Blessing had a lot of relatives, and they might have decided that Jake was responsible for his death.

But hiring somebody like Deacon Miller would be a strange thing for the Blessings to do. Another possibility was Ernest Dekker. Ernest might have found out about the old man's plan to retake the store and make Jake boss. Ralph had said that he was going to tell one of the other salesmen — Dandy, as Jake remembered — and the word might have gotten back around to Ernest. Hell's Fringe was the ideal place to do away with somebody, since little or nothing that happened out here ever got to a court of law.

After dark they approached Purcell, which was on the Canadian River west of Violet Springs, and Jake had a foreboding as they slowed down. The car was cool but otherwise comfortable, dimly illuminated by lamps along the walls. Tom, who was developing a knack for sleeping on the hard wooden benches of trains, was curled up, dead to the world, so asleep that he'd gone pale. His head was against Samantha's leg. Jake had noticed that things were happening—looks, little exchanges—that suggested something was going on between the two of them. In Jake's opinion Tom didn't know enough about the world yet to pair off with some woman, any woman, particularly one as mature as Samantha King. But then Jake wasn't exactly an expert at pairing off. He saw her again as she looked coming out of the river earlier today; she'd had more composure than he'd had after being shot at and pushed in a cold river.

Jake reached up and touched his ear, which had begun throbbing with the train's vibrations.

In the car were a handful of passengers: three drummers, one of them snoring so loudly you'd think he'd choke, and a couple of rawhide-stinking cowboys. Deacon Miller remained on Jake's mind. If he had gone straight down the river road, he'd have arrived at Purcell, where they were about to stop, and he'd probably be checking trains. When the Westinghouses clamped down for the Purcell station, Jake's worry b came as palpable as the vibrations of the car. He moved to the little fold-down conductor's seat at the front of the car, behind the door, and put his hand around the pistol in his coat pocket.

Outside, someone walked slowly by the car and Jake saw what appeared to be a derby hat. But the lone figure strolled on, and disappeared, and soon the train powered noisily out of the station. One of the drummers at the front of the car eyed Jake nervously when he went back to his seat.

Miss King extricated herself from under Tom's head and sat beside him. "Did you see something?"

"Guess it wasn't him."

She looked at his ear. "You'll have to have that dressed."

Jake thought about the instant of time back on the river when he'd looked a bullet in the eye. The train was up to speed, whacking along on roughly laid tracks. They would be crossing the Pottawatomie and Shawnee Reservation now. There was nothing to see in the blackness of the window except the soft reflection of a wall lamp across the aisle. He leaned back, still feeling as jumpy as a cat.

"What are you thinking about?" she asked.

"I don't know," he breathed out. "Not sure we shook our friend."

"Who is he? Tell me what you know about him."

Jake shook his head. "His name is Jim Miller. Off and on, he's been a house 'detective' at some of the row-house hotels in Fort Smith. I believe in his younger years he was an enforcer out here in the Fringe. White man's sheriff. In these whiskey towns, they hire men who make sure no debts are left unpaid, no bartenders or dealers get killed by customers, no Indians give em any trouble, that kind of thing. Last I heard, he'd come up in the world. Working for the railroads as an enforcer. But that's just saloon talk, I don't know it to be true. People always want to make a big deal out of men like him. I've been hearing rumors about him for years now. He apparently mixes with the horse crowd. I don't know whether you noticed his horse."

"The one you shot?"

"Yeah," Jake said grimly. "That's a walker, and it was worth several thousand dollars."

"Why's he after you?"

Jake shrugged. He tried to look unconcerned.

Tom, asleep on the seat, started making noises of fear, and Samantha reached across and caressed his temple until he stopped. Again, Jake was surprised by her tenderness.

She changed the subject. "Have I brought you bad luck, Jake?"

"I've been traveling out here over twenty years and never had much trouble. Since I met you, there's been flood, dynamite, poison water, and now a hired killer on my tail. All we need's an earthquake."

"Who do you think hired him?"

"Don't know, but now that I killed his walker, he's got a personal reason to finish off the job."

"Does it have something to do with your job? These mortgages?"

"Ralph Dekker called his business Dekker Hardware, not Dekker Land Company."

"You don't like your new boss, do you?"

"That's no secret."

"Why are you staying with them?"

Jake snorted. "Fifty-five-year-old man looking for a job in a depression? I wouldn't look forward to it."

"Want to go partners with me?"

"Partners doin what?"

"You're worried about your company being in the wrong hands. Quit them and set up your own hardware company."

"You're joking."

"No I'm not."

"So now you're making me a job offer," he commented. "Boy, we really have come a long way, haven't we."

Her big eyes were directly on him. "I think we'd make a good team."

"How old are you, Samantha?"

"Old enough to write a check," she said.

"Twenty-three, twenty-four?"

"Does it worry you that I'm a woman?" She looked at him with a little hint of flirtatiousness — or was she making fun of him?

"That doesn't make any difference to me," Jake grumbled. "Some of the best business people I know are women." He scooted down in his seat and put his hat over his eyes.

She lifted up his hat like the lid of a can. He only gave her the evil eye. He was too frazzled to keep up this conversation.

"You provide the know-how and I provide the capital."

Jake slid back up in the seat.

"I'm serious as sin."

"Okay, Sam. I'll take you seriously, but you answer me a question first."

"Ask it."

"If you've got a stake, what in the world brought you out here to invest it?"

"Because it's a place where the doors are still open. It isn't all sewed up. Even a woman can make money if she can find out how things work."

Jake reached into his pocket and pulled out the piece of paper that he'd found in her suitcase. "Is that what this is — people who know how things work?"

She didn't reach for it. "You've been in my suitcase?"

"I opened it in Tuskahoma to see if it was yours." She was smiling, which annoyed him. "So you came down here to round up a few people, find out how things work, and then just go after it?"

She raised her eyebrows. "How should I do it, Jake?"

"'How things work,' as you call it, isn't worth knowing. It's changing too fast. Sam, did you ever make money yourself?"

"Not a lot. My family did. It's in the blood."

"I don't doubt that," Jake said. "I do appreciate the offer, but I can't take it. Ralph has asked me to stay on."

"But he's not running the place anymore."

When he didn't respond, she went on, mildly, "You trust your old boss, don't you?"

"Why are you always asking me about the people I work for?" Jake didn't hide his irritation.

She turned away from him. "I guess you don't take propositions from women."

He felt a flash of anger, but then for some reason he relented and laughed. "Look. Ralph is hoping to pay back the debt on the store and take over again." He didn't add that Mr. Dekker had offered him the position of boss.

"How'll he do that?"

"Borrow some money, I guess. He's already gone to St. Louis to do it."

She looked out the window. The train was slowing. "So you feel bound to Mr. Dekker?"

"I reckon so."

"Why?"

"Ralph and I always got along."

"Do you know him very well?" she asked.

"Well enough." Jake wanted this conversation to end. "Anyway, I'm obliged to wait and see." He scooted back down again.

"So you're getting rid of me," she said.

"I'm not getting rid of anybody," Jake said. "I think we'd better stick together tonight. But you ought not hang around Guthrie. Deacon Miller is a bad son of a bitch, if you'll excuse the language, and now he's a mad son of a bitch because I killed his horse. He gets his job done however he can."

As if thinking aloud she said, "I do have to go to St. Louis. Maybe I'll go back to Fort Smith in a week or two and make you one more offer."

He opened one eye. "You do that."

"Boy, you take the cake. You are cold to the touch, mister."

He pretended to nap, but actually Jake couldn't anywhere near sleep. His nerves felt like they'd been sandpapered. He'd have given a dollar for a jigger of whiskey. Deacon Jim Miller. He couldn't stop wondering why somebody like that was after him.

When they pulled into Guthrie, he still hadn't napped and was in a tired, foul mood. He woke Tom up to help him get out the team.

The mules, having apparently not ridden on a train since the Battle of Chickamauga, had decided that the world was too jiggly and nervous a place, and neither of them would move off the stock car. After they'd at last been pushed down the ramp, they planted themselves, as fixed and firm as marble statues. Tom yelled Indian at them and that didn't work, Jake pushed them and cussed and popped them on the nose, all with the same lack of results. Tom went looking for some coffee and couldn't find any at this hour, and finally Jake, thinking that he should have sent these two worthless relics to mule hell where they belonged, pushed Lee half a block before he got the idea and started walking. Grant, with Tom's help, eventually did likewise.

Samantha stood around watching all these activities with little interest, brooding, apparently put out with Jake. After getting everything squared away at the stable, they went looking for a place to stay.

·12·

TOM HAD BEEN so asleep on the train that what had happened only that day felt as if it happened a month ago. He had fallen off the edge of the earth into a sounder sleep than he had ever known in his life — sleeping and speeding away from what was, what used to be.

As they walked through Guthrie looking for a hotel, Tom watched Sam, wondering how long she would stay with them. She was supposed to leave them now, but Tom kept thinking that somehow that was impossible.

They ended up in a room on the second floor of the Christian Boarding Hotel, a quiet place on a hill at some distance from downtown.

WE RENT TO ALL OF GOD'S CHILDREN
AS LONG AS THEY PAY IN ADVANCE.

The clerk, a prissy man, acted worried about giving them a room. He kept asking questions, until Jake, tired and frazzled, demanded the key and turned heel and climbed the stairs, leaving Sam and Tom standing there. "So is it Mr. and Mrs.?" the clerk asked for the second time, glancing after Jake. Sam gave him a big smile and said, "Why yes, and this is our dear son." She wrapped an arm around Tom's shoulder. "Isn't he a handsome boy?" she said. Tom felt his face go hot.

The clerk's smile was as thin as a clothesline. "Oh, then he must be your *step*son?"

"Oh, by no means," Sam said, almost maliciously. "This is our own *dear* boy."

Going up the stairs, Sam gave Tom a look, as if to say that it was their joke. After they'd all settled into the room, Jake stood at the window looking into the dark street. "I don't know if our friend Miller made it to Guthrie or not, but I think we ought to keep a watch. Are you good and awake?" he asked Tom.

"Yes sir," said Tom. "I slept on the train."

"Okay. Let me have a couple of hours, and I'll watch the rest of the night." Jake pulled off his boots, lay down on the bed, and was asleep before he could pull a blanket over himself.

Sam poured water from the pitcher into the washpan and quickly bathed her hands, arms, and face. To Tom's amazement, she then came right up to him, took off his shirt, and with a wet towel bathed his hands, his arms, and his face. Her left hand took his arm, then held his chin, while she washed him. Her face seemed to glow, so close to him in the lantern light.

The room was eerily peaceful. They kept silent because of Jake, who had turned his back to them and was snoring lightly. After she'd finished washing Tom, they just sat for a while, she in a rocking chair and he on the floor beside a steam radiator with his shirt still off. She'd loosed the top buttons of her dress in the warm room and taken off her shoes, and her eyes were playing over his shoulders and neck. Their eyes met. Sam scared him in a way, with her shocking decisiveness.

The room was luxuriant with steam heat, reminding him of the bathhouse in Durant. Sam glanced over at Jake and got up and paced across the room as if to test his wakefulness. She quietly left the room, and Tom remained where he was. After a few minutes, she returned, went to the window and looked out, then gestured to him to come with her. He followed her through an unlocked door into a room similar to theirs, with one bed and no light. Not knowing whether Miller was out there, Tom felt like they shouldn't leave Jake asleep and unguarded, and after she sat down on the edge of the bed in front of him, he was still thinking about returning to the other room. But then she took hold of the back of his left thigh. He reached over and touched her cheek and she pulled him unceremoniously onto the bed. Soon his pants were off, and she moved about taking off things, achieving successive incarnations of nakedness in the dark.

He continued to worry about leaving Jake, even when he was sitting on his knees in the bed and she was lying beside him, propped on her elbow, and her hands moved lazily over his thighs to his hard penis. He touched her breasts, even the nipples, which felt marvelous and soft and tight.

"Don't you know what to do?"

"Sure."

But he was bluffing, and she laughed. "What does this feel like?"

"Extremely good," he admitted.

"Stand up on your knees." He straightened up, causing his penis to stand out more prominently. "I like this," she said. "Mmm. I like it so much I think I'd like to eat it."

He was closing his eyes, although the room was so dark it didn't make any difference. "Eat it . . . ?" His voice fell away. She took her hand away and left him kneeling there with an achingly hard dick reaching for the heavens. "Don't."

"I can't eat it?" she said.

"Well . . . that doesn't sound practical . . ."

She laughed and took her hand away. "Then you tell me what to do. Here I am. I'm lying here on this bed beside you. Naked as the moon. What will you do with me?" She reached out and briefly touched it again.

"I think I know," he said.

"I'm waiting. You tell me."

"All right." But he couldn't think what to say next.

"You want to do it? From the back?"

"Yes ma'am," he said huskily.

"You sure you know where to put that hard thing?" she teased him.

"I think so."

"Let me get you off one time first. Otherwise you won't be much good for me."

"Okay," he said uncertainly.

To his surprise, he felt not her hands on his penis but something soft and round and wet, coming over the rim of it and sliding down, and it was a long couple of seconds before he realized that the thing around him was her mouth and she was doing what she'd said — or she was about to do it, and he dreaded her biting down on him but couldn't quite make up his mind to push her away. In fact she did bite down gently with her teeth, but he was by then launched beyond the rational, floating somewhere where having his penis chewed on was not so impossible a thing. She was standing up on her hands in the bed, with her mouth traveling slowly down the shaft of it, her hair against his belly, and he wouldn't have thought of pushing her away.

Tom heard a noise in the hall, steps approaching the door. To his horror, there was a fumbling at the door and it immediately opened, and there stood two men with a lantern. All he could think to do was jump from the bed and grab his pants and try to put them on, while the men stood there looking amazed.

Sam was the first to speak. "Get out of our room!"

The clerk's eyes were white orbs in the lantern light. "Oh, my *Lord!*" he said.

"Whooee," said the customer, looking at Sam.

Sam tried to get them to leave, but the clerk became dogged in his insistence on fully finding out what was going on. He went down to their other room and noisily opened the door without knocking, startling awake Jake, who took up the pistol and almost shot him.

"I have lived to see it all!" the clerk exclaimed, oblivious of the pistol.

The conversation that followed was so embarrassing that Tom's ears turned off. All he heard was the nasal tone of the clerk, insisting on telling Jake details that Jake didn't want to hear, once he'd gotten the general idea. Others in the boarding house came out of their rooms to see what was going on. Tom just sat there, his conscience secreting shame, although even from the depths of his humiliation, he could see how annoying this man was. Sam offered to end it by paying for the other room, but the clerk wouldn't talk to her at all, and Jake concluded the matter by telling the man to please get out of the room, they'd solve it tomorrow. Finally the three of them were again alone, Tom with only his pants on, she with her clothes askew and her hair streaming down.

Jake didn't look happy. "What time is it? Oh, the heck with it, I'll be staying up the rest of the night. Tom, you can sleep on the floor. Sam, you sleep on the bed if you want to." He gave them both a dark look, as if he were about to say something. But then he just shook his head and added quietly, "Tomorrow, we'll have to be going about our business."

◆

Sam was gone early the next morning.

Jake said nothing else to Tom about the incident, that night or on Sunday, and the very lack of a rebuke made Tom feel worse. He appreciated Jake not saying anything about it, yet at the same time almost wished that he *would* say something. He was painfully ashamed. He had betrayed Jake by leaving the hotel room unguarded. He slept only briefly the rest of the night, and all the next day he would be slowly realizing — not thinking in words but nevertheless realizing — that he could no longer afford to be so careless and ignorant of the world. He had to navigate better. He had to make himself more aware, gain better control of his own behavior. Life was different now, time itself had become different, rolling along more quickly beneath his feet, and he had to catch up and stay up. That was all there was to it. Without a word from Jake, he understood these things.

Waking to Sam's absence, though, was like waking from a turbulent, marvelous dream. He longed for her immediately. Jake and he went down to the dining room for breakfast, where a couple with a child, seeing them, furiously whispered to each other and left the room. Sitting at the table, Tom screwed up his courage to ask about Sam. Jake said that she'd apparently gone back to St. Louis. "She didn't say goodbye to me," he said flatly. "Tom, I don't know whether our friend the Deacon is going to show up in Guthrie or not, but when we go out there today, I want you to keep your eye out. If you see him, get out of the way fast. Understand me?"

"Yes sir."

As if talking to himself, Jake added, "I'd like to send you to Fort Smith, but we'll have to collect some money first. We've just about spent what little we did collect in this durn traveling circus. Be a negative proposition unless we get something done."

As they walked downtown, Guthrie struck Tom as a real little city, with its brick buildings and straight streets. Everything about it testified to a busyness of the recent past, but unfinished, roofless frameworks of buildings were scattered like raw skeletons all over town, with exposed wood already greyed by the weather, rotting before it was painted. Big-windowed stores offered such things as bright red and green china, lithograph frames, and canopied brass beds but had few customers. Owners and clerks lurked in their own stores, looking guilty and worried, as if they were ashamed of having such fine places with no one visiting them. The more Tom saw of the city, the less inhabited and stranger it seemed.

The one place where there was a crowd was the land office, where men milled around a dusty yard, talking, spitting, watching each other with sharp-eyed glances. They were edgy, desperate, swaggering around the yard telling tales, trying to find out the score or talk up a deal. Wagons trickled in and trickled out, all moving southward with the chill wind. Among the three or four peddlers circulating in the crowd was a tiny Indian woman with a basket. *"Shoooelaces! Shooelaces! Buy laces, you penny pinchers!"* she called out repeatedly.

Tom saw her the same moment Jake did. It was Mrs. Oke, the lady who owned the hotel they'd stayed in the night of the flood. Jake went over to her. "What are you doin clear up here, Mrs. Oke?"

"Hello, Mr. Hardware," she said simply. "I'm selling shoelaces. You gonna buy some from me?"

Jake reached into his pocket and bought two pair from her. "Do you have a place to stay?"

"Rollin like the tumbleweed," she said. "An old woman ain't got no family, might as well see how far she can go, hey? I walk this far. You takin care of the handsome young man?"

Tom smiled at her. "I'm glad to see you, Mrs. Oke. How are you?"

"Oh, I'm all broke down and puny, but that's the way of old things. Did the white woman pull through?"

Tom felt a pang like something sharp sticking into his side, and couldn't answer. "She's fine," Jake said, not elaborating. Jake went on talking with Mrs. Oke, asking her questions and leaning down to hear her answers.

The crowd was getting noisier, with men talking about the land rush in the Cherokee Outlet, complaining about failing to get land, and about cheating, and claims that had to be abandoned, and trying to make it to planting season. The sky had clouded up again today, and winter was in the air.

While Jake talked to Mrs. Oke, a black-bearded man nearby was reciting his tale of the land run to a cluster of people. ". . . Thirst, hell, we was all dry as seeds. I seen a woman fall on the line before the gun went off — fell like a gunnysack off her wagon. Weren't enough land fer all that bunch, and the cowboys was still in there, takin plots before we had a chance. Damn cavalry tooting around, supposed to run em out, but they didn't. Gun went off, we all whooped out, and time you got there, everwhere you come to was stakes already plugged in the ground. I finally found a piece. Got it marked out like they said, two stakes, left my whole bunch guardin it, lit out to the land office there in Enid. There was tents far as you could see, and more lawyers than tics on a hound! Stood in a line fer three days — wasn't exactly a line, neither, more like a big old pushin mob. I finally got to the front and argued with some damn clerk that claimed I had the wrong section, so I give in and hired a goddamn lawyer right there on the spot, paid him near all the money I had, he paid the goddamn clerk, just walked over and made change in that crooked bastard's pocket while he was busy cheating somebody else. Biggest bunch of crooks I ever seen in one place. I went back to my claim with the papers, all right, but stripped bare of money for groceries, which was too expensive to buy anyway. I'm goin back to Texas where I got kinfolk, to hell with free land."

"Sir, do you still have the claim to this land?" someone among the listeners asked, a man with a high, large forehead, a clean-shaven thin face, and a remarkable mop of curly grey hair that flew out behind him as if he was standing in a headwind.

"Why you ask?"

"Because that land has some value, no matter how poor it is."

"Sold the damn claim fer about what I paid that goddamn lawyer. You a goddamn lawyer?"

"I have been many terrible things in my career, sir —"

Another man, beside him, said, "Uh-oh, here he goes."

"I've been a drunkard, a seller of patent medicines, an actor on the less-than-great stage, a seducer of women, a beggar, a taker of drugs, a cynic — and I must concede that it all began with my being a duly empowered barrister at the bar in the state of Kansas. I had the finest law library in Arkansas City, more than a hundred tomes, inherited from my teacher, and I sold them one at a time when I embarked upon a checkered career, the peaks and valleys of which shouldn't be described in mixed company."

"So you are a lawyer?" asked the puzzled Texan.

"Like all questionable habits, the legal trade has its charms, sir, and I have returned for a comeback. If you should need my services, I offer reasonable rates. I am, as they say, between offices, so ask for me by name, Leonard LaFarge, contesting lawyer."

The Texan still was puzzled. "Another lawyer's the last damn thing I need."

Tom noticed that Jake had turned away from Mrs. Oke and was listening to the exchange between the Texan and the lawyer. "Hello, Leonard," Jake said. "What's going on?"

"Why, Monsieur Jaycox! I haven't seen you in weeks, my man. Have you, too, abandoned our poor village?"

Jake glanced at Tom. "Tom Freshour, meet Leonard LaFarge. And don't listen to a word the old rascal says."

LaFarge smiled as he shook Tom's hand. He said to Jake, "But your countenance is clouded, my friend. Is the hardware business all that bad? You couldn't be as poor or as sober as I am. Shall we go off to a house of spirits where we can discuss these and other weighty matters?"

"I quit drinking in the daytime, Leonard. But there is something I'd like for you to find out for me."

"Investigation is my true calling. What do you need to know?"

"Deacon Jim Miller," Jake said. "I need to know who he's working for."

Leonard's voice lowered. "Pray tell, why?"

"I want to know what he's doing now, who he's worked for in the past, whatever you can find out about him."

"I can tell you in a word, Jake. Leave the man alone."

Jake told him an abbreviated version of what had happened while the lawyer stood quite still, his grey mane of hair blowing in the cold, dusty yard. Tom noticed how quickly LaFarge changed from jovial to serious. "The man's life is hardly an open book. Anything I might find out would be susceptible to rumor."

"Anything's better than nothing. Just find out what you can."

"At your command. I'll try to have a report for you as early as tonight. Meet me at the Golden Wall."

Tom followed Jake as he departed from the yard. They walked on through town, past the newspaper building, where printing machines were whacking away, breathing out the sharp smell of ink. A newsboy stood outside selling an issue with a large headline: OPEN WAR IN ENID.

They went to the telegraph office, where Jake sent a telegram to McMurphy at Dekker Hardware Company:

NOT MUCH LUCK YET BUT AM SENDING IN CURRENT
COLLECTIONS WILL CONTINUE TOMORROW IN
CHOCTAW DISTRICT JAYCOX

Tom glanced down at the note and tried to guess whether it meant that they were going south again. A surge of yearning hit him — all of the longing and feeling about Sam that he had avoided today washed over him at once. He wondered where she was now, whether on a train, and whether she was asleep or awake, or thinking of the scenery going by or of Jake or perhaps of him.

·13·

JAKE HAD NO intention of going back to the Choctaw district, but until he'd found out a few things, he preferred for Ernest not to know where he was. Ralph Dekker had asked him to go along with Ernest until he got back from his trip, and Jake guessed he'd try to follow instructions. He wanted to send a message to the old man to find out whether he'd returned from St. Louis yet, but it wasn't safe to do it. Ernest cultivated a warm friendship with the delivery boys at the telegraph office. During the flood, Jake had happened out of the building one morning to see Ernest handing one of them a paper-money tip and the boy smiling and scraping like he was talking to the king of England.

Guthrie was — or had been — one of Dekker's few "overlapping towns," for no logical reason belonging both to Peters and to Jake. Jake decided to call on his five most active customers today, for now shucking the whole funny business of the mortgage transfers. By late afternoon he and Tom had traipsed around and pulled in more than two hundred dollars. He discovered that Pete Crapo (the worst salesman on the staff) had been through town a couple of days earlier, putting pressure on customers to sign the transfers; two had signed, but two others who hadn't given Crapo a dime did give Jake some money on their accounts. This confirmed to him that salesmen ought to be collecting money rather than trying to get mortgages on their customers' property, and they ought to be doing it in their own districts. They should be making steady progress on the debt, not threatening to close people down.

Jake would send Tom to Fort Smith tonight with the money and mortgage transfers that they'd collected. Tom could find out whether Mr. Dekker had gotten back from St. Louis. Jake's one concern was that he might be sending Tom from the frying pan into the fire. But Fort Smith was surely safer than out here, and it wasn't Tom whom Miller was after.

Off and on all day, Jake had been wondering how much to tell Tom, and he finally decided that since he himself still didn't really know what was going on yet, and since his own arrangement with the old man was still hanging fire, the cleanest approach was just to give Tom instructions and not burden him with too many confidences. Jake already knew that Tom had a good memory; anything he heard once he seemed to effortlessly remember.

They stopped at the Quality Café, a smoky crowded place where a little man by the name of Stub Adder dished out the best twenty-five-cent suppers in Oklahoma Territory. Stub was always attending furiously to his cooking, and he wasn't much for conversation, but he'd once told Jake that he was a "reformed range cook." He used to work on ranches and on cattle drives, which he claimed had spoiled him because of the way cowboys protected and praised even a tolerably decent cook.

Jake ordered two bowls of Stub's goat stew, cooked with tomatoes, onions, brown sugar, peppers, and whatever else — and he was pleased to see the expression on Tom's face as he tasted it and slipped into a trance of eating. Jake got a kick out of it when the kid enjoyed his food. Tom had been so rigid and skittish at the table when he first came to Mrs. P's that Jake didn't see how the boy could even digest his food. Although he was still stiff at the table, he looked like he might be uncoiling a turn or two.

They had a cup of Arbuckle's coffee and cobbler for dessert, and as they were finishing up, Jake told him how to proceed once he got to Fort Smith. He should be at the store at opening time to deliver the collected money and legal papers to the treasurer, McMurphy. He wanted Tom to keep an eye out for Ralph Dekker but not to ask about whether he was back from St. Louis. "Ask Edgar, maybe, but nobody else. As soon as Mr. Dekker's there, talk to him alone and tell him what happened in Violet Springs. If he has any messages for me, he can send them with you. He may want me to come to town right then. I'll be in Enid, which is north of here in the Outlet. You can tell the old man that, but don't tell Ernest or anybody else. I told them I'd keep traveling in the south, and I'd just as soon they believe it. After you've talked to Mr. Dekker, buy your train ticket at the last minute, straight through to Enid. Meet me there at the Plain Talk Inn. Can you remember all that?"

Tom nodded slowly. "Yes sir," he said, but he looked confused. "Is Enid where they're having the war?"

Jake laughed. "They're having a little dispute over where to locate the train station. It ain't a war. Don't believe everything you read in newspapers."

When Jake put him on the train, he repeated, "Enid. Plain Talk Inn."

◆

After Tom was gone, Jake worried a little less about Deacon Miller showing up, but he still felt as restless as popcorn in hot oil. He kept seeing the boy's face through the window as the train took off, imagining that he saw fear in his expression. Was he making a mistake sending him back there? He wandered over to the Christian Boarding Hotel with a newspaper but wasn't able to read.

As a hardware peddler, Jake was hardly the type to attract the attention of high-rent gunmen. Now and again over the years, he'd seen Deacon Miller in saloons, and he always wore the black clothes, and a lot of times he'd have a young aide-de-camp dressed up the same way trooping along with him. People would whisper all kinds of things about him — that he was mean as a scorpion but that he acted so polite about it that one of his many victims was said to have died saying "Thank you, Deacon." Jake figured such stories to be mostly cock and bull, but whatever his manners were, it was probably true that the man was a professional killer. The question was who he was working for now.

Sam was on his mind, too: her strange offer on the train yesterday, the way she'd gone distinctly cool toward him after he'd turned her down, the way she'd acted last night when Tom and her had been caught by the hotel clerk — not angry or ashamed or even defiant; on the contrary, more annoyed than anything. She was a real woman of the world, unafraid of what others might think, she made that clear.

The sound of a piano floated through the window, and he set out for the Golden Wall Saloon to find Leonard LaFarge.

Jake knew Leonard pretty well. He'd first met him years ago in a saloon in Fort Smith, where for a while Leonard had set up office for law-related tasks including everything from investigation to courthouse work. At some point, for reasons Jake never fully understood, Leonard left the area and became a traveler — a hobo, he called himself. After he returned to the border country from his wanderings, he and Jake got to be occasional drinking buddies, both in Fort Smith and in Guthrie. They were completely unlike in many ways but somehow enjoyed each other's company. Lately, Jake had decided to try to keep himself a bit more sober in his dignified years, and he'd been seeing less of his old friend. Leonard had the brains to be a good lawyer, but he spent too much time philosophizing in saloons.

He was sitting at a table in a corner of the Golden Wall without a drink, looking forlorn until he saw Jake come through the door. "Why Jake! You've arrived! Buy yourself a drink and get me one while you're at it — tequila — he has a bottle for me." He was very pleased when Jake returned, holding out the drink with its little worm in the bottom. *"Con gusano, ah! Excelente!"* He lowered his voice dramatically. "Beware the women. They're as starved as wolves for business. One of them approached me this very night, offering her services in exchange for future legal representation. Of course, I told her that I deal strictly in cash."

"I hear you work for nothing half the time."

"Only for clients *in extremis.*" Leonard sighed. "Unfortunately, most of the people I know lately are in that condition."

Jake glanced around at the three women desultorily working the other tables. The Golden Wall was indeed pretty slow tonight. "Well, I can see they're bothering you to death, Leonard."

"Museum specimens," Leonard grumbled. "Famine reigns when the whores offer credit: one of the oldest rules of bad times . . . See the old biddy with the six-year-old pinafore and the fifty-year-old face, the one with her eyeballs protruding? She'll be dead within the year. I tell her as much, too, just about every day. She's a snowbird."

"Too bad," Jake grunted, hoping not to encourage Leonard to launch into tales of his own years as a wandering hobo and morphine fiend. His stories of that part of his life were entertaining, but Jake always suspected him of inventing half of it. It was one of the rituals of their friendship for Leonard to bring it up and Jake not to act very curious.

"Snow. Cocaine. An inferior drug with superior addictive properties. There is no honor among snowbirds. I've heard it on good authority that their brains turn into a black syrupy mass." He held up his tequila and peered at it. "Ah, but this gentle fairy, I love her more than all my past mistresses." He widened his eyes. "A worm is at all their hearts; hers, at least, is visible. But let us not be lugubrious. Let us talk about your would-be executioner."

"Let's do. What'd you find out?"

"Given more ample time and resources, I could have reconstructed the scoundrel's entire biography, but with only part of a day, I have the following information: He came from Texas. He started to gain his notoriety around Ada, in the Chickasaw Nation."

"Hell's Fringe," Jake muttered. "He came after me in that vicinity."

"It seems that Ada is dominated by three cattle operations — three families who remain in a state of constant warfare with each other."

"That's been going on a long time. I sold Ada when I had the south route."

"I happen to know a little about the place, too. There's an attorney down there by the name of Moman Pruitt who's achieved a legal record. He's gotten three hundred men off scot-free of murder charges."

"Three hundred, huh?"

"That's correct."

"That's probably only a couple of months' work in Ada."

"Mr. James Miller, alias the Deacon, got his start in Ada working for one and then the other of these cattle outfits. How he avoided getting himself killed I don't know, but they say that he was regarded as merely an instrument, a professional, someone who did the will of others. Some say that he had an office in town with a sign out front that said 'Killer for Hire.' One of the men in Marshal Nix's office swears that's true. Anyway, about eight years ago he left Ada and briefly went to work for Pinkerton's Detective Agency, which he quit, the story goes, because they were too slow and scrupulous for him — which is about like saying that General Grant was too concerned about the comfort of his soldiers to conduct warfare. Off and on, he has worked for the Paris Hotel in Fort Smith, that most democratic of whorehouses. He also worked awhile for one of my favorite humanitarian enterprises, the Santa Fe Railroad, doing what sort of iniquity I don't know. So far as I can find out in an afternoon, he's never been tried for murder."

"Why?"

"Don't know. I guess he plays the borders well."

"That all you found out?" Jake asked.

Leonard shrugged. "All except that he's apparently a King Lear."

"A what?"

Leonard raised his expressive eyebrows. "Not a lover of the female gender."

Jake leaned back, frowning. "So you couldn't find out anything about who he's working for now."

Leonard shook his head. "Like I say, he's been employed at the Paris. He may bounce the place in exchange for his board. Who else he's working for I don't know. I do hope you're satisfied with my intensive investigation. My bill is your hospitable company, sir."

The mention of "King" made Jake wonder if by some chance Leonard knew anything about Samantha. "You lived in St. Louis, didn't you?"

Leonard took a sip of tequila and smacked his lips with pleasure. Leonard was a drinker who truly liked his drink. "Lived there? Of course I did. I did my apprenticeship with one of the most distinguished legal minds of St. Louis. Surely I have told you about Colonel Caruthers."

"Ever hear of a woman named Samantha King?"

"They called the colonel merciless, but a more gentle man

never walked the earth. He taught me all that I know . . . King, Samantha, what? No . . ." He frowned. "I do hear a dim chime in the dark abyss of the past, but I can't place it."

"Was there some prominent family in town called King?"

"Unfortunately, I didn't rub shoulders with the prominent." Leonard stared appraisingly at the worm.

Jake remembered the stationery that Sam had written her list on. "What about this place?" He took it from his pocket and showed it to Leonard, who held it away from his face. At the top of the sheet, a luxurious banner with fancy lettering wrapped around a substantial-sized building.

"The King Hotel! Why of course! The King was one of the more opulent houses in the city. The most opulent, no question of it. Considerably above my means at the time. Why do you ask?"

"You mean it was a whorehouse?"

"Oh, I'd hardly use such a crude appellation. A gaming and pleasure palace, it was." Leonard looked fondly at the stationery. "Marguerite King, impresario of the demimonde. Politicians in her pocket, leaders of the merchant and banking world. The queen of the King. Even Colonel Caruthers spoke admiringly of her, as I recall." He handed back the paper. "You ask much of me, my friend — to look back three decades and remember such things. This is ancient history." He took another sip, frowning. "But the King does come back. I recall it all the better because I never went there. I only dreamed about it. I thought it would be heaven to go just for one night. A Circean palace of voluptuaries. Thinly clothed temptresses whirling in torrid pirouettes, *nymphes du pavé,* cloud storms of perfume." He looked at Jake. "You realize I am only speaking from rumor and youthful imagination. Why are you asking about the King Hotel?"

Jake looked toward the bar. "I've met a woman —"

"Sir! This is desertion! A woman? You are a lifelong member of the honorable fraternity of bachelors." He rolled the little curl of worm around in the remaining tequila, grinning at Jake through his crooked teeth.

"I wish you'd go ahead and drink that nasty thing," Jake said. "I can't stand the suspense."

Leonard obligingly took the rest of it, with the worm, in one mouthful. He scowled as he swallowed it, sniffed once, and looked more serious. "Start from the beginning, Jake. Tell me all. Unburden yourself. A woman? From the King?"

They'd gotten through a second drink before Jake had finished telling about his brief acquaintance with Samantha King. Leonard was intrigued. "Where is she now?"

"She left this morning to go back to St. Louis."

"So at first you thought she was merely an accident you happened upon, and you discovered by means of this piece of paper in her luggage that she was interested in business, your business — is that the sum of it?"

"Guess so."

"And you still don't know why she latched on to you?"

Jake stared, shaking his head slightly. "Like I say, she claims to want to go into business out here, and she was thinking I'd make a good partner because I know the territory."

Leonard was still grinning.

"She's just a kid," Jake said. "She just doesn't act like somebody with her head set on running a business."

"How does she act?"

"She goes for whatever she wants, I'll say that much."

"Jake, you are being circumlocutory. Are you telling me that this woman is decisive? Did she go for you?"

"No, no!" Jake said, feeling his face flush. "Are you crazy? She's twenty-something years old."

"Your courier?"

Jake looked at him, not denying it.

"Aha! We've finally got it! You repulsive old devil you, you're jealous! And what look is this? What *is* happening with my old dried-up husk of a friend?"

"Good God, Leonard, shut up."

"I'd say she has good taste. That young man is extraordinary. Is he an Indian?"

"Tom grew up in the orphanage down near Durant. I don't think he knows what he is."

"Orphan. That explains it. He looks young and old at the same time." Leonard stared at him a moment, tapping his fingers on the table. "Anyway, she wants to launch this partnership without your contributing any money to it? Wave her golden wand and transform your dull, grinding, limited life from helot to capitalist, while you, being in the habit of thinking small, don't trust this opportunity and naturally suspect her motives. Her being a woman and all. Do I have it right?"

"Shit, Leonard. No. These are bad times. Things are worse than uncertain. The store's about broke. Ernest Dekker's set on turning it into nothing but a holder of mortgages —"

"Whoa. Hold it. Back up. Go slower."

Jake took a drink and thought about where to start. He pulled one of the mortgage transfer agreements out of his coat pocket and handed it across the table. Leonard squinted at it. "What villainy is this? I can't read fine print in this light."

Jake told him about the bank's threatened foreclosure at Dekker and his assignment to get owners to sign property mortgages against debt.

Leonard puzzled aloud. "So they want you to collect *land* mortgages against debts?"

Jake sat there for a minute, sipping, thinking. "Tell you what, Leonard. Do you still know people in St. Louis?"

"I do: a man who was a young lawyer when I was. He now has a solid practice, excellent contacts, a sober mind — just my sort. I've been in touch with him recently."

"How would you like to do some more finding out for me?"

Both eyebrows shot up this time, and he grinned. "Do I smell payment for services rendered? I'm all ears, Mr. Jaycox."

·14·

WHILE JAKE ACTED confident about Tom's traveling alone with the envelope full of money, he had given him a sudden nervous burst of advice before he stepped onto the train. "If some jaybird asks you what you're doing, let him know he can mind his own business. And don't get in any card games. Sharps ride the trains sometimes. And for pete's sake, don't get tangled up with any ladies. And don't forget to eat some durn food, even if you don't think you're hungry."

The urge to go to sleep hit Tom as soon as the train got up to speed, but he worked hard to stay awake. He needed to keep his eyes open to protect the packet, which had over three hundred dollars in it. He untied the string, took a cautious peek, and sniffed at the shaggy, folded, greasy bills. The Reverend had often spoken of the filthy stench of money, but he noticed nothing particularly filthy. A couple of signed mortgage papers lay neatly inside the envelope.

It was hard not going to sleep. The ceaseless rocking movement made him drowsy, and he kept slipping off, dropping his head and jerking back awake. He got up and paced the aisle a couple of times, then sat down and tried some of the mental games that he used to play in the classroom to stay awake. Sam and Deacon Miller kept coming into his thoughts, stitching his sleepy head with unconnected images. He fell into a confused, flickering, half-conscious state, and the man across the aisle and the several others in the car were all wearing black suits, but there at the rear of the train stood Sam King, wearing a deeply cut black dress, and she began walking toward him with a wolfish smile. He woke with a little shout.

The man across the aisle, muttonchop-bearded and nothing like the character in his dream, was playing a game of solitaire. He glanced at Tom. "Little nightmare there?" Tom didn't answer him. He blinked his eyes and wiped his face, too dazed to be embarrassed. "Take a bite, settle your stomach." The man offered a twist of tobacco. Tom reached out and took it, putting some in his mouth without thinking.

The man continued playing cards with himself, chatting in Tom's general direction about bad dreams. "I knew a farmer, claimed he never had em except during the planting season. But now my brother, he was a banker, God rest him, he had bad dreams every night . . ."

Tom fell into a reverie about Samantha, but soon his mind drifted to something that had happened three or four years ago. It was during summer, when heat waves were boiling up from the ragged dirt, and he was clearing bottomland for new planting the following year, struggling along with a sulky plow through brush and debris, avoiding stumps, when he noticed one of the boys coming down from the building across the field. It was Benjamin Bunch, one of the Reverend's spies, one of the saved, a boy who had chosen total compliance. He sidled alongside Tom with an ominous look of self-satisfaction, announcing over the rattle of chains, "You're in bad trouble. Supposed to go to the office now." As he watched Benjamin Bunch retreat across the field, it occurred to Tom that he could leave, just stop what he was doing and disappear into the woods, and maybe he could even stay alive out there, he really probably could. But he didn't do it. Instead, he unhooked the plow and rode the mule across the field, took her to the pasture, and walked dutifully, head bowed, into the office to receive his punishment for whatever transgressions he had lately performed against Reverend Schoot's rules.

That day the Reverend assigned him the punishment "reserved for the truest wickedness," of being locked away in the windowless cellar of the old building with its baleful smells of the past, where Choctaw Confederate soldiers and children had been buried under the house, according to what the Reverend called "the superstitions of ignorant Indians."

In the cellar you got one bucket of water and a bucket for slops. During part of the day, light would briefly enter through cracks in the floorboards, and Tom found things to do, exploring the gloomy room, making spears of old hoe handles and throwing them at targets, anything he could think of. Too quickly the feeble light would dim, and there came an endless passage of darkness during which he wasn't able to see his hand in front of his face. Fleas and spiders crawled over him, and he climbed to the top of the brick steps in an effort to get away. When he finally was let out of the basement, he'd be well covered by bites and temporarily blind, and sometimes have to go from there to the dusty, sagging "sick wing," where boys always lay ill with slow fever or flux, tended by the saved, the good ones — the "little reverends," as the unsaved secretly called them. In that place, your exemplary life could end in joyful death.

Tom looked at the greenish black, gummy tobacco in his hand. It was dawning on him how terrible the stuff was: of all the leaves he'd ever eaten, this was the worst. It kept him busy awhile, nearly getting sick, going back to the water closet and spitting it all out and realizing he had left the money and papers, then rushing back to his seat where the big envelope lay undisturbed.

♦

For the rest of the journey he concentrated on staying awake, clamping his jaw shut, grinding his teeth, avoiding sleep at all costs. Traveling was comforting to him — the swaying of the car was soothing; it made him unreachable, safe . . . *Awake thou that sleep.* The wall of sleep pushed inexorably against him. *Love not sleep* . . . The man across the aisle continued to play cards and occasionally talk, but Tom was scarcely aware of what he said.

The station platform in Fort Smith was quiet. The night was windless, bracing, cool. Jake had suggested that he hire a ride to the boarding house, but he was glad for the chance to walk. His legs badly wanted to walk. Up the hill, the Parker jail loomed against a moonlit sky, and climbing toward it he heard the forlorn sound of someone singing in the jail.

"Oh, I know a girl who's a gonna leave her mother . . ."

The song soon died out. It was coming from the far side of the building. As he walked by it, Tom smelled fried pork and urine. Edgar Wyatt, the elevator man at Dekker's, had told him about the Parker jail. "Use to keep em down there in the basement like barrows in the slaughter pen — one big room, nothin there but a bucket of water and bad company. Be in that place awhile and you'd just as soon march up them thirteen steps and git it done." The cellar jail was now vacant in favor of the new jail, a large brick addition on the building's other side consisting of one giant room with a three-story cage in it.

Going by the defunct cellar prison, he could almost see the old despair leaking up through the bars of the tiny window. Again he thought of the Reverend, and of his basement hell hole.

At the top of the hill, across the street from the jail, Tom saw flickering lights and moving shadows coming from the office of Dekker Hardware. He walked over to a corner of the open lot alongside the building. Men were in the big office, standing in a circle around one of the tables. Tom took a few steps closer to the window and saw that they were all stripped to their vests, with loosened ties, smoking, a single lantern on the table illuminating their faces. A couple of bottles sat on a small table off to the side. Mr. McMurphy, the fox-faced treasurer, wearing his usual green clerk's cap, was holding down a big unfolded paper, while Ernest Dekker, in a stiff collar and red tie, was talking, pointing his burning cigarette at places on the paper. The window was shut and Tom couldn't hear what he said. When one of the men turned and looked out the window, he slipped into the shadows and hightailed it up the street.

Within twenty minutes he had climbed up the stairs at Mrs. Peltier's and hid the packet of money and papers under the mattress in Jake's bedroom. He paced around the sitting room, thinking of the faces in the lantern light at the store, wondering why they were meeting so late at night.

He was now wide awake. He slipped into Mrs. Peltier's kitchen, took an apple from the barrel. It was a fine thing, being able to take food from the pantry at night! He decided to go for another walk, and slipped out. A little way down the street he passed an old sleepy-eyed black mule in the harness of a cane mill, still working. The furnace beneath the evaporator glowed red, and a smell of cane was in the air. The old man who was tending it went inside a shed to get another bind of cane, and the mule stood breathing a slow cloud of steam, resting from his endless circular path. Tom thought about Grant and Lee, and tears almost came to his eyes. Walking up to the mule and holding out the core of the apple, Tom was abruptly struck by the thought that he was free, and it was like a ball of energy flashing up his spine and hitting the roof of his skull. Free. It was the first time he'd felt it, alone, by itself, the pure feeling: free. The old mule lipped in the apple, and Tom backed away and hurried on to the avenue.

He felt like he could fly, racing down the wide board sidewalk. He was his own master, he could read a newspaper or a book, *any* book he could get his hands on. He could wander this town all night if he wanted to. Could drop everything and go off to find Sam. Oh, he missed her! Every time he thought about her, he knew that he had to see her again, soon.

He'd walked almost to the bridge before he knew where he wanted to visit. Edgar Wyatt's house, of course. Hack and Joel were staying there. Edgar would forgive a late night visit. And he could ask Edgar whether Mr. Dekker was back in town.

The elevator man's house was pretty far out Riverfront Street, beyond the edge of town — Joel had described it well enough that Tom was confident of finding it. A couple of the notorious row hotels on Riverfront appeared to have been flooded out. None of them seemed very busy late on Sunday night, although a woman stood in soft light in one doorway, calling out, "Hey cowboy, come talk to me." He hurried on past, thinking yes!

He found Edgar's house on a little rise, near a grain elevator and warehouse. Behind his house were sheds and an outhouse and a tiny field of dry cornstalks. There were no lamps lit, and Tom lingered awhile outside, but then built up his courage and walked up and rapped on the door. Edgar eventually appeared with a rifle over his arm and a worried, sleepy face, pulling up suspenders with one hand.

"Tom? What you doin out this time of night? I thought you and Mistah Jake out in the territories."

"He sent me back on the train. Are Joel and Hack here?"

"Little one's gone. They let him go a couple of days ago."

"Let him go?"

"Fired. That's what I heard, anyway."

"Fired Joel? Why?"

"Don't know." Edgar lowered his voice and looked away. "Say he had whiskey on his breath."

Tom didn't believe it.

"That's what the mens in the stockroom say. Course, you can't believe most of them. They been lying to me long as I can remember. Come on in. Too cold to stand in the door." Tom went in and stood by the stove. The room had a cozy, sooty smell. The ceiling was low, and hooks on the wall dangled with wraps. A small bathtub stood near the stove, and a mattress lay on the floor. Edgar came up beside him at the stove. "Mr. Jake okay?"

"Y-yes." For some reason Tom felt an unexpected chill now that he was beside the warm stove. A cold wind came up outside, fingering its way through the walls. His jaw went tense. His elation of a few moments ago had disappeared. Joel gone? Tom moved a half step closer to the stove. "Is Mr. Dekker back in town?"

"Mr. Ralph? I ain't seen him. Last week, you know, he was up on the fifth, watching out the window every day. Maybe he got tired of the scenery, decide to stay home."

"He went to St. Louis."

"Well, see, you one step ahead of me. I didn't even know that. They don't talk to me, Tom. I'm just back there puttin up with the mens in the stockroom. Much trouble as they give me, I oughta be paid once for my job and once for wranglin with them fools. Every new white boy think he gotta mess around with me, and every one I got to set straight. Been puttin up with that long as I been there, and it's only because I'm black, too. Got so I can smell it comin. They get to scrutinizin me . . ." Edgar sniffed and held out his big hands to the fire. "You lucky you can pass for white, I'll say that."

"Where is Hack tonight?"

"I wouldn't know. Hack has done moved. He come around here a couple of times, but I ain't been seeing him very much."

"Where's he staying?"

"Don't know for sure. Seemed like I heard something about the Paris Hotel. Don't you be going to that place."

Tom hung around a few minutes longer before leaving. Mist rose up off the river as he brooded down Riverfront. Back in Jake's parlor at Mrs. Peltier's he paced quietly, looked out the window, and eventually lay down, unable to turn off his mind. Without getting on his knees, he said the prayer.

♦

Monday morning, before the sun was quite up, Tom hurried to the store with the delivery envelope. One of the in-store salesmen sat behind the long front desk with a big catalogue in front of him, chewing a straw and reading a newspaper. He looked at Tom without saying hello. The room was strangely empty, with most of the displays gone or partly disassembled. In the big office, a tall bespectacled man called Loop sat working snuff in his lower lip and pounding the keys of a typing machine, as if unaware of anybody else in the room, *clap, clap, clap, ting, thwap.* Mr. McMurphy glanced up at Tom from beneath his eyeshade, held out a hand, and took the packet from him, quickly counting the money. He looked at the mortgages and began writing them into a ledger. Tom turned to leave, and McMurphy asked, without looking at him, "Where's Jake?"

"He's still in the territory."

"Is?" McMurphy looked skeptical.

"Yes sir."

"Wait here a minute."

McMurphy returned with the salesman called Jack Peters, who right off asked, "Say Jake's still out?"

Tom nodded warily.

"What'd he bring in?" Peters asked.

McMurphy showed Peters the ledger. "Couple of mortgages, little over three hundred dollars."

Peters looked at the treasurer knowingly. "Where's the boss?"

"Ain't here yet. Maybe at the bank." McMurphy gave Tom a hooded glance. "What's your name again?"

"Tom Freshour."

"Go to the stockroom, tell Edgar to put you to work. Mr. Dekker'll have some questions for you."

Tom walked back through the wide, dark room and up the half-flight to the shipping floor, which was completely jammed with boxes and crates, stacked higher than he could believe. The entire room was filled with stock. The huge curtain door on the bay of the shipping floor was open, and three boxcars stood beside the platform. There was no fire in the stove, probably because of the danger of things being this close around it. Three of the stockroom men were playing cards on barrel tops, with a fourth acting as lookout. They looked up when Tom came in, and one of them muttered, "Just one of the Indin boys. Nobody folds."

"Hey, boy. Where you been?" one of the card players asked with a sneer. He was a young, carrot-haired man named Jim.

Tom didn't answer him. During the flood he'd learned that Jim was among the stockroom men he had to ignore. He'd taunted Tom for the way he spoke. "Where'd you learn that fancy talk — they teach you that in the teepee?" he'd say.

As the elevator descended, Tom stood by waiting.

"I'm talkin to you."

"Play cards, Jim," another muttered.

"One of your little buddies got the boot. Little black one. Little buttercup nigger Indin. His own buddy got him fired."

"Shut up, Jim," said another card player.

Tom walked over and stood directly across from Jim. "Who got him fired?"

"Why, his bunkmate. The little chorus boy who hangs around the front office. They must teach you Indin boys real good."

Tom was normally slow to anger, but he wasn't completely unschooled in fighting. What Jim said incensed him, and he pulled him up, dragging him over the bench, and when Jim tried to take a swing at him, Tom pushed him against the pillar by the elevator shaft. Jim was stunned for a second, then he got a pocketknife out and opened a six-inch blade. "Well, well. I always did want to cut me an Indin."

The elevator platform arrived, and Edgar walked out of the gloom. "Put that thing away."

"Keep back, nigger," Jim said without looking.

Edgar came toward him. Jim turned and slashed the air. Edgar caught his wrist and took the knife and pitched it backwards, through the opening between the elevator and the floor, into the basement. "Pull that again and you be the one git a red necklace."

"Cut it out," one of the others said, glancing nervously out the bay. "You'll get us all in trouble."

Edgar kept an eye on Jim. "Come on, Tom."

As they glided smoothly upward on the wide platform through the dark shaft, Tom felt a little dizzy. "They's a spell on this place," Edgar grumbled, pulling the rope. "Ever since the old man left, I don't see nothin but spite and orneriness."

"He said Hack got Joel in trouble? Is that true?" Tom asked.

Edgar continued to work the rope, for a moment not answering. "All I know is the little one was after Hack about somethin."

"After him?"

"Gettin after him about somethin, like he was tryin to get him to do somethin — or not do somethin. They was pretty close-mouth around me, so I don't know what. Next thing I knew, the little one be gone, and Hack had done got in such a hurry all the time that he don't say much. But when it's somethin I can't do nothin about, I don't worry about it. That's my rule. That's the way I keeps food on the table. Better take some of that medicine yourself."

As they passed the floors on the way up, Tom noticed that the building was more than half empty. They ascended all the way to the fifth floor. "You wouldn't know it by them fools downstairs, but they is work to be done. Roll them nail barrels up to here, all of em . . ."

"What's going on, Edgar? Why's so much stock in the shipping room?" Tom asked.

Edgar shook his head. "Some kind of sale, I don't know." Edgar looked at him, his expression fierce. "You in the big world now, boy. Got to make a livin. It don't fall down in your lap. Can't be lettin fools pick fights with you. And don't be askin too many durn questions."

Tom's thoughts, though, lingered on Joel. How or why had Hack gotten Joel fired?

He looked down the long aisle of the upper floor and out the window. Despite so much of the stock being down on the shipping floor, the store's smells were concentrated here on the top floor — excelsior, oil, raw wood, iron. He could see across the river, far into the Nations. A guard with a rifle was walking down the pathway in the jail yard, past the gallows in early morning light. Tom thought about Johnny Pointer, who killed his own friends while they slept. He noticed another smell, pipe tobacco — a big standing ashtray full of burned pipe tobacco. It was the ashtray the old man had used, and it smelled fresh, as if he had been here recently.

◆

All day long, Tom kept wondering about Joel.

He spent most of the rest of the day moving things to the shipping floor. The stockroom men acted strange, in bursts working hard loading the rail cars, but then stopping and lurking in edgy groups, playing dominoes and cards, ducking out of sight on the few occasions when front-office men came back. Already about half of the stock in the store had been hauled out, and the rest was on the way. They talked in hushed tones, giving Tom the creepy feeling he was back at the orphanage. Once Tom heard someone downstairs yelling so loudly that it reverberated up the elevator shaft. In early afternoon he was briefly on the main floor, and saw several men hurry into the big office and slam the door while the catalogue salesman, hunched over his newspaper, glanced sourly after them. The regular business of the store seemed to be suspended.

He had a brief encounter with Hack, but he was in a big hurry, rushing out the back door to make a courier delivery somewhere. Tom tried to catch up with him and ask him about what had happened to Joel, but Hack said he didn't have time to talk.

Near quitting time, Tom was straightening cases of screws on the third floor, thinking about Sam, who never quite left his mind, when he heard someone stomping up the staircase. Jack Peters appeared out of the shadows. "Better get downstairs. Boss wants to talk to you."

In the big office, the bespectacled secretary was poking away at the typing machine on a corner desk. The room was laced with tobacco smoke and the smell of nervous sweat. The short one with the stub cigar in his mouth and the derby hat was sitting by a map, while salesman Marvin Beele sat at another desk, sorting a pile of what looked like the mortgage papers. Jack Peters remained standing by the door. Ernest Dekker paced around the room, dropping ashes, stopping and looking at the map, preoccupied.

Tom had been there a minute before Ernest even seemed to notice him with a brief, sour glance.

McMurphy was the one who finally spoke. "So Jake ain't doin so good."

It sounded like a statement rather than a question, and Tom didn't respond.

McMurphy looked at Dekker as if waiting for him to say something, but Ernest started pacing again, slowly up and down the room, glancing out the window. He constantly wiggled the cigarette holder, creating a trail of ashes. *Thwap, thwap, thwap, ting* went the typing machine.

"I'm wonderin whether we ought to send somebody else down there, sir," Peters said. "Hell, I'll go down there." The fat salesman's tone became innocent sounding when he was addressing Ernest.

McMurphy's eyes followed Ernest. The treasurer had a nose tic, one of his nostrils opening and closing in a little contraction of muscle. "Heard this morning that Shelby got four thousand more acres up around Tulsa," he commented.

The man in the derby hat asked around his cigar, "Who f'om?"

"Buncha Indians, lost their butts on a big cattle operation."

The lawyer took out his cigar and scowled at it. "I did hear about it. Creek tribe. They're easy to work, they're so ignor't. Army ordered them to clear all the herds off the Outlet before the land run, and most of em ended up in Tulsa. I hear you can't sell a steer now, can't hardly get em on the train. Say it's one big cattle yard, prices down to nothin, lot of outfits goin broke."

While this conversation went on, Ernest Dekker continued to pace and smoke. The room was charged with a kind of restless energy that Tom had never felt before. They all were hanging on Ernest, waiting for him to decide something, but his preoccupation appeared to be total. McMurphy asked, "You want to send Jake a telegram and tell him to get back to the plan?"

Ernest looked at him and nodded.

McMurphy said to the secretary, "Okay Loop, take this down, telegram, general delivery, to W. W. Jaycox, Guthrie. Tell him we want to see twenty signed mortgage transfers from the Choctaw Nation before he steps foot back in here."

The typist, slouching over his machine, blinked through round spectacles. "Twenty?"

"Remind him about the bounty," McMurphy added drily. "Maybe that'll get him off the dime."

The typist put a new piece of paper into the machine and started tap-tapping on it again. Marvin Beele had finished counting and sorting his papers, and he went over and handed them to the lawyer. "Looks like nine hundred acres," he muttered, chewing fast, glancing toward the door. Tom got the impression Beele was trying to make himself as invisible as possible.

The lawyer plugged his cigar back in and started looking through the papers. "Where are we now?"

"Fort Gibson area," Beele said, glancing at the pile of maps on the large table.

"Go into the other room for that," Ernest said. It was the first thing he had said since Tom came in.

The lawyer picked up the map and went into the little adjoining office, with Beele and the treasurer following. Tom could see them through the windowed door, and he noticed that eventually McMurphy took money from a green box and gave it to Marvin Beele, who folded it into his pocket. Peters sidled over toward the door as if trying to hear what was being said in the small office.

Ernest, still pacing, spoke to Peters. "You going out tonight?"

"Yes sir!" the fat salesman said. "Train's at six-thirty, sir. You want me to double up and hit the Choctaw territory? I can bring in fifteen thousand acres down there without even trying."

Ernest shook his head. "Keep working your territory. We've got enough confusion around here. And get some big fish, Jack. You're making twelve cents now. One hundred twenty dollars per thousand acres. At that rate, you could get up a pretty good bundle."

When Peters left, only the typist, Tom, and Ernest remained in the room. Suddenly, Dekker stopped pacing in front of Tom. His eyes, Tom saw, were murky and agitated. "What's Jake up to?" He spoke in a voice low enough that the secretary couldn't hear over the sound of his machine.

"I beg your pardon."

"Jake. What's he up to?"

"I don't know, sir."

"Has he been talking about me?"

"No sir."

"Did he get into some kind of scrape out there?"

Tom withdrew into himself in the same way that he'd always done at the academy — watching the skin, looking at the corners of the eyes, at the expansive eyebrows, grey-flecked.

"Answer my question." The eyes got wider. Ernest seemed to be on the verge of great anger.

From years of experience, Tom had learned that lying just started him playing the inquisitor's game. Truth was the best weapon, lying was the last resort. "Yes," he said flatly, without the "sir" — going neutral and cold, defying the rules of respect enough to derail his inquisitor. *Thwap, thwap, ting.* Tom felt dizzy, his own partial reflection in a pane of glass like a black shape. Inside him was a peculiar stirring.

"What kind of scrape?"

"Somebody shot at him."

"Shot at him," Ernest said sarcastically. "Who?"

"I don't know," Tom said.

"He okay?" Ernest asked.

"He's fine," Tom said.

"Jake's been having all kinda problems. I don't like my men getting reputations."

Tom didn't reply.

"And he left Guthrie to go back collecting?"

Tom barely nodded. Volunteer no information. Answer only what you have to.

"That friend of yours, Joel," Ernest Dekker said. "We had to get rid of him. That was a real shame."

Tom said nothing. His hackles were up now. The situation felt all too familiar.

"Had high hopes for that boy."

Tom said nothing.

"I can tell you're smart. They trained you boys right. You can do real well with me or you can do real poorly." He pulled back and narrowed his eyes. "What kinda Indian are you?"

"I don't know."

"Aren't all of you Choctaws?"

"I have no information about my parents." Tom's face had gone hot.

Ernest Dekker looked at him disdainfully. "You talk fancier than a white boy, but I'm not sure you've got the hustle this other one has." He was about to add something else when Marvin Beele came out of the small office in a hurry. Beele hesitated, as if he wanted to speak to Dekker, but changed his mind and left the room.

Hack appeared at the door. He looked startled to see Tom here. He glanced back and forth between Dekker and Tom. The treasurer came out of the office and saw Hack and held out an envelope to him. "Take this to Bradley." Hack was quickly gone.

"Finished with that telegram yet?" Ernest asked the secretary. "Just finished."

Ernest Dekker sighed and said to Tom, "Run that to the Main Hotel telegrapher." He took a nickel out of his pocket and put it on the edge of a desk. "That's for you."

In twilight, Tom walked up the avenue. He was in a tumble of thoughts, with the mood of the big office still overhanging him. *We had to get rid of him* kept echoing through his mind. He was worried, too, about the message he was supposed to telegraph Jake. If he sent it to Enid instead of Guthrie, Jake would probably get it, but then what? Would Jake leave Enid, canceling the plan for them to meet there? Maybe he should wait and take the message to him, and that way not lose touch.

Walking along the tracks in the middle of the avenue, Tom heard a loud rumble and looked up to see the single headlamp of a trolley approaching him like a giant eye. He saw no animals pulling the trolley. There was an odd humming sound in the air, coming from the overhead cable that ran down the street. The only trolleys he'd ever seen were pulled by animals. Electrical trolleys were another hole in Tom's acquaintance with the world. He knew that electricity somehow propelled dots and dashes through the telegraph, and lighted bulbs, but he had no idea that it could propel streetcars. Fort Smith's Trolley and Generating Company had been out of commission for almost a year due to financial problems — long enough for it to have died back as a subject of conversation. But it had reopened that morning and was running maintenance checks. Electrical power was dawning on this town in a lurching, lights-on, lights-off fashion that caused many to regard it as a questionable gimmick whose main purpose was to fleece investors.

As the trolley thundered by, sparks of fire rained down all around him, and for some reason he looked up at the front of the Main Hotel, where a few people had come to windows to look out. In a window high up, a woman briefly appeared who looked almost like Sam.

The lobby floor of the Main was another first for Tom, with its little white octagonal tiles that crunched under his feet. The lobby was luxuriously appointed with gas chandeliers, Persian rugs, Corinthian columns, and platoons of leather rocking chairs, occupied at this hour only by a couple of lounging newspaper readers. A Western Union sign hung above the desk.

He stalled, sitting down in one of the leather chairs, picking up a newspaper to read, the *St. Louis Post-Dispatch*. DISORDER IN RUSSIA read the left column; ARMY OF UNEMPLOYED read the right. He looked at advertisements for women's clothes, and his thoughts drifted off to the woman he'd seen in the window. She could not really have been Sam, but all day he'd been thinking of her, seeing and feeling and smelling her the way she'd been at the bathhouse and in bed with him, the way in bed she'd crawled on him, the smoothness of her thighs, the grandeur of her buttocks, the way she spread her legs around him . . .

A loud ringing sound caused Tom to jump. He looked up and saw the man behind the desk go to a box on the wall, pick up a thing hanging off a wire, put it against his ear, and then begin talking at it. By now Tom had run up against enough mysteries to have learned that his best bet was to sit back and wait for things to explain themselves, although it was slightly embarrassing to see this man talking into a box. The two men sitting in rocking chairs paid little or no attention to the clerk, and Tom decided that whatever the clerk was doing was not uncommon at the Main Hotel.

"St. Louis?" the clerk said into the box. "Yes. Yes. That's to Barnhill Bank and Trust. Okay. I've got it. Yes."

The mention of St. Louis reminded Tom that he should find out if Mr. Dekker Senior was back in town yet. That was the one obvious thing that he should do before sending this telegram.

He left the newspapers folded as he'd found them and hurried to Seventh Street and walked eastward until he found the address Jake had given him, a two-story house with a broad front porch. There was a light on in one of the front rooms, coming through the glass in the front door, and he slowly approached it down a brick sidewalk. No response to his knock. The light encouraged him to walk around the house. The back porch had an icebox on it, a line of water dripping from the ice door. A dog barked somewhere in the neighborhood. When he knocked on the back door it cracked open, and he saw the light coming from the front room. The kitchen was dark. "Hello?" he said tentatively. "Mr. Dekker, are you home?" He bumped into a table and heard a clink of glass. On the table he dimly saw a plate with the remains of a meal on it. He walked toward the lighted front room, through a short hallway where something lay on the floor — a canvas hunting coat. Through a dining room with a long table, into a sitting room, where a single steady gas fixture on the wall was burning. He called, "Mr. Dekker? Hello?"

A fire had almost died down in the fireplace. The room was in disarray, with papers from a desk spilled onto the floor, a drawer left open. Two stacks of books appeared to have been taken off a shelf and dropped nearby. Tom glanced back at the smoking fireplace. The silence in the house became more ominous.

A leather album sat open on a table, and he glanced at it. On the first page was a formal daguerreotype, apparently of Mr. Dekker as a young man. He had a hawkish, emphatic, purposeful face that shone with self-sufficiency. He looked like a man who did not hesitate. "The Pelham Studio, St. Louis" was engraved on the bottom of the portrait. In another daguerreotype the same man stood with his wife and three children, all turned toward the father, as if waiting for him to decide. The oldest was a daughter and the youngest a sickly-looking boy. Ernest, the middle child, at perhaps eight, was already brooding.

Raised as neither child nor brother, Tom didn't know much about flesh-and-blood families. Books in the academy library contained edifying passages here and there regarding the duties and responsibilities of sons and daughters, which sounded disappointingly similar to the duties of orphans. He had scarcely known enough about families even to wish that he was part of one. There were families in the Bible, but in them fathers sacrificed sons, and brothers were treacherous. Jesus seemed to be mostly annoyed by families, by all their duties and rules. Now in the world, though, Tom had witnessed some of the expressions of flesh-and-blood mothers and children — the simple motions of caring — enough to yearn for this condition he knew so little about. But this photograph of a young family, turned toward the austere father, did not excite that yearning.

Tom stood in the single pool of light in the house, fascinated by the photograph album, paging through it. There was yellowed writing on the bottom of some of the photographs. On one page, halfway through the book, was scrawled

M. King's daught.
Left b.

The photograph was a formally posed portrait of a little girl, perhaps six years old. She was a beautiful child, with long hair and very clearly defined and arresting eyes. The coincidence of the name . . . Hair rose on the back of his neck when he realized that the eyes were shaped like hers, indeed so was the face. Did a lot of little girls look like this?

Tom heard a creaking somewhere in the house. He turned and cleared his throat and said, "Mr. Dekker, are you here?" He got a candle from the mantel, lighted it by the gas lamp, and carried it around to the entrance hall, where a staircase led to the second floor. Near the bottom step was a piece of paper, and looking up, Tom saw things strewn all along the stairs. His pulse quickened.

Again he called out and waited. Nothing. He should probably leave, because if Mr. Dekker was asleep, or if he arrived now, he might think Tom was a thief. But curiosity drew him up to the second-floor landing, where he could feel air drafting through the house. A window rattled somewhere. Two doors were closed, one open. Through the open door, he saw a dark shape sitting in an easy chair by the bed, slumped forward. Tom went slowly into the room and knelt down on one knee, passing the candle under Ralph Dekker's face. The forehead was crushed, a single messy hole at the bridge of his great flaring nose, and blood was spattered on the wall. Tom had smelled death before in the orphanage's hasty funerals. *I'm not afraid,* he told himself, looking directly into the elusive gaze of the dead eyes. One of them was floating in blood, the other was clear, and in the whole expression of the face there was terrible grief.

Tom knew how to act in crisis. He knew what to do. You stood up and you walked out the door. You held the banister and took one step at a time down the stairs. You didn't rush. You went to the back door and out, you walked at a regular pace to a different street, and you retreated through the black night.

One block at a time, you guided yourself back to the boarding house. You kept quiet, slipped in. You took off your shoes at the door and walked up to your room and lay down on the couch. You put all thoughts of telling someone what you had seen out of your mind. When you yearned for some relief, some comfort, you found it however you could — you got Jake's pillow from the other room and held it tightly to your chest.

·15·

JAKE AND Leonard LaFarge met Monday night at the same table in the Golden Wall. By the flushed look on Leonard's face, a significant portion of the ten dollars Jake had given him for expenses was in his stomach in liquid form. He stood up when he saw Jake, his curly grey hair winging backwards. "Come with me, my man. I tire of this mausoleum. We need a livelier locale."

Leonard hurried through the streets with Jake following along, headed "downtown," which in Guthrie was down a hill in the area around the tracks, called Sin Gulch, where cribs and barrel houses and sawdust dance halls occupied buildings that had managed to look worn out in less than five years. Downtown was rich with the smells of beer, ash and coal from the train track, the smell of five-cent cigars that poured out of open doors of bars, the sounds of tric-a-trac, faro, roulette. Heavy-eyed men stood listlessly in front of red curtains.

A tout at the door of a dance hall saw them coming. "Come INto the PROtest Saloon! See the GIRLS, foolish virGINias REcently IN from the COUNtry, ALL wearing transPARent GARments! SEE them here!"

"You devil," Leonard said to the tout. "You assume that because this hair is grey I'm therefore a lecher. Well, you've got it backwards. Wait until you're four hundred years old and a candidate for the old folks' home!"

"Haven't seen you in a while, Professor LaFarge. Where you been?"

"I've been seeking an honest man, you young devil. Go back to your flimflammery."

"FAM'ly fun, OLD-time MUSic, SQUARE dancing . . ." the caller shouted, grinning after them.

They entered a crowded room with a sawdust dance floor at one end. It had to be the busiest place in town, but they found a rough table and barrels for seats at the other end of the room from the band. The train track ran in the gap just outside, perilously close to the back wall. A woman with a raw red face appeared. "Whatcha want?" She was chewing.

"Rye whiskey will do for me, from a bottle with a label, if you have it."

With absolutely no expression, she switched her gaze to Jake.

He ordered a beer. The odor of urine and sweat and fetid breath filled the place. It was noisy — a three-piece string band at the other end, sawing out rough hill-country music. On the dance floor a wild mix of people whirled and stomped to the harsh rasp of the strings: an awkward, toothless old man slowly flapping his arms like wings; a young, stiff, pomaded cowboy dancing a severe box step with a tiny partner; women from thirteen to fifty dressed up in small ways with a feather, scarf, or a gingham dress. These were not saloon girls but civilians. Yet at the end of the long room where Jake and Leonard sat, a row of shadowy booths lined the wall, with strange noises coming out of them. People sat in each other's laps, kissing and spooning, and occasionally a woman gave off a little yelp when the man went too far. A louder yelp caused a ornery-looking bouncer to bend down and peer into the booth with a threatening expression. The fiddle band went through "All I've Got Is Done and Gone" and "Broken-Legged Chicken," then stopped for a break.

"Popular place," Jake commented. The air was excited, combustible, crackling with energy.

Smiling across the table at Jake, Leonard said, "Here, my friend, you have the gayest among the butterfly chasers, frothiest of the land-rush refugees, human birds of passage on their way to the next imaginary crops. Tent camps have sprung up north of town now, have you seen them? People from Ohio, from Arkansas, Kansas, from Michigan and Minnesota. They saw the handbills put out by the Atcheson, Topeka, and Santa Fe Railroad, and certain other philanthropic institutions. They papered the walls of the United States with those handbills, describing the amazing, expanding, infinite Oklahoma Territory, its uninterrupted twelve-month growing season, pure coursing water on nearly every acre — I'll bet you didn't know these things, Jake — diamonds the size of nuts lying right on top of the ground, bottomland of unparalleled richness. And all of it free! Free for the asking! And so these people, who are poor, who've never made it through the debt cycle with all their legs and arms intact, never enough to catch up — quite understandably they heed the call. Strap their belongings onto the old wagon and make one more journey. Some of them have already lived in a dozen places, or fifteen, never able to sink roots, so why not! One more try." He looked around the room and said wryly, "Clodhoppers of the world. Proletariat of the soil. They come here, spend their last dollar on beer, mix with our bootleggers, our con men, our highjackers and cowpunchers, a few light-skinned Indians who can pass the door, a few professional women — an unusual mix, ah yes, all enjoying the marv'lous mild depravity of the Protest Saloon and Dance Hall in the heart of Oklahoma Territory! Did you know, Jake, that the Congress of the United States has declared this territory to be the official trash depository of the nation, a kind of sinkhole located conveniently near the middle, into which Indians from east and west, landless peasants, outlaws, all can be swept together, thereby keeping the other parts as tidy as possible. I tell you, we are witnessing a mighty social experiment. This is the Australia of America."

"What have you been drinking, Leonard?"

"Notice the barwomen, long of jaw and strident of voice. The grangers feel at home with them. Transparent garments, ha!"

"You oughta be a tout," Jake declared.

"I have been a tout. A fine one. In Louisville, Kentucky. I was so successful that customers gathered round just to listen to me. I was a one-man show. The boss fired me for keeping the customers outside listening to my golden rhetoric."

"So did you find out anything about Samantha King today?"

Leonard put on a sly look. "I did. More than I expected to. In a single telegram from my trusty colleague in St. Louis." For a moment, Leonard looked around the room. "All right. Your Samantha King is Marguerite King's daughter out of wedlock."

"Go on."

"Samantha went to boarding schools in another city, where she apparently led a wild and carefree life until her mother died or was killed. Then she moved back to St. Louis."

"What do you mean, 'wild and carefree'?"

"Those are my informant's exact words. He either didn't know more or didn't want to say more."

"Her mother was killed?"

"She died under suspicious circumstances. Suffocated, something like that. There was some suspicion of murder, but that's inevitable with a woman like Marguerite King."

Jake thought about Samantha's odd blend of secretiveness and brashness, her air of having both a past and a purpose.

"Her mother'd made a boatload of money, but I don't know what condition her estate was in when she died. I'm afraid none of this will help you understand her daughter's current interests, but the long and short of it is that the young lady may be telling you the truth, Jake. She may be that rarest of archangels, the kind with *dinero* to give away." Leonard smiled evilly.

A train was coming into town on the tracks in the gap just beneath the saloon wall, brakes squealing. Right by their table two windows went up and a group of drunken, shouting men were lining up, to Jake's surprise unbuttoning their trousers, whooping and laughing. The building shook like an earthquake when the train went by, the band scratching out "The Devil Take a Yaller Girl" and the crowd of men pushing and shoving each other for a chance to pee out one of the windows.

"There, you see!" Leonard shouted. "Piss on the mighty railroads. Oh, I am a true anarchist in my soul, but be careful how you aim those things, men! It's coming back on us!"

Jake stood up. "Let's get out of here."

As they walked up the hill, Leonard was suddenly in a bad mood. "One of those mudheads got me broadside."

"Did you look at those mortgage papers?"

"Yes." Leonard took a copy of the mortgage transfer agreement out of his pocket and gave it back to Jake. He was wheezing. "Flimsy as it looks, this little document . . . it's clever . . . Sit down a minute, I'm out of wind. My lungs . . . aren't what they used to be. I fear I'm allergic to . . . being pissed on." They sat down on a bench outside the newspaper office. The cold felt good to Jake after the saloon. There were several shadowy bundles around the land office. It looked like people were sleeping in the yard.

"I've got my breath," Leonard said. "As to these mortgages, all I can tell you is that . . . normally . . . mortgages on land aren't the most desirable way for a supplier to secure cash debt. Little hunks of real estate aren't very liquid. However, things are different now. There's a lot of scheming going on over real estate, what with all the remaining Indian land up for grabs and all these people pouring in." His gaunt face turned severe in the dim light of the street. "There are interests, very large interests, turning a greedy eye to this region. Half the Indian domain is worth the attention of big capital, my friend. I assure you."

"What do you mean?" Jake asked.

"The Indians had a hundred and forty million acres, more or less, before allotment began. They figure that when the Dawes Commission is finished they'll have kept about half that. It's the last big grab, my friend. Seventy million acres is worth the attention of almost anyone."

"Ernest is asking us to get these mortgages signed on land still owned by Indians, as well as land in the white territory. Is that legal?"

Leonard looked disgusted. "Oh, come now, Jake, don't be naïve."

"What makes it so valuable all of a sudden?"

Leonard pointed back down the hill. "There's your answer. There and in the tent cities. Tens of thousands have been lured here on promises that few of them found. Free land! The place is teeming with land-hungry wretches, ten for every one who gets a quarter section, lured by the publicity of the railroads and banks. If I were an economist, I'd write a treatise on it. Never has a market been created so fast and so unscrupulously. They've come here for free land and now they're talking themselves into leasing it for two dollars an acre per year. This place will be paved by sharecroppers in ten years. I hear them at the land office every day. They're here now, and they're ready to lease at any price."

"One of my customers down south was talking about a syndicate —"

"Yes," Leonard said darkly. "I've heard that word myself."

Jake stood there. A picture seemed to be forming, but he still didn't quite get it. "I need to find out more."

"My best informant on the subject of land dealing has moved to Enid, along with everybody else."

"Let's go see him. I was going to Enid, anyway."

"Honest work for honest pay — my lifelong . . . credo," Leonard wheezed. "But I've heard they're having a civil war up there."

"It's not that big a deal," Jake said. "I was up there three or four weeks ago."

"What exactly do you want to find out?"

"Whatever I can."

· 16 ·

Tom's survival instinct told him to tell no one about finding Mr. Dekker, to do nothing, to disappear into the walls. A half-breed, a newcomer to this town, someone who worked for the store and who had gone to Mr. Dekker's house at night — if he went to the authorities, they'd ask him questions and decide that he was a suspicious character, someone who knew more than he was telling. And in fact he did know more. He knew that Ernest Dekker had usurped his father (surely everyone knew this) and that Ernest was taking apart the store. He knew that Jake strongly supported Ralph Dekker and opposed his son, and that someone named Miller had tried to kill Jake. But for Tom to speak of these things would only make him more suspect. Lying low was the only thing he could do. He could not report the death. Someone else would have to find Ralph Dekker.

Jake would surely come when he heard. He hoped that would be soon.

All day Tuesday, he waited for the shock to run through the building: Ralph Dekker has been found dead! But it didn't happen, and by the end of the day he was exhausted by the sheer burden of what he knew, and of waiting. He couldn't tell Hack. He couldn't even tell Edgar, because if he reported it, the authorities would wonder why Tom hadn't. He was stuck with the bad news until somebody else uncovered it.

Late Tuesday afternoon, Jim, the carrot-haired man who'd brandished his knife at Tom the previous day, approached him in the shipping room with a lame smile. "It happened just like I fig-gered. They fired me. Done fired about everybody. I don't give a hoot about this place anyway. I'm moving back to the hills. De-cided to clear up my accounts." He frowned, looking up at Tom with his chin jutted out. "Yessir, I don't mean for you to take it bad, me jumpin you. It weren't your fault." This sounded like an apology for starting the fight, and Tom had the crazy impulse to tell him about Ralph Dekker. *Go ahead,* something inside him urged, *tell him, tell someone, get rid of this secret;* but common sense prevailed. He wished Jim good luck and left.

He ate supper at the boarding house that evening but was bad company at the table — he knew that he was — and the bachelors sensed his mood and treated him gingerly. He wondered if per-haps he could confess his secret to Mr. Haskell, who was a very de-cent man, but he didn't think it would be wise. One way or an-other, Mr. Dekker would soon be found. He just had to keep his mouth shut.

Everything had become muddled, confused, dangerous. The mysterious firing of Joel, the clearing out of the merchandise, the fact that he was supposed to go to Enid but probably shouldn't, since as soon as Jake heard about Mr. Dekker's death he would surely come to town. He was beginning to feel that he had never left his past. He had started a new life, but the past was catching up to him. Here again he had found the mood of Bokchito — se-cretive, hazardous, people driven by powerful hidden motives. When he heard the yelling from downstairs again, he leaned his head back against the brick wall and thought about the Rev-erend's fits of temper, which had never seemed quite genuine to Tom. They were intentional displays, tools in his routine of tyranny. Ernest Dekker sounded more desperate.

Tom found newspapers and read them front to back, and they helped take his mind off all these things, and there were a few books in the parlor of the boarding house, which carried him to places far away.

The store emptied of salable goods, leaving less and less real work to do, and as the merchandise disappeared the stockroom men went along with it, fired two and three at a time. He found a hiding place on the fifth floor, near a gas lamp; on Wednesday he spent virtually all day there, reading. He had taken one of Mrs.

Peltier's books, a "novel," which was a long made-up story about a little girl who lost her mother and spent her entire childhood looking for her, barely missing her many times, until page 350, near the book's end, when she found her just in time for the mother to die. In his hiding place behind barrels, leaning against the gritty bricks with the yellow light around him, Tom almost cried at the book's conclusion. It was the first time that he had ever felt this way over the loss of a parent, and it was a made-up story.

All of his reading provided a concentrated dose of information, as well as keeping his mind occupied. From the newspapers he learned that the box in the hotel was a telephone, and he read about the electrical plant in Fort Smith, and about crimes, and he looked at the advertisements, which were full of clues about the world. The other thing he did to keep his mind busy was pay attention to things at the store — the hurried, evasive movements of men in and out of the office, the strangely guilty behavior of the salesmen, the way Ernest seemed to stay in there, and to send out his messages through other parties, usually McMurphy, or through messengers.

When Tom went to work on Thursday, the few remaining workers in the stockroom were alarmed because it was apparent now that all of them were being fired. Three others had just been let off by McMurphy. "Leaves Pat, me, and one other fellow working back here," Edgar grumbled. "This place like a hainted house." At the mention of ghosts, Tom thought of Ralph Dekker. Was it possible that his body still hadn't been found?

Late in the afternoon, Tom was about to leave to go home when he saw, across the dark empty showroom, three strangers, wearing pistols, going into the big office. A group of men stood around the front desk, whispering, and he sensed that it had finally happened. He turned and went back up the stairs to the second floor, hoping to be able to listen through a ventilator to what was being said below. Working on this floor, he'd noticed that the typewriting machine and voices could be heard through the black metal grate, which was above a little-used adjoining room behind the big office. Tom wanted to actually hear that Mr. Dekker had been found, but the door between the two rooms was shut and the words were barely audible.

". . . several days," he thought he heard. ". . . like he done him-self in."

". . . don't believe it," said a second voice. Ernest's?

The reply was quiet and careful sounding, but Tom could only hear ". . . place tore up . . . couldn't find a note . . ."

Both voices were muffled and echoing, and Tom had a hard time understanding them. He lay flat on the grating, looked down, and there to his surprise was Hack, standing with his back against the wall with a slightly pleading expression. Someone else was in the little room, a man in a black suit, and he stood with his ear against the shut door, listening to the conversation in the big office. Tom couldn't see who it was, but when the man turned, there, very close, floating in the scarce light below, was the face of Deacon Jim Miller. Tom felt ice on his spine, and involuntarily jerked away. The face took on an inquisitive look, as if hearing something, then looked directly upward, squinting toward the grate. Tom moved out of sight, but he could hear Miller walking out the door of the room toward the stairs.

He got up and hid behind a bin. Miller appeared at the top of the stairway and began moving slowly down the aisle toward the grating. Tom waited until he had passed and then slipped down the stairs, walking on his toes.

He knew that the back door was locked; the only way out was through the showroom, past the gathering of men around the sales desk. Two of them Tom had seen Monday evening when he was looking through the office window. Both had neatly trimmed beards, wore stiff collars and watch chains dangling from their vests.

"Hey!" Mr. McMurphy called out. "You. I need to talk to you."

Tom wanted to run but didn't. He made himself walk up to McMurphy, who was the only one among the nervous group of men paying him any attention. The others were watching the big office, talking in undertones about the constables.

"Is Jake back in town yet?" McMurphy asked sternly.

"No," Tom said.

"You sure?"

"Yes," Tom said.

McMurphy looked at him a minute, then said, "Well, we're cutting down the men in the back, and I'm going to have to let you off."

Tom didn't reply. Any minute, Miller was going to come back down the stairs.

"Here's your pay for four days this week." He put four dollars on the desk, and Tom thanked him, picked it up, and headed for the front doors.

Tom supposed he should feel bad about being fired, but he didn't. In fact, he was so relieved to be out of the store that when he got back to the boarding house, he felt too giddy even to eat dinner. He slipped down to the parlor and found a morning paper and took it back to Jake's room. But he couldn't concentrate, even on reading; he couldn't get Hack's expression and Miller's dead-fish eyes off his mind. At least they had finally found Mr. Dekker. Tom had thought that once the news was out, his own sense of urgency would go away, but he felt trapped in the room, restless and moody. He went out and walked down to visit the mule at the cane press. It was soothing to watch the grizzled docile animal plodding in his circle. The old black man who fed cane into the press didn't seem to mind Tom. After a while, he went back to the boarding house and paced in the room, and then lay down and tried to go to sleep.

◆

He heard someone at the door, a slight shuffle and hesitation, and looked up just in time to see it open and a dark shape slip into the room. He rolled out of bed and did the only thing he could think to do — he lunged across the darkness and tackled the form before it got far from the door, hitting it in the middle and knocking it down.

Before they hit the floor he knew who it was. "I'm sorry! Oh, I'm so sorry."

"Knocked . . . the . . . breath out of me," Sam said.

He crawled up to her face and said again, "I'm very sorry." He touched her cheek, her shoulders and arms, only to confirm she was really here, in the flesh. "Why didn't you — ?"

She sat there getting her breath back.

He went and turned up the gas in Jake's room and left the door open, soft light entering the room. Her face was somehow different, and he was afraid he'd really hurt her. She remained sitting and he sat with her, and they talked in whispers.

"Is Jake here?"

"No, he's in Enid. But I think he'll be back soon. Maybe tomorrow. Do you know what happened?"

She nodded. "I read the newspaper about Ralph Dekker."

They sat knee to knee. Tom told her about getting fired and seeing Deacon Miller. He asked if she'd just arrived, and she said that she'd been in town a couple of days. "I wish I'd known you were here," she said, glancing worriedly into the other room.

She reached over and put her hands on his shoulders and looked at him sadly. "Are we safe, Tom, are we safe?" She kissed him, an experience they'd previously had only in hurried circumstances. Sitting quietly on the floor, they kissed in a wide-open, vulnerable, urgent kiss. She looked into his eyes and sighed. "You're a beautiful boy, you know that."

"Beautiful?" Tom said numbly. He looked back at her, at the curl of dark hair falling down beside her face, the glow of light on her skin, her green eyes. The set of her face reminded him a little of the faraway look she'd had when she was recovering from her head wound.

She gazed away toward the light in the other room. "I'm sick of arrogant men, ignorant little roosters prancing around. Trying to impress you. You can't even like them, you know. It's impossible." She started taking off Tom's shirt, a button at a time. She pulled it partway down. She stood up and took off her own blouse and dress, leaving on only her camisole and underwear. She went around Tom and knelt behind him, touching across his back. "Who did this to you, Tom?" She had asked this same question both times before. "Who made a whipping boy out of you?" Her voice was close to his ear. "You can't let them do that."

Tom didn't know how to answer her. He had started shivering. He wanted to make love with her and yet was not sure that he could.

She put her lips on his shoulder and neck. "You have so many scars. Can you feel that?"

He gritted his teeth as she kissed the scars, and he felt a surge of anger. She reached around his belly with both arms and for a moment rested her chin on his shoulder and her hands in his lap.

He didn't answer her. Her body against his back and her breath on his neck gave him a sense of power, radiating from the whole middle of his body, but her questions about his back terrified him. He felt as if he was crawling around in the most luscious blackberry bush, with big thorns raking across his skin.

"We don't have to talk," she whispered, opening her hands and moving them lightly against his pants. She took them away, and he heard a sound and then, with her naked breasts touching his back, she started to unbutton his pants. "Take your clothes off." He took his shirt all the way off, and, after some hesitation, his pants, embarrassed at the way his penis popped out so straight and tight. She took off her underpants and stood in front of him. "Take hold of me."

He wrapped his hands around her hips and could not believe how velvety soft and full they felt, how the palms of his hand seemed to fit around them so well, his little fingers at the bottom almost reaching underneath.

Her teeth glinted in the light. "That's for you, Indian boy." She lay on the rug beside him. "Feel me. Put your hands all over me." He happily obliged. ". . . You like those, don't you. Feel the tips of them. The nipples. Kiss them."

He kissed one of them and couldn't stop, felt it swelling tight in his mouth. She whispered, "Let's go to the bed."

They went into the bedroom. She stood up on her knees and he did likewise, opposite her on the soft mattress, his penis against her belly. She reached down and took hold of it. "This thing is unsafe," she taunted him. "We need to put it away some-where . . . Put your fingers inside me." He reached around behind again and touched the wet place between her legs. "Inside," she said, no longer whispering. She took his hand and put it against her front, and guided his fingers down the line of her opening, and inside. "There. Right there, umm, yes. Don't be afraid of me, I won't break," she said. She leaned back on her hands, her breasts up as he gently moved his hand where she had put it. Tom was suddenly desperate to get inside her. She leaned forward and nudged him, and he fell down backwards and almost off the end of the bed. Straddling his hips, she took hold of his penis with both hands and bent it back, causing Tom an ecstasy of pain, but as she started to come down on him, she stopped when hot juice snapped out of him, and some went up her front, even hitting her chin. "Ohh," she said, "my poor little hot boy. You got that stuff on my front."

"I'm sorry," he said.

"I'm going to make you lick it off," she said, sounding vague, dreamy, half here.

He felt slightly abashed, but wasn't well enough versed to know that he was supposed to be ashamed. His penis wilted some and he felt a lessening of the tension to put it inside her. She lay on her back and spread the sticky liquid across her breasts and belly, aimlessly. He did as she suggested, licking her like an animal cleaning another animal, across the globes of her breasts and her belly, and even into the fur, and when he did so she arched her back and moaned and closed her eyes and it seemed less that she was playing with him. She urged his head down further and said breathlessly, "There, Tom, down in there."

Tom was less self-conscious at these things than he was in the preliminaries. He was so untutored in even the normal superstitions of sex that here he was more like an animal than a human. The only instruction he'd had was from animals, among whom the licking of genitals wasn't unusual. He almost liked the salty taste down there, but he definitely liked the way she moaned, which changed as he went on, from comfortable sounding to sounding more like she was in a fever of some kind, or having a scary dream. He raised his head, looked at her, and saw the shine across her skin, the little dampness at her brow, and it was as if he had her in his power. He had forgotten for the moment his own need to put his penis into her. With the tip of his tongue he caressed the little hard marble inside her.

She sat up and pushed him again. "Lie down. I'm going to show you something now." She held his penis, not moving, just holding it in the warmth of her hand, closing her eyes as if she was willing it to go hard again, and then lightly moving it as it went tighter. He didn't have the same helpless urgency as before, and she got up and crawled on top of him, enveloping him, her breasts squeezed up tight across his chest, and she kissed his mouth. Again he felt the strange shiver of her melancholy. "I can't let you do it. It's too big." She was using the vague teasing voice again, at once urgent and feigned, but then quickly she raised her hips and pushed it into herself. It felt warm and tight but not stunningly different until she began to move, rising and coming down, and this he liked very much. Her hair dangled down across his face, and he took hold of her buttocks and even felt down where his penis went into her.

He was quite sure that this wasn't a dream, only the thought drifted through his mind that he had been here before in a dream. Holding her bottom in his hands as she raised and slid down his shaft was the best thing that had ever happened to him. Her flesh seemed to loosen in his hand. *I can die now,* he thought. She chewed on his ear, making little noises that sounded almost but not quite like noises of frustration. She held herself up on her hands, her hair coming down around him in a shroud, and he put his hands on her breasts. Her mouth was open, panting, her upper lip coming away slightly so he could see her top front teeth glinting in the light. He began to push gently upward as she came down, causing her again to exhale with each thrust. A trickle of sweat slid between her breasts. He was amazed at how easy he felt, how casual, as if he had done this a thousand times before.

She pulled him over and soon he was lying in the cradle of her legs, propped on his elbows so he wouldn't crush her, and she laughed at his careful motions at first. "Come," she said. "Come on, Indian boy, you can do better than that." Somewhat irritated at her taunting, he pulled back and came into her more firmly, and she grabbed his buttocks with both hands and let them ride up and down. "Come on," she said, slowly turning her head from one side to the other, eyes closed. "Come on, my big Indian boy. Do away with me."

Questions, from the most trivial to very large ones, flashed through Tom's mind even as these wondrous events were occurring. Why did she call him that? She moved her legs up so that they crossed in the air, above his ass, and one of her fingers wandered into his anus. This both excited and frightened him, and now he did wonder: Is everything allowed? Absolutely everything? In the back of his mind was the fear that the door would suddenly open and the outside world would catch them at this. Deacon Miller drifted in, his face looking up through the ventilator, the thin black hair, the longish nose. For some reason, Tom saw the Reverend's face, too, the way it would always flush when he beat you with his belts or his riding whips, the way he breathed a certain way, heavy and regular — so heavy that at times it seemed like the whole room would fill with his breathing.

She was looking up at him with her eyes wide, as if in fear. "Oh," she said. And he was alarmed and almost stopped, and she said, "No, don't, you got me now, you got me," and she grabbed him by the neck and pulled him down and kissed him long and hard and yet somehow gently, moving her tongue around inside his mouth as he rocked back and forth on her. At the instant before his ejaculation, she turned her head to the side with an expression of terrible pain. "Oh God!" she said, sounding both angry and hurt, and then she repeated it, "Oh God!"

His ejaculation into her was a scary tumbling eruption of pleasure. When he pulled out of her and fell beside her on the bed, he heard himself laugh, but then again, without apparent reason, he felt the starburst of anger he'd felt moments before, only more strongly.

"Tom?"

He stared at her and had the strange sensation that they were both lost and drifting.

"Oh Tom," she said mournfully.

Sometime later she sprawled across him. "You got me," she murmured again, and soon fell asleep, dead weight across him, breasts crushed against him. One flesh.

♦

Before the earliest stirrings of morning, Tom turned and looked at the window curtain, which had ruffled slightly. He'd left the window cracked open so that he could hear outside. He had been having a very confused nightmare in which the Reverend was trying to kiss him. The Reverend had taken off Tom's clothes, taken down his shirt. The white curtain stirred again.

·17·

ON THURSDAY, Jake rode the train with Leonard LaFarge to Enid, hoping to visit a man there who Leonard said knew the real estate game.

The ride from Guthrie to Enid wasn't far in miles, but at Leonard's request they took the train instead of using the wagon — west thirty miles to Kingfisher, where they had to catch another train that was crowded and uncomfortable. The passenger cars were remarkably shabby, with mud, dents, and scrapes outside, bullet holes, broken windows, and aisles as dirty as a public street, stacked with luggage. All seats were taken in the four passenger cars, and they were forced to stand. Thousands of would-be settlers were still roaming around the newly opened territory, trying to find affordable pieces of land to lease before the worst of winter set in. Sharing their car were a group of Russians, a pack of young sunburned Irishmen who'd been on a track gang in Texas, one severely clean, straight-postured, black-clad German family, probably from Pennsylvania, and, sitting right across from them, seven prostitutes in brightly colored décolleté glory, their sharp perfume doing battle with other, less sweet smells in the packed car. As they traveled into the low, rolling Cherokee Outlet, the smoke of prairie fires wafted in the windows — fires set by settlers making early preparations for spring plowing, or flushing out rogue cattle herders who were still occupying Outlet lands.

Leonard and Jake stood at the back of the car, surrounded by sacks and boxes of household items jammed into filthy aisles, including a new "B" Hot Blast #7 that towered behind them, a huge stove with fancy nickel foot rails, capped off by a nickel swing top that looked like a horseracing trophy. Jake could see by the wired-on tag that the stove had been furnished by Master's Hardware in Little Rock — which in more normal times might have concerned him.

Leonard turned to Jake and said in a low voice, "Have you noticed the gamy young canaries next to us? Those Texas maidens can take you to the Great Beyond, I tell you. Alas for them, in this savage land."

Jake looked at him blankly, irritable because he had to stand. He wished that they'd just used the wagon. The conductor came through the car and called, "Settle down low in your seats as you approach South Enid! There'll be trouble there! Get below your window."

"What trouble?" Leonard called out. "We don't have a seat." Leonard had a naturally stagy, doleful voice, which caused some of the prostitutes to laugh at him.

"Better get down in the aisle," the conductor said. "They've been hitting every train going through South Enid."

A quick babble of questions in three or four languages went through the car as people slouched in their seats. The bosoms of the women were further emphasized as they scooted down. Leonard said to the conductor, "I'm accustomed to the normal leavings of boot mud and tobacco spittle, sir, but this car has stable droppings in it. Have you used it to haul cattle?"

Ignoring Leonard's question, the conductor jammed his heavy watch back into the pocket on his jutting belly. "Get down, all of you!"

"This martinet is serious," Leonard said toward the women, who laughed again. They seemed to think he was wonderful entertainment. "What are we in for — do you ladies know?"

"They throw things at the train every time it goes through," one of them said. "I've been through it a dozen times already."

"Sho nuf, hon," said another.

The youngest looking of the women, whose face and scrawny chest turned red when she spoke, said vehemently, "Well, you didn't *tell* me about *this!*"

"Oh no, hon, it's not that big a thing. They're just fussin over where to put the town site. Them in South Enid want the trains to stop there."

"And to think that three months ago there was nothing here but the chirp of the cricket, the lonely call of the meadowlark, the distant lowing of cattle," Leonard said. "Now we have twelve thousand and more of these mudheads camped in the pasture, fighting a civil war over property values." He took a bottle from his coat pocket and offered the ladies a drink, and they were soon passing it around, to the discomfort of the already uncomfortable German family sitting across the aisle. The Irish contingent, farther up, were joking and shoving and cuffing one another — boys afraid of women but trying to impress them.

Jake stared out the window. As the train curved around the prairie toward South Enid, he saw ahead what looked like a white squarish object close to the railroad track. Very close indeed. "Looks to me like there's . . . something on the track."

Leonard polished the bright red lipstick off his bottle with a handkerchief and offered Jake a drink, but Jake was looking intently out the window. "There's a house across the track."

"Across the track?" Leonard forgot the bottle in his hand, squinting out the window. "And a mob beyond it," he said wonderingly. "By God, there are thousands, and they don't look friendly."

The engineer laid on the whistle but he didn't slow down. "Prepare yourselves," Leonard announced to the car. "Those clod brains have put a house on the track!"

The German matron, who had a little pinched-up face, suddenly let forth with a thin high scream, unleashing confusion. Jake couldn't believe that the engineer wasn't at least slowing down. The thing across the track was not a shed or an outbuilding but a genuine two-room house, with a damn lot of lumber in it, sitting on two heavy beams.

The train blasted into the house at full throttle and lurched heavily. The Hot Blast stove in the aisle behind them tipped forward, crashing to the floor, its fancy fittings popping off in all directions. Leonard tumbled into the laps of the Texas whores and Jake went the other way, into the German family. The train pushed ahead, slowed, its wheels chewing through lumber, and the mob outside started pelting them with rocks and other stuff — heavy clods of dirt, cow patties both dried and fresh, and chicken heads flew at the car. Windows shattered. Women screamed, particularly the ones under whose dresses Leonard was trying to hide. The Irish boys took to the aisles and energetically fired back, trying to throw rocks and dirt and dung out the windows despite the cramped quarters, in the act breaking more windows and causing more damage. Jake was amazed at how many people had gathered to throw stuff at the train. All of South Enid appeared to have come out, some attacking, others sitting on makeshift chairs around fires, laughing and waving as the train went by, as if it was all just a picnic game.

"We'll be murdered!" Leonard declared from somewhere under a dress.

"If you don't get out from under there, darlin, I'm gonna charge you three dollars."

"Meingottinhimmel!" bellowed the German man, having been hit by a fresh patty.

"Yeiiii!" his wife again screamed.

They finally passed through the body of the mob, and for the remaining distance to the terminal in North Enid, passengers picked glass and dirt and dung off of themselves and out of their hair.

"Ladies, please!" Leonard said, emerging from his sanctuary and getting swatted on the head. "I'm trying to extricate myself. My God, you Texas girls are made for fighting, aren't you? Are there broken limbs? How many casualties have we taken?" He passed around the last of his bottle.

People got off the train at the Rock Island terminal, angry, dirty, excited, some with cuts and bruises. The engine had a window frame hanging around the headlamp. Jake and Leonard went off to a huge tent saloon to get a drink, and others trooped along with them — all of the women from Texas, several of the Russians, and the track gang, one of whose eyes was swollen up big as a coffee cup from being hit by a rock. A cold wind blew through the circus tent saloon, and customers hunched down in their coats and shawls. Leonard raised his drink and toasted, "To the day we learned the meaning of the 'rock' in Rock Island Line. May this ghastly day never be forgotten!"

"Aye! Hear, hear!" exclaimed the Irish boys, who stood nearby, remaining at a shy distance from the women.

"*I* sure won't," said the vehement, blushing young woman. "This is my *first* day as a whore, and somebody threw a *chicken* head down my dress. I coulda stayed home and had my *brothers* do that."

"Don't call yourself that, darlin. Say 'professional woman.'"

"My dear young lady," confided Leonard LaFarge. "If this is your first day, let me warn you away from the profession. My work has allowed me to become acquainted with the lives of numerous ladies of the night trade, and I know that it promises little."

"Well I *sure* ain't gettin no promises from my mean old daddy and my six brothers! Ever one of em eats off the same plate as *rattlesnakes.*"

Leonard lowered his voice. "You see those young Irishmen over there. You'll not find a better husband than an Irishman. They work hard, worry little, and can be trained to deliver their wages directly to their wives. The one with the swollen eye is an especially brave fellow. Why don't you make his acquaintance, offer him succor."

"I don't *want* a husband," she said emphatically, squinting her eyes angrily at Leonard. "Any man from now on tells me what to do has to *pay* me."

Leonard smiled anxiously. "But there are other ways. I know a woman who owns a restaurant. She makes four times what she could ever make in this line of business."

"Just who are *you* telling *me* what to do? You sound like some kinda jack preacher."

Leonard backed off another step. "Have it your way, my dear, but you'll be faced with vagabonds of all manner, with their stinking breath and slovenly behavior. You will sit on a bench against the wall and they will point at you, as though buying a lard hog. High-jackers, cowpunchers, bullwhackers, confidence men, cutthroats, refugees, thieves, saloon swampers — I assure you that after you have dealt with your first hundred, you'll yearn for the sweet company of your six brothers."

Her truculence melted a little. "What do *you* know about my brothers?"

"Darlin, don't listen to him," said the older woman, giving Leonard an angry look. "You leave her alone."

"As you will, madam," Leonard said.

He and Jake went outside, where hundreds of tents, spreading in every direction, flapped and bulged in the wind. North Enid for the moment seemed unaware of the railroad war. Hammers were pounding away at nails. Stacks of lumber and shingles were scattered through the broad dusty streets. Shielded from the wind by tents and paintless buildings, men huddled around fires, puffing on their pipes. Jake noticed that there were a few more women in town than last month. New signs were up, barbers' poles were in place. In spite of the depression, Enid was taking shape on the wind-blasted plain. They strolled through the burgeoning honk-a-tonk district, where tents and a few makeshift buildings boasted green baize tables and roulette wheels. A medicine man was giving his spiel to two boys and one haggard-looking Indian.

A storekeeper Jake knew saw him and hurried across the street. "Jake, where the hell you been? I want to order some goods."

"I'll come by when I can."

"What's going on at Dekker Hardware?"

"Why do you ask?"

"A man named Peters tried to get me to sign my property to em. I told him I deal with W. W. Jaycox."

"Good for you, Bill. I'd do the same thing."

"Well, my credit is good. Damnit Jake, you know that. Can you come in today? I'm flat out of stock."

"Soon. Maybe tomorrow."

They went to find a room at the Plain Talk Inn, where Leonard promptly went to sleep. Jake bought a bath. Cramped up in a little tub in not particularly warm water, he fell to worrying about Tom — whether he'd made it to Fort Smith, when he'd be able to catch a train out here.

At sunset they got in line at an outdoor food concession, this evening serving baked beans, dove, cucumber pickles, and sauerkraut. Everybody crowded into three bench tables under a tent roof, most of them gossiping about the railroad dispute. There were rumors that the cavalry was on the way. The war in fact was part game, part serious. No one had yet been killed, although the people of "Government Enid" were apparently undertaking ever more desperate acts to get the train to stop at the South station.

After supper, they walked down the well-worn dirt path to

South Enid, where Leonard's real estate informant, a man named Gus Wall, kept his office. There was a good deal of commerce between the two Enids despite the conflict. Near a creek they saw, about a hundred yards away, a group of men who were busy doing something to a small railroad bridge — twenty or thirty of them, busy as ants. A couple of men were climbing nearby telegraph poles, working on the wire. A lookout with a rifle noticed Jake and LaFarge, and they hurried on.

Jake had heard of Gus Wall, but hadn't met him. Wall had the reputation for being a sharp operator. Jake hunkered down in his coat. With nightfall the wind was getting cold. "Tell me more about him."

"Gus Wall's biography will have to be written on asbestos paper," Leonard said. "He could swallow nails and spit out corkscrews. But he knows what's going on." Leonard stopped. "This has to be it."

Against the crimson sky stood a clapboard shack with GEN-ERAL LAND DEVELOPMENT painted in large white letters on its side. A lamp was lit in the shack. They opened the door into a little room, unfurnished except for one small table in a corner and three ladderback chairs. Sitting at the table reading a newspaper was a short, stout man, as ugly as galvanized sin, with a several-day-old beard like dirt on his face and a nose like a failed potato hanging down over his mouth. A pistol lay on the table in front of him, and he glanced up quickly when they came in, as if deciding whether he needed to use the gun or not. His welcome was tepid, but Leonard hurried to break out a new pint bottle of labeled whiskey, which lightened Wall's mood somewhat. He found three tin cups.

Leonard tasted the whiskey and smiled benignly. "They almost killed us today coming in on the train. How'd this railroad dispute come about, Gus?"

Wall looked at the whiskey in his cup. "Rock Island struck a deal with some Cherokees, had em take their allotments near the track where North Enid is now. Soon as the Indians got clear title to the land, the railroad bought it right back so's they could speculate in prices. But the federals — secretary of the interior — got riled, told em no town site could be built within three miles of an allotment, and that wasn't the location of the town site up there, no way, this here's where it was." He pointed at his table. "Been at it ever since, fightin over which it'll be. We tried everything we could to get the train to stop here. Bunch of us got together and passed a law makin it illegal for a train comin through Government Enid not to stop. That didn't do no good, since it's hard to arrest the son of a bitch when he's going fifty mile an hour. So the government stepped in and told the railroad they had to pick up the mail here, they didn't have no choice. Railroad said okay, built a damn mail tree. Mail hangs in a sack, arm sticks out of the express car and grabs it, breaks the sack and spills it all over the goddamn ground most of the time, but they claim they're pickin it up."

Leonard rolled whiskey around in his mouth and swallowed. "Who'll win this conflict?"

"Government's gonna win," said Gus Wall, with a hint of a smile. "That's why I'm here instead of up there. You staying here or North?"

"North."

"If you walked trackside this evenin, you seen what they're doin. Can't get the son of a bitch to stop any other way, so they'll try a little more track modification. See if that bluffs em out." Wall looked up. "Course, I don't have nothin to do with it, but I figure the old boys that run this railroad up in Chicago will tell the government to go to hell until they start losin some money on the deal. It don't take too many derailed trains to amount to a good sight of money."

They had another shot of whiskey and talked, the wind whistling around the tiny shack, and Wall eventually asked Leonard what brought them.

"Jake has a couple of general questions about the real estate game." Leonard looked at Jake. "Jake, you want to do the talking?"

Jake had already decided his only chance of getting any answers was to go straight to the point, whether it was risky or not, so he didn't hesitate. "I work for a wholesaler who's trying to turn our customers' debts into land mortgages, both here in Oklahoma Territory and in the land that still belongs to the Indians."

"I know it."

Jake glanced at Leonard.

"Dekker Hardware?" Gus Wall said.

"How'd you know?"

"Some of your customers around here been tellin me about it. Mentioned your name as the regular salesman. Said another fellow was up here trying to get em to sign the mortgages. Some of em gettin pretty agitated about it."

Jake wasn't really surprised. Word traveled fast in a town that was still being built. "Have you seen those particular mortgage papers?"

Wall shook his head. "Nosir, I haven't, but I've heard them described."

"Do you think they're legal for real estate in the Indian territories?"

"Legal?" Wall smiled. "You askin me?"

"Just askin your opinion."

"You ought to answer that one," Wall said, looking at Leonard. "Ain't you the lawyer?"

Leonard fiddled with his cup. "It's against federal law for whites to hold or transfer land held by the tribes. I assume that after the tribes are broken up, the government'll try to restrict transfer of allotted land for a period of time — say a few years."

Wall stood up, took a step to the window in his office, and looked out. "Try to, yeah. That's the word. Course, you know well as I do that legal in this country is what works, illegal's what don't work. And you know how people are. They're going to have a hard time making 'illegal' or even 'restricted' stick when it comes to tradin land. You're about as like to tell a man he can't talk land as he can't talk horses. Indians much as whites. Some of these old Indians with big families get a big allotment, you give em that land and tell em they can't trade it — that's about like dealin them four aces and tellin em they have to fold now, come back and play later."

"I'd say it's more like giving them a stake and telling them to wait a while before they gamble with it," Leonard said.

"Indians I know ain't exactly what you'd call dyed-in-the-wool land traders," Jake said. "Their land always has been owned in common."

"They're learnin here pretty quick," Wall said. He was silent for a moment at the window, wind fingering through the cracks, ruffling the lantern flame. "Long and short of it, Mr. Jaycox, there ain't much chance that a white court of law will invalidate a mortgage signed by a debt holder to a white supplier or a white banker — and they'll all be white courts of law and white banks here pretty soon." He turned from the window and offered a smile, a thin-lipped gash across his homely face. "No. What I been thinkin about, tell you the truth, ain't whether some of these old boys working up syndicates and such will get away with it, but what they're aimin for. What they're gonna do with all that land."

"What do you think they're doing with it?"

Wall took a sip of whiskey. "I've been sitting out in my office here of an evening puzzlin over just that question. Now, I know that you can resell land, or lease it for farming. Lot of times these farmers who're desperate for a piece of anything to plug a crop into will pay more in one year's lease than you paid to buy the land. But that's just money, gentlemen. That ain't big money. There's some big special interests keepin up with the Dawes Commission. They ain't the types just to lease farmland."

Jake and Leonard eyed each other.

Gus Wall hesitated, still gazing out the window into the near darkness. "You know, there's a lot of people workin in that commission. Writin rules and exceptions to rules. And I've been hearing about interests — not just banks on both sides of the river, but interests from back east — who're keeping up with em and helping them do it practical."

"What interests?"

Wall turned from the window. "Let me ask you a question, Mr. Jaycox. Did your people at Dekker Hardware tell you to work hard in any particular areas getting these mortgages signed?"

This time Jake was surprised. He hesitated but decided to go ahead. "Yes, they did."

"Where at?"

Jake unfolded the piece of paper listing counties and areas that McMurphy had given him, and held it out. Wall put it on top of the newspaper on the table and studied it awhile. Eventually he looked up at Jake. "Anything about this seem peculiar to you?"

"Well . . . those areas aren't necessarily where the most debt is."

"Just say your boss don't give a damn about which areas have more and less debt. He's lookin to get certain land. Seems like he'd be lookin to get hold of good farmland, don't it? But this here list ain't where the most bottomland is. What do you reckon it might be?"

"Minerals?"

"Let me put it this way. I been hearing that some of the lawyer types over in Muskogee keeping up with the Dawes Commission are from New Jersey and Pennsylvania. And I've also been hearing about some men been roaming around the territory out here, drawing maps about where they figure oil might be. I know for a fact that there's already some land up here in the Outlet been bought or leased for that purpose."

"Yeah, and hasn't one outfit gone broke trying to extract oil?" Jake said skeptically.

Wall looked at Jake. "The question you're asking me is why are your people so interested in getting mortgages on the land. I'm tellin you that there are reasons you might not have thought of, besides farming and coal. And rock oil is one of them. I hear it's about played out in Pennsylvania, and there's some old boys have made a bundle of money on it up there. Might like to find some more of it. Tell you something else about the company that went broke up here trying to dig for it. I got interested and found out a few things about them. The curious thing ain't that they went broke." He raised his eyebrows. "It's how much money they had in their pocket before they *did* go broke. Gentlemen, we are lookin at a big bidness, and it ain't doin nothin but gettin bigger. If it does get started, it could put coal to shame."

Sitting in the shack talking, Jake had become more uneasy than he had been before he came. The conversation seemed to be drawing to a close and he stood up. "I guess we better be getting back. Thanks, Mr. Wall."

Wall took another long look at McMurphy's list and handed it back. "By the way, it's too bad about your old boss there at Dekker."

"What do you mean?" Jake said.

"Him being dead."

Jake's heart leapt in his chest. "Where'd you hear that?"

Wall squinted at him. "In the newspaper. Didn't you know about it?" He picked the paper off his desk and handed it over. PIONEERING FORT SMITH WHOLESALER FOUND DEAD;

POLICE SAY SUICIDE. Jake read quickly through the text: "... found this morning ... single bullet wound in the head ... son Ernest Dekker mourns his loss ..."

The news caught Jake completely unawares. He was stunned. He didn't know what to do or say, except to get outside the shack. He thanked Wall and walked out into the windy night, under the stars, where he hit the path at a near run, Leonard struggling to keep up with him.

"You all right? Where you going? Jake?"

"Telegraph office. I'll see you back at the hotel."

·18·

O N FRIDAY, Tom woke up remembering that he had to go to the train station in case Jake arrived today.

But here she was, on her side, breathing next to him, hair spread lushly across her shoulders, one breast peeking out from her folded arm.

He wanted just to keep watching her breathe, but he also wanted to wake her up and talk. Round-faced and young in her sleep, she reminded him of the photograph he'd seen in the album in Mr. Dekker's parlor. Her eyes briefly came open and she rolled onto her back, groaned, for a moment staring at the ceiling before closing them again. People were moving around the boarding house, and he worried about Mrs. Peltier coming in to clean the room. She would kick them both out if she caught them here together.

"What are you looking at?" Sam said, eyes still closed.

"You."

"Don't."

His eyes fastened on her sleep-dried lips.

She glanced at him with slight malevolence and turned onto her side, away from him.

Waking up with her presented a new problem of decorum. There might be certain things you were supposed to do and not do. He wanted to talk to her, but after you slept with a woman, what did you talk about? She showed no signs of wanting to talk about anything at all, so he eventually stole away to the bathroom.

He came out and put on his pants and walked around the room hoping to wake her. Still she slept, and he sat down on the edge of the bed and watched her for some time longer.

She was frowning and making noises of fear, and he finally reached out and touched her shoulder. She flinched as if she'd been bitten by something, and her green eyes opened.

"Were you having a bad dream?"

"Ohh," she said, rubbing her face.

"I have those sometimes."

"I'll bet you do," she muttered.

Tom stood up and walked over to the window while she staggered out of bed, went to the toilet closet, and shut the door. Then she came out and poured some water from Jake's old pitcher with a rose on the side and desultorily washed her face. Drying it off with a frayed white towel, she gave him a little look. Tom couldn't stop watching her. It was hard enough not watching her when she had clothes on. She glanced at her face in the cracked mirror. "God, I look like last year's bird's nest."

She poured the remaining water into a glass, drank it, and put down the glass. She opened her own eyes wide and stuck her chest out at him. "You just sitting there with your big eyes. Leave a lady some privacy."

"Tell me . . . Tell me about your past," he said.

"Oh, Tom." She turned back and glanced at herself again in the mirror. "It's too early in the morning."

"I want to know more about you," he said.

She picked up Jake's hairbrush and ran it through her hair. "You think you want to know about me, Indian boy."

"Why do you call me that?" Unexpectedly, and for little reason, Tom found himself pitching headlong into a dismal mood. Ten minutes before, he had been in bliss just watching her sleep.

She brushed her hair vigorously and turned around. "I have a lot on my mind. When will Jake be back in town?"

"I'm going to try to meet him at the station, but I don't know when he's coming. Do you want to start a business with Jake?"

"Maybe," she said blandly.

Although he tried not to show it, Tom felt desperate. What had changed her from last night? She was swerving away from him at just the moment when he was hungriest to know more about her.

He wanted to grab her by the shoulders and shake her and make her like she had been last night. He had to know about her. "Did you go to school?"

"Oh, Tom!" She looked exasperated. "All right, you win. I don't like prattling about the past, so listen fast."

Tom sat on the edge of the bed, and she talked while she moved around and quickly dressed. "My mother was a business-woman. She started out with nothing and she worked up to own-ing a hotel in St. Louis. Her work kept her busy. She didn't have much to do with me. She was a strong woman, and a lot of people counted on her, but her work kept her away from me." She looked at Tom. "How is it they say it? She never much talked to me as a daughter."

"Who was your father?"

"I don't know. That's one of the things she didn't discuss."

With her underthings now on, she walked over to the window and stared out. "She sent me off to Chicago to school when I was seven years old. Mrs. Adams' Ladies School," she pronounced as if the words tasted bad. "After that there were other schools. I was a wicked child, but she paid them well enough to keep me, as long as I didn't burn the place down. Which I did try to do once. Actu-ally twice, at different places." She walked over and picked up her dress. "You ever try to burn down that orphanage?"

"No."

"Maybe you should have." She put the dress on over her head. "Anyway, my mother wasn't interested in my coming back home. A few times I visited, but she didn't want me there. I almost for-got what she looked like. When I grew up . . ." She hesitated for a moment. "I wrote her a letter and condemned her. I 'disowned' her, if you can do that. I became an orphan by choice."

As Sam talked, she turned farther away until he couldn't see her face. "She seemed to be satisfied with that. She never insisted that we meet, never tried again, and I was too young and con-ceited to give in, even when I felt like it. But she kept supporting me, sending money to an account, and I never had the strength to turn it down. There was a lawyer-guardian, a man I hated al-though I didn't know him. There I was, taking money and hating her for it. Maybe if I had turned it down, I would have realized younger . . ."

After a moment Tom prompted, "Realized — ?"

"I'm talking, you just listen."

He could hear the huskiness in her voice, but he couldn't see her face. "I wanted to change my name, but I was too young to do it legally. I grew up, I got more reckless. I had wild friends, school friends — people who were mostly well off with money. We thought we were doing things that no one had ever done before. Drinking, hurrying around, using opium. We had séances. We became vegetarians, took the water cures, whatever new thing came along. I guess you don't know about those things, do you, Indian boy?" She turned around and looked at him almost angrily. She made a dismissive gesture. "Anyway, that's about all."

"Did your mother's first name begin with *M*?"

She looked puzzled. "How'd you know that?"

"I saw a photograph of a child who looked like you," he said.

"Really."

"In a family album."

She waited for him to explain.

"At Mr. Dekker's house I saw a photograph of a little girl who looked like you."

Her eyes fixed on him, unblinking.

"I went there Monday night. Jake asked me to see if he was back in town from St. Louis."

As Tom told her the whole story, she looked increasingly puzzled. "It said what?"

"It said 'M. King's daught.' And then it said something like 'Left b' — the letter *b*."

"Can you go over that one more time?"

He repeated the details, start to finish, from the moment Ernest Dekker gave him the nickel and told him to deliver the telegram to Jake. As he retold it, she seemed to turn pale, lips slightly open, and she wandered into the other room and wandered back. He got up and started making the bed.

"I'd like to see that photograph," she said.

Tom felt nervous and despondent. Someone walked down the hall outside the room. "That man who shot at us in Violet Springs is in town, Sam. Like I said, I saw him at the store. I'm worried about Jake arriving here without any warning."

"So Jake is on his way back here?" she said vaguely.

"I'm sure he will be as soon as he learns about Mr. Dekker."

They talked some more as she helped him finish the bed, but they were both preoccupied. It was time for him to go to the train station. When the coast was clear, they hurried down the stairs and out the back door. "I'm staying at the Main Hotel," she said. "Room three-oh-three. Come after dark. Don't fail me, Tom."

◆

The station still smelled of the flood, of dead fish and river silt. Because of its closeness to the store, Tom decided not to hang around there between trains. He checked the schedule, got the arrival times of the three trains that Jake could be on, and promptly left. With nothing to do but wait for the first arrival, he decided to walk down along the river.

The air was cold and damp. New huts made of driftwood and scraps of tin had already been set up here and there along the Arkansas, amid the willow and scrub trees, and there were people fishing. Slowly walking upriver along the shoreline, looking through the fog across to the Choctaw Nation on the shore beyond, Tom felt unsettled. Last night was like a wonderful dream, another of many unbelievable events in his new life. In less than a month, he had seen a man hanged, a hotel float away in a torrent, and the land turn to water; he had seen a substantial business turn into a brooding empty hulk abuzz with rumors and secret dealings; he had read newspapers and a novel; he had found a dead man sitting in his house and been chased by a murderer in the company of a beautiful woman; he had bathed with this woman and made love with her and slept all night with her and talked with her about her life. There seemed to be no end to vivid and strange experiences, yet the curve of Tom's memory kept leading him into his past, pulling him through the curtains back into his drab life before the flood, as if there was something important that he'd left behind in the backwoods of the Nation. Looking across the river, he imagined that he could almost see the building in the fog — improbably large, looming tall with its fifteen chimneys and two-story arched brick arcades in the front, porches on both the first and second floors, its high windows with broken shutters like rotten teeth.

He didn't just hate the academy. It wasn't that simple. After all, it was a privilege to grow up doing something besides farm chores, a privilege to learn to read and have a chance to sharpen his mind. He knew that to be true. Yet staring across the river into the mirage, Tom could not forget that it was Friday, the day of his reckoning, the day that every other minute of every other day at the orphanage pointed to, when the implacable, austere, fixed mouth read his sins, large and small, and told him to take off his shirt and kneel at the post. Tom thought about what Sam had said about taking her mother's money, about not being strong enough to turn it down. He had been the same way with Reverend Schoot's sins and punishment. He did not believe in them, he did not accept them, but he took them even when he was smart enough and physically large enough not to take them. The Reverend had his unbending certainty and his cunning and his guns. When boys escaped Bokchito, they always ended up back there — either that or they would be reported dead. You will never get away. That's what he had always told himself.

He turned and walked along upriver. There was a surprising amount of activity in the strip of scrubland between the rows of tracks and the river. The shanties on Coke Hill had escaped the flood. He smelled coal and wood burning in open fires. A baby cried somewhere, a mother fussed at kids. There were little camps of hobos — men with the distant, disengaged eyes of perennial wanderers.

An old man was fishing with a cane pole near a wrecked boat dock; a black woman, who looked nearly as old as he, stood nearby, also fishing. She baited his hook for him. The old man appeared to be blind, or nearly blind, and Tom was surprised when he turned toward him and said, "What are you doing here?"

"Just walking," Tom said.

The old man blinked his clouded eyes and smiled a little. "Bet ye wonder why an old blind man still goes fishin this time of the year."

"No sir . . ."

"Well, do ye or don't ye?" He smiled again. "I'll tell you why. Time you get this old, you don't know whether you'll see the spring. I'm the oldest white man on the frontier."

Tom almost believed it, by the look of the old man's face, wrinkled and savaged by time, eyes with a blanked-over silvery haze.

"I'm near a hundred year old," he said.

"Tellin the trut," muttered the old black woman. "He de oldest white, I de oldest colored. We a pair."

"Ye a white man or a Indin?" the old man asked. When Tom didn't answer him immediately, he turned to the black woman. "What is he?"

She squinted at Tom. "Cain' rightly say. He well favored, though."

"So are ye a Indin or not?"

"Part Indian," Tom said.

"Well, good," the old man said. "We got that settled." He stood there for a minute, sensing his pole, then pulled up his line. "I got any bait on here?"

"Doin all right," the old woman said.

"Know where I sleep at night?" the old man asked Tom.

"No sir," Tom said.

"In the fort."

"Which fort?"

"Can't ye see the fort behind you?"

Tom turned around. "No . . ."

The old man pointed up the hill. "Right there, see those twenty-five-foot rock walls? See those towers on the ends?"

"Took de walls down," the old woman muttered, as if she'd said it many times before.

"Yes," the old man said, "they sure did. They took the walls down. And I was here before they ever put em up! I was here when there was nothing but a timber fort. I lived through it. I was fifteen year old when they come through St. Louis roundin up boys to be in the army. My daddy sold me to the army for two dollars. This was before the War Between the States, before the Mexican War, before any goddamn war except the British. They brought us up here on barges, a hundred of us. Give us uniforms. Had to git up at four-thirty in the morning and stand in the parade ground, march around and do exercises accordin to this little Blue Book, they called it. Had to defend the frontier!"

"You did?"

"Did what?"

"Have to defend the frontier."

The old man burst out laughing. "From what?"

"I don't know — Indians?"

"I thought ye said *you* was a Indin?"

"I'm part Indian," Tom said again.

"What type of Indin would you partly be?" the old man asked.

"I don't know."

"Well, come over here and I'll tell you. I can read faces."

Tom didn't move.

The old woman sighed. "Ain' cotchin no fish today. Still too muddy." She glanced over at Tom and shook her head. "He won't hurt ya, don't worry."

The old man held out his hands and when Tom moved over he touched his face, the ends of his fingers gently moving across cheekbones, forehead, chin. While the fingers played over his face, the air seemed to Tom to go strangely quiet, even the sounds of the river receding.

The old woman glanced over and said wryly, "He a dangerous type?"

The old man dropped his hands and went back to fishing, as if he had suddenly lost interest. "Most of em died," he said sadly. "We had slow fever and malaria worse'n they do now. Cholera. Smallpox — they give that to us on purpose. Took us all to what they called the longhouse and inoculated us with it to git it all over with at once. Our officers was drunkards, to a man, ever god-blessed one of em. Did nothin but drink, some of em. They had parties and balls, and more balls and parties. Seem like every night. The most Indins I seen was the ones they invited to them parties! They'd be in there just a-dancin around like a bunch of wheelin windmills. Didn't invite the enlisted men to the parties, nosir, they invited the god-blessed Indins instead! Said they was civilized Indians. Hoped they'd bring purty women, ye see, since there wasn't much in the way of white women around. All us enlisted men could do was hide in the shadows and watch the officers and Indins having a good time, peekin in the windows like little boys — Indins, Indin women, maybe a coupla white women would be in there, and us with no women a-tall."

"You makin up for it in your old age," the old woman sighed.

"It weren't healthy livin like that!" the old man said vehemently. "You know what us boys lived for out here on the wild frontier?"

"What?"

He turned his silvery eyes toward Tom. "Mail. That's what. Goddurn mail. That's what your brave boys on the frontier thought about. Messages from the outside world. Any kind of god-blessed message, they just couldn't wait to git it. Me, I never got no mail," he said.

"Nary a stitch," the old woman said.

"I seen others like me die from not gettin no mail. But I lived, mail or not! Lived to help build the rock fort. I was still in the army then, ye see. I stayed. Don't know why. Just did. Stayed right here. Was the only one to live through it. We built the rock fort — biggest, shining, most beautiful thing you ever did see. Hundreds of tons of limestone. Mortar — lakes of it! Fort Smith! It cost the U.S. Treasure aplenty, they was shippin gold out here by the bar-relful to pay for it. Guard towers on the ends reaching up to the clouds. Big parade ground. Took us years to build it. Officers' quarters — that jail up there was the officers' quarters, and I helped build it. And ye know what?"

"What?" Tom was genuinely interested.

"About the time we got her built, the fancy boys up in Wash-ington decided it wasn't no reason for her after all, and they told us to tear her down again. Yessir. That's when I quit em. Decided if they was fool enough not to know whether to build a fort or tear it down, I wasn't workin for em no longer."

"Sho did," the old woman said.

"I stayed in the neighborhood." He sniffed. "Farmed. Raised cotton in the bottoms right up there around the bend. Got re-venge, too," he added portentously.

"Revenge?"

He beckoned for Tom to come closer. He had a smile of sheer wickedness on his sunken-jawed face. "C'mere. Come close, lemme tell you what I did."

Tom took a step closer, and the old man reached out and put a hand on his shoulder. "I built a house."

Tom smelled his papery old breath. "House?"

"Yeah! Built her with the rock they tore outa that fort. Used the spare mortar they had done left. Used the wood casements they was about to let rot. I built the purtiest blessed house that ever was. How do you like them biscuits?"

"That's nice," Tom said.

"Well, damn right it is. It's what I mean when I say I sleep in the fort. Take it from the oldest son of a bitch on the frontier, my young friend: revenge is sweet." He cackled. "Sweetest revenge that is! Just ponder that, Mr. Indin. I've got some serious fishin to do."

"What kind of Indian am I?"

The old man smiled worriedly. "Well, I reckon you'll have to find out yourself." He pulled out his hook. "How's my worm?"

"Look fine," the old black woman sighed. "No fish want him, though. River's still too high."

Tom had a while to wait, and he walked on, up one of many trails to the army graveyard on the hill beyond Judge Parker's gallows. He walked among the small, weathered, older grave markers, and among the more recent graves of Civil War soldiers. Graves reminded Tom of the basement at the academy. He walked on quickly toward Coke Hill. Many of the people who lived in the shanties scattered around the hill were colored — blacks and Indians, bloods of all sorts — living in thrown-together structures made of driftwood, sticks, rags, old boards, tin. Smoke floated slowly in lumpy coruscations in the quiet damp air. He went toward the few "real" houses on the hill, which were old and musty smelling, with boards bending out and holes in roofs. At the corner of a building a horse stood with his ribs sticking out like a washboard. This oldest part of town, near where the fort had been in the old days, was inhabited by blind poverty.

He went back to the station for the first train in from the territory. Jake wasn't on it. Tom left and wandered the riverbank for several more hours, then returned for the second arrival and again was disappointed. The last train was due to come in after nine o'clock that night, plenty of time for him to go back to Mrs. Peltier's for supper. But he didn't look forward to the prospect of answering questions that the men were likely to put to him. He continued to fear that Mrs. Peltier would have little sympathy for someone without a job and that she might ask him to leave the boarding house.

Back on the riverfront, tired and hungry, he made a nest in the weeds and took a nap. He slipped into a vivid dream about trying to build a house out of the academy building, trying to take bricks out of the walls and carry them through a dark forest to his site; but each time he went for more bricks, the Reverend was there, right beside him, marking his name down in the book, and the bricks wouldn't be pulled from the walls . . .

Tom woke up shivering in the cold night, sat up, and looked across a moonlit ribbon of river. He walked over to meet the last train out of Oklahoma Territory. It didn't show up, and the stationmaster told him that there'd been a big wreck just south of the Enid station.

"Railroad war," he said grimly, and proceeded to look busy. The next train coming from that direction, via Red Fork, was at eleven o'clock Saturday morning.

When he walked out of the station, a boy came gliding up to him in the dark on a soft-tired bicycle. "You Tom Freshour?"

Tom nodded.

"Been lookin for you all day. Telegram. Can you read?"

"Yes."

He gave Tom a yellow envelope, and Tom read the telegram in light coming through the door.

WHAT HAPPENED KEEP YOUR EARS OPEN ABOUT MR D
BE CAREFUL WILL BE BACK AS SOON AS I CAN GET
THERE JAKE

He sat down on a bench, holding it in his hand. He was relieved to hear from Jake, relieved to know for sure that he was coming. It was the first message from afar, from anybody, that Tom had ever gotten in his life — except for the yearly Christmas letter from the Presbyterian Mission sent to everybody at Bokchito — and the mere fact of it, addressed to him alone, made him feel good. He understood what the old fisherman had meant today about the soldiers yearning for mail. He looked up the hill above the station, where lights burned in several windows of the Dekker building, lights even from the top floor. He thought of the old man, dead in the chair beside his bed.

He thought of Sam.

She'd invited him to come to her room tonight. He had grown uneasy about Sam, although his urge to see her outweighed it. The more he was with her, the more uncomfortably unlike her he felt. She was so far beyond him — older, a woman from the city, a woman of experience — why would she care about him?

Lightheaded from hunger, he walked through the streets into the lobby of the Main Hotel, with its legion of empty wooden chairs all lined up like soldiers, past the hard gaze of the clerk at the front desk, up the wide staircase to the third floor. He tapped on her door. No answer. He tapped again. Finally he tried the door and it was open. The room was lighted by a single lamp sitting on a dressing table in front of a mirror. Sam was sitting there, completely still, in front of it.

♦

As he approached her, she remained sitting at the straight-backed chair in front of the mirror. She glanced at him without turning around. "The boy made it back." Something was stuck into the mirror's frame with the lamp just in front of it. She was wearing an ivory-colored dressing gown.

Tom walked up to her and could see that it was the photograph from Mr. Dekker's album.

"Is it you?" he asked.

Sam stared at the picture. She seemed to imitate the child's expression unconsciously, and her face looked eerily the same. Her eyes were shiny in the immediate glow of the lamp.

She continued to look at it. "What do you know about your mother, Tom?" she asked.

Tom didn't particularly like talking about mothers and fathers. It was like talking about how old he was. He knew nothing about it, and it made him feel stupid.

She waited. "Can't you answer me?"

"Well, I have a mother. Or had one. I wasn't born in the orphanage . . ."

"I didn't think you were born from a pumpkin. But then this *mother* of yours was gone forever, and your father was probably gone before forever." Her eyes narrowed. "And you became a little Christian Indian. After fifteen years of never seeing her, never knowing her name, never knowing if she's an Indian or a white woman, is she still your mother? Was she ever your mother, really?"

"I don't think my mother's alive."

"She might be. And would you protect her? Let's say she walked in that door and I threatened her, would you protect her from me?"

"I shouldn't have to protect her from you."

She snorted at him. "You talk like a lawyer."

Her mood was quickly spreading over him like a bruise. She seemed careless and angry.

"You don't get knocked off course, do you, Tommy? You're all worked up inside, but you act so stiff and straight and young. At least you do now. And look at you. Look at yourself! That was one thing your mother gave you. She must have been a beautiful woman, Tommy. Everything's new. You're excited. You're free, you're out, like a child in springtime. But life starts getting to you. One of these days, Mr. Whipping Boy, you might just throw the account book out the door, like our storekeeper did."

Her eyes had wandered from him back to the photograph stuck in the mirror frame. "There's such a lot of tears and sentiment about children. People cry and moan about them. They worry about if they're with their mothers, or if their fathers are alive, or whether they have a nice Christian orphanage to live in, and when they die, they worry about whether their little souls have flitted up to heaven where they belong. Did you ever think, Tommy, that the children would be better off without our sentiment and tears?" Her eyes played across the photograph. She took a deep breath. "Forget it. Don't listen to me. I feel Irish when I drink a little. I begin to sound like my mother. I saw her drunk. A couple of times. She was like a different person. All her proper English accent forgotten. As Irish as the day is long. It was her best-kept secret."

She sighed and stood up and put on a tired smile. "You must be hungry. I have plenty of dinner left — I didn't eat much. You don't mind eating after me, do you?" A small table on wheels with a white tablecloth and several dishes stood against the wall. When he hesitated, she turned and looked at him directly, her back illumined in the lamp, her front dark. "Go on and eat," she said. "Don't start looking at me."

She took him by his arm, guided him over, and sat him down. There was a whole baked chicken, potatoes, stuffing, green beans, pie, a fresh loaf of bread. She brought over the other chair and sat down opposite him, served him food, and poured both of them some wine. He ate hungrily but self-consciously. He was grateful to her for the dinner, but as she sat there drinking and watching him, he felt like a boy who had accidentally blundered into an adult occasion.

She offered him a glass. "Would you like wine?"

He tasted it — another first — and shuddered. It was intriguingly terrible, and he sipped again.

"Why'd you turn against your mother?" he asked her.

"She was a madam, Tom. Her hotel was a casino and whorehouse. Some of them were younger than me, you know. Her girls. When I was fifteen, I was in St. Louis and visited the hotel without her knowing about it. I met a girl and started talking to her. She thought I wanted to work there. She was thirteen years old and already a veteran." Sam looked tired. "I was almost never in St. Louis. She kept me away. I was supposed to stay in Chicago, where people didn't know about my mother. I was supposed to become a perfect lady."

She drank the rest of the wine in her glass and stared toward the soft gaslight coming through the window. "I grew up in Chicago. The young ladies I knew in Chicago got married or they quickly became old maids, hiding in their fathers' houses: the sheep and goats got separated, but as far as I was concerned they were all headed for the slaughter. My acquaintances became less respectable. I didn't want to get married. I didn't want to sit in parlors with my finger crooked around a teacup handle, talking about the weather. I didn't want to be a schoolteacher. I wanted to be out in the world — with a business of some kind, but that didn't seem possible. I became what they call a sporting woman."

She gave him a pale smile. "After my mother died, I'd seen enough of that life to understand why she kept me away. I started thinking that maybe I'd been unfair to her, but it was too late to do anything about it. Anyway, she left me what remained of her estate. I was her only child. She had no one else."

Another wince went across her face when she looked at him. "So. There you have the long life of Samantha King up to 1894. But the past is a bucket of ashes, Tommy. Now I can do something in the world, and I will, whether I'm a woman or not. Whether I have a past or not. I will."

"What's a 'sporting woman'?"

"Oh Tommy, I took money from men. I wasn't a whore exactly, but I did."

He felt a little dizzy, from her strange vehemence and from the wine. "Why?"

Sam's jaw tightened, her eyes flashed on him with jade intensity. "Don't act stupid, Tommy. Be ignorant, but don't act stupid."

Abashed by her fierceness, he didn't respond.

For a moment she looked into her own thoughts, then her eyes focused on him again. "Why do you put down your fork when you talk?"

"We were taught to," he said.

"Well, for heaven's sake," she said irritably, "you'll starve to death." She rose and began pacing. She seemed restless and preoccupied. But after a while she turned, and with a purposeful smile said, "Enough of that. Do you want to take a bath?"

She went into the bathroom and shut the door.

He walked to the window and looked out on the neat row of gaslights down the avenue. He continued to explore the glass of wine with sips, waiting for her to come out. In the novel Tom had read that week, a sophisticated, evil man was always standing by fireplaces and windows with a glass of wine, but Tom wasn't a sophisticated anything. His feeling of how much older Sam was, how much more experience she'd had, was deepened by her story. The more he knew of her, the more formidable she became. The door opened and she swooped back in, her dark hair down around her shoulders. "Do you want to take a bath? There's plenty of hot water."

The tiled bathroom was huge, the tub was the largest he'd ever seen. Tom was awed by the hot water gushing out of the spigot. He'd heard of "running hot water" but could not believe the profusion of it. Hurriedly, he took off his clothes and got into the tub after it was filled. She washed his shoulders and back with sweet-smelling soap.

She knelt down and washed around the front of his neck and chest and down around his belly, smiling at him and giving his wine-numb lips a little kiss. "You have no idea what a lady-killer you could be."

"Lady-killer?"

"I want to keep you for my own, Tommy." Her face came close, and the intimacy of the moment was overwhelmingly sweet to him — the closeness of her face with the steam on her glowing skin, her breath on him. "You don't know that you're beautiful, do you?" she said softly.

Tom smiled awkwardly, embarrassed and excited at once.

But as she rubbed the soap down past the water on his belly and on his penis, it was already hard. The nightgown was falling down from one shoulder, revealing the globe of her right breast. "I think I'll join you." She stood, took it all the way off, and remained there as his eyes feasted on her, then she stepped into the tub and sat down slowly in front of him, actually between his legs. The water rose all the way to the rim. He loved her smooth back and the feel of her buttocks between his thighs. She leaned against him, pushing him against the tub, the two of them lying back, her breasts tipping up out of the water. She wiggled slightly against him. He glanced around at the huge bathroom, the gleaming brass fixtures, and his partial dizziness again made him uneasy. The wine.

She laid her head back on his chest and said softly, "You're not like other men. I hate the way most of them act, the little cocks. As if they knew everything, as if they *owned* everything — women included. Their possessiveness makes me sick ... What's that against me?"

"Against you?"

"That thing I feel."

"Nothing." He scooted back.

"It feels like something to me." She completely turned around, sloshing water over the tiles, and reached out, taking him again first in one hand, then putting both hands around it, holding it very gently and moving her hands up and down in the water. She leaned over and put her mouth down around the tip of it, at the moment protruding from the water. He closed his eyes, and when he opened them she had slid her mouth down it until her face was under water. She came up for air but kept her mouth around the tip of it before going down again. Tom shut his eyes.

In a few minutes they stepped out and quickly dried off, and she got a bottle of oil and put it all over him, neck to toes, saving his penis for last, which she liberally and slowly anointed. Finally finished, she handed him the bottle to use on her. He did as she had done, using both hands, starting at her shoulders and moving down her breasts and belly and thighs. She put the nightgown around her shoulders, leaving the front open, went in and lay down on the bed. On the way out of the bathroom, Tom passed a full-length mirror and stopped. It was the first time he had ever looked at his own erection in a mirror, and he was oddly excited by it. Yet again, the luxury and spaciousness, or something else here, made him feel edgy. Maybe it was wine: he didn't like the distanced feeling.

"Yes, you have a fine one," she said lazily from the bed. "Did you ever use it on anybody before me?"

"No." He almost laughed. The dark wooden headboard loomed above the bed.

"Why not? What about one of those boys at the orphanage?"

Tom did laugh now, one gawky burst.

"I'll bet they all tried to get their hands on you."

He came over and lay beside her on the bed, propping his head on his elbow. "Another boy, you mean?"

"Why not? I loved a woman once."

He pulled back. Women and women? He remembered a mare at Bokchito that would sometimes cover other mares when she got into a certain mood, as if she were a stallion. And of course some of the boys did do things to each other, at risk of a severe judgment.

"Who was she?"

"Oh, it wasn't for long." She reached out and lightly touched the back of his shoulders with a languid look of concern. "What kind of people ran that crazy orphanage?"

"What?"

"Was it the teachers?"

"The Reverend was the only teacher. The other teachers who came to work there always quit after while. None of them stayed more than a few months." Tom tried to sound dismissive, hoping she wouldn't ask too many such questions.

"Why'd they quit?"

"Maybe the place was too melancholy for them."

"Melancholy?"

"It's so far away from everything." Tom kept trying to signal by his tone that he didn't want to talk about it.

"Did the Reverend do funny things with the boys?"

"No."

"But he did this," she said, the palm of her hand still resting on his shoulder, her fingers touching his back. Her tone was almost casual. As if it was that simple, as if he could just say "yes" and that would be all there was to it.

Tom was suddenly angry. It swarmed into him so abruptly and with such force that it was almost like a blow to his head. Her questions, her seeming casualness, the way she was directing him as she must have directed other men, the tension he always felt in her presence, had felt from the first morning he saw her, the unceasing desire and anticipation, the fact that it was Friday, reckoning day — whatever the causes, his mood turned instantly sour, and he saw himself tearing the hotel room apart, crashing the table into the mirror and kicking over the furniture.

But he didn't, of course. He didn't. He just lay there on the bed staring up at the ceiling, the sudden rage making him feel barren, blank, hopeless.

Remembering.

Not the beatings but being locked in the basement for three or four days at a time with nothing but scraps to eat and bugs crawling over him, while he tried to sleep in that place of endless blackness, where day and night were almost indistinguishable; where, after a while, nothing made sense.

"What is it?" Her face floated close over his.

Tom realized that he didn't trust her. He felt out of his element, like a boy, a child out of place in her fancy hotel room. He had to leave.

"Tom, what is it?"

"I'm sorry," he said, sitting up on the end of the bed. "I have to go."

"What did that man do to you, Tom?"

"Nothing!" Again the anger hit him so hard that he wanted to strike out.

"It's a wonder you didn't die from this, you know. Your back's been turned into a sea of scars."

He held up both hands in front of him as if to fend off blows. "I don't want to talk about it." He got up and went to the bathroom and put on his clothes. In the bathroom mirror his own face looked as if it belonged to someone else. He had a dizzying urge to make some connection with what he knew, with his past — to talk to Hack or find Joel or someone. Anyone.

He left quickly, out the door and down the hall. Before he knew why, he was running in the middle of the tracks down the broad avenue toward the bridge.

· 19 ·

J AKE WAS LYING AWAKE in a narrow cot in the first light of
Friday morning, after a night of trying to sleep with the news
of Mr. Dekker fresh on his mind, when the walls of the Plain
Talk Inn began to shake. There was a ripping sound and a
tremendous crunch and an unearthly metallic shriek, and he
started up from the edge of the cot, tipping it, causing the whole
precarious torture device slowly, gracefully, to fall to the floor.
Earthquake? he wondered, struggling to get up.

When he and Leonard got out into the street, North Enid was
in general turmoil, and the talk was running fast and loose. It
seemed that the good citizens of Government Enid had caused a
train wreck. An engine and twelve cars had been scattered around
like toys, throwing out large quantities of wheat, lumber, and
pressed oil. It hadn't been a passenger train, but according to rumors flying up and down the streets, at least twenty people had
been killed. It later turned out that only two people had been
killed, but North Enid wasn't in a mood to be accurate about such
things. By the time the sun was all the way up, a crowd was having
a spontaneous town meeting in the street, with aroused citizens
talking about drafting an army for self-protection against Government Enid. People in Government Enid, rather than sulking
around guiltily, were said to be having their own meeting, openly
debating what to do next to show their further appreciation to the
Rock Island Line.

"These poor fools will think war if an army of Pinkertons shows up," Leonard commented. The telegraph line had been cut, businesses were closed, and the whole place had gone haywire, with people running around like ants from a burning log. While looking for somebody to hitch a ride with back to Guthrie, Jake and Leonard heard a different version of the wreck from everybody they talked to.

They caught their ride at McKenzie's Livestock Corral, where an anxious meat purveyor was hooking up a team of six horses to a big old drayage wagon, stacked with slaughtered carcasses that he was rushing to Guthrie before they went bad for lack of the daily shipment of ice from Texas. It was the kind of wagon that was often pulled by oxen, open but with high sides on the bed. It could haul ten thousand pounds, and the driver didn't mind having a couple of extra riders, as long as they weren't from Government Enid. Leonard took a seat next to the driver; Jake rode in the back with the carcasses, bouncing and rattling and jerking around with a couple of melting blocks of ice and a growing puddle of meat juices. A thirty-mile-an-hour wind raked down from the northeast.

"Leonard! You want to go with me to Fort Smith?" Jake yelled.

"No," Leonard yelled back, holding tightly to the seat. "Much more of this and I'll be in the same condition as your friends back there! I've traveled the entire world, short of the polar extremities —"

"What?" yelled the meat purveyor.

"I've lost a taste for travel! Even Fort Smith seems a great distance."

"I *need* you, Leonard! I need a lawyer!" Jake yelled as a carcass whanged into his leg.

"Fort Smith is infested by lawyers! Go to any saloon."

The meat purveyor glanced at him sourly. "You a lawyer?"

"I am, sir."

The man's grimace deepened and he didn't speak again for the entire trip.

Jake eventually found a way to hold on to the side and not be thrown around so much, but the heavy carcasses couldn't be prevented from shifting and tumbling into his lap. By the time they arrived in Guthrie, near noon, he was battered and bloody, but at least most of the blood wasn't his own.

At the Guthrie stable where he'd left the mules, Jake washed his hands and face and tried to wipe some of the gunk off his clothes. "I'll pay you good money, Leonard. Be my lawyer for one week. I'll pay you fifty dollars."

"What do you need me for?" Leonard asked, softening.

"I intend to find out what happened to Ralph Dekker. You know the courthouse. You know the law. You know how to find things out. I don't. I wouldn't do anything but get in trouble."

Leonard looked suspiciously at the mules, who were standing side by side with their eyes closed. "This trip to Fort Smith wouldn't have anything to do with those ancient, malicious-looking animals, would it?"

"Why, those fine animals are veterans of the Civil War. Leonard LaFarge, meet Grant and Lee."

The mules continued to appear to sleep, although even with their eyes closed they somehow obstructed Jake's efforts to get them into harness. Leonard went off to get his cardboard suitcase and came back still grumbling that he couldn't believe Jake wanted to leave now, after the morning they'd had. Jake got on some less dirty clothes and stuffed the bloody ones into his suitcase.

They embarked early that afternoon for Fort Smith. Grant and Lee had apparently gotten accustomed to the leisure of the stable, and they were uncooperative, lurching between dead slow and breakneck speed. They'd walk for a while, so slowly that Jake was afraid they were about to keel over in the traces, then, pow, as if a gun had gone off next to their ears, they'd take off. His attempts to control their pace had little influence. Yet by late afternoon they were piling down a section-line-road shortcut not far from Tulsa. Tulsa was north of their path, but the route was slightly the lesser of evils.

Jake didn't yet know exactly what he was going to do when he got to Fort Smith, but he was grimly fixed on getting there as fast as possible. One thing on his mind was the telegram he'd sent Tom the night before, right after he'd heard the news from Gus Wall. Today he realized that anybody crazy enough to kill Ralph Dekker wouldn't think twice about doing the same thing to a snoopy half-breed boy. Maybe he should send another message to Tom, telling him just to forget about the whole mess, quit the job, and stay entirely away from the store.

The mules kept him well occupied. He yelled at them and Leonard yelled at him, complaining bitterly about his driving, as they crashed and wobbled down a grooved, cattle-mauled, hard-packed road. "I have a delicate stomach, I have hemorrhoids! Mr. Dekker is already dead, it's no use hurrying. If we cross the river tonight, we'll be at Tulsa. Tulsa on Friday night!"

He'd been complaining all day, and Jake was only half listening to him. "What's wrong with Tulsa? I thought you preferred it."

"Preferred it to what? Slow down, damn your eyes! Watch out for that tree! God's hooks! You're going to break a wheel. You're going to kill us."

When they could smell the Arkansas River ahead, the mules chose to slow down to a walk.

Leonard was bent over. "Gad, my stomach's going, for certain."

"Don't worry, Leonard. However much it hurts, there's always worse."

"I don't need your optimism, I need opium."

"What good would that do?"

"Opium is an anodyne, an anesthetic, a soporific, and a narcotic. With the help of all of these angels I might survive."

"You're drinkin too much."

Leonard gave him a dirty look. "And you have such a tight jaw that you look like you could bite a crowbar in two. Why are you in such a hurry? Why rush to arrive in Tulsa, the pit and abyss of the world? These poor mules will die of heart attacks if you run them any more."

Jake tried to relax his jaw. "They run when they want to and walk when they want to. I don't have anything to do with it."

"Well, you're conveying to them a general sense of urgency. Are you worried about that shavetail Tom Freshour? Is that why you're trying to kill us?"

Jake glanced at him, surprised that he knew, since he'd said nothing about it. "Last night I sent Tom a telegram asking him to find out what he could about Mr. Dekker. Now I'm thinking it wasn't such a good idea."

"Well, you can't do anything about it in the middle of the prairie."

It was late in the day as they approached the river — the sun just down, the wind almost still, a dippered moon rising in an azure sky.

"Don't worry about the boy, Jake. I detected in him a certain hardness."

"Hard-on, more likely."

"Oh? Is he rooty for the heiress?"

Jake raised his eyebrows in assent.

"Is the feeling reciprocal?"

"Appears to be," Jake said.

"Oh? Is this something that you actually witnessed? Come now. Tell me the good parts."

Jake told him a shortened version of what had happened at the Christian Boarding Hotel, which delighted him so much that he appeared to forget about his stomachache.

"How old is Tom?"

"Too damn young for her."

"Do you fear that she'll merely use him for a handy stud and cast him off?"

Jake didn't answer.

Leonard sighed. "There are worse fates, you know."

"This woman came to Fort Smith on a train with a list of people that included me, then stuck to both Tom and me like a bedbug ever since."

"But particularly to Tom," Leonard said innocently.

Jake looked at him irritably. He was going tense again, preparing for the fight he assumed the mules would give him at the river. To his relief, they pulled right through the mud onto the planked barge, as if it had never occurred to them to act balky at water. The ferryman, a gruff young white man, emerged from a lean-to near the river. He poled them across, floating quietly downstream. Jake and Leonard sat on the back of the wagon.

"You know, Leonard, I worked for that mean old devil for nearly twenty-five years."

"And you don't think he killed himself."

"There's something I haven't told you."

"Uh-oh."

Jake told him about Mr. Dekker's plan to retake control of the store and put him in charge.

Leonard took out his bottle and uncorked it. "*Now* I understand your grief. Ralph held the keys to your advancement, from lowly salesman to prime minister of the hardware store. And from such heights, yet unsavored, art thou cast down." He quickly raised and lowered his bushy eyebrows. "Have a slug and assuage thy well-earned grief." Jake shook his head and Leonard took a delicate sip. "It is possible that the old man did himself in, you know. Maybe he failed to find the necessary finances in St. Louis and decided a pox on it all. He wouldn't be the first strong man who broke because he couldn't bend."

Gazing out across the smooth, darkening river, Jake shook his head. "He wasn't a person to kill himself."

"That's what they always say." Leonard took the last taste of whiskey from his bottle and pitched it into the river.

"I just wonder why Deacon Miller followed me into the Fringe and tried to kill me. Miller's a hired gun. He doesn't do it for sport. Who paid him?"

"You've got this all figured out, I can tell by your tone," Leonard said drily. "You figure Ernest Dekker is the responsible party for all of it."

"Look at it this way: The old man wants to make me boss. Maybe Ernest finds that out somehow and decides to pay a visit to Deacon Miller. Meanwhile, the old man goes to St. Louis to get money, and he comes back to town. Maybe he has money with him, maybe not — we don't know. But next thing you know, he's dead. Somebody tries to kill me, then somebody does kill him. Seems to me that there might be a trail to that scent."

Leonard glanced at the ferry operator and said in an undertone, "Speaking of scents, I wish the breeze was blowing the other direction. Between the mules and Charon here . . . Tell me about the sheriff in Fort Smith. The new one."

Jake shrugged. "He's tight with Ernest. Big horse-track gambler."

"What about Judge Parker?"

Jake looked puzzled.

"For argument's sake, let's say you're right and Dekker Junior is the guilty party. You do realize that it isn't a good idea for you to go barreling into town playing lone Pinkerton. A man like that has more than one way to cook your goose."

Jake looked at him irritably.

"Pugnacity alone won't solve your problem. You need somebody on your side. Some kind of ally. You could pay court to the judge, inform him of your suspicions and see what he thinks about it."

"What good would that do?"

"It might make you a little less vulnerable, that's all. This concerns Indian Territory. Parker's been a friend to the tribes. The federals don't like him because he doesn't believe they've given the Indians fair treatment, and he's been public about it. He knows that there are more schemes to take over Indian land than red ants in Texas. Big capital wants this territory opened up, and they've used his 'bloody court' as one of the reasons for white settlers to take over and 'civilize' the place."

Jake shook his head. "You know, I worked across the street from the judge all those years, but I don't really know him any more than to tip my hat . . . I'd hear his voice coming out of the courtroom window now and then." He stared off. "Never watched a hanging. I was at the store quite a few Saturdays when they had them. Heard the trap drop a few times. Never did understand why people like to see that."

They bumped against the north bank of the river, and Leonard looked up and sighed. "Tulsa."

·20·

TOM LEANED against a bent and rusted iron fence, still panting from his single-man race down the avenue between sentinels of street lamps. He had run out on Sam because her questions made him feel trapped and because her life story gave her a past, a flawed and particular and far-reaching whole lifetime of pastness, transmuting her from radiant force and pure mystery into the demarcations of flesh, and the more human and real she was, the farther from her he seemed — like a kid squinting across a wide gulf of experience toward a figure far away. She made him afraid of his own past, too, afraid that it would somehow cohere out of the gloom, that it would be thrust into his hands like a heavy suitcase.

He wanted to talk to Hack. He had Jake's telegram in his pocket, asking him to find out what he could about Mr. Dekker's death. But more than that, Tom wanted to know what had happened to Joel — exactly what had happened — and why Hack had been so actively avoiding him.

Tom held on to the iron fence in front of this dark rambling clapboard wreck, its sign above the door barely readable through mist blowing up from the river: PARIS HOTEL. The fog dampened the sound of a piano coming from the hotel and cloaked the occasional figure who hurried by in obscurity. He didn't relish going into the big old drooping building, but now was better than tomorrow, when Hack would be working and hard to catch.

Tom loitered up and down the fence, drumming up his courage, then finally went in, passing into the familiar odor of a dilapidated building, layered with a half-dozen other smells — dry rot and flood and cigar smoke and borax cleaner and strong perfume and the thin suggestion of vomit. A long-haired, skinny night clerk sat dealing out rows of cards to himself beneath a frosted glowing lantern. In the corner of the room a black man in a high white collar was playing the same rinky-tink piano music that Tom had heard coming from saloons everywhere, only his playing was different. Instead of pounding mechanically on the keyboard, this man watched his hands with an expression that was effortless, serene, amused, while his fingers pranced, capered, and spidered across it. Three people besides the clerk were in the lobby. On a couch a large woman bulged out of a ruffled violet dress, vacantly staring, as if she was unaware of the music or anything else, and two young Indian men sat across from her in rumpled duck jackets, one with his eyes shut, the other mumbling to himself. This inert trio was a strange audience for the dazzling music. Tom stood there a moment listening, before walking up to the clerk to ask where Hack Deneuve was staying.

The clerk looked up from his cards with a smiling mouth and menacing eyes. "Hello there, chief. Wouldn't just be coming in from the Flint courthouse, would you?"

"I beg your pardon?" Tom said.

The clerk was thin to the point of being skeletal, with a large skull on a long stalk of neck. "Money's good, we don't care what you are, chief. This town has a dozen good houses in it, and we're the only one that'll take bloods. We don't want no tattoo-skin Comanches, a course. Long as you're dressed white and look okay. Been real busy here since that strip payment."

Tom had read about it in the newspaper: the government last week had distributed two-hundred-dollar payments to Cherokee people for the purchase of the Cherokee Outlet.

The clerk went back to his cards. "Never did see so many prosperous bloods. They come acrost here lookin for some fun. I tell em all, I say, you want to turn real estate into white nooky, chief, you have done come to the one and only place in this fair city, the Paris Hotel and Society Parlor. So how bout you, young man, what can I do you for? Most of the girls are off tonight because it done finally tailed down from all the strip bidness, but now I think I just *might* be able to scare up some socializin for you."

"Can you just tell me what room Hack Deneuve is in?"

The clerk instantly became less friendly. "That'd be one-twelve. Not sure I'd be visitin him now if I was you."

"Why not?"

He just shook his head and went back to his card game.

Tom went down a long cold hallway filled with a fragrance of smoke that wasn't quite like tobacco. Sounds came through doors and gaps under doors — conversation, somewhere a bed squeaking, and, from a room down the hall, rachitic, wheezing laughter. He was standing by a lamp when a woman appeared in front of him.

"Well," the woman said, looking him over. "Well well well well." Smiling broadly, with big healthy-looking teeth, she took him by both arms and pulled him firmly into a room. She had black hair, wild on her head, as if she hadn't combed it after sleeping, and she was wearing the scantiest costume imaginable, scarcely reaching her knees. In the gloom he saw that she was short of stature, neither comely nor uncomely, and that she projected a powerful impression. "Well well well," she said again, still holding his arms at the shoulders with a tight grip, inspecting him. Tom was alarmed but mesmerized by the woman's wide eyes. She nodded. "You in the market, honey?" She came up close to him and rubbed across his front with one teasing hand. "Are you?"

"Am I what? I'm here to see a friend."

She began to unhook her top, and in the imperfect light her entire costume seemed to disappear from her magically, and she clamped herself against him with the suddenness of a praying mantis, her sweet-water perfume overwhelmingly strong. Looking down at her bosom, crushed against his chest, Tom's thoughts began wildly switching this way and that.

"I came to —"

"A pure, young, mettlesome Indian man like you must want it bareback. Am I right?" She soon had his shirt off and was taking down his pants.

"I'm here to see a friend . . . one-twelve," he repeated unconvincingly. He tried to back away but wasn't equal to the raw force of her blandishments. She kissed him passionately, wrestled at his clothes, pulling his pants to the floor, and rubbed her body provocatively against him.

With one hand already around his penis, she said, "Well! What is this sweet oil on you? What'd you do, honey, get all ready for me?"

She shoved him lightly and he stumbled out of his pants. There he was, standing naked against this wild woman from nowhere, who now walked him backwards until he collapsed onto a bed, where she fell down and kissed him on the mouth, pushing her big tongue into his mouth. Shortly, she got up astraddle him. Tom knew that he could jackknife out of her clutches, but inside himself he was running around in circles, and before long he had begun to get hard. Quickly, and without ceremony or buildup, she raised up and slid it into herself, making a little sound of seeming pleasure. "I do take money," she said, rising and coming down at first very slowly, keeping him inside her, "but I don't strictly do it for money, not when they're like you, honey. Unh, now you're getting there. I been called crazy, unh, but I love strong young fresh Cherokee Indin men like you. What's your name?"

"Tom," he said, too stunned to ask hers.

Tom was beginning to enjoy it despite himself. The window was open and wet patches of air snaked into the room. The woman propped herself on the bed with both hands, her hair dangling down around his eyes almost like curtains, her face close to his.

"I specially like em young and fresh. I was made to give it to young, fresh — yeh, like that, that's it, now you getting it, mmm, bring it on to me, chief, talk to me." She spoke loudly and in a disjointed and unconvincing way. "You hung like a Cherokee chief. Are you a chief?"

"No ma'am. I'm not even a Cherokee."

He was beginning to notice what the bed smelled like, when he heard something in the room and looked over and saw a shadowy form in the doorway, apparently just leaving the room.

"Not a Cherokee?" She arched backwards, thus bending his now perfectly hard penis until he rose up in pain.

"Ouch! That hurts, ma'am."

"Not a Cherokee, did you say? You telling me you didn't go to Flint courthouse and get payment?" Tom extricated himself and crawled out of the smelly bed, stumbling around looking for his pants, which had been thrown into a corner. Before he had them halfway on, he was pushed headlong out the door, which slammed hard and was locked. Stunned almost beyond embarrassment, he looked both ways in the hall and pulled the pants up. He put out a hand against the wall and stood there a moment, eyes closed.

He crept past an open door, afraid that someone else would lunge out and grab him. Several people were sitting together inside, passing around a pipe, smoking some pungent substance. "Come in, join us," said a woman, giving him a come-hither gesture. A fat man with sleepy eyes said, "Nother blood? I ain't smokin with a damn blood." The woman still beckoned. "Come on in, stallion." Tom backed away from the open room and approached 112 at the end of the hall. He started to knock on the door but hesitated when he heard sounds inside. He stood there with his fist suspended, wondering whether what he was hearing through the door were sounds of pain or pleasure. Whatever it was, he decided he couldn't interrupt it. He backed away, unnerved, and retreated down the hall.

Through the open door, he heard snatches of conversation from the gathering of people who were smoking. Their tone was clandestine and insinuating in a way that sounded strange to Tom. Later, he would understand that this was the twilight world of prostitutes and drug takers and small-time criminals, with their other language, their intimacies, their cynical, casual, upside-down view of everything from the law to the pleasures of the flesh. Now he understood only that they were people — not ten thousand miles away, not across the world, but people here, all around him — whose beliefs and desires and fears were completely unlike what he and Hack had learned in their previous life. What they believed or cared about Tom didn't know, but he was sure that if they were standing in the weedy, dusty yard of the Armstrong Academy after Thursday marching practice, listening to the weekly harangue about the terrible justice of God, they would probably not be scared or angry but merely uninterested. He understood a little better why Hack was staying here.

Tom eventually went back downstairs and sat on a threadbare love seat across from the abundant woman in ruffles. He tried to decide whether to wait or come back. The woman appeared to be as unmindful of him as she was of the piano music or the two others who were here, one of whom was snoring lightly. The clerk glanced suspiciously at him through smoke rising from his ashtray.

For a while Tom just sat among the little flock of lost souls in the whorehouse parlor, listening to the music coming out of the black man's fingers, sat there thinking how fast and dangerous the world was.

He was about to leave when a group of drunk country men came in the door, white men with sunburned faces and big Adam's apples, walking in a clump of slouching, stumbling, pushing, sideways movement, as if they were one lurching organism with several heads, all talking at once. This single entity of lanky, long-jawed men — there were five of them — was arguing almost continuously, making small threats toward one another that suddenly ballooned into promises of mayhem and murder. They separated, and two of them pulled out pocketknives, crouching as if about to attack, ready to cut each other's throats. Their chattering died out to baleful silence, the black man playing the piano got up and went softly out a side door, and the desk clerk said, "You men take your fightin outside," to which there was at first no response, just more slouching, crouching, and knife-waving intimidation, and then one of them said, "Aw, we ain't got no reason to scrap," and just as abruptly as they had prepared for battle, they clumped back together in a shoving, chortling, drunken bevy, all beating on the counter and demanding tail. The clerk said there was no one available tonight, and once again they got louder and more argumentative.

A figure appeared at the top of the stairs, a man of medium height and thinning hair with a large-bore pistol in his hand, whose identity, without his black duster, took Tom a second to register.

Tom turned his face away, surging with fear, and he thought

about running but decided it was better just to sit still and hope that the man didn't notice him. The two Indians in the parlor departed quickly. The lady in ruffles remained, but she was barely of this world.

"You gentlemen please leave the premises?" said Deacon Jim Miller to the cluster of men.

"Ain't no gentlemen, jist as white as you are, come all the way from Springdale," they said, all talking at once.

Miller lifted his pistol and let it drop down, cocking it. "I'm pleased that you're not listening to me," he said with no particular emphasis, so quietly in fact that Tom wondered if the men even heard him. "The last time I shot a hillbilly's testicles off? He put on quite a hoedown."

"Didn't come here to git our testicles shot off," said one of them, looking startled. "Come to git some tail, money's as good as anybody else's."

Miller slowly aimed the pistol at the general area of their midsections, and they became so frozen with terror that they didn't seem to know what to do, whether to disperse or huddle together even more tightly, trying to hide behind each other. Tom assumed that Miller was just scaring them, that he had no intention of shooting them, but the clerk said sharply, "Let em leave under their own steam. I don't want no more dead men to have to explain."

They began to retreat, the whole clump moving backwards toward the door, a couple of them wiggling around like they had scorpions in their pants, and then they were all five trying to get out at the same time, none wanting to be last. Miller looked almost disappointed when they finally managed to get out the front door, falling in a great tangle of skinny limbs down the steps, struggling up, and running off. He followed them, two shots rang out, and screams faded into the night.

Tom got up, going for the same door the others had used. Glancing over his shoulder, he saw Hack Deneuve on the stairway landing, his dark-ringed eyes fixed on him in surprise.

It wasn't until he was in the street and hurrying back toward the boarding house that Tom felt in his pockets and noticed that they had been cleaned out. He decided it was unimportant, since he'd had less than a dollar in pocket change. Not until later, lying on his couch at Mrs. P's, did he remember the other item he'd been carrying.

♦

Tom woke up the next morning with those same haunted eyes fixed on him. Hack stood at the end of his bed, smirking. Tom raised his head slowly off the pillow.

"What'd you run away for?" Hack asked. "Deacon scare you off? Come on, let's get some breakfast."

Tom didn't say much at first. He got up and did his ablutions, and directly they left the house and walked down Texas Avenue. It was after six, and the streets were waking up, with sweet smells from the large bakery down on the west side permeating the cool air, a milkman rattling by, a barbershop near Garrison Avenue opening, the barber standing outside in his shirtsleeves snapping an apron clean. The first horseless streetcar of the day rolled heavily by, looking less threatening to Tom now that he knew about it.

They went into a café off Garrison with a sign in the front window that said DEPRESSION DINER: COFFEE AN' 5 CENTS. A stranger probably wouldn't have seen anything unusual about Hack, but as they began to talk, Tom noticed remarkable changes in him. In the past, Hack had been quiet and on the slow side; now he acted energetic and nervous. He used to not smile very often, but now he had an almost compulsive grin that continually melted into a little grimace of uncertainty and doubt. His eyes appeared to have gone more deeply into his face, and there were those rings under them, as if he wasn't getting enough sleep. He talked more, and bragged much more — about getting privileged information from important people.

"I knew they were gonna fire you. I hear things before they happen." Hack smiled with the queer twist at the end. "I know the right people, Tom. I can help you get a job." Tom acted interested, and Hack rambled on. "With money you can get anything — horses, land — it'll buy anything. Women," he said, pointing with his thumb in no particular direction. "All they want is your money. They'll do anything for it."

Tom asked nothing about Deacon Miller, although Hack made little hints about him. Nor did he yet ask Hack anything about Joel. Hack seemed hungry to have a friend, somebody to show off to, but he had something on his mind, too — some purpose, something he was leading up to, and finally he got around to it.

"Hey, I'm taking a trip today. You want to come with me? I'll pay the tickets. I've got an idea that I think you'll like."

"A trip where?"

"The territory," Hack said. "Muskogee."

Tom didn't reply at first.

Hack added quickly, "I'm delivering papers. I've already been there three times."

Tom chewed the last of his doughnut before he said, "Delivering papers where?"

Hack looked around the sparsely attended café and leaned over the table. "This stuff is secret," he said. "I can't talk about it. I'm not supposed to know what I'm delivering. Look, why don't you go with me. It won't cost you anything. I'll tell you what's on my mind on the way."

Tom thought of Jake's telegram. Now was his chance to get answers to some questions. But he had to wonder why Hack was being so friendly all of a sudden, after so long avoiding him around the store.

"You can't tell anybody you're going," Hack added. "This has to be totally secret. It's just you and me."

Tom went back to the boarding house and got a few things together, wrote a note to Jake telling him where he was going, and went to the station early in order to meet the first train coming in from the territory. Again no Jake. Jake might have decided to drive the wagon all the way back, in which case Tom felt a little better about not waiting to meet him.

The train to Muskogee left that afternoon, and Hack showed up wearing a black duster and galluses, looking like a younger version of Deacon Miller, which was both funny to Tom and a bit eerie. He was carrying a soft leather satchel, along with a small suitcase.

They took the Iron Mountain train west into the Cherokee Nation. As they rolled across the flatlands of the Arkansas River Valley, Hack began to talk about Bokchito. His face became heavy, the darkness around his eyes deepening. "How many times did that *sinti* beat you, *Chalak?*"

Sinti, one of the Indian words covertly used by some of the boys at the academy, meant "snake," and *Chalak* was the shortened version of *Chalakki okla,* "Cherokee," Tom's old secret nickname.

"How many times every week?"

Tom tried to shrug it off. "Enough."

"Yeah, you were one of the lucky ones." He looked at Tom directly now. "I'm going back, you know."

Tom at first didn't understand.

Hack added, "Back to pay the Reverend a little visit. You want to go?"

"I thought we were going to Muskogee."

"We are, but from Muskogee to Durant is one straight ride south on the Katy Railroad. It'll be no problem getting there. We can hide in the woods until night. Make our visit. Take a train back to Fort Smith. No one will know we've been there. It will be our secret."

Tom had known that Hack had some reason for inviting him to go along with him, and he'd planned to act receptive, if for nothing else to keep him talking. But he hadn't expected this. Before he even fully comprehended, his skin started tingling, as if his body grasped what Hack was saying before his mind did. He looked out the window and didn't reply.

"You remember Motey Campbell? Motey was my friend. I saw the report that the Reverend sent in when he died. He wrote that Motey died of a fever. I thought I'd go crazy because I couldn't do anything. Hey, now I can do something." Hack kept making his new, nervous, melting, worried smile.

"How'd you see this report?" Tom asked.

"It was my day of reckoning. A Tuesday, as usual. I went in, and the Reverend left to go to the privy. He told me to wait. I read what was on his desk. 'Motey Campbell, age thirteen,' it said. 'This unfortunate boy died on the Sabbath, August 19, of a sudden fever. He rests with his Creator.' "

Tingling and jumpy, Tom wanted to get up and walk away, but there was nowhere to go on the moving train except to pace the aisle. The idea of revenge reached out and wrapped its cool fingers around him. Suddenly he and Hack were old friends having an angry, intimate, whispering argument.

"Say it, man, you want to go with me." Hack poked him in the ribs.

"It's the past. Just forget it."

"I say we do him like he did us."

"There are other ways."

"What other ways? Name them."

"We could write letters describing the place. We could send them to the tribe."

Hack scoffed. "Oh, yeah. That's a great idea. Two breeds — kids — against the Presbyterian Mission."

"So what do you want to do, go over there and beat him up? Make *his* back bleed? You're crazy."

Hack smiled. He was trembling a little. "Feel under my coat," he whispered.

Tom reached out and felt the hard thing under his duster. He was wearing a pistol.

"We're yellow if we don't, Tom. Yellow as dandelions."

Tom completely gave up trying to be the clever detective. "Where is Joel?"

"What does that have to do with it? I told you already. He left is all I know."

"Edgar said that you had some kind of argument with him."

"Hey, that old nigger doesn't know what he's talking about. Think about what I'm saying to you now, man. Don't change the subject."

"Tell me about Joel first."

"I told you all I know. He just went. They fired him, he went. He didn't tell me where. Look, are you with me?" Something about the turn of Hack's mouth told Tom that he was lying.

Tom looked out the window. They were nearing the river again. Across its brown surface a fire was raging in the scrubland near the bank, blazing across the water, with three men standing around on a sandbar watching it. The billowing black smoke looked like a ragged beast with its head lifted to the sky, its arms stretching out. Tom wondered if what was always in the back of his mind, the source of his nightmares, was not the fear of going back to Bokchito but the fear of wanting to. Wanting to so badly that he would secretly smolder inside until he walked through the door that he'd so often dreaded, until he looked into the Reverend's eyes with the Reverend's own dead-fish expression and declared that there was no outside authority, no way out, because this was *his* day of reckoning. Finally *his*.

Revenge is sweet, the old blind soldier had said. Just by thinking about it, Tom could taste it, as vivid and bitter and sweet as the wine that Sam had given him last night. But he remembered Mr. Dekker's dead eyes and wondered what killing left you with.

They stopped in Hanson, a raw-looking place with a store and a cotton gin, a cattle yard near the station, where a few stacks of fiber bales and twig crates of chickens sat on the shipping platform. They had a fifteen-minute layover during loading, and they got off the train to stretch their legs, Hack putting his delivery satchel under his arm and walking close beside Tom. Inside the little station they looked at Wanted posters, Hack with an arm dangled around Tom's shoulders. Bank robbers, train robbers, killers. Tom remained partly under the spell of Hack's idea, but the sudden chumminess, the way he stayed so near him, got on Tom's nerves. He was pushing Tom, trying to boss him, giving him that insinuating, melting smile.

Some miners got on the train at Hanson, and their car quickly filled with tobacco smoke. The language they spoke sounded German. At the academy they'd been introduced to several languages: a little French, German, even some Hebrew. Tom had never really understood why the Reverend absolutely forbade any Indian language. Getting caught speaking even single words was as bad as getting caught using obscenities. The boys were beaten for it.

"Did you ever wonder why he didn't let us talk Indian?" Tom said aloud.

"I don't wonder at anything he did," Hack replied.

The train back up to speed, Tom looked out the window at the reds and greys and browns of early winter in the wooded hills. As they crossed a narrow river valley, he could see northeastward all the way to the majestic blue Boston Mountains. The tobacco smoke in the car became intoxicating, and Tom rode along in a partial daze with Hack's fantasy of revenge riding right along with him. Hack seemed to have become a different person, as if during the last month or two he had walked through a mirror and turned into his own opposite. The old Hack had been gentle, deliberate, and without much apparent guile; the person sitting beside him was threatening, conspiratorial, and full of secrets that he hoarded like gold coins. Tom didn't need Jake's advice not to trust him. It came naturally. Yet wrapped all around and among Tom's mistrust were a thousand strands of intimacy based on their old friendship.

They got off the train at Fort Gibson and took a mule-cart taxi to a fifty-cent hotel at the south edge of Muskogee. It was called the Acme, and in its lobby three shabby, bearded men sat around as if they'd been there for a week without moving. On the counter lay a stack of crudely printed magazines and pamphlets with titles like *The Voice of Labor, Industrial Solidarity,* and *Birth Control Review.* "Them go for a dime apiece," the clerk said with a tobacco-stained smile. "Good readin for bad times, fresh outa Chicago."

The only furnishings in their little square room were a chair, a slop jar, a tin cuspidor in a corner that was stained amber by innumerable misses, and a low home-built table by the one sagging bed. Wire mesh was nailed over the transom, and a single kerosene lantern provided light.

In the room, right away Hack started acting peculiar. He laid the delivery satchel on the floor by the bed, unstrapped and set his holster on the table, and loaded his pistol. It was a twenty-dollar .45-caliber revolver, of a kind sold by Dekker Hardware. He sat on the bed, opening and closing his hands around the walnut handle, aiming at the wall, pretending to shoot a cockroach that was walking up it.

"Pchou!"

Tom sat down on the chair. "What's in the satchel?"

Hack lowered the pistol to his lap. "Don't know. Ain't supposed to know. Ain't supposed to look." He glanced down at the satchel and added, as if it didn't matter, "It's for somebody name of Crilley. I've come here before, always take it to his house on Sunday."

"Who's Crilley?"

"Have no idea." Quickly, Hack raised the pistol at the cockroach. *"Pchou!"*

"Did Deacon Miller teach you how to shoot?"

"Taught me what I need to know," Hack said cryptically. He suddenly looked glum. "What do you know about the Deacon?"

"I know he tried to kill Jake."

"I warned you about Jake. He's out."

"Did Miller teach you how to kill people?"

Hack peered at him through the gloom, head back, eyelids partly closed. "So you won't go with me? Are you yellow?" He slowly raised the gun and aimed it at him. *"Pchou!"*

He was trying to make Tom mad, trying to stir him up, but Tom wasn't going to play his game. "You could get yourself killed, Hack. The Reverend sleeps lightly. He keeps a gun by his bedside. You remember him hunting birds during picking." His own memory was vivid: at harvest time, the Reverend in the popcorn field making quick, twisting shots with his double-barrel shotgun, dragging two doves at once out of the sky, so close together that they hit the ground almost at the same moment. Every bird season he liked to show off to the boys that way.

Hack sat there fiddling with the gun, looking at him with the ringed, sleepy eyes. Tom was beginning to wonder whether he should even remain here with him. He got the feeling that Hack was trying to get used to handling the gun, but also Tom felt that he was part of what Hack had on his mind — the gun and him together. He didn't understand the looks Hack was giving him.

"I feel wild sometimes at night," Hack said suddenly. He twirled the pistol's cylinder and snapped it shut. "Hey, listen to me. My blood is boilin."

Tom looked away, uneasy.

"Girls!" Hack said sarcastically, taking off his shirt. He had already taken off his pants. "They're good for making money. That's all. Girls, *pfft*. The Deacon doesn't waste his time with girls."

"Does Deacon Miller work for that hotel where you're staying?"

"Sometimes."

"Does he work for the store?"

"Why do you want to know?"

"You're asking me to help you kill somebody. Come on. Talk to me."

"Why are you askin about the Deacon?" Hack looked at him intently, his face trembling with a ferment of emotions — shame, fear, pride, anger, bitterness, everything bubbling up at once. "The Deacon belongs to no one. He *takes* what he wants! It's that simple. He has *power,* man!" Hack picked the gun up again and held it out. "Here! You want to know what power is? Let me show you something. Take it. Go on. Take it!"

Tom looked at the gun a moment and finally took it.

"Aim it at me. Aim it at my heart."

Tom hesitated.

"Go on," Hack said sharply, eyes flashing. "Aim it at me!"

Tom aimed hesitantly, from the waist.

"Now feel it in your hands. It's loaded. Feel the trigger with your finger. Feel the handle underneath your palm. You can snuff me out for good, Tom, it's up to you. That's God. Not some man walking around in a dress two thousand years ago."

Tom lowered the gun. "Did Miller teach you that?"

Tom could see that his refusal to act impressed bothered Hack. He looked wounded. They talked more, Hack assertive but unconvincing. Their conversation kept ending in bruised perplexity.

When they were readying to go to sleep, Hack started acting agitated again. He had taken off everything but his undershirt. He turned down the wick and got into bed, and immediately rolled over and said, "You know, there's a way to get satisfaction without girls. I can show you."

At Bokchito some of the older boys did things to each other at night, but as far as Tom knew, Hack hadn't been among them. "No," Tom said quietly. "I'm going to sleep."

Hack started trying to tickle him and play with his chest. Tom didn't like this at all and pushed him away. "You're acting crazy."

Hack jerked up from the bed, snatched the gun from the table, and lay down on his back on top of the blanket. Tom watched as he licked its barrel, slowly, all around. Tom almost laughed, but Hack put the barrel into his mouth, just the tip at first, and to Tom's amazement, he cocked the pistol and plunged it clear into his throat. Hack's penis had risen up tight across his belly.

Tom was frozen.

Hack took the gun out. "I can show you something." He was like a coiled spring. "Look. Hey, you know how that *sinti* used to beat us? He did it because he liked the way it made him feel. Just to get hot. You want to see? It's better if you take your clothes off. Hurry." He waved the gun threateningly toward Tom, eyes dancing crazily. He took the belt from his own pants. "Take em off. Go on!"

Tom was really afraid now, but he knew that he'd better not act that way.

"Come on, man," Hack taunted. "I'll shoot you."

"What is all this with the gun?"

Hack again looked vulnerable and afraid. "Come on," he pleaded, and held out the belt to Tom.

Tom, sitting on the edge of the bed, took it. "What do you want?"

"You do it to me," he said. "You'll see. You don't have to take off your clothes if you don't want to." Hack got down on his knees by the bed and took off his undershirt and, now stark naked, knelt there in the light of the lantern, still with an erection so tight that Tom could almost feel it himself. Across his scarred back were fresh red and purple stripes. Somebody had beaten him recently.

In the lantern light in the dank little room, looking into Hack's upturned, beseeching eyes, Tom understood something now: Hack wanted to turn white into black, east into west, pain into pleasure, men into women; he wanted to escape his past by returning to it with a vengeance. Tom dropped the belt onto the floor in front of him. "I just want to know what happened to Joel."

Hack smiled with the bitter twist at the edge of his mouth. "Will you go with me to Bokchito if I tell you?"

Tom leaned forward and put his face close to his old friend's and said quietly, "We're different now, Hack."

"I'm going back to Bokchito, *Chalak,* that's how we're different. You can go with me or not."

"Is Joel dead?"

Hack's new, worldly smartness leaked out of his expression. He looked away. Eventually he sat down on his haunches and crossed his hands over his nakedness. A train was coming into town from the south, and as it went by they didn't talk. When the clattering and squealing brakes had subsided into silence, Hack said, "He gave out information. Somebody got him to talk, maybe the same person who killed old man Dekker. Somebody killed the old man and stole something from him, some paper, money, I don't know. Now they're tearing up the damn store looking for whatever was stolen. They started Thursday night turning it upside down."

"What do you mean, Joel gave out information?"

"A courier can't give out information, man. He broke the rule. He knew what he was doing. These men don't play around. What they're doing is a lot bigger than a barrel of nails and a roll of barbed wire, man. A lot bigger. They're going to own half of the Indian Territory."

"Did they kill Joel, that's what I'm asking you."

"It was none of my business, man. I don't know."

"Did Deacon Miller do it?"

"Look, I'm his boy. I belong to him. I'm learning from him. I'm learning what I have to. You better learn something, too. Because you didn't learn *nothin* from Reverend Schoot," he added vehemently. "Nothin! How to eat *pig* food. Sit on your butt all day reading Latin verbs. Latin! How to be some kind of useless, fake white man, which is worse than a nigger. Take that to the bank and see what you get for it."

With black anger in his heart, Tom rose, went over to the window, and stared into the night. "Joel only used to be a friend of yours. Is that it?"

When he turned back, Hack was standing up, putting his pants back on. "You think you're so righteous. Well, you're dead if you go back to Fort Smith. You were dumb enough to have that telegram in your pocket at the hotel. They took it to the Deacon. I was there when they gave it to him."

"What difference does that make?"

"Your salesman friend is *out,* man, he's gone, he's scheming against the boss. And since you had that telegram in your pocket, so are you. You can't go back."

"So they're going to do him like they did Joel?"

Hack looked weary, but he opened his eyes wide at Tom, flashing anger. "Joel was weak! He was dead anyway. He was already crazy. He was shaking all the time, he was having bad dreams, he was seeing things. He talked all the time about Bokchito. Man, he was dead!"

"Who'd he give information to?"

"Whatever happened, he did it to *himself*. I've had enough of this."

They had little else to say to each other. Hack sank onto the bed and curled into a ball. After a while Tom, completely exhausted, lay down beside him, back turned, and silently said the Lord's Prayer over and over, waiting for sleep to come.

· 21 ·

TULSA HADN'T BEEN quite as bad as Leonard feared. During the night, they heard only a few shots, at some distance from the hotel, although the sound of bawling cattle was loud from every direction. Large herds had been driven to all nearby railheads to clear out the Outlet before the land run, so the town was temporarily bustling. Exhausted from his lack of sleep the previous night and from driving all day Friday, Jake did sleep that night. It was Leonard's turn to suffer. At breakfast he looked pallid.

"I'm not long for this world, my friend."

"Life of sin, Leonard."

"And I suppose you're going to finish me off by driving the way you did yesterday."

"Have some breakfast. You'll feel better."

Leonard surveyed the ham, potatoes, bread, eggs, and pumpkin pie before him. "A good solid shot of brown whiskey is my only hope."

Jake changed the subject. "I wonder if they've got rock oil around here. This is one of the places on the map that Ernest wanted us to get mortgages signed."

"I'm sure we can find out if we stop at a friendly saloon," Leonard said hopefully.

The boy who was waiting their table came around to pick up dishes, and Jake asked him, "Could you give me about a quart of coffee, please — in two bowls. I'll bring em back."

It was Saturday, and when they went to the stable their wagon and team were standing outside the yard, lined up with four or five others, ready to go. That was a good sign. Market day was already heating up, the air all dust and excitement. The stableman had cleared out last night's wagons and was using the yard for a temporary cattle-holding pen. Jake gave Grant and Lee the coffee, which they sucked up with gusto. Jake had gotten so he kind of liked these old worthless mules.

A half-dozen cowboys who'd received their wages for the week were racing up and down popping off six-guns, scattering a group of Indian girls, in town from one of the schools. Cattle were putting up a racket. Along the street, men leaned against posts, hats down over their eyes, talking livestock. A lot of "lost" cattle from Indian operations were shipped out of Tulsa. Tulsa was in the Creek Nation, but in fact the local whites controlled the town, and it was generally known that a number of them were rustlers and thieves who avoided prosecution by stealing only from Indians. This was Dandy Pruitt's territory, and Jake had heard many a tale from him.

The mules were unperturbed by the noise and bustle. Picking their way through town, Jake and Leonard passed a hunter peddling game off his wagon: turkeys, quail, rabbits, and small deer carcasses hung on a line. Some beautifully dressed buckskin suits of the type made by Creek Indians lay across the boards he'd propped up for his table. The hunter's name was McCann, and Jake had seen him all around the eastern part of the Nation for these many years. He pulled up. "How do, Mr. McCann."

McCann smiled through sooty teeth and nodded. He had a sinewy, dark, clean-shaven face.

"Been doin okay?" Jake asked.

McCann shook his head. "Game's done fell off, what with so many folks scratchin around. Got the place about cleaned out. I been doin a little wolfing up here for the ranchers. Keeps me busy."

"What are they offering for wolf pelts now?"

"Like I say, that's one thing that's holdin up. They're running so many cattle these days, makes it damn easy on the old wolves. Smack Henderson over to Bar BQ's lost a dozen calves. He's offerin twenty dollar for a full-grown loafer caught on his place. Seven-Up's offerin about eighteen."

"That is good money," Jake said.

"How's the hardware trade?"

"Like everything else." Jake felt a twinge in his stomach at the mention of it. "You still selling game to the big cities?"

"Not here lately. Old boy that was shipping it said they quit eatin deer in New York City. Said it wasn't in fashion no more, whatever that means."

"He was buyin things besides deer, wasn't he?"

"Yeah, but he was only givin me fifteen cent for prairie chicken, a dollar fifty for a brace of quail. I had to be selling him deer for it to be worth my while."

"Maybe deer'll come back in fashion," Jake said with a grin.

McCann shook his head. "Won't be enough of em left, time that happens. With so many white settlers moving in here, they're killin em back. It's got so I'm lucky to put up one deer. Time was, I'd put up half a dozen in a slack day. Take me a line of mules into the Winding Stair and make em earn their oats comin down. Them days is done, and I ain't young enough to learn a new trade, unless it be somethin like working in the slaughter pen. I don't relish that." He smiled wanly, as if he was embarrassed at talking about his troubles.

"Mr. McCann, you ever hear about rock oil in these parts? Digging wells for it."

"Well, there was some old boys up on Sue Bland's place trying to dig some kind of well. Didn't find nothin. Folks generally said they was crazy."

"You think they are?"

"Oh, there's oil out there. I know where a few seeps are. I don't know what good the stuff is. Can I sell you somethin today?"

"We're travelin light . . . How much you get for one of those buckskins?"

Mr. McCann and Jake did a little bargaining over a buckskin suit and struck a deal. Jake asked Leonard to put it into his suitcase.

As they jogged through town, Leonard glanced at him furtively. "Perhaps we could stop and replenish my carrying bottle."

"You can't drink in the morning, Leonard. Not if you're going straight."

Leonard gazed wistfully as they passed the last shack on the edge of Tulsa that looked like it might have liquor for sale. The mules were still walking, warming up. Jake snapped the reins, eager to get down the road.

Leonard was silent for a while. Then he looked irritably at Jake. "Who told you I was going straight? I certainly said nothing about that."

The road to Muskogee was over fairly flat country, but this was the lawless borderland between the Creek and Cherokee nations, place of train robberies, stomping ground of the Daltons and their like. Only fools rode through it with an easy mind.

Somewhere in the flatlands above Muskogee, they stopped at a country store to water the mules. There was a rough trough outside holding rainwater, and Grant and Lee took a good drink. The screen door slammed behind Jake, and he walked into a shadowy room with a few plank shelves. An old black man sat behind a long board, staring at him, chewing. At first Jake thought that there was almost nothing for sale, but on the dusty planks here and there between the mouse poison were cans of tomatoes, some melons, turnips, and a few other items. For thirty-five cents he bought a loaf of bread, two cans of milk, and a melon. He tried to engage the proprietor in a conversation, but the old man was close-mouthed. A shotgun stood conspicuously available. He'd probably been robbed. The freedmen — former slaves of Indians, many of them — were the worst hit by the latest outbreak of border lawlessness, and the marshals and tribal lighthorses didn't typically do a whole lot about it. Jake walked out of the gloomy store and pitched a can of condensed milk to Leonard, who looked at it as if it was a dead rat.

"Milk? Don't they have anything healthful to drink in there?"

"How bout a piece of bread, Leonard?"

He took a piece and chewed sulkily at it. Patches of dried thistles encircled the rain barrel. The afternoon wind had picked up. "What a place," Leonard said, pulling his waistcoat around him. "It looks abandoned. Who's running the store?"

"Old freedman." Jake split open the watermelon with his knife and offered Leonard a hunk. "Thank God for this year's melon crop."

On they drove, through the afternoon, and their luck held —

no thrown shoes, no broken wheels, no robbers — into Muskogee. It was past dark when they felt their way up the dark streets. Muskogee was much like Tulsa, on the edge of the Creek Nation, a rail and cattle head, but it was older and closer to Fort Smith, and the Creek Agency and Fort Gibson were nearby. It was a good-sized town, with more than fifty businesses, a power plant for electric light, a couple of mills, and a handful of schools. Its streets were washboards, with holes and pits and minor washouts, good for breaking horses' and mules' legs. And Muskogee stank with the best of them tonight, the sulfuric aroma of well water being almost as strong as the smell from the outhouses.

A large part of the downtown had burned down around the first of that year, and Jake went to a hotel where he'd stayed when he last traveled this territory, a boxy two-story building. The hotel was unpainted, dirty, decrepit, with greasy-smelling pillows, but Jake didn't have the spunk to ride around in the dark trying to find something better. It was just a place to lay their heads.

Leonard perked up considerably at the opportunity to go out and get his reward for remaining sober all day. "Shall we celebrate our safe arrival?"

"You're a grown man, Leonard," Jake said grumpily. "You want to kill yourself with popskull whiskey, go ahead and do it."

"Well, I certainly don't want to drink in the presence of such Methodist attitudes."

"I ain't a Methodist," Jake grumbled. But he decided he could use a drink himself.

They found a nearby saloon and lined up at the bar. Leonard ordered tequila and looked happy for the first time all day. "You know, I've been thinking about your situation." He took a sip of tequila and smacked his lips. "It's a losing proposition."

"You're in a good mood."

"It's one thing to have your job and your pension snatched from you, another to lay your head on the chopping block."

Jake scowled at him.

"If Dekker Junior really does know that his father intended to install you in his place, whether he's a killer or not he will certainly be ill disposed toward you. Also, you don't have any authority in the matter of his father's death. You're not a marshal. You're not a relative. Ergo, you should keep your distance."

"Only authority I've got is the truth."

Leonard grunted. "That and a nickel might buy you a cup of coffee, but it's short currency against a local big shot. Authority, my friend, consists of one or both of the following items: money and ropes to pull."

"Well, I've got four hundred dollars in the bank and an old calf rope."

"The four hundred won't qualify, I'm afraid. And the rope is no good unless it's tied to the private parts of certain local officials, which I assume is not the case."

Jake again fell to worrying about Tom. All day he'd been worrying about him. Once more he told himself that he shouldn't have sent the telegram. "I'm going to hit the pallet. We have a ways to go yet."

· 22 ·

THE MOURNFUL SOUND of wind going through the four-bit hotel briefly wakened Tom to early morning, and he saw Hack, wearing his duster, sitting on the stick chair looking out the window with his satchel in his lap. Tom didn't see him look inside the satchel, but he had the impression that Hack had just done so. Later, when Tom really did wake up, he was unsure whether this scene had happened or whether it was a short, vivid dream, like an eerily tinted photograph: blood-red sunlight coming through the window, and an expression on Hack's face that was at once baffled and decisive. Whether it had been a dream or not, Hack was now gone from the room, and he'd taken the satchel and everything else that belonged to him.

There was no note from him and no message left with the hotelkeeper.

Tom went outside, and as he walked along the tracks toward the station, he realized that it was nearly noon. He'd never slept this late in his life. Across the track in a muddy field, two little boys flew a red paper kite, and he stood around the tracks awhile, brooding on the playing children, oddly envious of their fun. He felt very uncertain and strange. The sky was such a solid winter grey that Tom doubted this morning's vision of Hack, with its apocalypse of red sunrise.

In the cold greyness of midday, Hack's revenge scheme seemed even more hopeless. Even if he succeeded, he'd be seen by someone and hunted down. Watching the two boys trying to keep the rag-tailed kite up in the gusty wind, it occurred to Tom that Hack might have brought him out here because he secretly hoped that Tom would stop him from his mission.

Whatever his intention was, in fact now Tom was the only one who could stop him. Around a bend in the track he saw a train, about to leave for the south, and he cut across toward the station, wondering if this might be the train Hack was catching. On the station platform a posted schedule showed that this was the second and last southward train for the day. Tom had no money to buy a ticket. He walked along beside the already moving cars, blinking in the coal smoke, his eye on the wide-open door of an unoccupied cattle car.

♦

It was over a hundred miles to Durant, and this cold, splintery, dusty, smoky floor was the ultimate test of Tom's ability to sleep on trains. He actually did sleep some, although it kept crossing his mind that he was freezing to death. No one bothered to kick him off at the stops in Eufaula and McAlester. Black smoke covered and settled into his clothes and exposed skin.

In Durant he got off and waited outside the station, shivering, hoping to see Hack, but only one person, an old man, got off here. Whether Hack had arrived on the earlier train Tom had no way of knowing, but now he had to decide. It was about twelve miles to Bokchito, and it would be well into the night before he could walk the distance.

He had come this far.

He walked down the gloomy track toward the Blue River bottoms, trying to brush the black dust from his clothes. The lonely call of a whippoorwill penetrated the dusk. The wind for a while declined to a cold breeze, and the uniform grey sky broke into moving clouds. At the moment of silence before night, he was hungry and cold but somehow beyond those conditions, animated by nerves. He had seen no sign of Hack at all. Walking in deepening shadows into the night forest, he now doubted that Hack really had come down here. He was chasing a fantasy, returning to Bokchito alone.

At a little stream, Tom drank — the first thing he'd put in his stomach that day — and washed some of the soot off his skin. His new shoes were as broken in as they ever would be, but still they cut his ankles, and eventually he took them off, tied them by the shoestrings to a belt loop, and walked barefoot, his feet numbing in the cold. A few miles from his destination, he stopped and with a box of Paris Hotel matches made a fire in one of the tracks and sat close to it. The wind was picking up again. He slowly added sticks, listening to the coyotes and owls. Though Tom feared Bokchito, he felt a mysterious homesickness and kinship with the land itself.

He talked to himself while his feet warmed. "He's probably not here. He was just bragging . . ."

The fire cheered him. He had the thought, now for the second time, that even if he died tonight, he would still have been lucky. Jake was a friend, almost a father. And Sam, he thought, frowning into the flames. Why did thinking of her always make him ache? The attentions of a woman were still new and marvelous, but the better he'd gotten to know Sam, the more uncertain of her he'd become — of her grandness, her freedom, but also her secrets, her unspoken desires, the designs that she couldn't or wouldn't explain. In the hotel room two nights ago, she'd been so angry and melancholy, calling him Indian boy and whipping boy, asking him if he had ever had a mother . . .

In the windblown firelight Tom saw the girl child's photograph from Mr. Dekker's album. He could see it as clearly as if it were there in the flames — her game smile. He wondered if there was some kinship between Samantha and him that made them more like brother and sister than anything else. But then he had all kinds of uncertain feelings running around in him. He felt like his new life and past life were not as utterly separate as he had assumed — that somehow they were both of the same cloth, or were converging.

He looked away from the fire in the direction of Bokchito, and in a flash of blue moonlight he saw the Reverend in his mind's eye. A fierce soldier of God standing amid the smoking, twisted, blown-apart battlefield of human desire. God is compassionless, cold. Our fate is sealed before the moment of birth. Nothing we do matters until or unless we are chosen. Those who aren't chosen — the great majority, even at Bokchito — are not to be encouraged or discouraged. They are merely to be managed, put up with, the sick of soul, the half-alive, shades in the bleak waiting room of the flesh, doomed from their first breath of life to eternal torment.

Nearby in the forest, a bobcat made a sudden unearthly scream that Tom felt on the back of his neck. Staring into the dancing flames of the fire, he thought of another photograph in Mr. Dekker's sitting room, the picture of Dekker as a young man with his family — hawkish, fierce, as purposeful as a hunting animal. Upstairs in his room, slumped in a chair, the old man had looked so very different, his resoluteness crumpled once and for all around the bullet hole in his forehead. He had realized something before he'd died, made some discovery more painful than death.

With sensation warmed back into his feet, Tom found a walking stick, put out his fire, and went on down the narrow road, where the tall bottomland trees rose around him, their limbs clashing in what again was becoming a stiff wind.

It was sometime in the middle of the night when he passed the far fields of the academy farm. Crossing what the children called the big bridge, over the Blue River, he was in a curious state of mind, partly due to the cold. He still had no indication that Hack had been down the road, and for a moment he felt hopeful. Perhaps he could look in a few windows, sleep in the scalding shed, and then quietly disappear tomorrow morning. When he finally approached the great building in the forest, patches of moonlight and darkness were moving across sheds, trees, uncut brush, and all of it was terribly, depressingly the same.

The sight of the academy building took the energy out of him, like a blow to the stomach. He could have lived his entire life without ever coming back here. A tall brick structure as large as something in a city, improbable in this lonely country, grand and desolate and grim, with colonnaded porches on the second and first floors, many chimneys, and one pure decoration: a round, leaded attic window that looked almost like something in a church. One wing of the building had been added at a later date, its brick of a lighter color. Most of the boys' rooms were in this wing, on both floors. The Reverend lived in the old, main part of the building, in three rooms. A few of the saved ones — the flock — lived on the second floor directly above his rooms. For the last hour or so,

Tom increasingly had hoped that he wouldn't have to enter the place. With no definite sign of Hack anywhere along the road, he'd hoped that he was on a wild goose chase.

The only sounds were from the wind. He heard nothing at all coming from the boys' rooms, no bad-dream crying. There was a dim light in the Reverend's room, which seemed slightly odd. Tom stepped onto the porch and looked through the shutter of one of the large, low windows into the sitting room. Beyond the cracked door of the Reverend's bedroom a lantern was lit. Why the light at this hour, past midnight? It was difficult to see through the shutter, but it looked as if there was a rocking chair lying on its side, dumped over in the sitting room. Tom very carefully tried the front door and found it locked. None of the windows appeared to be disturbed or open.

He went around to the dilapidated back porch, where the door was standing partly open. By the porch steps, he glanced around but wasn't quite prepared for what he found. At the edge of a patch of moonlit weeds beside the building, he saw — and slowly went up and touched with his bare foot — Hack's satchel. It didn't even cross his mind to wonder why Hack had brought it with him instead of making the delivery and then catching a later train, because there was no question now that he had to go inside. He took the dangling shoes off his belt loop and laid them beside the satchel.

In the complete darkness of the back hallway, the building's smells provoked in him an instant melancholy. He stood still for a moment trying to collect himself. Then he walked on through the hall to the door leading to the Reverend's library, where the musty smell of the books was agonizingly familiar. He reached out and felt across their dry spines, as if to confirm that he really was in this place. Still he'd heard nothing except a creaking here and there in the house — no doors opening, no one walking down the stairs. The Reverend's office door was half shut, and he opened it gently, the room dimly lit by the lantern behind it in the adjacent bedroom. He walked quietly to the open bedroom door, seeing the lantern on the dresser and the capsized chair. The Reverend's bed was messed up but unoccupied. Had Hack come and taken him outside at gunpoint? Was Hack lurking on the grounds and the Reverend gone patrolling? He'd seen no lights anywhere else in the building.

Back in the office, he glanced around. The heavy kneeling block sat before the Reverend's desk. How many Fridays he had walked into this room and heard his defects read to him, the Reverend always sitting while he read, using his most monotonous, clerkly voice, implying that this was the standard and unavoidable inventory of living — poor attentiveness in school, failing to sit up straight and eat in silence, bad washing after fieldwork, improper care of uniform for marching practice, improper language, and so on and so on — he could hear the droning voice coming out of the square block of a man, but always with a hidden edge of anticipation beneath. Then he would ask Tom to remove his shirt, to kneel here.

Everything was the same in this room. The Reverend's own books, all lined up in the same order, *Institutes of the Christian Religion* prominent among them. Various books on education and the training of boys. *Antichrist on the American Continent* — Tom had always looked at that title and wondered about it. He took it down and flipped through the pages. It was a big, illuminated book with color plates and drawings throughout — mostly of Indians, with various tribal names beneath the plates, all grotesque, exaggerated renderings, naked devils and monsters dancing around fires with blood-dripping spears.

A terrible, bitter grief welled up in him, and he wanted to tear the book to pieces. He must not even throw it down, he realized. He set it down quietly and started to go back into the hallway when he had the feeling that someone was standing nearby watching him. He looked around the room until his eye lighted on the filing cabinet. "The annals of shame," he'd once heard the Reverend call it. He walked around the desk and found several keys on a ring in the top drawer. As he picked it up he heard something, a voice somewhere in the timbers of the building. Hurriedly, he tried keys until one of them opened the cabinet drawer. Folders in it were put away in three carefully demarcated groups, and he found his own name in the back section. In his file were several pages with the single word RECORDS printed on the top. Each of these pages was a listing of transgressions, pages and pages of them going back for years, each with the appropriate "judgment" listed. The Reverend apparently spent a great deal of time copying the pages of his "book of sins" in his fastidiously plain script. Tom's life appeared to consist entirely of transgressions, until he found at the back of the file a single yellowed piece of paper, dated *14 July 1880*, with a tilting spider's scrawl written across it: *"To Whom it May Concern the Enfant in Question was received as a Foundling at Osi Tamaha Where he was Left near the Big Tree by Party or Partys . . ."* Tom deciphered as much as he could of the rest — *"possibly Apache . . . delivered to the Skullyville Agency . . . Captain Sam Sixkiller High Sheriff & Warden"* — but he had to do it quickly, because he unquestionably heard a muffled yell somewhere in the building. He dropped the paper back into the file, shut the cabinet, and retreated back down the hall.

At the basement entrance, a coolness leaked through the bottom of the door. He stood there thinking he'd readily go to hell before he would descend those stairs, but there was a light coming through the crack, and another, louder cry, and definitely it came from there.

He pushed open the thick door and went down. At the base of the half-rotted stairs, beyond the graveyard — mounds of both marked and unmarked burial places of orphans and Civil War soldiers — past huge barrels that at one time had been used for water storage, in a small pool of light coming from one lantern, Hack knelt in the dirt with his shirt off and his arms tied behind him. Standing by him, with his short braided horsewhip in one hand and a pistol in the other, was the Reverend James Schoot.

He saw Tom at the base of the stairs and said, "You're just in time for judgment, Mr. Freshour. Come and join us."

♦

"Your friend Mr. Deneuve came to do me harm," the Reverend said, with the fixed blankness on his face that Tom had seen so many times. His arm fell hard, the whip snapped across Hack's back, causing him to topple into the dirt. "Get back on your knees." Hack struggled up, with stripes of blood on his back visible from twenty feet away. The Reverend talked while he did it, as always, in a tone controlled but excited and only partly connected to the flailing arm. Tom had heard it so many times. *I am a stronger and more vital animal than you,* it seemed to say.

"You are a threat to God's work. You are pestilent in His eyes."

The sight of the Reverend beating Hack, the terrible familiarity of this place, the dirt and rotten smell permeating the damp, grief-filled darkness made Tom weak in the knees, nauseated. He hid behind one of the huge containers, breathing, trying to gain control of himself.

"Come here, boy."

With his back against the vat, Tom looked around it and was surprised to see the Reverend coming toward him, with the pistol held at the ready. Tom ran back into the darkness. The Reverend pulled off one ear-splitting blast, the bullet eating air close to his head. Tom went around a corner and stopped, waiting to see if he would follow, his pulse pounding. Tom had one advantage, thanks to the Reverend: he knew every nook and cranny of this stinking basement.

Hack had just stood up. Walking back to him, the Reverend said, louder, "Kneel down, boy. Now!" Tom found a rock and threw it into the darkness near them, hoping he would waste a shot on it. The Reverend shouted at Tom, "If you don't come here now, I will send this sinner to his final judgment. Do you hear me? I'll count to ten, and if you haven't come here into the light, slowly, with your hands in the air, his sickness will be over. It is in your hands. One, two . . ."

Tom came partway out so that he could see better. Hack was still standing, and the Reverend kicked him hard in the knee. There was a sickening crunch, Hack screamed in pain and fell to the ground, and the Reverend aimed the pistol toward his head. ". . . four, five, six — you don't think I mean it?"

"I'm coming," Tom said.

"*No!*" Hack wailed. "Don't. He'll kill us both!"

Tom didn't know what to do. He didn't believe that the Reverend would execute Hack. Tom had no weapon, but during one of his exiles down here he had whittled on some old hoe handles, using a piece of metal he'd laboriously sharpened on the foundation rock. He'd made primitive candles out of tightly twisted paper, talked some matches out of the boy who brought him water, and practiced spear throwing. He had spent hours and hours doing this, until hunger and darkness prevented him. He and some of the other boys had hunted in the woods, too, with spears and bows, homemade from ash saplings, and he'd gotten good enough to kill an occasional rabbit with a spear. He ran to the corner where he remembered leaving the spear, and felt across the damp rough rock.

"Seven . . ."

Finally his hand found three of them. He grabbed one, swiveled around, and threw it toward the Reverend. He'd thrown without looking, and it missed, but the clattering caused the Reverend to crouch down. Tom knew that he would come after him now. He took the remaining two spears and moved back from the wall into the darkness so he wouldn't get cornered.

The Reverend leaned over and picked up the lantern. He took a step toward Tom, but then saw Hack trying to crawl away and changed his mind. He placed the lantern back on the ground and quickly counted, "Nine, ten! This is your last chance, Mr. Freshour. Do you want to kill your friend?"

"Don't come!" Hack bellowed.

Tom was just opening his mouth to say he would come when to his astonishment the Reverend aimed the gun at Hack's head and pulled the trigger. He shot him once, in the temple, and Hack thrashed in the dirt. The Reverend looked up, and the sight of his face in the shadowy yellow light, the inert black eyes — the awful, indifferent fixity looming above Hack's death tremor — changed something in Tom forever. By inborn fact of temperament, against all odds, Tom had stubbornly resisted what this man had tried to make him believe — that there was evil in the world, that there were people who were in the grip of evil, in whom it eclipsed anything else. Partly because the Reverend so avidly believed it, Tom had resisted this knowledge, but now he knew that the Reverend had been right, because he was one of them. In his heart this man was an inflicter of pain, a killer, and whatever good he did was finally nothing beside it — null and void, zero, utterly meaningless.

Without thinking it in words, Tom at last became a believer.

Turning toward him, the Reverend raised the pistol and aimed it in his direction. Tom fell to the dirt and scrambled to the side.

There was another blast and a thump near his hand. He had missed, but the flash had revealed the Reverend. Tom stood up. Using all of his body, he launched another of the sharpened handles. Just as the pistol went off again, the spear struck the Reverend in the shoulder and he grunted with surprise and pain. The gun fell from his hand, and slowly he leaned over to retrieve it.

Tom never hesitated. Giving the Cherokee death gobble that the boys used to make when they wrestled, he ran toward the Reverend. The noise made the Reverend hesitate just a second, causing a hitch to his movement as he brought the gun up, and when he straightened, Tom rammed him with the sharpened stick in his belly. His mouth hinged wide open in surprise, and he staggered backwards against a pillar and roared in pain as Tom pushed the spear home. The gun went off again, a wild shot, and Tom kicked it out of his hand. The Reverend tried to pull the spear from his gut, and he bellowed again as a red stain blossomed across his front. He pulled it out but was bleeding lavishly; he fell to his knees, crawled, then stood up and stumbled toward the stairs, crashing into something and falling again. Tom darted up the stairs ahead of him, slammed the door, and bolted it. He stood outside the door gulping air, and he heard the Reverend dragging himself to the top of the stairs.

"Let me out," he said weakly.

Tom didn't reply.

"God will forgive you, sinner," he groaned.

"No," Tom said.

"Then you will go to hell," the Reverend said feebly. "Please," he panted through the door. "Let me out."

Tom wondered why none of the boys from this side of the building had come at the sounds of gunshots in the basement, and guessed that they were afraid for their lives. He had a chance to get away without being seen, and he took it. He ran to the back door and fell headlong down the steps. He lay on the ground a moment, winded, stars bursting in his head. Lying there, he saw Hack's satchel, left on the ground. He crawled over, grabbed it and the shoes, and ran for the barn. With luck he could hold on to a horse long enough to get away from here.

Part Three

· 23 ·

TOM HAD TAKEN one of the Reverend's team horses and ridden through rapidly falling temperatures. The day came, and he was riding into the face of real winter weather coming down across the plains. He made the St. Louis and San Francisco tracks and followed the old, washed-out military road that went alongside it, north into the Winding Stair Mountains. He didn't know how hungry and tired he was until he fell off the horse from exhaustion. He led the horse down to a gully under a trestle, out of the biting wind, and went to sleep on the ground.

After a nap filled with wild visions, he woke up feeling stiff and strange. The sky was grey and closed in, with a curtain of greenish darkness approaching from the northwest.

What he'd done last night seemed like a dream. He felt unmoored, adrift, almost to the point of not being sure who he was anymore. The horse was standing nearby with his head down, and Tom noticed Hack's satchel on the back of it. When he'd saddled him, he'd tied it on and forgotten about it. He walked over and unbuckled it. At first he just looked inside without touching anything. Then he put the satchel down, took out five neat envelopes, and lined them up on the ground. Five bundles of twenty-dollar bills. He counted a bundle. There were twenty-five of them. Two thousand five hundred dollars in all.

Inside the satchel was also a letter, a plain envelope with *John Crilley / Muskogee / I.T.* written neatly on the outside. It was sealed.

He walked up the embankment to the railroad track and stood looking toward the south. Although he'd been traveling northward, he still was not far from Texas. Texas was like a different country, he had heard. People went there and began new lives. *GTT,* they wrote on their cabin doors — gone to Texas. He could go there and start a whole new life. A third life. Find a place and settle in, maybe pass for a white man — a white man with money. He sat on a rock and put his head down, unconsciously running his fingers through his hair. He thought about those evenings when he and Jake came home to Mrs. Peltier's. The good suppers, sitting with the men playing cards, the easy acceptance they'd shown him. The way Jake obviously cared about him. He thought about the danger Jake could be in. And Sam King. Thinking about her weakened and bewildered him.

If he returned to Fort Smith and confessed the truth, he would be hanged. For an instant, he saw Johnny Pointer being dragged to the gallows, begging not to die. Tom sat, hands slowly running through his hair, thinking hard. Had anyone known that he was leaving Fort Smith with Hack? The note he'd left for Jake was the only evidence. If Jake wasn't back yet, he could destroy it.

Stubbornness had made Tom avoid the habit of lying. At Bokchito, the ultimate defiance was to not be a liar. I am not saved, he had always admitted, I am not chosen. But he knew he could lie and keep a straight face about it. If he returned to Fort Smith, he had better be able to.

He went down the embankment, untied his horse, and rode north.

♦

Monday morning, well before light, Jake sat on the edge of his bed under a wall lamp, admiring Tom's flawless hand — his gracefully double-backed *D,* sweeping *J,* and evenly inclined letters:

Saturday Morning

Dear Jake,
  In case you arrive while I'm gone: I am going to Muskogee with Hack Deneuve. He knows about what has been going on and he

may talk to me. Deacon M. is staying in the Paris Hotel. I saw him at the hardware store, too, and believe that he works for them.

They fired me on Thursday.

Sam is here, staying at the Main Hotel. She came back from St. Louis to talk to you.

I'll be back.

Tom

Jake had read the note when they'd arrived last evening, but he'd been almost too exhausted to comprehend it. The last few miles of their day-long trip from Muskogee had consisted of open warfare with Grant and Lee. Fighting with two thirty-year-old mules was worse than fighting two eight-hundred-pound boulders, since these particular mules were not only obstinate almost beyond belief but also they looked at him out of their beady eyes with a hard-edged glint of triumph, as if bragging about it.

Jake had actually begun the day feeling affectionate toward them. They'd acted fine coming out of Muskogee, traveling at a good clip. But around Sallisaw they started getting stiff, and pretty soon it wasn't a matter of their walking at whatever pace they wanted, but absolute, intractable, full-bore balk. It would have been easier to have shot them than what he ended up doing, which was to trudge along beside them with a jerk-line arrangement, pulling and pushing and kicking and carrying on. Leonard was no help, since all he did was sit in the wagon complaining about his stomach. Between the mules and the lawyer, it was a long day.

And here was Tom's note, which let him know that whatever difficulty he'd had getting here might be the least of his troubles.

He had suspected that Deacon Miller was working for Ernest, but seeing it delineated in Tom's clear hand made it unpleasantly plain. But was Miller *openly* working for him?

Yesterday it had been obvious to Jake that Ernest had hired Miller, but the closer he stared it in the face, the more peculiar it looked. Why would a businessman — a businessman with Judge Parker's crossbeam a hundred yards from his front door — hire a killer to stalk an employee? Why not just fire him? This was the wrong side of the river for that kind of behavior.

Jake left Tom's note on the table so Leonard could read it when he woke up, went down to the kitchen, and chugged a cup of cold leftover coffee. He hurried up the alley to the wagon yard, where he ignored the mules, who were still off in mule dreamland. He snugged a borrowed saddle onto a brushy-tailed mare that he sometimes used in town, and in the chill last blackness of night rode her at a gallop to the store. He let himself in the back door with his key and walked into the unlit shipping room.

He found matches in a drawer of the shipping desk and lighted the wick of a lantern, and what he saw — or didn't see — made him wonder whether its meager light was playing tricks on him.

The shipping room was empty except for a few crates and barrels here and there. Downstairs, he found the main display room to be similarly empty. The long front desk had a single catalogue sitting on it, but there wasn't much else in an otherwise stripped room. Mystified, Jake walked back up the stairs to the second floor, and from there up another flight, and another, finally to the top, discovering one floor at a time that the building was stockless.

He walked through the stark void of the store with increasing disbelief. Back downstairs, he went to the sporting goods storeroom, which was also barren of goods. Beneath a wallboard display of the 102 bullets currently for sale by the Winchester Arms Company was the old man's desk. Several drawers were open and papers hung out, as if someone had rifled through them.

He sat in Ralph's chair and breathed the vaporous cold, trying to fathom the store's emptiness.

Across the front room, the big office was locked, but he had a key and let himself in. Lantern held high, he surveyed the place. The air was sour with lingering tobacco smells. In the wastebasket were a few notes that looked like property descriptions. He entered Ernest's small inner office, made sure the blinds were shut, and set down the lantern on the desk. A standing ashtray was full of the butts of pre-rolled cigarettes. Across the top of the desk was a large sheet of thick paper. It was a map of the Indian Nations and Oklahoma Territory, with ovals and circles drawn in various places, along with tiny squares which generally appeared around towns all over the map. It was a detailed map of the areas that the salesmen had been told to collect. The little squares were apparently places where mortgages had been signed. In a top corner was a series of numbers, crossed out, leading to a final number: *130*. The one area where there weren't a lot of squares was the Choctaw Nation, where Jake himself had been sent to collect. He found a pencil in a drawer and did a quick sketch of the map, roughly copying some of the details.

Putting the pencil back, he noticed a commonplace book in the back of the drawer. He sat still for a second, listening to the building, then pulled it out. On one page was a draft of what appeared to be a telegram.

> *To: Master's Hardware, Little Rock:*
>
> *Am clearing inventory at prices severely reduced below supplier costs. Will sell complete stock. Total supplier cost fifty-three thousand dollars, to be sold at twenty thousand, negotiable to eighteen cash purchase. If interested in buying, please contact me immediately.*

Jake looked up. He thought he'd heard a sound somewhere in the building. Quickly, he glanced through the rest of the notebook. Somewhere at the back he found a page that included a short list of names with dollar notations:

Shelby, $4
Bradley, $1
John Crilley, $10

He shut the back door and walked outside, beyond the wagon yard to the place where he'd tethered the brushy-tail. He stood beside her for a minute, listening. Morning was coming to a cloudy and very cold day for this early in winter. He rode to the Main Hotel and asked after Miss King.

The clerk gave him a funny look. "Afraid she's not here. Miss King is popular this morning. She left earlier. With another gentleman."

"Another gentleman?" Jake said.

"Two other gentlemen, actually."

"Did you notice who it was?"

The clerk shook his head. "You're welcome to leave her a note, sir."

Jake looked at him, trying to decide whether to push it. "Can you tell me what these gentlemen were dressed like?"

"I wasn't here. Another clerk mentioned it."

Jake took a pencil from the desk and wrote a note to her, saying that he was in town now and asking her to see him.

Back at Mrs. Peltier's, Jake found Leonard still in bed. Almost as soon as Jake shook him, Leonard swung his legs out and put his feet on the floor, as if intending to get right up, but that was as far as he got. Leonard was generally hard to wake up. He had to bitch himself awake in the morning. Today he wiped at his face and stared at the wall and with a sleepwalker's vacuous expressiveness cursed the one responsible for waking him up. Finally he breathed a theatrical sigh, wiped his face several more times, got up, and padded across the room to the water closet, muttering.

Jake fired up his little gasoline burner, boiled some sheep-herder's coffee, and when Leonard came out he handed him a cup of it without a word. Leonard started drinking, still muttering and knocking, like a boiler trying to get up to steam.

Jake sat down at his table, spread out his copy of the map from Dekker's office. He thought about what he'd seen at the store. By the time both of them had swallowed a couple of cups of coffee, Leonard had reentered the land of the living and was asking questions. "You say there's no stock at all?"

"It's empty as a hull. Stripped. I saw a draft of a telegram to Master's Hardware in Little Rock. Apparently he sold the whole inventory to them for less than half what it cost."

Leonard had already read the note Tom had left for Jake, and now he read it again. He eventually got up and began slowly pacing. He stopped and pointed at the *130* in the upper right corner of Jake's copy of the map.

Jake looked up. "You tell me."

"How many salesmen are there at Dekker?"

"Eight or nine, counting the front desk."

"How much total debt do each of you carry."

"Varies according to how much we turn over. I was carrying over twenty thousand in the northern district, but it averages less than that. Maybe fifteen."

"So the store's got over a hundred thousand dollars accounts receivable?"

"Hundred twenty, maybe. Nobody's paid up this time of the year, even when things are normal. It takes a while for everybody to clear their debts after the crop's shipped. Some of them wait until the last minute before spring ordering. And of course this year —"

"How much is he transferring these debts at?"

"Twenty-five cents an acre is what he told us."

Leonard sat down on the bed and stared at Jake. "Then the 130 is how many acres are already signed over."

Jake raised his eyebrows.

"A hundred thirty *thousand* acres," Leonard said, shaking his head. "You have to take this to somebody."

"What do you mean?"

Leonard held up fingers and enumerated. "Widely respected merchant dead under suspicious circumstances. Son turns wholesaling company into a shell for land scheme. Bankers implicated. A man in town who recently tried to murder you. Solid indications that you are persona non grata. Far be it from me to be a voice of reason, Jake, but either you talk to somebody like Parker or you leave town. There's no other reasonable choice."

Jake squinted at the map. "I'm wondering why he dumped all the merchandise. It won't take the store long to go down with no stock to sell. Word will get around. Customers will start jumping ship."

Leonard got up and walked over and looked out the window. "You told me he was a gambler. This is his big bet. He doesn't care about the store. He's turning it into land."

"But if he can't legally own tribal land — ?"

"Gus Wall was right about that. The white courts will probably go along with just about anything tied to an actual debt."

"It ain't fair to take somebody's property at twenty-five cents an acre."

"It's just a mortgage, Jake, a guarantee of repayment. The debt holder has the full right to buy it back."

"With what?" Jake said. "Are you saying the government will go along with this?"

"Judge Parker used to try to keep the sooners out, but Congress chopped his district in half. He no longer has authority over there. It's gone beyond one judge's ability, anyway." He looked at Jake. "Did you find anything else this morning?"

Jake poured another kick of muddy coffee. "I tried to find Sam King. You saw on Tom's note —"

Leonard nodded.

"Well, she wasn't there. She disappeared with 'two gentlemen' early this morning."

"I mean at the store, when you were snooping in the office. Did you see anything else there? Anything at all."

Jake shook his head. "There was somethin in the back of a notebook about Bradley and Shelby. That's probably Shelby White. Those two are with the Mercantile Bank. And there was a third name — Crilley, I believe."

Leonard, who'd been combing his long grey hair back with his hand, stopped dead still, his mouth open. "Crilley?"

"It was just the names written out with dollar amounts behind them. It was nothin. One dollar after Bradley, four dollars after White."

"One dollar means a thousand, Jake. He's using accounting shorthand."

"Well, then, Mr. Crilley, whoever he is, hit the jackpot, because the number after his name was ten."

Leonard stared at him with a strange, lowering intensity. "John Crilley," he said quietly.

"That's right. There was a first name on his entry. Who the hell is John Crilley?"

"You told me the boy — Tom — is in Muskogee?"

"Yeah. There's his note," Jake said, pointing at the table. "It's bad luck we didn't see him when we were there."

Leonard picked up the note and scanned it again.

"What's on your mind, Leonard? You look like your eyes are going to jump out of your head."

Leonard again stopped at the window and glanced out. He

said with dramatic flatness, "Get your hat, Jake. Let's go." He was looking down on the street.

Jake got up to look out, when someone came into the hallway below. Without a word, Jake grabbed Leonard by the shoulders and pushed him into the water closet, whispering, "Be quiet."

There was a vigorous knock on Jake's door.

"Mr. Jaycox. I have a message from Miss King."

"Put it under the door, please."

Before he could do anything, the door opened.

·24·

TOM RODE PAST wind-clashing trees on a rock-scattered road through the Winding Stair. By dark he had made it to Poteau, where he tied the horse in a shed beside McCurtain's General Merchandise and fetched from the saddlebag one of the envelopes full of money. He went inside the store and from the triangular stacks of cans along one wall got a tin of beef and a tin of green beans, took them to the front, and paid for them with one of the bills.

The storekeeper, a friendly, grave man of about Jake's age, didn't act like there was anything remarkable about Tom or his twenty-dollar bill, but the huddle of blizzard refugees who were sitting around the stove stopped talking and watched him. The storekeeper opened the cans and loaned Tom a table knife. Dazed from the cold, Tom walked toward them and sat down on a wooden box. At first he ate quickly, wanting both to vomit and to devour the entire contents of both cans in one swallow. As he knifed down the jellied beef and beans, the others eventually began talking again, in English and in Choctaw that he didn't understand well.

Around the stove were four men and five women. The oldest man had ramrod-straight posture and wore a floppy hat; two younger ones sat slump-backed, staring moodily at the floor. Among the women was a sultry young one wearing a fringed dress, who watched Tom eating. For some reason there were no children here. Two of the women were talking about the pros and cons of metal roofs, which were popular on settlers' dugouts.

Then they all talked about stoves, different models of stoves, cook stove and heating, fondly describing their shapes, sizes, and trim, how large a space they could heat, even the particular qualities of warmth put out by each one. It soon became apparent that none of them currently had a stove. "Twenty years ago was the first time I saw one in a house," the older man with a floppy hat said wistfully. One of the younger men, with the smooth, beardless face of a full blood, said that when the tribe's land was split up, he was going to sell his acreage and buy the best stove in the catalogue.

"Will you carry it on your back?" Soft Hat asked him.

Full Blood looked puzzled.

"Sell your land and you'll have no place to put your fancy stove," Soft Hat said.

"I plant in the bottoms."

"But if somebody else owns that land, you won't be able to plant there no more."

"We always plant in the bottoms."

Soft Hat laughed. "But somebody else will *own* the land!"

"What difference does that make?" Full Blood said casually. "Plenty of bottomland." Soft Hat said something back in Choctaw, and they carried on in that way for a while, talking faster. Tom was reminded that the Choctaw his pals at Bokchito used when they dared to talk Indian was a dim echo of the real thing. He glanced around at the faces of the people here and felt completely unconnected to them. In his state of mind, they seemed like lost wanderers from some distant land. He felt vaguely ashamed — of what, he didn't know.

Looking into the flames of the stove, he remembered the Reverend's picture book with naked savages dancing around fires. Would the Reverend always be in his thoughts, darting around, whispering, judging him? Did killing him only bring him to life? What Tom had read in his file had almost no meaning: *Osi Tamaha . . . Big Tree . . . Apache*. From long ago, he remembered some conversation about Apache from one of the younger boys, and all he could recall was that the very word terrified him. Then there was the old woman with the bathhouse at Durant . . .

His thoughts drifted to Samantha King, and he was scalded by a sudden raw desire to see her. He glanced at the young woman in fringe, who was watching the knife he was using to eat with.

He got up and limped around the store, his heels sore and his thighs tender from the long ride. The store had clothes, and he spent the remainder of the twenty-dollar bill on a plain brown pair of cowboy boots and a fur-lined sheepskin coat. He wasn't unhappy about abandoning Sam's ankle-cutting shoes once and for all.

As he was about to leave, the weather refugees were still talking about stoves. "Ain't worth selling your land," Soft Hat was saying. "You could buy a fine stove for forty dollars, cash." With no hesitation, as if pulled by invisible strings, Tom reached into his pocket, withdrew the envelope of money, walked over, and gave Full Blood two of the twenty-dollar bills. Seeing the look on Soft Hat's face, Tom gave him the same amount. He went on around to the others, handing forty dollars to each of them. Somewhere in the back of his mind, a voice was saying that this was the most foolish thing that he could possibly do. After the first two of them had received money, the others waited in dazed silence, as if they were afraid to move.

The young woman in fringe was last, and she gave him a desperate, sudden smile. "Take me with you," she said.

Tom looked at her a moment and realized that she was serious, but he was too stunned by the whole situation to reply intelligently. He just reached out his hand as if to touch her and said, "Take care, sister. Get your stove."

The young woman looked as if she was going to faint, which alarmed Tom, and he was turning to go when the storekeeper came out from behind his counter. "Friend, can I have a word with you?" he said. "That weather's dangerous. Do you have to travel?"

Tom nodded.

The storekeeper searched Tom's face. "I had a cousin freeze in a norther."

Tom shook his head. He wanted to talk but was too wrought up to say much.

The rest of the journey to Fort Smith was over gentle hills south of the Poteau River. Now he was headed away from the wind, but the old road and the train tracks were well covered with snow, and in some places he had to guess his way. He got to the bridge over the Arkansas, where the wind howled and tore at the river below. He had intended to let the horse loose before he came into town, but he'd only die if he did.

Not knowing what else to do, Tom took the horse to the stable that Jake used, got him unsaddled and fed, and turned him loose in the sheltered yard, where in the shadows he saw the outline of a mule. He walked over and there was Grant standing asleep. Tom patted him and rubbed his old hairy chin, unconcerned about being bitten. On the other side of the yard, as far away as possible, was Lee. Tom went over and hugged him around the neck.

Down the alley in Mrs. Peltier's back shed, he put the satchel into the bottom drawer of an old cobweb-covered dresser. He walked straight through the back door and up the stairs, meeting no one on the way. Jake wasn't in his room. He looked around for his note to Jake — the evidence that he'd been with Hack — and wasn't surprised that it was gone.

With a last spasm of energy he managed to pull off his new boots. On the couch in Jake's parlor, finally warm, he lay down and immediately slipped into a half-sleep. Several times he was wakened by comings and goings in the halls. He heard people talking, but remained locked in an unrestful stupor.

A couple of hours later, the door opened and in walked a man carrying a lantern with long grey hair streaming across his shoulders. Disoriented, a little scared, Tom lifted his head from the couch. He recognized the grey-haired man: Leonard LaFarge, Jake's friend he'd met in the land-office yard in Guthrie. He was pale.

"Tom?" he said, walking closer to him with the lantern. "Tom Freshour?"

Tom sat up and put his feet on the floor. "Yessir?"

"*Ecce homo,*" LaFarge said wonderingly, peering intently at him. "You look . . . older."

♦

Tom asked after Jake, and LaFarge immediately began pacing. He told Tom about Jake's and Sam's abduction by Deacon Miller. He then described what had just happened to him. He had been "kicked out by the U.S. commissioner," he said. "Which makes it unanimous. He was my last hope. No person associated with the law in this town wants to hear about this. All day I've been waiting for people. I saw the sheriff and he fobbed me off. I went to the marshal's office, and they told me they needed proof of something that serious. Proof! I finally went to the U.S. commissioner — I *know* Claude Baines — and what does he say but that in the absence of suspects in custody he has no authority."

LaFarge stopped pacing and stared at Tom with big expressive eyes, jaw jutting out, wild hair sticking out in all directions. "They look at me and think, There's old Bindlestiff, old Copper Nose, he must have finally sprung a leak. That's how the courthouse crew thinks. He's prob'ly only tellin half the story, they think. Deacon Miller? White man's sheriff, high-stakes man, they think. He don't work for no piss-ant pay, they think. That salesman must owe somebody a right smart amount of money, they think. Missing links!" LaFarge spat. "The descent of man, verified! That's why I quit this trade."

Mr. Haskell came into the room while LaFarge was making his speech. "Hello, Tom. You doin okay?" Mr. Haskell was Tom's favorite boarder at Mrs. Peltier's — somebody he felt like he'd known although they hadn't talked that much.

"Yes sir. I'm okay."

Tom asked Mr. Haskell what had happened, and he calmly related what LaFarge had told him about Jake's and Sam's disappearance, while the lawyer continued to pace and mutter.

LaFarge came over and plopped down, and the three of them sat for a moment in silence. "I can't believe the way they treated me," LaFarge said lamely. "Law enforcement in this town is all being paid off. Without exception."

"Sheriff's up for hire," Mr. Haskell said. "Everybody knows that. I doubt the marshal is."

LaFarge glowered at him. "Parker. He's the only one left."

Mr. Haskell looked at him skeptically. "Think I'll take a quick turn around town and ask around. We'd feel pretty dumb if we found out the two of them were sitting somewhere in a saloon, drinking a beer."

Leonard LaFarge waited until Mr. Haskell had shut the door.

He looked down at his hands, folded on the table. "Did you go to Muskogee?"

Tom had prepared for this question. He had thought about it much of the way back, coaching himself in the lies that he hoped would keep him out of trouble, practicing them in his mind. The report of what had happened to Reverend Schoot would take a day or two to get out, but he might as well put a gun to his own head as admit having had any part of it. If he hesitated, or if he acted odd about it, he'd be caught. He had no choice but to lie.

But in the face of this news about Jake, all of his preparations became insignificant. Ignoring LaFarge's question, he put on his boots and coat. He went to Jake's bottom drawer, where Jake kept an old pistol. As he stood up and slipped it into his coat pocket, he noticed a beautiful, lightly dressed buckskin suit with a short fringe lying on top of the dresser.

"That's for you," LaFarge said.

"What?" Tom said.

"A gift. Jake bought it for you in Tulsa."

While Tom made ready to leave, LaFarge paced back and forth, talking as if to himself: "It was daylight, and they took him right out the front door, which gives me hope. Miller isn't known for doing his work in front of witnesses." He looked up and saw that Tom's hand was on the doorknob. "Wait! Don't leave. Do you have any idea what they might want to find out from Jake? What they might be looking for?"

Tom shook his head.

LaFarge sighed. "This isn't just about Jake and Samantha King, you know. It involves certain big shots who don't like people interfering with their plans. They can have you killed and not think twice about it."

"I know," Tom said. "They already killed Joel."

"Who's Joel?"

Tom went through the door.

First, Ralph Dekker's house.

Through a dark town gone quiet in the falling snow, he rode down Seventh Street. The back door was unlocked, and he walked into a torn-up kitchen. He found a lantern in the corner, and when he lit it he saw that all cabinet doors were open, drawers emptied out and stacked off to the side. In the sitting and dining rooms books had been thrown on the floor, every door was open, couches and chairs sliced up with stuffing pulled out, and in one place several holes were knocked into the wall. The house had been turned inside out. Tom saw Dekker's family album in the heap of books. For a few minutes he wandered through the rooms. They had searched frantically for something, here and at the store. He remembered how lights had been burning on every floor of the nearly empty store building the other night.

He stood for a moment in the sitting room amid the clutter, holding up the lantern, his breath thick in the cold. The house was silent. His eye drifted to the fireplace, and he recalled the dying fire he'd seen here on Monday night. He knelt at the fireplace and held the lantern close to the ashes and probed them with his hand, picking out a little piece of ash and looking at it.

He had found what they'd been searching for.

Rising from his knees, he looked over at the stairs and remembered the terrible look on the old man's face, sitting in his bedroom.

Straightaway, Tom rode to the Paris Hotel, where the same skeletal clerk sat at the front desk playing solitaire, with no one else in the lobby. Tom went up to the counter; the clerk glanced at him and went back to his cards.

"Hello, chief. Colder'n a wood-yard wedge in December out there. I never seen nothin like it this time of year."

"I'm looking for Deacon Miller."

"Been here before?" the man said to his cards.

"Yes sir," Tom said quietly. "One of your employees tried to rob me a few nights ago."

The man glanced up again, as if slightly worried by Tom's quietness. Tom was looking not at him but just off to the side.

"Do you have any idea where Deacon Miller is?" Tom said again.

The clerk squirmed irritably and moved his ashtray on the counter so it was between them. "He don't keep his time with me."

"I'm not asking about his time, I'm asking whether you know where he might be. He has a friend of mine with him."

"That boy ain't with him," the clerk rushed to say, picking up his cards and shuffling them busily. "He went somewheres else. Earlier."

Tom turned his eyes to him now, giving him one of the Reverend's patented looks: death mask mixed with an incongruous, elusive dash of friendly concern. He said nothing.

"Besides which, even if I did know where he was, I couldn't tell you." His eyes bugged out as he dealt his cards. "Don't mess with me, chief."

Tom leaned across the desk on his elbows and slowly moved the ashtray aside.

"I'll call out the *dogs* on you," said the clerk.

Tom pulled out the pistol, cocked it, and aimed it at the clerk's face. "The dogs are already out."

The man shook his head. "Deacon don't never tell me where he's goin! All he said was somethin, I heard him say somethin, somethin . . ." He trailed off. "He said somethin about Park Hill. Which I don't know *nothin* about. I just heard one of em say it. Park Hill is all I know! Mister, please, if he was to find out I told you —"

Tom left him babbling at the front desk and headed for the Main Hotel.

◆

A lingering sour feeling that somewhere he went wrong. He is plowing into unmerciful cold. He tries to avoid waking up to the wind and noise, but hears something calling. Turns away. Turns away. A bad headache is keeping him company, but a five-pound ball-peen hammer is waiting above the murky trench of sleep. He sees a man who beneath his duster is dressed in a high collar, striped tie, full-length coat, like somebody who might be reading Frank Leslie's Illustrated Newspaper *between acts at the opera house, only the look on this man's face is not casual . . .*

The closer he got to awake, the colder he was. Finally venturing to open an eye, Jake discovered that he was on his belly, with his hands behind and tied to his ankles, his face against splintery planks in a prying, probing, stunning wind. He heard the clacking of wheels and smelled manure, a pile of it two inches from his face, and a plank wall some distance farther. Hog-tied, freezing, he managed to cock his head back and see into a hurricane of eerie grey-green light. The hurricane was dust and hay and dried manure; wind was coming through four-inch gaps in the wall planking. He realized that it was a bull car, a livestock car with stalls, and either it was moving at ninety miles an hour or it was heading into a brutal wind.

At some distance away through the furious bands of light, he saw Sam. He remembered her name with no difficulty, although a number of other basic matters still floated around in his head, looking for a berth. Like why, exactly, he felt a certain mistrust of her when they were clearly headed toward hell in the same hand-basket. She was sitting with her ankles roped together, her arms tied, and secured to a hitch ring on the wall.

"Aah! Aah!" She was making a strenuous attempt to yell through the gag.

Jake tried to speak but only a croak came out. He tried to move his hands and they were completely numb from lack of circulation. The only way he could move was to turn on his side and wiggle like an arthritic snake toward her, raking down a considerable distance of splintery, manure-splattered flooring. When he got there, he saw that her face was stiff around the gag. She kept trying to talk through it while he chewed and pulled at the rough hemp knots on her legs until he got them free.

It took her a minute to stand up, and she was able then to use her fingers to get the gag off, and then to gnaw the ropes on her hands. She was wearing some kind of thin dress jacket over her top, and underneath that, what looked for all the world like a short nightgown, which left a quite long remainder of her wearing nothing at all. By the time she finally got loose and started working on Jake's ropes, most of what had happened had come back to him. The man at the door had been Deacon Miller, who had tried to talk Jake out of the boarding house and into the buggy, saying that his employer wanted to have a talk with Jake about some missing money. That failing to work, he had aimed his .44-caliber pistol at Jake's heart and repeated his request. Jake had heard something behind him, and that was all he could remember.

Sam spoke close to his ear. "We're gonna freeze, Jake." After she managed to untie him, Jake stumbled around in the car, getting the feeling in his arms back, trying the door. Grainy hot smoke occasionally raked through, stinging his skin. He found part of a dirty Pullman blanket piled in a corner and took it back to her. She offered to share the blanket, but he realized that it wasn't going to do the job. One of the stalls next to the front wall had a large pile of piss- and manure-soaked hay with a partly frozen exterior shell. "We've got to get under that and squeeze together," he said. "Keep the blanket on." They managed to build a nest in the hay and manure pile, tasting and breathing a considerable amount of it in the process. Pushing up against each other, they both shivered in waves. Jake was fully awake now, and he was too mad to freeze.

"What *is* this?" Sam shuddered.

"I think we're heading into a norther." In a storm like this, the temperature could drop twenty or thirty degrees within a few minutes, and people sometimes got themselves killed out of sheer confusion. He remembered that Tom was out here somewhere, and it worried him. The two of them pushed their bodies together in as many places as possible under the dung pile.

"Any idea where we're going?" he asked numbly.

"I don't know. I think we crossed the river."

"Didn't hear them say anything about where they were taking us?"

"No."

"How long we been traveling?"

"You were already knocked out when they tied you in here," she said, her teeth chattering. "Then they hit you again. I thought you were dead."

"How long?" Jake said gruffly.

"Maybe two hours. We sat for a while somewhere."

"How'd they get you?"

"Came into my hotel room early this morning while it was still dark. They didn't say anything. They just came in and hit me."

Warming above the frost point, his brain throbbing, Jake reared back and looked at the bloody lump on the side of her head and got even more aggravated. Sneaking into a woman's room and knocking her out while she was asleep was a pretty low form of behavior.

She sneezed violently three times, groaned, and pressed right up against him.

Jake wondered if Miller had put them on a train for the same reason that he'd followed them into Hell's Fringe — to kill them outside of Parker's jurisdiction. Miller was too smart to murder respectable-class people in Fort Smith. Only a fool or a drunk would do that. But if someone froze to death somewhere in Indian Territory . . .

"You have any idea what they're up to?"

She didn't reply. She just lay hard against him, shivering. Even through curtains of head pain, in a pile of manure, Jake, who had been without a woman for a good while, was beginning to experience a certain responsiveness to Sam's being so thoroughly, physically, all up and down, against him this way, which annoyed him for too many reasons to think about.

Eventually she seemed to warm up a little. Jake pulled back to see if she was okay. She was staring. He tried to answer his own question. "Maybe they're taking us out here for some kind of questioning. Miller said something to me about missing money."

When he pulled his body away from hers, she snuggled right up to him again. His frustration returned. This had to be one of the most miserable situations of his life. Lying under a pile of manure with a blind headache, helpless, embarrassed, up against a beautiful young woman.

"I'm sorry, Sam, I'm truly sorry," he said crossly.

"For what?"

"For getting you involved, and for the discomfort I'm causing you, lying here like this," he said stiffly.

"If I could wrap you around me like a blanket, I'd do it," she said.

Contemplating this image, Jake kept looking at her, checking on her, afraid she was freezing. His own headache was beginning to do strange things now, making noises, knocking holes in his thoughts.

After a while — he didn't know how long — she said, "I have to tell you everything. Before we both get killed. I want you to forgive me."

"I forgive you," he said drowsily.

"Not until I tell you!"

He was going out.

"I was using you, Jake."

"What's that?"

"I was using you to get to Ralph Dekker."

· 25 ·

M R. HASKELL, Leonard LaFarge, and Tom sat at the dining
table in the boarding house. It was past midnight. LaFarge
was drinking something from a coffee cup. Mr. Haskell had
just gotten back from making a run on the avenue saloons,
where he hadn't seen or heard anything of Jake. "Dead quiet out
there," he said. "People hiding from the weather."

"I have an idea what happened," Tom said.

LaFarge's eyes crinkled in puzzlement.

Mr. Haskell sniffed and stared, looking slightly pained. He
started to say something, but the lawyer beat him to it. "What?
Speak. Tell us."

"I don't know for sure, but there's some lost money," Tom said.

Mr. Haskell said, "How'd you find this out?"

LaFarge held up his hand. "What money, Tom? Do you know?"

"Ralph Dekker brought money back from St. Louis. Ernest has
been searching for it since the police told him his father was
dead."

The two of them waited for more, but that was all Tom had
to say.

LaFarge's eyes remained fixed on him.

"They started going through the store last Thursday or Friday.
Now they've ransacked Mr. Dekker's house."

The lawyer looked baffled.

Old Mr. Potts shuffled up to the doorway in his bathrobe and
seemed to peek at them over some imaginary barrier. "Why, looky

here," he said in his odd, mild voice. "Tom grew up since the last time I saw him. I like your new coat, Tom. And your stogies. What's wrong with you? You porely?"

Mr. Haskell gave Mr. Potts a sour look.

LaFarge asked Tom, "Any idea where they took them?"

"A hotel clerk heard something about a place called Park Hill."

"Park Hill near Tahlequah? That's a seminary of some kind, isn't it?"

"They shut that place down," Mr. Haskell said, "two, three years ago."

There was another silence, and Mr. Potts ventured, "You look like death eatin crackers, boy. Ain't been drinkin that whiskey, have you? How many years has it been since I seen you? Seems like yesterday." He looked back and forth between them with his little cracked blue eyes.

"I know a man who works for the railroad," Mr. Haskell said. "I'm going to see what I can find out."

Mr. Potts followed him down the hall. "What's wrong, Yankee? Have we lost a man?"

LaFarge went to the window, cup in hand, and looked out. "What does Samantha King have to do with all this?"

Tom shook his head, trying to indicate that he didn't want to talk about her. Questions about Sam made him feel trapped. He didn't know how far to trust LaFarge.

"You know her pretty well, I take it," LaFarge persisted.

Tom looked down at his boots, amazed at what was pouring through him. Once again he was swamped by images of annihilation — throwing over the table, kicking holes in the wall, running everybody out. It had happened in Sam's hotel room, in the Reverend's office, and now again.

Everything appeared small and distant, even his hand on the table. Coming across the room toward him, the grey-haired lawyer seemed to walk a great distance. "You have to excuse my nosiness, Tom. Jake did tell me quite a lot about you. He was so concerned about you that he nearly jostled out my innards racing across Indian country, trying to get here in a hurry."

Tom was on the edge of the chair, staring down at his boots, his thoughts still jumbled. He looked at the door leading to the hall and imagined going through it. Not even opening it, just moving through it, into the night. Escaping.

LaFarge sat down across from Tom. "I'm not asking out of puerile interest."

Please, Tom thought. *Let go of me.*

LaFarge sighed, rubbed his face, and assumed a calmer tone. "We can't do a thing until Mr. Haskell comes back. You look like someone who could use a hot bath. Would you allow me to get up some hot water?"

The craziness receded almost as quickly as it had come. He felt under control again.

Soon after Tom sank into the bath, LaFarge knocked on the door and brought him in some food — dinner scraps negotiated from the kitchen, which Tom devoured in about one minute while in the bathtub. But to Tom's discomfort, LaFarge then stayed in the little bathroom and started telling him his life story. There was a small window looking eastward down the street through which the lawyer watched while he gabbed, occasionally wetting his lips from his cup. Tom had switched ends in the bathtub so that his back wouldn't be toward LaFarge.

"I did everything at least once," he said. "I was a traveling player, a hobo, a merchant seaman, a day laborer, a pharmacist's assistant, a drug addict. The pharmacist I worked for introduced me to morphine sulphate. Happy dust, they call it. Fashionable women crush a lozenge in a napkin and breathe it like it was delicate perfume." He pulled together his fingers and made as if smelling it. "I learned to inject it into my bloodstream with a syringe. You push the curved steel horns and shoot it directly into your blood." His eyelids descended. "Presto, you are in an atmosphere of purest tranquility. Nothing can bother you. But there's a hitch: you must have it constantly. More and more of it. Without it you grow uneasy, flighty, hideously, sleeplessly exhausted. You have chills and sweats. If it's been too long, you feel an incredible drilling agony in your arms and legs." He gritted his teeth as if in pain, then he glanced down at Tom with a crooked-toothed grin. "Jake hates this story. He thinks I'm exaggerating.

"I wandered to Europe in quest of my elixir. You can buy it there in little cardboard cases, divided into cells, each cell lined with wool, a little glass globule sealed with wax and filled with the drug. I had a black morocco case to carry around everything I needed, needles, spoons, and so forth." His eyebrows raised, then he set down his cup, unbuttoned and rolled up a sleeve, and showed Tom the scarred inside of his forearm. "I did that all over my body. Sticking myself."

LaFarge seemed oddly cheerful about his scars. He almost looked amused. Tom was suddenly interested.

"I traveled on to Asia, where they grow the poppy that makes the drug. Trying to get as close as possible to the fountainhead. One evening I was standing alongside a man near the stern of a hundred-ton rusting hulk of a ship in the Indian Ocean. I can remember the smell of hemp cord rising up through the deck. It was sunset, and we were hoping to see the green flash. Do you know what that is?" He looked at Tom.

"No."

"Just as the sun sinks beneath the sea's horizon, there is sometimes an instantaneous flash of emerald light. But it's very elusive. As many times as I'd looked for it, I'd never seen it. But that evening we actually did, and just after it happened my companion said, 'As soon as we know, what we know is gone.' He'd been to China, and at the time I thought it was just opium talk.

" 'What we know is gone.' Please, sir, I thought, tell me something new for the price of admission. Strangely, during the next few days I couldn't get his remark out of my mind. It began to dominate my thoughts entirely. I realized that it was my drug habit I was thinking about — eating oblivion, wanting oblivion. I had sacrificed the necessary in hopes of gaining the superfluous. All of my traveling was a trick I was playing on myself, an illusion of adventure, a way to skip across the surface. Standing on the same spot at the stern of the ship a few days later, I understood that I had no choice but to throw my drug kit or myself into the ocean. Otherwise I could travel the entire surface of the earth and see less and less, and know less and less, and hate myself more each day."

He glanced back at Tom, looking slightly sheepish, holding out his nearly empty cup. "Of course, I still have my vices . . . I can't remember why I'm telling you all this. Did I have a point?"

"Why do you smile about your arms?" Tom asked.

"The scars?" LaFarge narrowed his eyes in mock defiance.

"Why, sir, I'm proud of those. They're the record of my travels, the blue pictorial myth of how far I've traveled. Besides," he added with a grin, "what else can I do?"

LaFarge looked out the window into the night and took a last sip. The wind was getting through the cracks around the window, causing the flame to waver. He turned, suddenly frowning, looking almost severe. "You know, Jake did talk quite a lot about you, Tom. He said that you were a smart young man who could do what you put your mind to. Jake's language suffers from understatement. You are *not* any young man." He sighed and looked at Tom almost gloomily. "I believe that you are a most unusual young man."

Tom blanched.

LaFarge put his cup down on the windowsill. "I'm a pretty good judge of character. I have a knack for it. You are blessed in more than one way, Tom, but particularly on the top story. You are intelligent, alert, unafraid. You don't appear to be hampered by pridefulness, which is the worst blinder of all. I see why Jake feels the way he does about you." He raised his eyebrows, as if inviting Tom to respond.

Tom stood up, quickly dried himself off, and went upstairs to Jake's room, where he put on an undershirt and a pair of Jake's pants.

LaFarge followed him. "Jake found a notebook belonging to Ernest Dekker which had a very interesting note in it. The name of a man in Muskogee. It implied that money was given to this man. If I had some confirmation of that note, I could go to Judge Parker. I can't just tell him I saw a name written down. It's not enough." He shook his head. "I need a witness who can confirm that money was sent to this man."

Tom said nothing, but he was listening. He realized that LaFarge had been preparing him for this.

LaFarge stared out the window again, sighing. "You know, Judge Parker's a good man, but time has passed him by. He's hanging the wrong people, and I think he knows it. Ten or fifteen years ago, yes, they were the ones. The lawless element. The drunks, the spree killers. But that's not what he should be attending to now. Now it's the sharp operators, the Dekkers with their mortgage schemes. A whole new generation of thieves is loosed upon that poor land." He glanced back at Tom with a look of distaste. "Twenty-mile-wide grants of real estate to railroads. Walnut trees cut off tribal land. Illegal coal mining. The Dawes Commission. Land syndicates set up by Indian agents. White towns passing laws preempting real estate. It's not the few poor clods robbing trains, it's the men in suits. Blackface Charley Bryant, the Dalton Brothers, bah! They're not even the clowns in this circus. They're hardly even the ants carrying away crumbs." LaFarge shook his head again. "Parker's got the best of intentions, he truly does, but he's stuck in a rut. He's after the wrong people. And he's too smart a man not to know it."

He looked at Tom and showed his snaggle teeth in a brief bleak grin. "If we could get Judge Parker's attention, we'd have a better chance of getting Jake out of this. I believe that the best way to get his attention is to convince him that we know for a fact that money was sent, probably by courier" — he raised his eyebrows slightly — "to this man in Muskogee."

"What man?" Tom said.

LaFarge held up a hand. "Be patient. I'm getting around to it. You should know this first: Judge Parker's district used to include most of what is now the Oklahoma Territory and Indian Nations, as well as a big part of Arkansas. Four years ago the Congress divided his district and created a new federal court in Muskogee. Parker hates the judge who occupies the bench there. He even spoke against him in the newspapers, for which he was roundly criticized and accused of petty jealousy. He thinks the man's questionable."

"What's his name?"

"John Crilley. Judge John Crilley."

Without a word, Tom stood up and walked out the door. He didn't stop until he'd gotten to the kitchen steps, where he hesitated a moment and looked back through the dark kitchen into the warm house as if he was leaving it forever. He went out to the shed, got the satchel that he'd hidden in the bottom drawer of the old dresser, and trudged back inside, up the stairs.

He dumped out the bundles of money and the letter in front of Leonard LaFarge and calmly told his story. He lied about how he'd ended up with Hack's satchel, omitting the details of following Hack to Bokchito and what had happened there in the cellar.

He said that he woke up in the Muskogee hotel with Hack gone and his satchel left behind. LaFarge questioned him about what he thought had happened to Hack, and Tom said he didn't know but he might have gone south.

Lying didn't have any particular effect on Tom. He experienced no powerful emotions. His heart didn't even beat hard. Lying had no more immediate consequence than telling the truth. Everything else he told the lawyer was true — he just left out the trip to Bokchito. He admitted that on his way back to Fort Smith he'd spent and given away some of the money at a store in Poteau. LaFarge looked worried about that, but when he saw the envelope beneath the pile of money, all his skepticism melted. He picked it up, looking fixedly at the writing: *John Crilley / Muskogee / I.T.*

He held it out and said wonderingly, "God bless us, Tom, this is it. Will you go with me to see Parker?"

There was a quiet knock at the door, and before LaFarge could put away the money, Mr. Haskell opened it and came in, his face reddened by the cold wind. "I haven't got a bead on this place yet. My railroad man is out of town. It'll be tomorrow." When he noticed the money he looked embarrassed. "What the heck did you do, rob a bank?"

♦

Before Sam could really launch into her confession, the train came to an abrupt halt. The door slid open, and there stood Deacon Miller and two pals, looking none too warm themselves. Miller showed some irritation that they had worked free of their ropes, but he also seemed relieved that they hadn't frozen to death. Soon they were inside a little abandoned depot, which was being occupied by a flock of sleeping chickens. Then they were walking through face-stinging snow to a big brick building that stood over the crest of a hill. There was an equally large building nearby that was burned to its rock shell.

Jake knew by sight most of the big older buildings in the Indian Nations and Oklahoma Territory, but he couldn't place where they were. They entered the tall front door. Inside, several fireplaces were roaring, with someone rushing around feeding them, the wind moaning constantly and lanterns wildly flickering, threatening to go out. Jake's brain was about to go out again, too.

He heard Miller say something about wanting only one room to guard, and dimly he heard him threaten them against running away, but he remembered nothing at all about walking or being carried upstairs.

He woke up several times during the next few hours, noticing that someone was in a small bed with him, and that they were sharing two thin wool blankets. It was Sam. As they slept, the blizzard moaned around and through the building.

After nightfall, an old woman entered the room, bringing them shredded beef and beans, and two cups of coffee with hickory-nut butter in it — the sweetener called *canuchi* by the Cherokees. They ate in silence, and Sam got up and tried to comb the dirt out of her long hair with her fingers. To Jake's annoyance, they hadn't given her anything to wear. Both of them were still grimy with coal smoke, manure, and hay dust, but for Jake the headache, at least, was subsiding to manageable proportions. One of Miller's apprentices, probably the one who'd hit him on the head — white, maybe twenty years old, grumpy and sullen — was sitting in the hall near the door, and Jake talked to him long enough to learn that his informativeness did not go beyond where the toilet was.

After a while, Sam and Jake were sitting side by side in the bed, propped against the wall, the thin wool blankets over them. The blizzard still raged outside. They were fortunate not to be on the north or west side of the building. There was no stove in the room, but a length of pipe sticking out from a chimney added its own deep wail to the building's orchestra of wind sounds. The room was narrow and had five single metal-framed beds lined along one wall. On the wall opposite the beds there was one small table with a kerosene lantern, and above it hung a picture of a stern, luminous Jesus, providing the room's sole adornment and clue to the identity of this place.

"Looks like a school," Jake said. "An old school. I don't know. I figure we're in the Cherokee Nation."

Sam didn't reply.

"Sam, what were you about to tell me before we got off the train?"

She groaned.

"I may've had my eyes open, but I wasn't all there. Did you say that you used me to 'get to' Ralph?"

She looked over at him sullenly. "He owed my mother money. I came to collect it."

"Our friend out there is close to the door, so you better talk quiet. You mean that's why you came in the first place?"

She looked at the dirt on her arms and hands. "I can't stand this."

She sat still awhile, gathering herself. Then she began talking. "It was about the time I was born. Ralph Dekker borrowed money from my mother several times over a period of about five years for his business. She occasionally made private loans to people she trusted. Most of them paid her back. But her hotel defied the law in more than one way, and if someone didn't honor a debt, there was only so far she could go without resorting to those types." She indicated the door. "She once told me how galled she was by this man down in Fort Smith who'd taken a lot of money from her. He owed her over thirty thousand dollars. She named him and carried on. Ralph Dekker this, Ralph Dekker that. My mother was usually stiff with me, like I was some stranger in her house that she had to put on manners for. About this subject she seemed to let her hair down and talk freely to me. The few times we were together, she never spoke to me about anything relating to business or money, and there she was, all torn up about an old unpaid debt."

Sam looked away, toward the dark window. It was tapping lightly with crystals of sleet. "I hated her, Jake. But after she died I missed her worse than if she'd kissed me good night every day of my life. Now you explain that."

Jake felt like he was a long way from explaining anything to this woman. "So you decided to collect an old debt twenty-some years past due? Why?"

She continued to stare toward the window.

"Sam. They want some information out of us, something they think we both know about. Unless they satisfy their curiosity, I'm afraid they'll send us for a walk with their friendly boys, and that's gonna be it. Please, tell me the rest of this."

As if she hadn't heard him, she continued her story. "I must have sensed that there was more to this man than owing her money. She wanted to talk about it, but she didn't. Maybe he'd humiliated her somehow. Whatever grief she suffered was fine with me, at the time. I was sixteen years old and generally disgusted by her. But I knew there was more to it than money. Somehow I knew." She shook her head slightly.

Jake sighed impatiently.

"I went to see Ralph Dekker a week ago. The night he died."

Jake looked at her. "Wednesday?"

"No. It was Monday."

She went quiet again, heaved another sigh, and threw back the blankets. "I can't stand this. I *have* to have a bath." She got up and went out in the hall, long legs and all, and told the guard that she wanted a bath. He told her to either go to the toilet or get back into the room, and she started arguing with him. It wasn't long before she was cleaning his plow. "Getting me a little water's not going to hurt you. And damn you, I want some kind of clothes to wear!" Jake lay there listening until she said, "Boy, you are one big brave shithead, waving your gun at an unarmed woman."

Jake looked up at the Jesus on the wall and groaned to himself. He climbed out of bed and went into the hall, where their guard had the expression of a dog with his first porcupine. Miller showed up and acted eerily polite. There would be a "meeting" tomorrow, he said. He was "sincerely sorry for the discomfort," and of course she could have a bath.

This fake solicitude worried Jake worse than anything. The old woman eventually came to their room with two buckets of water, some soap and rags, a Mother Hubbard dress for Sam to wear, and a couple more blankets. Jake tried to ask her, in English and then in halting Cherokee, where they were, but she acted as if she didn't understand him. The water was ice cold, the air in the room seemed below freezing, and the building wailed with wind, but Sam unhesitatingly stripped down to belly naked. Jake sat on the bed, turned away, thinking, *Go ahead, don't give me any warning.*

"I don't care how cold it is," she chanted. "I don't care. I don't care." After she'd finished and put on the Mother Hubbard, Jake noticed her grab something from the coat she'd been wearing and slip it into a pocket. She crawled back into the bed. "Oh," she said. "Oh!"

Having dipped her hair into the water, she now rubbed it vigorously. Jake stiff-walked over to the buckets and washed his own face and arms. For good measure, he took off his shoes and washed one foot at a time. That was all he felt inspired to do. He knocked the dust out of his clothes, went back to bed, and crawled in with her. She was shivering.

"So," he said. "This was Monday, you say?"

"I went to see him about five o'clock Monday evening. I stood outside, on the steps of his house. I told him who I was and why I'd come. I said that my mother was dead, but as her sole legatee I'd come to collect the debt that he owed her estate. I told him that I wanted to talk to him in person, but I'd contact him through a lawyer if he preferred." She frowned. "At first he just stood there staring at me, like you might expect — acting as if he didn't know what I was talking about. He didn't invite me inside. But I could tell he didn't want me to leave. He was . . . interested. He kept looking at me." She sounded hesitant. "Finally he invited me in, asked me to sit down. He started pacing and asking me questions."

"What kind of questions?"

"First he said that he didn't know my mother, but then he asked me things that half admitted he was lying, like how had she died, had I been there, were we reconciled. I asked him what he meant by 'reconciled,' and he said he meant were we close. He wanted to know whether I was married. He didn't ask it casually or lightly like people will do."

"Whether you were married?"

"He demanded to know whether I was married."

"I don't understand what you mean."

"He had a set to his face, kind of mean, kind of confused. 'Are you married?' he said."

"Well, did you answer him?"

"I did, but I was getting nervous."

"Because you were a lone woman —"

"Oh, heavens no. He wasn't acting *that* way. I expected him to be suspicious and provoked. To tell you the truth, I thought he'd just tell me to depart the premises. I expected that. I didn't expect him to be asking all kind of questions about me." She was staring up toward the Jesus. "It caught me by surprise. It didn't even seem to have much to do with the money. At first I thought he was going to reveal something, maybe talk to me about my mother, but he didn't. He acted like my mother had, ten years before, the day she told me about him. As if he couldn't speak what was really on his mind. I had the strangest feeling, like I'd been there before."

She broke her stare and looked at Jake. "Anyway, there we were. I told him that I'd come to offer him a way to right what was wrong, and I earnestly requested some answer from him. He faltered a little. Finally he turned around and looked me square in the eye and told me to leave his house."

"Debt collectors are usually tobacco-chewing men in dirty black suits," Jake said. "And here comes one looking like you. I can see how it might throw him a little off."

She reached into the dress pocket and pulled out a small rectangle that Jake had to hold up close to his eyes in the dim light. It was a twenty-five-cent studio portrait of a young girl with long darkish hair and striking eyes. Jake's unhesitating, first thought was that it was a picture of Sam as a child. On the back was written, in what looked like Mr. Dekker's distinctive, looping hand,

M. King's daught.
Left b.

"Where'd you get this?"

"It came from a photograph album in his sitting room." She pointed at the last of the scrawl. "What do you think that means?"

" 'Left b.'? . . . Left before, left back, left . . . behind." A chill went through Jake. "Did he give this to you?"

"No. Tom went to his house later that night. You had asked him to find out if Ralph was back from St. Louis. Well, he did, and he found him dead in his bedroom. The photo album was on the floor in the sitting room, and this was in it. Those words were written beside the photograph as well as on the back."

"*Tom* found Mr. Dekker dead?"

"Yes."

"So Ralph got killed between the time you left and Tom came?"

She looked him in the eyes and nodded.

"You told me earlier that you knew nothing about who your father was. Is that right?"

"I didn't care, or thought I didn't."

Jake tried to see Mr. Dekker as someone who abandoned children and rued back on personal debts. All these years he had thought of the old man as a model of rough but honest dealing — a truth teller, stingy but straight. But he hadn't really known much about Ralph's past or his private life.

"So what happened to him, Sam?"

"I don't know. I left him standing in his house looking tired."

"Why wouldn't he talk to you?"

"He wanted to. Like my mother had wanted to. The way he was questioning me, asking me all about whether I was married and reconciled and all. That was as close as he could get." Her voice went small. "I don't judge him," she said, her voice barely audible in the sound of the wind. She closed her eyes and shockingly big tears popped out of them. "God knows, I can't judge anybody."

Jake didn't know what to say. "Hadn't your mother told you anything about who your father was?"

She looked at him and said nothing. She looked as if she was having trouble breathing. "Oh, Jake. My momma couldn't tell me the truth about whether the sky was blue or grey. She couldn't tell me the truth about anything. She was trying to keep me as far away as possible. She was trying to prevent me from entering her life."

"Why didn't you just go to Ralph in the first place about this debt business? Why'd you latch on to me?"

"I had no reason to trust him. I had to find out about him. Get whatever I could on him. Learn about his business. Find out whether he even had any money."

"From me," Jake stated, looking at her.

"That's right."

"And did I give you the information you needed?" Jake said.

She stared at the picture. "You told me he was going to the bank in St. Louis."

"And that's why you left Guthrie in such a hurry?"

"Yes. And he did go to St. Louis. He took forty thousand dollars in cash from his bank."

"Borrowed it?"

"No, it was his own money. All of his savings. He took it in cash."

Jake understood now. "That's why we're out here, then. Where is it? Do you know?"

"He told me to leave his house. I left. I left him standing there. I don't know where his money is." She looked away. "He was my father, Jake. He had the chance, and he wouldn't tell me. Something stopped him. The question about whether I was married was as close as he could get. He knew about me and was ashamed of me."

"Maybe he was ashamed of himself."

·26·

A
T TEN-THIRTY Tuesday morning, walking with LaFarge
through snow-quiet streets, up the ample entrance steps of
the new courthouse, into its ominously wide halls, Tom again
remembered Johnny Pointer's struggle against the marshals
as he was being dragged, now drooping, now stiff, yelling and sob-
bing up the thirteen stairs. Tom's sympathy for Johnny Pointer
was deepening. It was the loss of control and dignity more than
death itself that he thought about. Being reduced to a pleading,
frenzied animal. At least three times over the last few days he had
sensed it happening to him, or almost happening — the accustomed solidity of things melting away, and his own mind floating
somewhere outside himself.

The hollowness of the courthouse halls made him conscious of
his heart beating against his clothes. At LaFarge's request, Tom
wore the buckskin suit that Jake had bought for him in Tulsa,
flamboyant with fringe along the breast and arm seams. Tom almost laughed when he saw the image of the lawyer and himself in
the glass-paneled door at the end of the hall: a tall, slightly
stooped white-haired gentleman and an Indian in buckskin. An
Indian! LaFarge briefly hesitated before opening the door that
said JUDGE ISAAC C. PARKER, 13TH DISTRICT COURT.

He spoke to the secretary, a corpulent man with muttonchops
and cold eyes, who acted annoyed but asked them to wait in the
hall while he went off to the courtroom. LaFarge glanced at Tom

and tried to look reassuring, indicating the satchel. "Have faith. All we have to do is tell him the truth."

Tom had had an entire sleepless night to think about truth and lies, and about how dangerous a game he was playing, about what he could say and what he couldn't say, and the more he thought, the more complicated it became. He knew now why he had been for the most part defiantly truthful when he lived at Bokchito: because lies were like building rickety steps beneath yourself into the air, adding one more flight in this direction and then that direction, until sooner or later the whole thing is swaying in the wind, threatening to crash down. Now he was about to admit that he had gone to Muskogee with the person who was found, or soon would be found, in the basement with the dead Reverend Schoot. Admitting it to LaFarge was one thing, Parker was quite another.

The courtroom door at the other end of the hall burst open, startling them both. Two marshals, with big holsters and mouths set grimly beneath ornate mustaches, appeared out of a blue haze of tobacco smoke with a man in handcuffs and leg irons, blinking his eyes, stumbling awkwardly before them.

Leonard watched anxiously as the judge came down the hall with the secretary talking to him in an undertone.

The judge's hair was cotton white, and his face looked puffy and sickly. In the hallway he gave both Tom and LaFarge a brief handshake and smile. He smelled like borax soap.

"I recall you, Mr. LaFarge. Haven't you practiced in my court?"

"I did, sir, some years ago."

"Do you practice elsewhere now?" he asked pleasantly.

"Yes sir, in Guthrie. Not so long ago I returned to the territory and fell into my former trade."

Judge Parker smiled. "Did you try some other occupation?"

LaFarge looked slightly pained but answered him. "I tried several, Your Honor."

"Oh?"

"Yes sir, I traveled a great deal . . ." LaFarge cleared his throat.

Judge Parker looked surprisingly curious, as if he wanted to ask LaFarge more. Tom could not then know — few people besides Judge Parker and his doctor knew — that the judge was seriously ill. Tom could only sense that on that day, at that moment, standing outside his office, the judge was mild and almost disconcertingly open.

"And you?"

Tom realized that the blue-grey eyes were on him. "I worked at Dekker Hardware Company, sir."

"Sad news about Ralph Dekker. I didn't know him well, even though our places of work were close for many years."

"What we'd like to talk to you about relates to that subject," LaFarge said. "I was hired by my old friend W. W. Jaycox, who worked at Dekker, to help find out something about Ralph's death."

The judge's pleasantness began to fade.

"Mr. Jaycox doesn't believe that it was suicide."

A look of impatience, or weariness, started forming on Judge Parker's face, and LaFarge said quickly, "I realize that your time is limited, Your Honor, so I will get to the point. Inquiring about what happened to Mr. Dekker, we've stumbled across the fact that an attempt is being made to bribe the federal judge in Muskogee."

Judge Parker stiffened and narrowed his eyes.

"Judge John Crilley," LaFarge said.

"Please come into my office."

They walked past the secretary, who looked up suspiciously, into Parker's office, where he shut the door. They all continued to stand.

"Bribe him for what purpose?"

"More immediately to my concern, Mr. Jaycox has been kidnapped."

Judge Parker waited.

"Deacon Jim Miller, in the hire of Ernest Dekker, took Mr. Jaycox from his boarding house. Early this morning. Hit him over the head and dragged him into the street. I saw it happen."

Everything LaFarge said was making the judge look less friendly, which made Tom wonder if the lawyer knew what he was getting into.

"I presume there's some connection between these accusations?"

"There is, Your Honor."

"I have to go back to the courtroom in two minutes. Perhaps you can enlighten me within that time." There was a loud knock on the door, and one of the mustachioed marshals appeared carrying a packet of mail, which he put on the judge's desk. The marshal eyed the satchel that Tom was carrying and hesitated. "You can wait for us outside," Parker said to him. After the marshal left, Judge Parker looked at his watch.

LaFarge took a deep breath. "I'll try to put it in a nutshell. Ernest Dekker colluded with certain parties of the Mercantile Exchange Bank to obtain control of his father's business. He then called in the debts of his customers in Arkansas, Oklahoma Territory, and the Indian Nations. He is threatening to close their businesses if they refuse to transfer merchandise mortgages for land and improvement mortgages of their customers. Ernest Dekker essentially wants his retailers to sign over their customers' land wherever they're holding mortgages. He is selling these mortgages to a land syndicate that I believe will exploit the mineral resources, possibly oil —"

"What?" Judge Parker said.

"Rock oil, sir. Kerosene, gasoline, lubrication."

"I know what oil is used for, counselor," the judge said. "But I'm not aware of any oil trade in the territory."

"Lately in Guthrie, I've been hearing a great deal more about oil than coal. There's beginning to be a great interest in it, although at twenty-five cents an acre, it doesn't much matter what use they intend for the land."

"In your practice you've been hearing this?" Judge Parker said.

"Yes sir."

"Which *is* currently the practice of law?"

LaFarge nodded, looking wounded. "I do have a modest practice, sir."

"Please excuse my limited knowledge of the law, counselor. I am only a federal judge. But the last time I checked, white men couldn't own land in the Indian Nations. In certain arranged circumstances, they may be allowed to lease it from the tribal government for grazing. They may even 'hold' improvements — but they may not own land. The land belongs to the tribes, by treaty and by statute."

"That's where Judge Crilley enters," Leonard said.

Parker waited for him to explain.

LaFarge hesitated, and Tom saw him make a decision. "He is trying a case that reflects on this."

"What case is that?"

LaFarge's glance fell to the newspaper on the desk and he sniffed. He squinted, right hand going up to his stomach. Tom got the feeling LaFarge had lost the bridle. He suddenly sounded less sure of himself. "It concerns whether whites may . . . own land in the Indian Nations, be sold land, or in some way exploit its mineral . . . resources."

"This must be a rather undefined case, counselor," Parker said. "Who are the parties in it?"

"Sir, my immediate concern is that Jim Miller, in the hire of Dekker, has kidnapped Mr. Jaycox, along with . . . another. Another person." LaFarge sounded almost breathless, and Tom saw his gaze wander to the newspaper again. "Knowing how limited your time is, I hesitate to go into that part of it. It's the bribery of Judge Crilley that most concerns me."

The judge had become openly impatient. "Mr. LaFarge, you just said that it was the bribery you were most concerned about, then you said it was the kidnapping, now you've come back to the bribery. Which will it be?"

The office was cool, but LaFarge was sweating. Tom wondered when he was going to signal him to give over the money and letter. "I don't know the name of the particular case that Judge Crilley is considering, Your Honor. I should have admitted that. I haven't had time to investigate it."

"On what evidence are you making the charge?"

"Logic, sir, inductive logic." He added limply, "Based on fact." LaFarge looked stricken. His complexion had gone chalky and he looked sick to his stomach. He was sinking like a rowboat with the plug pulled out, and Tom didn't understand why. Only a moment ago he'd had Parker's interest.

There was a rapping on the door, and the secretary opened it and left it open. Past the stern-faced marshal, down the hall, people were filing back into the courtroom.

Tom unaccountably felt less afraid, despite the fact that the marshal was looking holes through him. He got the impression that the judge was more interested than he was acting.

"They're back in court," the secretary said.

Parker tranquilly rested his light blue-grey eyes on Tom for a moment. "If you have reason to do so, I admonish you to see a law enforcement official. Specific complaints will have to be made to them. It is beyond my power to protect citizens from harm, except by harsh punishment of the guilty."

Desperately, LaFarge said, "Your Honor, I came to you because you have always been a protector of the people of the Indian Nations. Their land is being stolen, and the new courts in the Oklahoma Territory and Indian Nations are the worst villains in it."

Parker's eyes flashed on him. "Are you just becoming aware of that, counselor? Many times over the years, recently converted protectors of Indian rights have come to me for one thing or another. Always, it seems, their newfound philanthropy is happily congruent with their own immediate interests. Now, if you have cause to talk with a federal marshal, please do so. I must wish you good day, gentlemen."

With his eyes Tom signaled to LaFarge, *Don't you want me to give him the satchel?* LaFarge looked alarmed. Had his nerve failed? Should Tom just dump the contents out on the floor? Surely that would get the judge's attention. But LaFarge took him by the arm with a surprisingly strong grasp and pulled him through the door.

They walked in silence for a few blocks, LaFarge huffing and puffing and looking green in the daylight. He went into a druggist and bought a little brown bottle of Dr. Poole's Stomach Relief and drank a slug on the spot, while Tom hung around a dark corner of the druggist's display case, gazing at a group of "sanitary instruments" with carefully printed labels: ELECTRIC BELT, PHIMOSIS DEVICE, PILE COMPRESSOR, SPERMATORRHOEA RING, and SOLUBLE SANITARY TAMPONS. Leonard LaFarge looked unsteady for a moment, then he walked out of the drugstore without a word, and Tom followed.

At a barbershop, LaFarge bought a *Fort Smith Elevator,* and they walked on to Mrs. Peltier's. The two of them went up to Jake's room and LaFarge fell down on the couch, still sipping his medicine, reading something on the front page of the newspaper. Finally he looked up and sighed. He held out the paper, and now Tom understood — before he took it — what had happened in the judge's office.

ORPHAN MURDERS BENEFACTOR
WORKED FOR DEKKER HARDWARE
MURDERS MINISTER AND THEN
COMMITS LAST MORTAL SIN
FOUND IN POOL OF BLOOD

Tom tried to read it and couldn't. His eyes and the words pushed each other away. He eventually looked up at LaFarge.

"Far be it from me to worry about one less Bible Jack in the world, but is this true? And were you with him, Tom?"

Just lie, Tom told himself.

LaFarge squinted, as if trying to see him through a clouded glass. "Can you answer me?"

Looking out the window into the grey daylight, Tom felt sweat running down his body. He took off the stiff buckskin shirt and went over to the washbasin, poured in water, and splashed some on his face and neck.

When he turned around, the lawyer was staring down at the floor, shaking his head. "We marched into his office! There we were, in the office of the most deadly judge in the United States, about to show him the goods, bragging about it! You were with this boy, this boy killed somebody, a preacher! And you now have the *money* that he was carrying! Tom, if we gave over that delivery parcel, it would seriously incriminate you."

"I know that."

"Well, why in heaven's *name* didn't you tell me? No, no, don't tell me anything. Nothing else. I don't want to hear another word. Jesus Cristos! What have I gotten into?"

Tom heard someone in the hall, and Mr. Haskell came in without knocking. "I found my railroad man. He says that Park Hill is being used, all right. Some men from Fort Smith using it for some kind of business dealing."

LaFarge seemed too exhausted to respond.

"I think we're wasting our time," Tom said. "We have to handle it ourselves."

◆

Unable to sleep any longer, Jake stood at the window, watching the night unbuild. A clear day was dawning. He'd been at this window awhile, trying to figure out their location, but there wasn't much to go by. They were on the back side of the building, looking onto a scrub forest. He'd already been to the toilet, under the watchful eye of Jesse James, the gun-toting eighteen-year-old in the hall, and while sitting on the toilet he'd heard men talking downstairs, one with the deliberateness of an Indian speaking English. A rooster crowed somewhere in the distance, and, as if it had been a signal, someone could be heard sprinting up the stairs and through the hall. Hurried words were spoken, and then it sounded as if they both went back down the hall.

Jake waited a second and opened the door. Nobody was there.

He went over and shook Sam, who was still asleep. Her eyes blinked open. "The man outside the door is gone," he said. "I'm going to look around. You need to wake up. If there's a way out of here, we ought to think about taking it."

Into the hall Jake walked, as if he knew what he was doing, to the unlit stairs leading to a foyer below. He stopped partway down and sat on the stairs. Below, to his left, the entrance hall opened through double doors into a big room. Several Dekker people were there, working around a long table. A prosperous-looking half-breed stood beside McMurphy, pointing at something on the table and talking excitedly, as if trying to please the unpleasable treasurer. Jake could hear a typewriting machine, and a brief burst of what sounded like Jack Peters's high-pitched laughter. Into the foyer through the double doors walked two men who at a glance looked almost like twins — slight of frame, distant of gaze, wearing bowlers, high collars, and twenty-dollar suits. They came to a place below the staircase where he was sitting, their hats not four feet away.

"Just watch the count. That's what we're here for."

"I think something's wrong."

"Look, it's not our problem."

"Those two are claiming three thousand acres. That's twenty-five allotments!"

"These people all have twenty children. Don't worry about it. They're not asking us to check every allotment. Just keep your eyes and ears open. We report what we see. We'll be gone from this place within the week. It'll be in the boss's lap."

As they sauntered back into the big room, McMurphy looked

up warily toward them and surely would have seen Jake if not for the dimness of the stairs.

Jake knew that if he and Sam walked together down these stairs and through the entrance hall, they would be caught before they got off the property. Outside, they'd leave prints in the snow. He got up and slipped back upstairs, to the end of the hall. He tried a couple of doors and found nothing but dusty rooms. He was going back to his room when he heard somebody rush up the stairs. Two men appeared in the hall, guns out, walking toward him. They took him by his elbows and escorted him back to his room.

As Jake entered, he saw Deacon Miller standing back, almost in a corner, as motionless as a statue. Ernest's lawyer came in and shut the door. He sat down and offered Sam and Jake straight-backed chairs, which they both declined. The lawyer jammed the cigar into his mouth but seemed to make an extra effort to speak carefully around it. "You're out here for an important reason."

"What's your name?" Sam said.

"I don't care about no smart talk, ma'am. Give me any and I'll have you took to another room and let the boys talk to you. They ain't the gentleman I am."

One of the two who had escorted Jake back to his room, the skinny eighteen-year-old, smiled menacingly.

The lawyer took out his cigar and gazed at it. "Now Jake, you and this woman have been scheming against Mr. Dekker. You was trying to work the old man into puttin yourself into his place. I know about that, and I know she's been going around town ask-ing all type of questions about his bidness. A certain courier told us that Miss King was going around asking questions. I also know you've been stealing collection money —"

"What?"

"While you've been consorting with this woman publicly all over the territory, setting up in fancy hotels, you've been taking cash from customers and keeping it."

"That's a lie," Jake said.

"We have the witnesses. Nobody likes to see a good hard-workin man go down to a brazen woman," he said with fake con-cern. "But if it goes to a jury, they'll know you wasn't the first one."

"You little dirtwad," Sam said. "You look like a jug with a cork in it."

A fleeting look of anxiety crossed the lawyer's face before he recovered and turned to Deacon Miller. "Take this here banty hen to another room, please, Deacon."

Miller walked over, clamped her arm, and shoved her through the door.

The lawyer followed Miller into the hall and spoke hurriedly to him, then came back in. "Let's get it over, Jake. The old man brought a considerable amount of cash money with him from St. Louis on Sunday or Monday last week, and that money is missing. You know where it is. Tell me and we'll let you go, free and clear, no further trouble, long as you keep your nose out of Mr. Dekker's bidness. Despite all the other things you've done to incriminate yourself, that there's all we want from you. It's your ticket."

Jake could feel the flush in his face. "I'll talk to Ernest."

"Can you tell him where his money is?"

Jake didn't reply.

The lawyer sighed and shook his head. "I don't expect you to believe it, but I'm the one that's trying to make this easy. I told him I'd try to talk reason with you. The money's his. You know that. He'll have it one way or the other. So let's just git it over and done with."

"I'll talk to him. Not to you."

The lawyer stood up. "Like I say, I hope you don't intend to bring him in here and provoke him. I warn you, he's in a mood."

They tied Jake to a chair and left him, and the longer he sat there without food or the chance to visit the toilet, the ornerier he felt. By the time his bladder had reached its limit, it appeared to be near noon. Eventually he started yelling, "Let me loose, I have to pee!" The skinny one ambled in and started to put a neckerchief around his mouth. "Let me go to the toilet, mister."

"Do any more yellin and I'll tie them knots so tight your blood won't move."

Finally the little lawyer reappeared and they took off the gag. "He's coming up. This is your chance. Tell him where he can find his money and we'll cut you loose."

"I need to go to the toilet."

"Ain't got time. He's coming now."

Ernest Dekker was hurriedly talking in the hall as he approached the room. ". . . You tell me. All I know is what's in the telegram. Goddamn these fools!" The door burst open and he flew in as if he'd been shot out of a cannon. Fat Jack Peters was in the hall, but he caught sight of Jake and beat a retreat. Ernest came up close, his face red. He looked angry. "Jaycox, you know what I want."

Jake looked him in the eye.

"You're pitiful, hiring a whore to do your dirty work. Hiding behind her skirts."

Jake stared at him for a minute. "If you're referring to Samantha King, she ain't a whore. She's your half-sister."

"I don't want *any* bullshit from you!" Ernest thundered. "Don't try to fiddle me around! I want to know where that money is. You're a dead goddamn son of a worthless bitch unless you tell me. So is she."

Jake looked at the lawyer and said, "Samantha King is Ralph Dekker's natural daughter."

The lawyer winced at this.

"Your father had an affair with a woman named Marguerite King, who lived in St. Louis. She had a child. That woman is your blood half-sister."

The lawyer was still wincing, watching Ernest, who rolled his shoulders, showed his teeth, and assumed a false calm. For a moment he seemed to drift off into thoughts far away, then he turned his eyes down to Jake.

"Will you tell me where my money is?"

"I knew your father was going to St. Louis to borrow money, but I didn't talk to him after he got home. I was in the territory and had no contact with him. I can get a hundred witnesses to tell you that. I was in Guthrie and Enid."

"You did talk to him before he left?"

"Yes I did."

"And you talked him into this little scheme."

"I didn't talk him into anything. Your father called me and told me what he was going to do."

"What's that?" Ernest's voice could almost have been mistaken for calm.

"He wanted to pay off the debt, keep the store going."

"And what else?"

"What else what?"

"What else did you plan besides paying off the debt?"

Jake was tempted to say "He planned to kick you out, Ernest," but he knew that it would be asking for it. "I need to take a leak. Would you mind letting me go long enough to do that?"

"Listen to me. I've looked on every floor of the store, in every crack. I've taken apart his house. I've got a hundred and fifty thousand acres of land mortgages and land options and I've got to pay for twenty thousand more today, outright. You won't stand in the way. I'm going to make this payment, and I'm going to make it on time. I've got a dozen people hanging by their fingertips. Bankers, investors, important people. And fifteen minutes ago I got a telegram saying that twenty-five hundred dollars that was supposed to be delivered to Muskogee was not delivered, and that the boy who was supposed to deliver it has been found *dead,* and the goddamn money is missing, and the man it was supposed to be delivered to is feeling *very* unfriendly toward me. That makes forty-two thousand five hundred goddamn dollars you've stolen from me."

"Mr. Dekker, uh —" The lawyer tried to interrupt him.

"Do you understand me, Mr. Salesman? I am not in a mood to be *fiddled* around. I want you to tell me *where* that money is. If you don't, I'll get it out of that woman. I don't care if she's the lost sister of Jesus Christ." Ernest put his face down close to Jake's. "You were making deals with my father, you son of a bitch. Slippin around behind my back. And then you killed him, or had him killed."

"I think we ought to stick to the subject, sir," said the lawyer.

Dekker looked at him with disdain, then back at Jake. "Our lawyer here thinks that you won't tell me where the money is if I tell you that I know you killed my father. He thinks that'll make you realize that you're so far up shit's creek that it's no use talkin. I think, though, that we better get down to the nut cuttin. Either you or somebody hired by you did it."

Jake was about to give up on his bladder. Even if they let him loose, he'd never make it down the hall.

"Now tell me where the money is, or the remainder of your life will be real unpleasant, Mr. Salesman."

"Oops," Jake said, cutting loose. "Now looky there, you scared the piss out of me."

"Teach him some manners," Dekker said, and was gone from the room.

· 27 ·

TOM WATCHED the whitened landscape go by through a little barred window in the caboose. It was declining toward dusk, but with the blizzard passed, the air was warming.

Mr. Haskell's friend who worked for the railroad had gotten Tom, Leonard LaFarge, and Mr. Haskell onto a freight train headed for Tahlequah. Starting out across the river, the lawyer filled Mr. Haskell in on a few of the details — the land scheme, the attempt to bribe a Muskogee judge — none of which surprised the old veteran much. They sat around a coal stove at the back of the caboose, Tom with the pistol that he scarcely knew how to shoot, Mr. Haskell with his bird-hunting shotgun, and LaFarge unarmed.

"Where's your gun?" Mr. Haskell asked the lawyer.

"My tongue is my weapon, sir."

"Paying these boys a social call, you ought to be carrying the difference."

"In my case, the difference is here." LaFarge tapped his head. "In the old brain box."

Tom spoke over the clacking of the rails, his own voice sounding strange to him, as if it was someone else's. "I know where Ralph Dekker's money is."

"You what?" LaFarge said. "For pity's sake, Tom! Then we should have brought it!"

"It's in the fireplace at the old man's house. Burned up."

LaFarge rubbed his stomach and stared. "Burned up? As in gone, evaporated? How do you know?"

"I went to his house. Stacks of hundred-dollar bills were put on burning logs. You can read the ashes."

LaFarge stared at him. "Who'd burn up that kind of money? Are you sure?"

Tom shook his head.

"Anything else you haven't mentioned? Do you know how this happened? I mean, since you know everything else."

Tom looked out the little window again. That was all he wanted to say. "The money's burned. They can see it for themselves. I don't know how it happened."

Gazing across the snow-covered land, Tom thought about Sam. Sam had been on his mind without cease from the first minute he met her, a steady, burning presence — she who had made herself an orphan, who had drifted and then taken her fate into her hands.

They were passing rows of squatters' shacks and dugouts near the rail line. In places along the blackened rails the snow had melted, and at one point a single young child sat playing on an ash and coke pile, staring at the train as it roared by not twenty feet away. Tom wondered about the boys at Bokchito — whether the mission would send another principal, or whether they'd let the academy fall into the dust, where it belonged.

"Tom!"

He looked at the lawyer. He hadn't been listening.

"That's all you know?"

He nodded.

A brakeman was riding with them in the caboose, at the moment lying asleep on a bench, and Tom realized that this was the first time a train hadn't made him sleepy. As they slowed, the brakeman woke up as quickly as a cat and without even glancing out said, "Okay boys, you got Park Hill coming around the bend. You goin huntin?"

"Might say that," LaFarge said.

"Watch out about gettin too close to the old seminary," the brakeman warned. "Can't tell what might be goin on up there."

"Why?"

"Some of the Indins in Tahlequah still use that place now and again for their little what you might call whoopie camp, if you know what I mean. There ain't no regular passenger service to Park Hill, so the boys down at the station make arrangements, just like you done, gettin rides for girls. Some of em come out of the Paris Hotel, they say. I wouldn't know about that. But I do know I have done rode this glory wagon with twenty of em packed in here tight as a tin of sardines."

"That must be very painful for a Christian man," LaFarge said.

"I tell you what. Cause even a old Christian man to get red in the comb."

"So certain Cherokee politicians keep the old seminary building as an out-of-town whorehouse."

"Well, it ain't no church-meetin place and ain't no stomp dance. This here's hard drinkin and plain foolishness."

The three of them got off in slush, a hundred yards from what looked like an abandoned station, and walked toward it as the train pulled on. They crept inside the old station, which currently was being used as a chicken house. The chickens were roosting. From the station they could see, over a hill, the tops of a couple of multi-storied rock buildings, one of which appeared to be burned out.

Mr. Haskell looked out the window at the back of the station. "Smoke's coming from the chimneys. I guess we're in the right place."

LaFarge got out his bottle of Dr. Poole's Stomach Relief and drank it slowly, making faces between nips. "Park Hill," he said. "The Cherokee Female Seminary. Isn't this where they put out the Cherokee newspaper?"

"Yep," said Mr. Haskell, finding a place not covered by chicken droppings to sit on. "Printed in Cherokee."

In Cherokee? Tom wondered to himself. *You could print in Cherokee?*

LaFarge held up his bottle to see what was left. He took a final couple of nips, screwed on the top, and set the medicine bottle down carefully.

"So you think they're here doing bidness with Cherokee politicians?" Mr. Haskell asked.

LaFarge looked vague. "They're doing something nefarious. I don't know what. And they're doing it outside Judge Parker's jurisdiction."

The old soldier looked sour. "Well, how do we handle it?"

"You two stay under cover — here, I guess. I'll go in and talk to them. If I don't come out within half an hour, it'll be up to you."

"Go up that hill and you'll be like a hen at a mass meeting of coyotes," said Mr. Haskell. "We could wait until later tonight. Scout the place out. Maybe sneak in."

LaFarge shook his head. "We have to talk to them. I think I can get their attention."

"How?"

"Don't worry. I think I can do it."

Mr. Haskell looked skeptical. "You're the brains, I guess."

LaFarge was at the door. He turned and said with aplomb, "Give me a half hour." He smiled and headed out.

Tom watched through the back window as the lawyer trudged up the hill. Mr. Haskell stood next to him, shaking his head. "That man's crazy as a professor with nine degrees, but I like him." He looked at his watch, cracked open his shotgun, and put two shells into it.

Tom suddenly became very aware of surfaces in the darkening ten-by-ten room — Mr. Haskell dressed in a boiled shirt, grey waistcoat, blue overcoat, and a comfortable hat that was turned up a bit. Tom was wearing the buckskin suit and his new coat. It was quiet except for the lulling sounds of the chickens. Tom picked one of them up and she didn't stir. Even though she was asleep, her feet quivered. Her little comb had fallen over her head like a pretty red hat, and the shine of her feathers reflected the last light coming through a broken front window. When he was very young, Tom used to play among the chickens at Bokchito whenever he could. Chickens were the closest thing he'd had to pets, and he still had an affection for them.

Mr. Haskell leaned against a wall. "Reminds me of the Wilderness."

"The Wilderness?"

"Eighteen and sixty-four. First of May." Mr. Haskell pushed the upturned brim of his hat higher and stared at the chicken.

It took Tom a second to realize what he was talking about. Haskell had a reputation for never telling war stories, presumably because he was a Yankee and outnumbered at the boarding house.

"General Grant had been in charge for a while, and he didn't mind throwing the men around, we knew it by then . . . You don't want to hear about this, do you?"

"Yes, I do." Tom pictured the graves in the basement at Bokchito — the soldiers beside the orphans. He had slept among those graves.

Mr. Haskell turned and looked out the back window. "I don't know why this puts me in the mind of the durn war. I must be nervous."

"I want to hear about it."

Mr. Haskell looked at him with a little smile, as if gauging whether Tom meant it or not. "Well. The general put us on the attack, and it was no going back. I never saw so much traffic as I did at the Wilderness. Long wagon trains of supplies. We were going after Lee, and the general was piling it on, putting everything he had to it. He brought out regiments of artillery that had been around Washington for most of the war. Movement all over the place. And prisoners — I remember one big old barn full of about sixty Rebels, and such a collection of long-legged, shaggy-haired, lantern-jawed specimens you have never seen. The South was running out of men by that time, and they were getting em out of the hills. We met em in the woods south of the Rapidan River and fought for two days in there. It was quite an event. So much shooting going on that the brush was catching on fire. I saw a two-foot oak tree that'd been cut down by bullets. Couldn't breathe half the time. And seventeen thousand of us dead, it turned out. We were convinced it was Chancellorsville all over again."

Mr. Haskell looked at his watch, and Tom got the feeling that he had suddenly become self-conscious, perhaps a little emotional. He cleared his throat. "I remember how the boys felt when they learned we weren't going to retreat. We were just going to keep driving south. The sons of bitches were singing. Hell, I was singing, too. We were tired of losing. And then they met us again a few miles away at a little old courthouse. They'd dug trenches and thrown up a breastwork in the shape of a horseshoe around this courthouse. It started raining. We tried every goddamn thing to overrun em. I never saw men act that way, before or since. They weren't men. They'd jump out of them damn trenches and fire, with men handing up guns until they fell, then another one would jump up in his place. Dead three-deep in the trench, and it didn't make no difference. The men weren't normal — on either side. They'd gone over the line. I figure most of us, Blue and Grey, were crazy. The Rebs finally pulled out, but they dug another line not far back, and so it went on, skirmishing and fooling around. In about a week's time, we had us another thirty thousand dead men. And you know what? In the evening time, you'd see trading going on between the two sides. Men meeting up between the lines, trading newspapers, laughing and talking, right out there in the open. We'd take them coffee and they'd bring us tobacco. Honest trading, all fair and civilized. Why, you'd have thought we were old friends."

Mr. Haskell turned back to the window looking up the hill. "All I can see is the top of that building. I guess it's no use watching. We've got about fifteen minutes."

The chicken stirred and purred in Tom's hand. Haskell looked at it. "Anyway, that isn't what I was going to tell you. That's why I don't talk about the war, one of the reasons. Old windbag gets going and he can't stop. One thing reminds him of another."

Tom glanced beyond him, through the glass toward the building over the hill.

"All I started to say was this old boy in our regiment bit off live chickens' heads and ate the durn things. He'd carry on, yelling, make all kind of noise, he'd grab up that chicken and bite its head off and *eat* it, then and there."

"Why?"

"Said it got his blood up for the next day. It was a sight I didn't particularly relish, him squishing and chewing on a live chicken head, but the worst part was that most of the times he did it, the next day we'd have a fight on our hands. It got to be a prophecy, like he had a direct line to the generals. Old Chicken Head would do his act, and sure enough, the next morning before light somebody'd be kicking us awake. You could usually tell when they woke us up with their boot like that, saying 'Keep it quiet, boys, keep it quiet,' that it wasn't going to be a day to loaf." Haskell's gaze wandered through the broken front window, and his voice had an edge in it again. "Cold Harbor was next. They'd pushed us to the limit by then. Lee would just dig in, fight, and retreat, then dig in again, and they were killing a lot more of us than we were of them." He hesitated, as if unsure whether to go on.

"What was Cold Harbor?" Tom asked.

The old man's face had grown stiff with emotion. "I don't know why they called it that. It was just a little old dusty crossroads outside of Richmond. That night we didn't need Old Chicken Head to prophesy a fight. We knew we were in for it. The Rebs had drawn up a long straight trench. We were so tired from marching that we couldn't think. That night, before the attack, something happened to us and we all started extra restless. We got desperate, I guess. It was like we all went crazy at the same time. We'd seen too many messmates fall in these trench attacks. We lost faith. It just fell through all at once, and you've never seen anything like it — men trying to find some scrap of paper to write their names on, pin it to their coats so somebody'd be able to identify their carcasses and notify their folks. Bury em with a name if they were lucky. Licking their pencils, trying to make the letters black. I don't care to remember that night. There ain't nothing worse than losing faith, Tom. I figure dying is nothing next to it."

"Did you?"

"Did I what?"

"Pin your name on your coat."

Mr. Haskell laughed, breaking some of the tension in the darkening room. "I did. Far as I was concerned, I was already dead. The next day Grant ordered an all-out assault. Fifty thousand of us attacking that line at once. I took a couple of minnie balls in the leg and a piece of something in the side, and by some miracle didn't get infected and didn't get nothin sawed off. Didn't get under a doctor, which was probably the luckiest thing ever happened to me. I ended up catching a train at a little old place called Hanover Junction, headed back north. There was a whole trainful of us, the halt and the lame, moaning all the way to Washington." He laughed. "I still remember thinking how God-awful that trainload of men looked. I was sure glad I didn't look that way. Took me a while to realize that I *did* look that way, bad as the rest of em." He shook his head.

Tom was standing across from him, still holding and unconsciously petting the sleeping chicken.

"You know, Tom, I don't mean to pry, but you looked just a little like that when I first saw you after you got back. Did you get into some kind of fight?"

Tom's awareness of the darkening room became painfully acute. He hadn't expected this question. "Might say so," he allowed.

"Were you the cause of it, or did it get done to you?"

Something happened to Tom now that had never happened in his life. Without warning, as if lightning had struck him, hot tears started pouring out of his eyes. At first he tried to hold them back, but he sobbed once, and then overwhelming waves rolled over him, and, still holding the sleeping chicken, he put his head down and stood there, grieving.

Mr. Haskell touched Tom's arm. "I'm sorry, son. I didn't mean to trouble you by asking that. Just forget what I said. And whatever it is on your mind, let it be. Give it time. Keep your faith."

Mr. Haskell took up his shotgun. "It's been a half-hour, and my time's up. I'm goin up there now. I don't want you with me. Go to Tahlequah. It's only five or ten miles from here. You've had enough trouble. Give yourself some slack, Tom. No reason for you to be in this." He stopped at the door and laughed. "And don't ever let nobody put you in a durn trench."

When Mr. Haskell left, Tom put the chicken down and dropped slowly to his knees, disabled by this strange experience of grief — for the sin he had committed, for the war, for the woman he loved, for the fathers, for the amazing world that was revealing itself to him, the evil wrapped inextricably around the good. Still on his knees, he rested his head on the floor.

After some time, he heard a crack and jumped as if it had been a whip across his back. Out the back window, he saw that Mr. Haskell had just reached the top of the rise, and in the gloom of near night, he saw him hesitate and shift the shotgun. He heard a second crack and saw Mr. Haskell fall backwards. For a moment Tom stood transfixed as the old man lay unmoving in the snow. A man in a black duster appeared over the rise. Aiming a gun at Haskell, he pushed the old man over with his boot. He looked down the hill toward the station and then disappeared back under the rise.

Tom ran out the front door and sprinted toward the winter-thinned brush at the base of the hill. He circled around and climbed the hill, slipping in the slushy wetness, wiping his eyes. Jake, Sam, LaFarge — he wondered if any of them were alive. At the top of the hill he could see both the gutted building and the other one, with lights in the windows. Near it, in the yard, were three buggies with hitched teams, and he walked from the woods toward the building, using the buggies for cover. Two men wearing high boots and western hats came out of the house, walking fast toward the buggies. They were talking excitedly back and forth in Cherokee. Someone at the front door yelled something at them, but they didn't even slow down. They were stout, middle-aged men wearing long dark coats.

As they climbed into a buggy, one of them spoke breathlessly, saying what sounded like "He . . . had . . . no . . . money." The other one caught sight of Tom just as his whip came down across the horses, and they lunged forward and clattered away.

A door in the big building slammed. Tom was close to the burned-out, roofless building, and he went against a wall around a corner in order to avoid two shapes emerging from the other porch. Broken glass littered the ground under his feet.

". . . down at the station," he heard one of them say.

"It's a goddamn old man."

"Look, we better check that damn station."

"Boss gone haywire, if you ask me."

"Yeah, well, he's got too damn much goin on out here at once't, that's for sure."

As they went down the hill, Tom heard them continuing to talk back and forth, fast.

♦

The apprentice with the pencil mustache had lank black hair, hollow black eyes, and a strangely expressive chaw-filled mouth that grimaced, sneered, and made loose lips. Watching this mouth was part of the unpleasantness. Although it didn't seem to Jake that he had blacked out for long, he had definitely gotten feather-headed. He wanted to tell the mouth that he could quit now, that was all he needed to do, he'd handled the assignment. But Jake was unmoored and mute, floating, at one point completely away from himself, doing a little watching and thinking on the outside, standing in the corner of the room like an angel, taking it all in — his head lolling there, looking like the hindquarters of bad luck, with his grey hair springing up, while the mouth paced around, as if he was mentally afflicted. He had whacked Jake in the skull,

shoulders, and neck with the butt of his gun, and now he was trying to decide what to do next. The angel-Jake didn't feel hatred
or anger exactly. He considered floating out of the room to look
for Sam, but feared that if he got very far away, he might just float
on, to wherever non-churchgoers went.

He really didn't want to lay down his knife and fork quite yet.
He had unsettled accounts.

The next thing he knew, he was looking at a squarish, fattish
face, so close that he could see the flakes of the eyes and could
feel the burning tip of a cigarette in the holder between his teeth
about an inch from his own chin. It was Ernest Dekker, peering in
to see if he was alive. Jake sure hoped that he was still alive, because Ernest's face was not his idea of the first thing he hoped to
see on the other side. He didn't know whether to play possum or
what. Ernest had asked him a question that he couldn't answer.
He hadn't heard it, even.

"Lookin for somethin?" Jake eventually said, which caused
Ernest to jerk upright as if he had been smacked on the rear end.

"You know what I want. Where is it?"

Jake tried to concentrate through the fog. "Funny way to get
an hombre to remember something. Knock him on his thinker."

Staring at him with his bloodshot, bulgy eyes, as if he was almost in a trance, Ernest said, "My father favored you. He gave you
the best territories. He liked you. Why'd you kill him?"

Jake kept trying to blink away a dark spot, and he realized that
part of the problem was his own hair, smeared with something,
down in his eyes. "I was two hundred miles away from your father
when he died."

"You had the woman do it, didn't you?"

Jake just shook his head slowly, a gesture that involved some
pain in his neck. "Nothin gets through to you, does it?"

"Gets through just fine, Jake," Ernest said contemptuously.
"You talked the old man into taking the money out of the bank.
Your woman friend was all over town asking questions about him
and me. She followed him in St. Louis. Our banker fully described her, and took her name."

Ernest let that sink in, and, as uninclined as Jake was to worry
about any charge made by Ernest at the moment, he did worry a
little. After all, he'd worried on his own.

"We're wasting time," Ernest said. "I've got three men downstairs trying to sell me ten thousand acres. I need it for the package. But I need my money to work with, Jake. That's why you're here. I want you to tell me where it is."

Jake didn't know what to say. Stubbornness was one thing, but this man didn't hear what a person said. It was like talking to yourself, and Jake didn't have the strength for it.

Ernest seemed to take his silence as caving in, and he added, mollifyingly, "Now, I know we've been dealing rough here, but you have to understand the stakes. This isn't some chickenshit invoice for hinges and screws. This is land, a lot of it. I'm willing to forget the past to get it done. All you have to do is get me the money back, and I'll consider the matter closed. You tell me now, right now, and I'll even offer you one more chance at part of the winnings. Jack Peters has pulled in over five thousand dollars, cash in the bank. Some of the others are doing even better. Dandy Pruitt can retire with a crapper in his house. You'll be able to do the same. We've still got over half our debts out here that aren't converted yet. I intend to bring in every cent owed to us for a second package, and you can cover the Choctaw Nation."

In his tied-up, bepissed, skull-cracked condition, his shoulders seizing up with bruises, Jake almost laughed at Ernest's playing at being magnanimous. But his claim that Dandy was going along with his game did get to him, and caused him to feel sorry for himself, which made him mad, which made him give up all caution. "You're being awful generous toward somebody you think killed your old man."

"What's done is done. I want to get this finished."

"Your father was a decent man to work for, Ernest. But he failed you. He should have kicked your butt out of the county ten years ago. Maybe you'd have grown up."

Ernest put the holder back into his mouth and looked at him a minute, an ash dripping off the end of his cigarette. "Taking the hard line? Well, that's up to you, Mr. Salesman. I'll give you ten minutes to remember where my money is. If you don't, I'll have your whore disposed of first. Then you."

"Which one of your boys will carry out that brave order?"

Ernest took out a watch and said, "The Deacon likes to handle women like her. He has plenty of experience. And you've got nine minutes and thirty seconds."

♦

Tom waited until the two men in long dark coats walked down the hill, then stepped out and went to the fallen Mr. Haskell. His mind was strangely clear when he knelt beside him. He'd been shot through the heart. Tom touched the old veteran's chest, and he dabbed his blood onto both of his temples. He picked up Mr. Haskell's shotgun, took a handful of shells from his pocket, and walked quickly around the fretting horses toward the back of the big building. Lantern light shone from windows on all three levels. Around the back stood several ramshackle outbuildings and a summer kitchen with a couple of fireplaces.

From against the back wall, he heard something from an upstairs window that sounded familiar, a snapping followed immediately by muffled expulsions. He realized what it was, and his fear walked out of him. He opened the back door and went through a big indoor kitchen into a hallway. In the hallway he saw stairs and went for them. Men were visible through two doorways in a room, where most of them were at the front, looking through windows. When he was halfway up the stairs, Peters, the large salesman, appeared above him on the landing.

Peters looked down at him with alarm. "What are you doing here?"

Tom aimed the shotgun at him. "Go back up and don't talk."

"What are you doing? You can't come up here."

Tom cocked one of the hammers on the gun.

"God —" Peters raised his hand and waved it at him as if to say no, erase that word, I didn't say it. Tom herded him down the hall, with him still waving his hand, walking backwards.

"Go in there," Tom said, waving his gun at a door.

"Look, I can't —"

Tom gave him a look that encouraged him to do as he was told. Peters twisted the knob and backed, stumbling, into a barely lit room where he rammed against a man sitting in a chair.

"*Wha?*" Peters yelled, jumping away from him. "Goddamn!"

It was Jake, with his head bloodied and one of his eyes swollen up. Tom got out the pocketknife that Jake had given him and sawed him loose.

"Sorry, Tom. They tied me up until I had to pee on myself."

"Don't worry." Tom picked him up gently and carried him over and set him on a bed.

"Hell, Jake! What's been going on up here?" Peters said with fake-sounding concern.

Tom took a step closer to him and said, "Sit down in that chair."

"*I* didn't have anything to do with this. I've just been doing what they tell me."

"Sit down and be quiet. Don't talk, and don't move." Tom sounded dangerously patient, and the fat salesman sank into the chair.

"Where is she?" Tom asked Jake.

"Other room. I don't know which one, Tom. The Deacon took her. I don't think you should —"

Tom went back to the open door and from there heard steps hurrying around downstairs. He kept an eye on the staircase and walked down the hall, as quietly as possible opening doors. He looked at the crack below for light. None. He checked another — dark again.

He was at the end of the hall, crouched over, when a door exploded open. There was the black-clad Deacon, holding Sam against him, with a handkerchief tight around her mouth, stripped to the waist and with red cuts all over her neck, her shoulders, her breasts. The barrel of the Deacon's pistol tried to find Tom. Having no clear shot, Tom dived to the other side of the hall. Two shots went off, missing him, and at that moment Leonard LaFarge appeared at the top of the stairs and thundered, *"Sir! It's over! Stop!"* and the Deacon turned and shot him. LaFarge fell to one knee, and Sam flopped like a sack of potatoes to the floor in front of the Deacon. Tom raised the shotgun, pulled a trigger, and nothing happened. The Deacon was swinging back to him, and Tom reached the other trigger and the shotgun bucked so hard that it almost flew out of his hand and the Deacon was lifted up and thrown backwards down the hall. He started squirming toward the pistol that he'd dropped, and Tom cocked the other barrel and walked over to him. The Deacon fell over on his side and rolled onto his back, and Tom put the shotgun right above his eyes, which vibrated as the light went out of them.

LaFarge remained on one knee on the landing, and Tom went over to him and helped him up. Tom carried him into the room Jake was in. Peters was still sitting there.

"What did you run into, Jake?" LaFarge asked. "You don't look well."

Jake was sitting on the edge of the bed. "You don't exactly look · like the queen of England yourself. Where'd he get you?"

"Left shoulder. Tom, there are six men downstairs. Some of them will use guns."

Tom went back out into the hall and put Sam's shirt over her. She had been severely whipped. She looked up at him and smiled, and she said in a confused, longing voice, "Tom . . ." Blood immediately came through the blouse that he laid on her, and Tom was staring at it when someone called nervously up the stairs, "Deacon! Come down here! Deacon! Boss wants to see you!" It was McMurphy, somewhere downstairs, and he sounded afraid.

Tom heard Ernest Dekker whispering, urging him, "Tell him to come down now, goddamnit. What's going on up there?"

Tom had always been physically strong, but his strength had sometimes been obscured by his clumsiness. It did not seem hard now for him to pick up the carcass of Deacon Miller and send it downstairs. He did not think about whether he could do it. He just did it — and the Deacon did not touch the three-and-a-half-foot railing. No part of him touched it. It was as if he flew or was shot out a cannon, into the high common hall, past the dangling rope where a chandelier used to hang, down the fifteen or twenty feet where he made an ugly sound hitting the floor below. Someone — McMurphy, he thought — screamed in unabashed terror. Doors downstairs were opening and slamming, and men were running across the floor.

Without any hesitation, Tom picked up Miller's pistol and held it out to Jake. Jake took it, and Tom then descended the stairs.

"Wait a minute, Tom!"

Jake went after him. On the one landing below, Tom turned and said to him plainly, "Stay upstairs."

Jake followed him nevertheless, holding tight to the railing.

McMurphy was standing in the hallway with a rifle, but he didn't so much as raise it. Instead, he turned and joined the men who were making an unceremonious exit out the front door, who included Loop, the secretary, Pete Crapo and Marvin Beele, salesmen, and the two city-dressed men Jake had heard talking in the hall. The sight of the flying corpse of Deacon Miller had knocked off all their feathers, and they were scattering.

Ernest Dekker didn't run. If his expression was any clue, he was frozen with terror. He had a burning cigarette in the black ivory holder in one hand and a pistol in the other. Tom hadn't raised the shotgun, but he reached the bottom of the stairs and walked straight toward Dekker, not caring at the moment whether he lived or died. Tom stopped five feet from Dekker. Jake dragged up beside him.

"What happened to Joel Mayes?" Tom asked.

"What?" Dekker looked stunned.

Dekker's right hand twitched, and Jake said, "Don't raise that pistol, Ernest. You can't get both of us."

"What happened to Joel?" Tom repeated.

"Who's that?" Dekker said, sticking the cigarette holder between his teeth.

"He worked for you."

"I had nothing to do with that."

Tom took a step and tore the cigarette holder out of Dekker's mouth with such viciousness that a large chip of one of his front teeth popped out with it. "You had nothing to do with *what?*" Tom said furiously.

Dekker's eyes got very wide. He put up a hand in front of his mouth. "I didn't tell him to do it. That woman was askin the boy questions about *my* bidness! The boy gave out private information! I'm tellin the truth. I didn't tell him to do it."

Tom slowly raised the shotgun and aimed it at Dekker's watch chain. Dekker's revolver clattered to the floor, and Tom heard a faint hiss.

"He killed him. *He* did it." Dekker pointed across the room at Miller's corpse.

"Darn it, Ernest," Jake said, smiling grimly, "look what you did to your britches."

· 28 ·

JAKE HAD a couple of knots on his head, a lot of bruises, and two shiners that made him look like a raccoon. He had a "concussive swelling," which for a few days caused him to have blackout spells. But soon he emerged from the fog, nourished by Mrs. P's chicken soup. Jake had the impression that Leonard had been running around busy while he was recovering. Tom had stayed nearby, and they'd already talked a little about what had happened. Jake noticed that he wasn't here this morning.

"You among the living, old man?" Leonard asked, sitting beside his bed and looking him over with a gaze so gentle and considerate that it almost worried Jake. Leonard was wearing one arm in a sling, and he had a pocketful of newspapers. Being sober seemed to cause Leonard to get down to the details faster. "Do you want to talk about this? You already know most of it."

Jake didn't like Leonard's emphasis on "most."

"Feeling well enough?"

"Yeah," Jake said warily. "Unless you know something I don't. Where's Tom?"

"You were a little amnesic for a few days, but there's no harm in that. I've been amnesic for several years at a time and look at me now."

"You risked your hide for Tom, didn't you?"

Leonard shook his head as if to discount it. "I don't know whether you heard, but they're finally bringing Mr. Haskell's body here tomorrow. Mr. Potts says he wants him buried close to the spot where he's going to be buried, so he can keep an eye on him." With his little squint, he said, "There are a couple of things we need to discuss." He handed Jake a newspaper article.

Reading it, Jake had a moment of dizziness. "What is this?" The article was about the murder of the principal of Armstrong Academy.

Leonard told Jake the story of the money that had been destined for Federal Judge John Crilley. "The packet didn't get delivered, and it seems that a little visiting committee went down to the Armstrong Academy to repay this man for his kindnesses in the past."

Jake laid down the newspaper. "Tom?"

Leonard combed his hair with his fingers. "I haven't questioned him in detail, but he had something to do with it. The long and short of it is that if all of this starts untangling, I'm not sure Tom ought to be around here. There's another problem, too. Word's already spreading that Tom is the man who finally broke Deacon Miller's medicine."

"So?"

"If Tom stays in this neck of the woods, he'll be dragging a pretty big deed behind him. People are calling him a gunfighter."

"Oh, *bull shit*," Jake said disgustedly. "Do you listen to that kind of crap?"

"Tom's the one who has to listen to it, not me. He's already had to listen to it. Three or four pimply boys have been hanging around in the street trying to catch glimpses of him."

"He was with that kid Hack in order to find out about Mr. Dekker. This is my fault for sending that goddamn telegram."

Leonard shook his head. "I don't think you had that much to do with it. I went to the Paris Hotel and asked some questions. That place has more morphine addicts and happy-dusters and drinkers of Dr. Thompson's Eye Cure than Butte, Montana. The word there was that this kid Hack was a case."

"Cut that finer," Jake growled.

"He was a young man with a desperate purpose. Maybe he'd been bullied into the relationship, it's hard to say, but he was living with the Deacon, learning how to swagger, talking a lot about revenge. He seemed to have decided to apprentice himself to the trade."

Jake was incredulous. "Gunplay?" The idea of a literate young man choosing the low life was beyond him.

Leonard glanced down at the newspaper. "This Reverend Schoot apparently made Christian soldiers of his orphaned savages by whipping them daily. I suppose that could either break you or do a lot to the willpower. Maybe Hack thought he needed to attach himself to somebody who was meaner and bigger and more cold-blooded than the Reverend. I don't know."

Jake threw back the cover on his bed angrily, knocking the newspaper onto the floor. "The bastard got what he deserved."

Leonard looked worriedly at him. "Do you realize that you are cursing a lot? Is it the head wound — ?"

"Get to the point."

"The point is that I think that Tom was involved in this." He picked up the newspaper and folded it with his one good hand. "He almost wants to talk about it. Which is another reason why I think he shouldn't stay around here."

"Where *is* Tom?" Jake started to get up, but a spell of dizziness hit him.

Leonard held out a hand as if to steady him. "Calm down, Jake. Schoot was killed where he lives, at night. You don't kill teachers or preachers, and he was both. He worked for the Presbyterians for almost twenty years. He was sleeping in his own bed. Tom's a half-breed with no family and no pull in the tribe."

Jake's face flushed with anger.

Leonard got up and walked over to the window. "I can see I shouldn't have brought this up, but now that I have, let me finish. I'm working my way to the touchy part."

Jake felt another gorge of anger rising. "What touchy part?"

"The undelivered bribe that Tom brought back. We handed it over to Judge Parker."

Jake blinked at him.

"You were out of commission. We had to decide what to do. We ended up in Tahlequah the other night — do you remember? You got out of the buggy and fell down in the mud, so you probably don't, but it took every trick this old scoundrel could muster to get the lighthorse to put Ernest in the hoosegow, even though he was a babbling wreck by the time we got there."

"I remember some of it. Where is he now?"

"He's in jail here. Parker brought him over, but he wouldn't have if Tom and I hadn't given him that delivery packet. Over two thousand dollars in cash and a letter in Ernest's hand bribing a federal judge was a pretty good something to show him. Ernest just might end up being Parker's last case, Jake."

"How's that?"

"Parker's sick. I didn't notice it the first time, but he's got that look in his eye."

Jake's brain was working better now, and he didn't like the conclusions he was reaching. "Tom's in trouble. That what you're telling me?"

"This thing could play out a lot of different ways when all the guilty parties start pointing their fingers at everybody else. But Tom wanted to turn over the packet. Day before yesterday, he dumped the money and the letter onto Parker's desk himself. Parker read it. You should have seen him when he read that letter. I thought his white hair would catch on fire."

"What'd it say?" Jake asked flatly.

"There was a case before Crilley which tested the right of a white holder of improvements on Indian land to alienate mineral rights. That's what it came down to."

"You mean sell the right to drill for oil?"

Leonard nodded.

"To who?"

"To an oil company headquartered in Pennsylvania. The 'contribution' to Crilley was for him to come to a favorable decision on that and to remain generally friendly toward Ernest Dekker, and it said so in the letter. It was Tuesday noon when we went to see Parker. That afternoon Dr. Eldon of St. John's Hospital sent over his report describing the upper torso of Miss Samantha King: 'Severely and mercilessly beaten by a cutting whip,' it read. That did it. You'd have thought that report was being read by half of the town before it was even in Parker's hands. All the gophers started running for their holes."

"What do you mean?" Jake grumbled.

"Before closing time Tuesday, they started trying to cut their losses at the bank. Chief Teller Bradley was fired by Chairman Shelby White. Yesterday, White put on a great show of outrage in the newspaper. He said that he 'suspected' the teller to be engaged in a 'highly speculative scheme that endangered the assets of the bank.' And today —" Leonard brought another newspaper out of his pocket and held it up.

WHITE RESIGNS

BRADLEY ACCUSES HIM OF BEING IN CHARGE

OTHER LOCAL MEN INVOLVED IN LAND SCHEME

DAWES COMMISSION LAWYERS MAY BE

IMPLICATED

Leonard grinned. "All over town they've got out the soap. I've never seen so much hand-washing at one time among the better class of people."

Jake again hazarded to stand up, and it took a minute to get his sea legs. He started to dress. "Where's Tom now?"

"Probably back to visit Miss King again. He's been watching over both of you. That's the other thing I wanted to talk to you about. Something's going on between Tom and that woman."

Jake felt like a hog on ice. His head would only turn slightly, and his right arm didn't want to raise more than shoulder-high. He looked at himself in his glass and decided that with two black eyes, at least he'd better shave.

"He's gone to visit her several times," Leonard went on. "He comes back here every time looking as if he had the measles."

"He's in love. Haven't you ever seen that?" Jake stropped his razor on the belt hanging down from the cabinet. He used the bowl of water already there to make up a handful of soap.

Leonard fell into a meditation while Jake wielded his razor. After a while he said, "Do you still believe that Ernest or one of his shooters killed old man Dekker?"

Jake shaved his throat, not answering.

"You know, I have a feeling that may be one of the things on Tom's mind."

Jake looked at him in the mirror.

Leonard shook his head. "It doesn't quite make sense. Forty thousand dollars or thereabouts gets burned in his fireplace downstairs, but he dies in his bedroom upstairs in a way that either was — or was made to look like — suicide."

"Burned in his fireplace?" Jake squinted at him through the glass.

"That's right. Tom found the ashes when we were still running around over here worrying about what to do about you. He told Haskell and me on the way to Park Hill. I went over and looked yesterday. He was right."

Jake continued staring into the mirror for a minute, thinking about Sam's description of going to see Ralph and getting thrown out. She'd said that she had no idea where the money was. "So who did it?"

"I'll answer your question with another question," Leonard said. "Can you imagine old Ralph burning his life savings?"

"No. But I couldn't imagine him losing the store to his son. And I couldn't imagine Samantha King being his daughter, either."

After Jake washed his face in the bowl, Leonard added, "Samantha visited him that night."

"You must have talked to her since we've been back."

"I went by the hospital yesterday." Leonard looked puzzled. "She really didn't act as if she was trying to hide anything."

Jake dried off his face and found a hat. "Want to go visit her again?"

"I have one more thing to tell you. Parker asked me — and Tom — to come to his office this afternoon at two-thirty. I got the message less than an hour ago."

"Does Tom know?"

"Not yet."

"And you think he's going to ask whether Tom was involved in this thing at the academy?"

Leonard sighed. "Seems a good possibility."

"Why didn't he ask him when he gave over the packet?"

"He was too interested in the letter itself."

Jake finished getting himself together, and the two of them went looking for Tom. The horse lot and stable Jake used was unusual in that there was seldom anyone there tending it, and the people who patronized it occasionally used each other's rigs without asking, so Jake wasn't alarmed at the absence of the mules and wagon. Leonard couldn't saddle a horse with one arm in a sling, so Jake did them both, although certain muscles in his shoulder and neck severely objected.

Belle Grove neighborhood was the fashionable section of town, with two- and three-story Victorian and Baroque houses, but Eldon's lying-in hospital was an older, modest, one-story cottage behind a wrought-iron fence. Jake found the doctor, a friendly, unbusy-acting man, in exactly the same place he'd found him the last time he'd seen him — sitting on the front steps smoking a pipe.

"She scabbed up pretty nice. I think she ducked the lockjaw."

"Lockjaw?" Jake was alarmed.

"I was watching for it. That whip had steel studs on it. She'll have some scars. She doesn't have her color back yet. I don't know whether she ought to be leaving so early."

"She left?"

"She and the young man tore out of here a few minutes ago."

"Did they say where?"

"I believe they headed toward the avenue."

Jake made it onto his horse in a fury of shoulder pain and galloped toward the avenue. The horse was a good saddler, but Leonard was on a snuffy little plowhorse that didn't like hurrying, and he was going all over the street behind, his injured arm flapping like a helpless wing. He was trying to say something to Jake, but Jake couldn't hear it.

At the avenue, Jake looked both ways. It was busy with wagons and people, but no sign of the mule wagon. Leonard rode up beside him, yelling, "Take it easy! Fall from that horse and your head might just decide it's time to cash in the chips."

With his horse snorting and whirling around, Jake surveyed every direction and galloped across to the store, and all the way around it, with Leonard following along, scolding him the whole way. Dekker Hardware was silent and abandoned. He rode back to the base of the avenue. There he saw them, on the long bridge to the Indian Nation, just past the midpoint. As he rode up to them, he saw that the wagon was stopped. Sam sat quietly next to Tom, her green eyes wet with tears.

"What's going on? You two going fishing?" Jake said to Tom.

Neither of them was quite able to muster a smile.

"You doing better, Sam?"

Still no answer.

Tom glanced at Jake. "I was going to send you a letter and money for the mules," he said stiffly.

"I don't care about that. Where're you two going?"

They glanced at each other, as if both of them were confused.

"Just gonna leave without a word?"

Tom stared ahead. Sam looked at Jake sorrowfully.

"Talk to me, for pete's sake!"

Sam finally answered, "I'm not going anywhere, Jake. I'm making a stand here. I'm serious about going into business. Tom says he won't be stopped. He came to the hospital to say goodbye and I couldn't let him go. I rode with him this far. Now we're just talking. He says he has to move on."

Jake saw how bleak they both were. He leaned on his saddle horn and tried to collect himself. "Okay," he said, holding up both hands. "I'm not trying to interfere with anybody. All I'm trying to do is find out the deal." He could see that Tom wanted to talk but couldn't, or didn't know how.

Leonard rode up behind him, puffing and wheezing as badly as the plowhorse he was riding. He took in the situation, threw Jake a look, and rode back twenty yards, out of hearing.

Sam abruptly got down from the wagon and went over and leaned on the railing, and Tom got off but remained by the wagon. Below them the river shone in the midday sun. Jake got down from his horse. Sam's cuts had been dressed with something that smelled like turpentine, and her unpinned hair came down all the way to her elbows. Tom was wearing the buckskin Jake had bought him, along with a wide headband. They were a wild-looking two.

Sam blinked at Jake through tears.

"The doctor doesn't think you —"

"Oh, don't say it. I can't stand another minute of you caring for me." She put a hand over her eyes. "*Both* of you! All my life, I couldn't find a decent man and suddenly *two* of the bastards show up at once!" She flung her hand disgustedly in the direction of Leonard. "Hell, they're coming out of the woodwork!"

Tom gave Jake another worried glance, and Jake now understood that she hadn't told him everything. Sam looked at Jake and seemed to read his expression.

Jake decided to sit down. He leaned against the bridge railing.

Sam composed herself. She stared out on the silent river for a full minute. It was very quiet out here, and cold, with only one other cart on the bridge, headed toward them from the Indian side. The mules were already half asleep, their nostrils gently steaming. Sam finally spoke. "I thought I wanted to get back the thirty thousand dollars that he owed her. I planned it. But when I went to see him, it all went wrong. I intended just to get the money from him."

"What happened?"

"He offered me five hundred dollars." She looked away in shame.

Jake could just see it. The sly old man trying to buy his way out at the cheapest price.

She shook her head. "I hated him when he did that, Jake. I hated him bad."

"How'd you get him upstairs."

"I didn't get him upstairs. He got himself upstairs."

"You shot him, though?"

"I didn't shoot him. Oh, I was ready to. I would have if he hadn't given me the money. That's why he changed his mind and suddenly remembered where it was. It was in his basement. He knew I was dead serious. I made him get his money and stand there and watch while I burned it. I didn't have to kill him. I did something worse. I showed him what he was worth and left him with it."

"So he did kill himself," Jake said — a statement rather than a question. He was thinking of the horror the old man must have felt, knowing that this was the daughter he wouldn't claim. *What he was worth . . .*

Jake got up. He gently took Sam's hand. "Sam, it was his doing. He made his own bed." He gestured at Leonard to come over.

Leonard did so, with one hand on his stomach and a wary look.

"Leonard, I'm asking you to do something that might be a little difficult."

"Yes?"

"Can you talk Judge Parker out of this thing? Can you convince him that it's unnecessary to talk to Tom?" He looked at him pleadingly. *Come on, Leonard, I know you can.*

Leonard thought aloud: "Well, Tom and I went to Judge Parker twice on our own accounts. We handed him the evidence. And he does know that Tom lost his job. I think it would seem normal enough for a young man out of work to move on . . ." Leonard's uncertain look became a grin, and he glanced at all of them. "They don't call me the man with the golden tongue for nothing."

Jake walked around the wagon and stood beside Tom. "Son, you go on. Trade those damn mules in and get yourself some decent horses. You got any money?"

Tom looked at Jake, shaking his head, a stormy look to his expression. Neither of them spoke. Jake held out his hand and Tom looked at it a minute, and instead came over and put his arms around Jake uncertainly. The two of them stood that way, stiffly, only for a moment.

"Do you know where you're headed?" Jake asked.

"I'll send you a letter."

"Well, don't get a job as a miner or a cowboy. Get a town job somewhere. And for God's sake, Tom," Jake said, reaching up and touching the side of his head, "get a damn hat. That band won't keep you warm."

Leonard held up a hand in goodbye. "If you ever decide to apprentice yourself to the law, Tom Freshour, call on me. I know a thing or two."

Tom walked over to Sam and whispered something in her ear that Jake did not hear. She turned half toward him and stopped. He climbed back up on the wagon and looked at them all one last time, as if drinking them in. Then he put his eyes ahead and started for the other side.

♦

Tom wasn't sure where he was going, but on the Indian side he turned in the direction he knew best — southwest.

He had whispered to Sam, "Even if we never see each other again, I won't leave you."

Over the last two and a half days he had gone to sit with Sam in